THE DEATH LIST

PAUL JOHNSTON

MIRA®

MIRA

ISBN-13: 978-0-7783-2481-2
ISBN-10:   0-7783-2481-8

THE DEATH LIST

Copyright © 2007 by Paul Johnston.

www.MIRABooks.com

Printed in U.S.A.

10 9 8 7 6 5 4 3 2 1

To Roula and Maggie,

hearts of gold

ACKNOWLEDGMENTS

During the ups and downs of my recent life, members of my family did what they could to help. My father, Ronald, was the first to read *The Death List*. I hope the open-heart surgery that he later successfully underwent was not brought about by the book. To those who provided generous hospitality in Herne Hill—Claire, Chris and Frances—this may seem an odd way to express appreciation. But there's no one odder than an author, guys....

I've also been fortunate to have had unstinting support from two superb crime writers: heartfelt thanks to my good friends Robert Wilson (Oxford 1976, and then the world...) and Julia Wallis Martin (London 1999, but almost Oxford 1976).

My agent Broo Doherty was quick to see the potential of the book. Her astute comments improved it immeasurably. I salute you, Broo.

My editor Linda McFall's insights were also essential. To her and to all at MIRA Books, most enthusiastic of publishers, my deepest gratitude.

'Tis not so great a cunning as men think
To raise the devil; for here's one up already;
The greatest cunning were to lay him down.

—John Webster

PROLOGUE

A heavy fog had come down over London that evening and the traffic was backed up all the way from the Lea Bridge roundabout to Hackney Central.

Jawinder Newton banged her hands on the steering wheel as the bus in front of her Peugeot stopped again. It was nearly eleven o'clock. Not for the first time, the monthly meeting of the Hospital Trust had overrun. September's report was full of unresolved problems and she'd had to fight to keep her eyes open. It wasn't just her demanding job—she was a solicitor in a busy local partnership that dealt with immigrants' problems. The fact was, she'd only been back at work for six weeks after maternity leave. She was finding it hard being away from her beautiful Raul. He would soon be eight months old and she already felt she was losing touch with him. At least her mother was able to look after the little boy when she and Steven were out during the day. She didn't know how people could entrust their children to outsiders.

The traffic finally cleared at the roundabout ahead and Jawinder turned right at Clapton Ponds. She found a parking place opposite the terraced house on Thornby Road and stretched for her bag. Before she got out, she turned on the interior light and looked in the mirror. She was a mess, her short black hair ruffled and her eyes bloodshot, but she didn't care. In a few seconds she'd be lost in Raul's delicate scent and listening to the miraculous regular intake of his breath.

Locking the car in the thick drizzle, Jawinder ran across the deserted street, house key in her hand. As she went up the steps, her heart missed a beat. Raul was screaming. Even though the nursery was at the back on the first floor, she could hear his cries clearly and immediately she panicked. What was Steven doing? Surely he couldn't have fallen asleep in front of the television. The noise was enough to wake the dead.

She pushed the door open, letting her handbag and briefcase fall to the floor.

"Steven!" she shouted, going past the sitting-room door. It was a couple of inches open and she could see her husband's head lolling on the back of the sofa. Jeremy Paxman was grilling some government spokesman on the television. "For God's sake, Steven! Can't you hear Raul?"

Jawinder dashed up the stairs, her heart pounding. The sound of her son's voice was piercing. It was making the hair on the back of her neck stand up and her breath catch in her throat. She ran into the nursery.

"What is it, my darling?" she said, picking up the red-faced child. His eyes were wide and filled with tears. He was alternately gulping for breath and screaming as if he were completely terrified. Jawinder had never seen him like this before. She clutched him to her chest and pressed the palm of her hand against his forehead. He wasn't running a fever. The poor thing. He must have had some awful dream. Did babies have nightmares? She cooed to him, stroking his back and feeling the heaving little body gradually calm down.

"It's all right, my beautiful, Mummy's home." She picked up the blanket from the bed and wrapped it round him. "Mummy's home to look after her little man."

Raul looked at her with huge, tear-filled brown eyes and let out a grunt of satisfaction. Then he smiled.

"My darling," Jawinder said, finding his bottle and putting it to his lips. "There you are. That silly Daddy. Let's go downstairs and find out what he's doing." She carried the sucking child out of the bedroom, her eyes narrow in fury. She was going to tell Steven exactly what she thought of his child-care skills.

When she reached the open sitting-room door, Jawinder looked over the dark hair on her son's head. She noticed now that the TV volume was much higher than Steven liked. He was always complaining about how loud her mother had it.

"Steven?" she said severely. "Didn't you hear your son screaming?" The remote control was on top of the TV. She went to take it and lower the volume, surprised by its location. Her husband normally put it between his legs, something she was sure he did to irritate her mother. "Steven?"

Jawinder turned and almost dropped Raul. She managed to stifle the scream that burst from her throat, but not before her son started whimpering. She moved him round to keep his eyes from what was on the sofa.

"Steven?" she repeated, her voice nothing more than a whisper.

But her husband didn't answer. He couldn't answer. A red scarf had been tied tightly around his mouth, making his cheeks pouch out above it. His eyes, the dark blue that had attracted her so much when they met in the bank five years ago—she'd gone to negotiate a loan for the partnership—that beautiful blue was an awful parody of what it had been now that his eyeballs were bulging like an octopus's.

Jawinder's knees were weak, her body racked by spasms that turned Raul's complaints to bleats of fear. She mouthed her husband's name, her voice completely gone.

Steven Newton was sprawled on the sofa, his legs wide. He'd kicked over the coffee table and a can of beer had drained onto the carpet. But the smell of alcohol that Jawinder disliked so much was not the one making her stomach heave. That was a visceral, far more repellent stench.

It came from her husband's midriff. His shirt had been wrenched apart and his abdomen cut open. In a cascade of blood, his inner organs had fallen forward over his groin.

Jawinder staggered to the door, keeping Raul's face away from his father. She pulled the door shut behind her and reached for the phone on the hall table. The remote handset wasn't there. She couldn't bring herself to go back into the sitting room to look for it. Fumbling in her handbag, she found her mobile and hit 999.

Her son started to cry again as she stammered out her name and address in a high-pitched wail. But she couldn't describe what had been done to Steven.

The horror of it would surely never leave her.

"Jesus Christ Almighty."

"Steady," Karen Oaten said. "There are enough unpleasant substances in this room already."

"Sorry, guv." Detective Sergeant John Turner, eight years in the job but still possessed of an unreliable stomach, managed to swallow the bitter flood that had risen up his throat. Inspector Oaten had no time for people with weak stomachs. She also had no time for people who called her "Wild" or "Oats," so no one did, at least to her face. She was a hard one and she wanted no distinctions made between her and her male counterparts, so "ma'am" was out and "guv" was in. Turner, from Cardiff, wished he could stop the rest of the team calling him "Taff," but he knew there was no chance of that. "What do you think?" he said. "Jamaicans? Turks?"

The inspector gave him an impenetrable look. In white coveralls with matching bootees, she managed to come across as both attractive and in control, her blond hair tied back in a bunch. She was also as smart as they came, a graduate on the fast track who'd be promoted out of the Metropolitan Police's Eastern Homicide Division soon, Turner was sure. He just hoped she'd stay long enough for him to pick her brains.

"Certainly looks like there's a drug connection." Oaten glanced at the hundred-gram bag of cocaine that one of the scenes-of-crime officers had found under the upturned coffee table.

Turner looked at his notes. "According to the wife, he never touched narcotics. He was a bank manager."

The inspector kneeled down in front of the dead man, pulling a gauze mask up over her mouth and nose. Her eyes were unwavering as they took in the wounds. "The autopsy will show that." She looked up at the pathologist, who was closing his bag. "Preliminary thoughts?"

"Cause of death, shock and/or loss of blood." The thin, balding medic looked at his watch. "It's 1:16 a.m. now. I'd say he died between 8:00 and 10:00 p.m."

Karen Oaten leaned closer. "Weapon?"

"Very sharp, double-edged, nonserrated blade. One of the wounds exited the victim's back above the left kidney, so it must have been at least twelve inches long, as well."

"More like a small sword than a knife, then," Turner said.

The inspector seemed not to have heard that. "I notice there's a contusion on his forehead."

"Indeed. I don't think it would have been enough to knock him out, though."

Turner swallowed hard. "So he was conscious when he... when he was cut up?"

The pathologist nodded. "Nasty. Very nasty."

"Calculated or frenzied?" Oaten asked. She was notorious for keeping her words to a minimum at crime scenes.

"The former, I'd say." The pathologist pointed to the lacerated intestines. "The pattern is pretty regular. Ten upward strokes by my count. The assailant must have had a strong arm."

The inspector's eyes had taken in the dead man's wrists. "There's blood here. He was bound."

The pathologist nodded. "Looks like by a thin rope, tied very tightly."

Oaten looked around. "Which was then removed. What does that tell us, Taff?"

"That he's calm under pressure." The Welshman's face darkened. "And that he's working to a plan."

The inspector nodded. "He left the body displayed. I wonder what that means." She turned to the doctor. "Okay, thanks. I want to be at the autopsy."

"I'll make sure you're kept informed of the scheduling." He moved away.

"All right, Taff, let's take a break." Oaten led her subordinate out into the hall. The SOCOs were still working, but so far they had reported no obvious prints or traces. There was no blood anywhere except in the sitting room and the door showed no sign of having been forced.

"You reckon this Newton might have been a dealer who got caught up in a turf war?" Turner asked.

The inspector raised her shoulders. "Possibly. You'll be spending tomorrow talking to the neighbors and his colleagues at work to see how likely that is."

Turner nodded wearily. "What did you get from the wife?"

Oaten shrugged. She had spent ten minutes with Jawinder Newton before she went to her mother's house round the corner.

After a shaky start the woman had got a grip and shown a lawyer's command of detail, but she didn't have much to tell.

"Does this look like a robbery scene to you, Taff?" the inspector asked, staring at the telephone's base unit.

"Hardly." Turner tried to smile. "More like the Hackney Ripper in full flow."

"Don't use the *R* word again," Oaten said sternly. "The media won't need any encouragement."

"Sorry, guv." Turner looked away. "No, it doesn't strike me as a robbery gone wrong."

"You didn't notice the laptop lead on the desk in there, then?" The inspector gave him a tight smile. "Dear me, Sergeant."

"The wife reported a laptop missing?"

"Correct. And the landline telephone."

"The handset?"

"Two handsets—one downstairs and one from the main bedroom."

Oaten and Turner exchanged glances.

"Interesting, eh?" the inspector said. "Maybe there was something that incriminated the killer on the hard disk."

"And the phones?"

"Numbers in their memories. We'll check the phone company records." Karen Oaten nudged Turner in the ribs. "Looks like Mr. Steven Newton might have been into more than just mortgages and small-business loans."

The sergeant was still trying to remove the sight of the victim's ravaged abdomen from his memory. He wasn't succeeding.

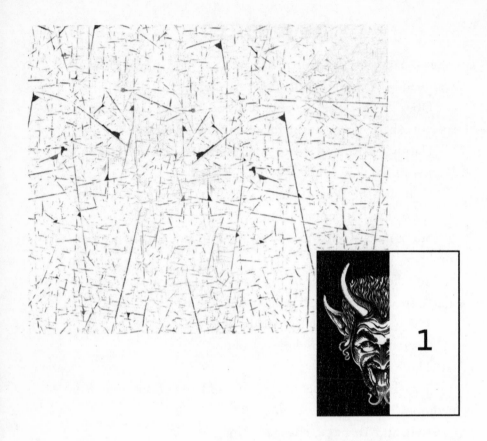

1

The day I made my deal with the devil started the same as any other.

It was one of those sunny late spring mornings when your soul was supposed to take to the air like a skylark. Mine hadn't. A few miles to the north, the white steel circle of the London Eye reflected the rising sun, its iris vacant and its pods already full of tourists who were more in awe of the ticket prices than the supposedly inspiring view. Suckers.

I was on my way back from walking Lucy to school in Dulwich Village. The stroll down there, hand in hand with my beautiful eight-year-old, chattering away, was one of the high points of every weekday. The other was when I met her in the afternoon. The uphill slog back to my two-room flat was the nadir. A blank computer screen was waiting for me there, and in the last month I hadn't managed more than a couple of album reviews. Today my next novel seemed as far away as the skyscrapers of Manhattan; tomorrow it would probably have moved on to Chicago.

I had to face up to it, I told myself as I walked along Brantwood Road. I was blocked, good and proper. Suffering from terminal writer's constipation. About as likely to make progress as the government was to increase taxes on the rich. It was time I came up with an alternative employment strategy. There seemed to be plenty of work available destroying the pavements for the cable companies. I stepped across the uneven, recently laid strip of asphalt and went up the path to my front door. Except it wasn't mine. I was renting it from the retired couple below. The Lambs were charming on the surface, but sharp as butchers' knives when it came to anything financial or contractual. I'd only taken the place so I could be near Lucy after the divorce. She and my ex-wife, Caroline, were round the corner in what had been our family home overlooking Ruskin Park. The way things were going, I wouldn't even be able to afford this dump for much longer.

There wasn't anything special in the mail—certainly no checks; a music magazine I was forced to subscribe to even though I wrote for it occasionally, the electricity bill, and an invitation to a book launch. Someone in the publicity department of Sixth Sense, my former publishers, was either stunningly incompetent or was winding me up. No way was I going anywhere near what they were calling "a low-life party" to celebrate Josh Hinkley's latest East End gangster caper. When he started, the toe-rag had half the sales I had. Now I was a nobody and he was a top-ten bestseller. Could he write? Could he hell.

I made myself a mug of fruit tea, trying to ignore what

Caroline had said when I gave up caffeine. "Brilliant idea, Matt. You'll be even less awake than you are now." She could nail me effortlessly. A top job in the City, daily meetings with business leaders, international credibility as an economist—and a tongue with the sting of a psychotic wasp. How had I managed to miss that when we got together? It must have been something to do with the fact that she was the owner of a body that still turned heads in the street. Who was the sucker now?

I logged on to my computer and opened my e-mail program. I had several writer friends who proudly said that they never checked their mail until they'd finished work for the day. I'd never had that sort of discipline. I needed to feel in touch with the world before I wrote my version of it. Or so I'd convinced myself. Deep down, I knew it was a displacement activity on the same level as arranging your paper clips or dusting your diskettes. When I was moderately successful, I still got a rush from unexpected good news, even if it was only my agent's assistant proudly telling me that they'd sold the translation rights for one of my books to some Eastern European country for a small number of dollars. It had been almost a year since something as insignificant as that had happened.

The contact page on my Web site was connected to my inbox. For the time being. I was struggling to pay the bill, so *www.MattStonecrimenovelsofdistinction.com* wouldn't be online for much longer. When my books were selling, I used to get up to five messages a day from fans bursting to tell me how much they loved my work. Now that I wasn't the apple of any publisher's eye, I was lucky if I got five a week. But I lived in hope. There was nothing like a bit of undiluted praise to crank the creative engine.

After I'd deleted the usual cumshot and cheap drugs spam, I

looked at what was left. A brief mail from the reviews editor of
one of the lad mags I contributed to. I'd sent him a message
begging for work and here he was informing me that my services
were not required this month. Great. That went the same way
as the spam. Then there was yet another message from WD. I
had to hand it to him or her. No, it had to be a guy—he knew
too much music and movie trivia. He was as loyal as it got. And
as regular. Three times a week for the past two months. I had
foolishly made a commitment on my Web site to reply to every
message, so I'd kept the correspondence going. But WD had a
solicitous way with words and I'd made my feelings about some
of the issues he raised clear enough. In short, I'd given him a
glimpse of the real me.

I double-clicked on the inbox icon and went into the file I'd
made for WD—giving all my correspondents their own file was
another displacement activity that had kept me going for days.

I ran down the messages, opening some of them. They had
started off as standard fan stuff— Dear Matt (hope first name
terms are acceptable!), Really enjoyed your Sir Tertius series.
Great depictions of Jacobean London. Squalor and splendor,
wealth and violence. My favorite is The Revenger's Comedy.
When's there going to be another one? To which I'd replied,
with the deliberate vagueness that I used to cultivate when I had
a publishing contract, Who knows, my friend? When the Muse
takes me. Dickhead.

WD was also one of the few people who liked my second
series. After writing three novels set in 1620s London featuring
"the resourceful rake" Sir Tertius Greville, I'd decided to pull
the plug on him. The books had done pretty well—good reviews
(sarcasm and irony, always my strong suits, turned a lot of review-
ers on); The Italian Tragedy had won an award from a specialist

magazine for best first novel; I'd had plenty of radio and TV exposure (admittedly mostly on local channels) and I'd done dozens of bookshop events.

Then, for reasons I still didn't fully understand, I had decided that "A Trilogy of Tertius" was enough. I wanted to jump on the bandwagon of crime fiction set in foreign countries. I didn't know it at the time, but jumping on bandwagons is a talent possessed only by the very brave or the very lucky. I was neither. My choice of country probably didn't help. WD wrote, Your private eye Zog Hadzhi is a superb creation. Who would have thought that a detective would prosper in the anarchy of post-communist Albania? I particularly enjoyed Tirana Blues. Very violent, though. I suppose you must have seen some terrible things on your research trips out there. I didn't tell him that I'd never been near the benighted country and that all I knew I'd learned in the local library. No one seemed to realize. The critics were still approving (apart from a scumbag called Alexander Drys who called Zog "an underwear-sniffer"), but sales plummeted from the start. By the time my intrepid hero had defeated the Albanian Mafia in the second novel, *Red Sun Over Durres*, they were down to a couple of thousand and my overworked editor had declined any further offerings from me.

I'd known the series was in trouble from the start. There was a strong correlation between falling sales and the number of e-mails from fans. But I hadn't expected my publishers to deposit me in the dustbin of unwanted authors with such alacrity. After all, they'd invested in me for five books and I was already planning a new departure to get myself back on track. But they were more interested in twentysomethings with pretty faces and, if at all possible, blond hair, rather than a thirty-eight-year-old former music journalist whose looks could at best be described as rugged and whose author photograph had scared more than one sensitive child.

Never mind, Matt, WD had said. You have so much talent that I know you'll be back in print soon. James Lee Burke went unpublished for years. And look at Brian Wilson. Decades of silence and then a great new album. He was trying to help, but he didn't succeed. I didn't have five percent of Burke's talent and, besides, I'd never liked the Beach Boys' warblings.

Normally authors who have been dropped by their publishers do their best to keep that fact from their readers. Not me. In what my ex-wife described as "a career-terminating act that Kurt Cobain would have been proud of," I decided to air my grievances in the columns of a broadsheet newspaper. I'd met the literary editor at a party and I thought he'd be interested in an insightful piece on the cutthroat nature of the modern publishing business. He was, but not for the reasons I'd assumed. I bitched about how much money my publishers had invested in me only to cut their losses before I made the big time, I whined about how the author's appearance was more important than a skilled turn of phrase, and I looked back nostalgically to the weeks I'd spent on the road chatting up booksellers—all thrown away at the whim of a callous managing director. Controversy flowed for almost a week, and then the literary world moved on to more pressing issues (the next bald footballer's ghosted biography, the kiss-and-tell story of a large-bosomed singer). And, too late, I realized that, by deploying my cannon as loosely as a blind-drunk pirate captain, I'd made myself unpublishable. Smart move. It got worse. A few days later my agent, a rapacious old dandy called Christian Fels, sent me an e-mail in which he graciously relinquished his representation of me. I had hit rock bottom. No publisher, no agent, no income.

At least WD remained supportive. Loved your piece in the

paper, Matt. Such a shame the people running publishing are so shortsighted. So what if so-called experts like Dr. Lizzie Everhead tear you to shreds in public. Don't lose heart. There's a story out there waiting for you to write! Typical nonwriter, I thought. Stories didn't hang around like pythons waiting to ambush passing writers. Stories were in writers' heads, hidden away like lodes of precious metal. You had to dig deep and hard to find them, and I wasn't up to that anymore. I was too dispirited, too cynical, too ground down. I could have done without being reminded of Lizzie Everhead, as well. She was a poisonous academic who'd taken exception to my use of the Jacobean setting in the Tertius books. She and Alexander Drys were my biggest hate-objects.

Then I clicked open WD's latest message and entered a world of pain and torment.

Something I'd noticed as I scrolled down the messages in WD's file was that the e-mail address was always different. I'd been aware of that before, but I hadn't paid much attention, assuming my correspondent was the kind of cheapskate who jumped from Microsoft to Google to Yahoo, setting up free accounts and giving himself all sorts of different identities for fun. Except WD was always WD, no matter what his e-mail server was. This time he was WD1612@hotmail.com.

Dear Matt, I read. Hope you're well. I've made the most interesting discovery. You haven't been honest with me! There I was thinking that your name was Matt Stone and now I find that you're actually called Matt Wells.

That was interesting. I'd never revealed my real name anywhere on my site or in the media. I was a music journalist before I started writing novels, and I wanted to keep my two professions separate. I had the feeling that people who read my interviews with the Pixies and my career assessments of Neil Young and Bob Dylan might not be too impressed by the fact that I also wrote crime novels. I should have realized that being embarrassed about what I did was a bad sign. But the point was, how the hell had WD uncovered my real name?

Don't worry, I won't hold it against you, my correspondent continued. After all, some of the greatest writers hid behind nom de plumes. George Eliot, Mark Twain, Ross Macdonald, Ed McBain, J.J. Marric—yes, I know, Matt, it is rather a downward progression in terms of quality and you're at the end of it, but you get my drift. I imagine you wanted to keep your two audiences unaware of your alter ego. Didn't your publisher's publicity department give you a hard time about that?

Who was this guy? Not only had he found out my pseudonym, but he'd latched on to the fact that my former publicist had spent years trying to get me to be open about my music journalism in order, as she put it, "to make people realize how cool you are." Well, I couldn't be any cooler than I was now in career terms. Cool, as in stone-cold dead. But how did WD know all this?

Anyway, Matt, I imagine you're wondering how I came by this information. Well, that'll remain my little secret, for the time being at least. If we come to an agreement, as I'm sure we will, I'll try to be more forthcoming.

Agreement? What agreement? The only time I'd made an agreement by e-mail with a fan was when a woman called Bev pestered me into meeting her in a Soho pub. She was bigger than I was, not to mention more pissed and substantially more determined to exchange saliva. Fortunately I was a faster runner. Just.

You see, Matt, I have an ongoing project that I think you

might be interested in. Before you get too uncomfortable, let me assure you that this is a genuine business proposition. And, as the blessed Zog says in *Tirana Blues*, "business only works on a cash-up-front basis, my friend." I seem to remember Sir Tertius saying something similar, except that gold was the commodity required rather than money. Your investigators are nothing if not careful in their financial dealings. It's a pity you don't share their acumen!

Arsehole. I was getting irritated now. When I got to the end of WD's message, I was going to have a lot of fun telling him where to stick his business proposition. The idiot probably wanted to flog me his life story. Why was it that people couldn't see how boring their lives were?

You're getting a bit hot under the collar now, Matt, so let's take a short break. Why don't you go downstairs and see if there's been another mail delivery? I know, it's a bit unlikely, but you never know your luck. Go on, Matt. No time to lose.

What the...? I leaned back in the ridiculously expensive leather chair that I'd bought with my first advance and had somehow managed to keep my hands on in the divorce settlement. Where did this guy get off? I looked at the screen. There was a gap between the line I'd just read and the continuation of the text. A gap that I was supposed to fill by going downstairs and— I sat up straight. How did WD know that I had to go downstairs to get the mail? Even the most wet-behind-the-ears crime novelists knew not to reveal their home addresses to punters. There were too many weird specimens out there, too many crazies. So how had he found out? Was he just guessing? Most people probably did have their studies upstairs.

I looked back at the message and scrolled down. It continued with the words I understand your confusion, Matt. You're wondering how I know that you have to go downstairs, aren't you? That's another of my secrets, to be revealed if you behave. Now, don't mess me about. GO AND CHECK THE MAIL!!!!

I pushed my chair back on its rollers. What the hell? I could do with stretching my legs, anyway. The pounding my body had taken playing amateur rugby league from my time at university until a couple of years ago meant that my muscles and joints stiffened up all the time. Besides, WD had piqued my curiosity.

I saw the brown paper package lying on the floor when I was halfway down the stairs. It was one of those bubble-filled envelopes, A4 size. There was something bulky in it. I wondered how it had landed on Mrs. Lamb's doormat without my hearing it. I felt a spasm of apprehension as I got nearer. Surely it couldn't be a bomb. I'd written about terrorism in the Balkans in the Zog books and I'd expected at least a verbal backlash from one or other of the armed groups. None of them even knew of my existence, of course. Until now?

I forced myself to walk forward. This was idiotic. WD was just playing games. Then I realized what it had to be. A manuscript. The fool was a budding writer who wanted me to vet his book. How many times had I been asked to do this? The same number of times that I'd told people, not particularly politely, that I was a writer, not a script reader.

I bent down, feeling the usual twinge in my right knee—that had been what had finally made me stop playing for the South London Bison. The package was weighty enough, but it wasn't solid in the way several hundred pages of copy paper would be. There were only two words on the envelope. *Matt Wells.* Now my correspondent really was taking the piss. Each word had been cut from a newspaper, my first name in a small black font and my surname in larger red letters. Who'd been reading too many crime novels?

I opened the front door and looked down the street, both right and left. There was no sign of anyone. Most people were at work, college or school and the others—retired people or au pairs—were indoors. There weren't even any builders in evidence, which made a change for Herne Hill. I knew the Lambs weren't around. They'd gone off to their holiday villa in Cyprus for a month. Whoever made the delivery had pulled off a clean getaway. As there was no address, it obviously hadn't come from the hands of a postman.

I felt the package in both hands as I went back upstairs. It was paper, all right—there was nothing hard or metallic inside. Reassured, I tore open the flap and emptied the contents onto my lap.

The money was new, the colors shining brightly in the light on my desk. There were five bundles of twenty-pound notes. Each bundle contained fifty notes, making a total of £5000.

My mouth suddenly felt very dry.

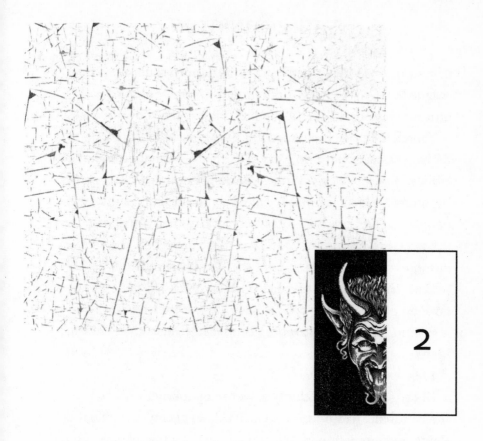

2

I sat in front of the screen again and scrolled down.

So, Matt, I read. Now you know I'm serious about my business proposition. In case you're wondering, there are no counterfeit notes. Pick any one out and ask your bank to check it if you want. No, it's hardly worth the trouble, is it? Before I go into the details of what I want from you, I'd like to blind you with science. Or, more particularly, blind you with what I know about you. It's always good to do your research on a potential partner, don't you think?

"Is that right?" I said under my breath. "And how am I supposed to do research on you, WD?" Or rather, WD1612. There was something about the combination of letters and numbers that rang a bell deep in my memory. My correspondent's earlier addresses had seemed to be the random numbers assigned by e-mail servers, only the letters seemingly having significance. WD1612. What the hell did it mean?

Your full name, continued the message, is Matthew John Wells. You were born on March 13, 1967, making you thirty-eight years old. Place of birth—London Hospital, Whitechapel. Height, six foot one; weight, thirteen stone six pounds; hair, dark, no sign of gray yet. Eyes, brown. Great author photo, by the way. Brooding, intense. That must have had the ladies falling over themselves to get their hands on you.

Yeah, right. I was still puzzled how WD had got past my nom de plume.

But, in fact, it's a bit more complicated than that, isn't it, Matt?

I felt a stir of disquiet.

Because you were adopted, weren't you?

My parents had told me so when I was Lucy's age. They'd always been straight with me and I'd never had the desire to go chasing after my birth parents, even though I was aware of a void in my life.

Don't worry, WD1612 continued. There's nothing to be ashamed about. Even though your real mother was a Cockney slapper called Mary Price. Good name for one of her kind! Except, I think her price was never more than a few port and lemons.

There was a gap of several lines. I let go of my cableless mouse and leaned back. Normally I could make out patterns in the cracks on the ceiling, rivers winding and splitting like the Amazon or the Nile. But now I couldn't see anything. My vision was dulled. Was the bastard telling the truth? What right did he have digging into my past? I blinked and ran my sleeve across my eyes. I was about to click on the reply button and terminate the exchange when I saw the next line after the gap.

KEEP READING, MATT! I realize you're pissed off with me now. You didn't know, did you? You didn't want to know. I just want you to understand that I do. I know everything about you. Your other mother, so to speak, is Frances, known as Fran, age sixty-three, address 24 Collingwood Grove, Muswell Hill. Profession—children's author. Surely she could give you some hints about how to get back into the publishing business. She still produces a book a year. The last one was *Milly's Excellent Adventure,* wasn't it? DO NOT STOP READING, MATT! I've got much more to tell you.

My heart was pounding. He knew where my mother…my adoptive mother lived. And the tone had changed. This was no longer a besotted fan; this was someone who was able to manipulate. I glanced down at the wads of money in my lap and pushed them to the floor.

Good, you're still with me! What else have I got for you? Father—not your real one, of course, even I couldn't find that out; I don't suppose your birth mother knew herself—father, Paul Jeremy Wells, born September 2, 1932, first secretary at the Department of Transport.

I felt my eyes dampen again.

Killed in a hit-and-run incident in Fortis Green, July 8, 2004. The driver who ran him down was never found. Would you like me to try to find him or her, Matt? My powers of research are formidable, as you can see. Just let me know. You attended Tumblegreen Primary School and Fortis Park Comprehensive. Your parents were—Fran still is—in the Labor Party, the old-style Labor Party, so no hoity-toity private education for you. But you were a good student, you got yourself two As and a

D (what happened in that Modern History A level, Matt?) and went off to University College, Durham, to study English. You were on the rugby team there, not the union game that the toffs play, but league, the sport of the northern working man. Bravo, comrade. You were a fast and slippery winger who scored a lot of tries. But you let your studies slide, getting yourself covered in mud most afternoons and pissed most nights, so you ended up with a pretty average two-one. Were Paul and Fran impressed?

The bastard had left another space in his text, no doubt because he guessed that I was smarting. WD1612 was really sticking it to me, the pretence of worship completely abandoned. Maybe he thought that the five grand bought him mocking rights. He'd soon find out otherwise.

No, they weren't, were they? And Paul was even less pleased when you went off to Cardiff to do a journalism course and got yourself on the staff of *Melody Maker* before it went down the toilet. Still, I suppose he must have been proud of you when *The Italian Tragedy* was published. And when it won that award. What was it? The Lord Peter Wimsey Cocktail Glass? Handy.

I looked up at the red display case on the bookshelf above my desk. The tacky piece of engraved glass stood there as a symbol of my pathetic career. I should have smashed it years ago.

Still, I read, Paul and Fran must have been pleased when you and Caroline got married. Caroline Annabelle Zerb (crazy name...), born Bristol, December 27, 1969. Studied economics at Durham and the LSE. City highflier. How on earth did you two get together? Were you her bit of rugby-playing rough?

I clenched my fists. He was getting very close to the bone. Caroline had been a bit naive about life when I first met her on the train to an Emmylou Harris gig in Newcastle. I'd always had a suspicion that she was initially attracted to me because I was well known in the university for my on- and off-field antics.

After that, WD continued, you moved to *Maximum*, didn't you? "The Mag for Lads who Live for Sex, Sport and Rock 'n' Roll." That must have gone down really well with Caroline's friends in the City.

Jesus, this was getting well beyond a joke. How much more had WD1612 dug up? He knew about Caroline as well as me.

Anyway, Matt, I won't bore you with too much about yourself. Just to add that your favorite musicians are The Clash, Richmond Fontaine, The Who, Joni Mitchell, King Crimson and the Drive By Truckers. Nothing if not Catholic, at least in your music tastes if not your religion. (Why do you boast of being an atheist on your Web site? Are you so sure that powers beyond mankind do not exist? Better to be an agnostic, my friend.)

Better to be a smart-arse, you shithead, I said to myself. He could have worked out my favorite music from my reviews—he didn't need to have seen my CD collection.

And you're a devotee of film noir and crime movies in general, particularly Hitchcock. Good choice, Matt! The dirty old fat man is one of my top five directors, too. When you're not reading the competition (who, let's face it, are doing a lot better than you), you're down at the South London Bison club-house getting shitfaced with your former teammates. The South London Bison. Record in your last season—played 21, won 2, drawn 1, lost 18. Not much better this year, are they? Still, win or lose, the mud tastes the same, I guess.

"Like it will when I fill your mouth with it," I muttered. "If you're dumb enough to want to meet up."

Last, but very much not least, you're the doting father of Lucy Emilia Wells, born King's College Hospital, Denmark Hill, January 18, 1997, currently attending Form 3M at Dulwich Village Primary School, home address 48C Ferndene Road.

Now there was a mist obscuring my vision. A sour taste had shot up my throat and my fingernails were cutting into the fabric of my jeans. The bastard knew about Lucy. What did he want with me?

Oh, I almost forgot, the message continued. For the past three months you've been going out with Sara Margaret Robbins, born London, August 22, 1971, reporter on the *Daily Independent*. Good-looking woman, Matt. God knows what she sees in—

Right, that was enough. I moved the mouse, intending to log off the e-mail program. Then I saw the pile of banknotes on the floor. WD1612 had shown me that he knew how to get at me and my loved ones, but he'd also given me five grand. It wasn't as if I had anything more pressing to do.

So I kept reading. —you. Let's get down to it, Matt. What do I want for my five thousand? Well, first of all, I need an act of good faith. Don't worry, it's nothing too difficult. But it does concern your daughter, Lucy.

He had my full attention.

To be more specific, it concerns her bedroom. You need to get round there and clean up. Someone's made a terrible mess. And, Matt? There's just one ground rule. Don't tell anyone about this. Not your ex-wife, not your girlfriend, not your mother, not any of your mates from the rugby club, and certainly not the police. I'll be watching. You'll never know when and where, but I'll be watching. And I'll be listening. So take the money and do what I say or the people dear to you will feel serious pain. I'll be in touch again soon and I'll be wanting an answer from you. Make sure I don't lose my patience. Now go!

I was out of the house like an Olympic sprinter on the latest dope.

It couldn't have taken me more than three minutes to get to the house in Ferndene Road. It had been half mine until Caroline bought me out last year—I put the money in a trust fund for Lucy—and I didn't like going back when my daughter wasn't there. Caroline didn't like it, either. She only allowed me a key because I needed to lock up after I picked up Lucy in the mornings and to get back in after school. I glanced at my watch as I ran. It was coming up to eleven. What was this mess WD1612 had mentioned? At least I had four hours until I went to pick Lucy up. But how long would my correspondent wait for an answer?

I slowed down as I approached the house, my knee suddenly starting to complain. It didn't take much these days. I'd been neglecting my fitness in general. The small front garden was full of bushes and trees that I'd planted, pink and white blossom in their full spring glory. I looked down at the paving stones as I went up the path. There was no sign of any strange footprints. The paint on the door was untouched and there were no scratches around the keyhole. Was this some kind of idiotic hoax?

I turned the key in both locks and opened the door slowly. The only sound was the hum of the fridge. Caroline's mail was strewn across the hall carpet. I left it where it was and went up the stairs slowly, turning my head from side to side. I couldn't hear anything out of the ordinary. Lucy's bedroom door was closed. That made my pulse rate soar. I knew for sure that I'd left it open that morning as I chased her downstairs to get her coat. I approached it cautiously, wishing I'd picked up a walking stick or even an umbrella from the front hall. After taking a deep breath, I turned the handle and pushed the pastel yellow panels back.

The stench that flooded my nostrils made me gag.

"What the fuck?" I heard myself say over and over again. "What the fuck?"

The first thing I saw was a large sheet of heavy-duty plastic. It had been laid over Lucy's bed and the floor in front of it. Then my eyes focused on what was lying on the bed, the source of the horrendous smell. Jesus Christ, could Lucy have been taken from school and brought back here?

But I quickly realized that the object wasn't human. I went closer, a handkerchief over my nose and mouth. Bending over the splayed creature, I made out yellow hair matted with blood and a canine snout. The teeth below it were bared in agony.

It was the neighbors' golden retriever, lying spread-eagled. Her name was Happy and she was what Lucy described as "a teenage dog," being not fully grown. She had been skillfully cut open, her rib cage cracked and her front paws stretched wide in what looked like a travesty of the crucifixion.

I got the message.

Lucy loved playing with Happy.

No one was safe.

It took me less time than I'd initially thought to clean up. There were only a few spots of blood on the pink rug and I managed to make them disappear. I went over to the window and looked out over the back gardens. The neighbors, Jack and Shami Rooney, were childless insurance executives. On decent days like today, Happy was left in the garden, where she had a kennel. I banished speculation about how the killing had been carried out and concentrated on getting the carcass out of Lucy's bedroom. It never occurred to me to disobey the command. Lucy would have screamed for days if she saw what had been done to the dog she loved.

I found a roll of large black bin bags in the kitchen. I was about to lean over the dog when I realized that my clothes would get covered in blood and other matter. There was nothing else for it. I stripped and, breathing through my mouth, managed to wrestle the body into a bag. At least rigor mortis hadn't yet set in. I wrapped it as securely as I could, putting the bloody plastic sheet in another bag and lashing the whole thing together with string.

Then it struck me. How was I going to get rid of Happy?

I washed myself clean in the shower and put my clothes back on. Then I went back downstairs and let myself out. There were some people in Ruskin Park, but none near enough to register me. I checked the street in both directions and headed home. The seven-year-old red Volvo station wagon that I'd inherited from my father was parked outside my place. I drove it back to Caroline's and opened the tail hatch. Waiting until an elderly couple with a Pekinese had passed, I raced upstairs and brought the bundle down. It was heavier than I'd expected, but it fit in the rear compartment easily enough. I closed and locked the car, then went back to check Lucy's room. I couldn't see any sign of what had been on her bed. My stomach flipped when I thought that my daughter was going to have to sleep there tonight, but

I had other priorities right now. I went down to the basement and found a spade.

Now what? How do you dispose of a dead dog in central London in broad daylight? I drove swiftly away, heading for Crystal Palace. I knew there was a public dump somewhere, but I decided against using that. There was too much risk that I'd be spotted or that Happy would be found. In the end, I drove out to Farnborough and took it into the woods behind a bridle path. Since it was a weekday morning, there was no one about. I dug a shallow grave, deposited the wretched animal in it and covered the hole as best I could.

I got back to my flat at two o'clock. The computer's screen saver was on, showing a collage of my book jackets that I'd been meaning to get rid of for weeks. I logged back on to my e-mail server and found a message from W1612D, this time via Google. The bastard was moving around the Internet like a ghost.

Matt, it said. I am impressed! Farnborough, of all places. I won't tell anyone. Here's the serious bit. Make sure you don't, either. Or Lucy will end up in a similar state. Or perhaps your mother. Or Sara. Or Caroline. Or anyone else you know. Do you accept my proposition, Matt?

I hit Reply and typed, What proposition?

The answer chime came quickly. I hardly think you're in a position to quibble, my friend. Besides, you've taken my money. Are you going to cooperate or do you want more innocent blood to be spilled?

I thought about it, but not for long. The fact was, I was shit scared about Lucy. But there was more to it than that. I'd been making up crime stories for years, and now the actual thing had literally landed on my doorstep. I couldn't resist responding to the lunatic who'd cut up Happy. Like every crime writer, I fancied trying my hand at real-life detective work. I reckoned I could do it better than the clods in Scotland Yard—no way was I telling them about my hotline to the sadistic bastard. It didn't occur to me that I was walking through the gates of the underworld.

Okay, I typed. But I don't want your filthy money.

Another chime. That's the deal, Matt. The money's yours. Don't make me angry.

I hit Reply again. Who are you?

Come on, Matt. I've already told you. Bye for now.

He'd already told me? WD? What the hell did WD mean?

Then, with a surge of apprehension, it came to me.

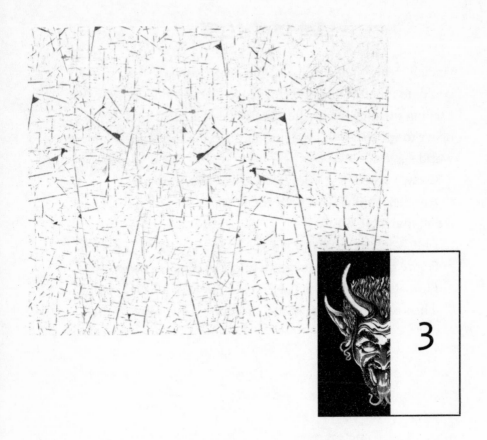

3

The sun was casting a dying red light over the Thames. The view from the penthouse was fantastic, worth every penny of the million and a half he'd paid for it. The place was packed with the equipment he needed, the far end of the huge living area taken up by an ultramodern gym. The watcher at the window closed his eyes and smiled. His story was going to be told, and by a professional writer. It had to be done right, with nothing missing—the way he remembered it from the beginning. He was the hero, he had fought to get where he was now, with all the power in the world.

He'd begun to realize his true potential the day his father hit him for the last time.

★ ★ ★

"Les?" His mother's voice was soft and warm, as it had always been. "You all right?"

He was in his cramped bedroom in the tower block in Bethnal Green. It was winter and there wasn't any heating on. His father had taken all the coins and gone down to the pub.

"That's a nice tank," Cath Dunn said, kneeling down by her son. "Where d'you get it?"

Les looked up from the model of the Mark One Tiger that he'd stolen from Woolworths. "Gran gave me the money. I fetched her shopping for her."

Cath smiled. She knew her boy wasn't being truthful, but she didn't care. He was a good boy, a lovely boy, with his light hair and nut-brown eyes. And he was so advanced for a twelve-year-old, he knew so much about things—airplanes and tanks, battleships and uniforms. She frowned, hoping that he wouldn't end up as a squaddie. She remembered how rude they were when they came home on leave, only talking filth and football. But no, her Les wouldn't be joining the army. He was far too sensitive for that.

Les shivered as his mother's hand stroked the back of his neck. He forced himself to concentrate on the turret assembly. Recently, every time she touched him, he'd felt the blood run hot in his veins.

He put down the model and stood up. "Mum," he asked plaintively, "can't we just go? You and me? You can get a job in a shop somewhere else. We can go to another part of London. He'll never find us. I'll look after you and…" He let the words trail away when he saw his mother's face crease and her eyes fill with tears. He put his arm round her thin shoulders. "It'll be all right, Mum. Honest, I'll protect you from—"

"From dirty Billy and his roaming hands?" His father's voice made them jerk away from each other. He'd taken to coming back from the pub stealthily and sneaking up on them. "Seems to me you're the one with roaming hands, son. You like the look of yer old mother, do you?" He stepped closer, his right arm raised. "You filthy little pervert!" He brought the hand down hard, but Les moved aside and was caught only a glancing blow on the shoulder.

"No, Billy!" Cath screamed.

"Shut your noise, cow!" Billy yelled, giving her a backhanded slap to the face.

"Stop it!" Les shouted as his mother went down. "That's enough!" He felt a strength he'd never known. Although his father was six inches taller than he was, his arms thick from years on the building sites, Billy was drunk. He didn't even see the straight right that broke his nose.

Les stepped back, amazed at what he had done. His father had crashed back against the wall, blood oozing through the gaps between the fingers that were over his face.

"You…you…fucking little bastard," Billy gasped, glancing at his cowering wife. "Tell him, Cath. Tell him what a bastard he is." He stumbled away, the front door slamming behind him a few seconds later.

"Are you all right, Mum?" Les asked, raising his mother to her feet. "What did he mean? I'm your son. I'm not a bastard."

Cath looked at him, her expression a mixture of sadness and pride. "Thank you, Les," she said, leaning forward to kiss him. "Thank you for getting him off me." Her skin on her left cheek was red and raised. "He's nothing but a pathetic bully."

"Yes, but I am your son, aren't I, Mum?" Les persisted. "What did he mean? What do you have to tell me?"

Cath led him into the dimly lit sitting room. They sat down on the worn velour sofa.

"Well, Les, strictly speaking you *are* our son. We did all the adoption papers when you were a baby. Billy didn't drink so much then and the checks they did weren't so tough as they are now. And...I wanted a baby so much." She started to sob. "I couldn't have any of my own," she said, her face averted from him. "There was something wrong inside me. He...your father...Billy...he hurt me. That's why he couldn't say no when I wanted to adopt."

"But...but who's my real mother?" Les said, his eyes locked on her.

Cath smiled nervously. "I am, son. I looked after you when you were a tiny little thing, I'm raising—"

"Yes, but who did I come out of?" Les said, his voice rising. He could find another way to put the question.

"I...I don't know." Cath tried to meet his gaze but failed. "Some poor girl who couldn't keep you. It was much harder then, being an unmarried mother."

Les sat back on the sofa and looked around the room. His mother did the best she could, but with so little money from her husband and nothing left over from her own wages after food and so on, the place wasn't much to talk about. A battered black-and-white TV with a ragged lace cloth on it, an armchair with the stuffing coming out and a wobbly table—that was about it. The badly fitted window was covered by a faded orange-and-brown curtain that moved in the constant draft.

"There must be somewhere better than this, Mum," he said. "There must be."

Cath shook her head slowly. "I can't leave your dad, Les. We're Catholics, remember? We can't get divorced."

Les felt his fists clench. He knew they were Catholics, all right. Father O'Connell made sure he knew what was right and what was wrong. Father O'Connell was an expert in that department. He was another one he'd pay back. But his father, who he now knew wasn't even his real father, was number one on his list.

"All right, Mum," he said, giving her a smile. He'd realized he was better off after hearing the news that he had been adopted. The piece-of-shit Billy wasn't related to him and that was a big relief.

He eyed his mother. And Cath wasn't a blood relation, either. That changed everything.

Les moved closer, his hand touching his astonished mother's breast. By the time she'd started to protest, he'd clamped his mouth over hers.

No, the watcher at the window said to himself. Not that. The writer wasn't going to get that. His loving mother's memory was sacred. Nothing could be allowed to cast a shadow on it.

He looked around the penthouse. If he'd wanted to, he could have invited a hundred people and still have had room for dancing. But he didn't know a hundred people. He didn't want anyone in his home, not even cleaners. It was his safe place, his hideaway—the opposite end of the scale from the dump in Bethnal Green where he'd grown up. His mother would have loved it. She would even have laughed if she'd seen the tanks— dozens of models, hundreds of soldiers, British and German, in the diorama he'd built of the Battle of El Alamein. Beyond that was the sand-covered layout he'd constructed of Lawrence of Arabia's assault on Aqaba, camels and horsemen charging across the Turks' lines. He might spend most of his time in the underworld, but he liked to live on the surface of the earth, too—the surface he made himself, not the one outside his safe house.

No, he thought. Matt Wells wasn't going to get anything about his mother. But his father's—his adoptive father's—story was another matter.

Billy Dunn had deserved everything he got.

It was a late December afternoon, three weeks after Billy had last hit him and his mother. He had been planning it ever since. He'd bunked off school several mornings to follow his father to work. He was carrying bricks at an office development in King's Cross. When he wasn't drunk, Billy Dunn was quiet, accepting the foreman's orders without complaint. But Les had seen the anger burning in his father's eyes and knew that it wouldn't be long before he started taking it out on Cath again. That wasn't going to happen.

He waited for the perfect day. There was heavy drizzle, mist, and people were walking the streets with their heads bowed, concentrating on avoiding the puddles and paying no attention to anyone else. He positioned himself behind a lamppost across the street from the site entrance. Late in the afternoon when the brickies were getting ready to pack up for the day, he slipped inside. He knew exactly where Billy was—on the recently started third floor. Only a few walls had been erected there so far.

He'd been watching his father and he'd learned how to sneak around. Being small, he'd already picked up a lot of skills like that at school. Avoiding bullies was better than standing up to them, unless there was no other option. He went up to the third floor, making sure no one had spotted him. Most of the men were on their way out, anyway. Billy was over in the corner, hunkered down and lighting a fag.

"You coming, Bill?" one of his mates called.

"I'll see you in the Crown," his father said, blowing out smoke.

The boy waited until the others had all left. Then he moved forward on all fours, keeping beneath a low wall.

"Who's there?" Billy said, mild alarm in his voice.

"The devil," his adopted son said in the most frightening voice he could manage. He knew that Billy, a lifelong Catholic who hadn't been to confession since he was a boy, had the weight of his many sins on him.

"What?" Billy said, dropping his cigarette and getting to his feet.

"The devil, and he's come to take you!" Les said with a wild yell, running forward with his head down.

He heard Billy's breath as it was expelled in the impact, then watched as he fell headfirst to the concrete surface at ground level. His body lay limp down there, the head shattered, but Les knew that Billy Dunn's soul was plummeting far deeper, into the very pit of hell.

The watcher saw the lights come on at St. Katharine's Dock across the river. To his left, Tower Bridge stood out in all its ridiculous grandeur. Vanity, he thought, all is vanity.

He glanced at his watch.

It was time to tighten his grip on the writer.

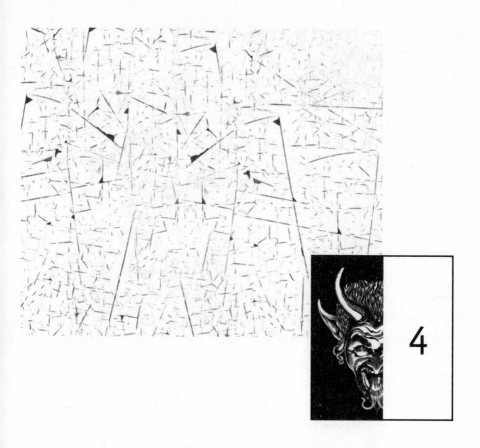

4

"Hello, Matt."

The voice made me start. I looked round and saw my good friend Dave Cummings's wife. She was a stooping, thin-faced woman who had never approved of our involvement with the rugby league club.

"Oh, hi, Ginny." I had to force myself to make conversation. "How are things?"

She gave a weak smile. "You know, same old same old. Kids, cooking, cleaning, ironing."

I didn't show any sympathy. This was Ginny's way of complaining that her husband didn't pay her enough attention. My loyalties, tested hundreds of times on the pitch and in the pub, lay with Dave.

We watched as Lucy approached with Ginny's kids, Tom and Annie. Tom was in my daughter's class and they got on well. As soon as I could, I drew Lucy away.

"Daddy, can I have an ice cream?" she asked, trying it on. I wouldn't usually have given in to her, but I needed to keep her sweet. This wasn't going to be a normal afternoon.

"All right, darling," I said, leading her across the road to the Italian deli in Dulwich Village. "Did you have a good day?"

"Yes, thank you." She gave me a blinding smile that made my heart skip several beats. My little girl's hair—raven like her mother's—was in a plait and her face was covered in freckles.

God, I loved her. I couldn't let anything happen to her. For all I knew, the bastard was watching us right now. I looked around as casually as I could. There only seemed to be the usual crowd of mothers and grandparents, even the odd father, but no one suspicious. Then again, this guy was smart. He wouldn't be standing in full view with a pair of binoculars.

As we walked up the hill, I went over the course of action I'd worked out. I was going to take Lucy back to Caroline's place first. I had no choice. If I took her straight to mine, her mother would be instantly suspicious. Lucy was only supposed to be taken there at weekends. I didn't want to raise any suspicions that, by changing the routine, I might have had something to do with Happy's disappearance.

The difficult part of the plan was if Lucy noticed Happy's absence. She often went to the garden fence and called the dog.

When we got to the house, I tried to shoo her straight upstairs.

"No, Daddy." She headed for the back door. "I want to say hello to Happy."

I bit my tongue. The less I said the better.

Outside, after calling the dog numerous times, Lucy gave me

a puzzled look. "Where is she, Daddy? Do you think something's happened to her?"

"No, of course not, darling. The Rooneys probably just kept her inside today. Maybe they thought it was going to rain."

Lucy peered up at the blue sky and frowned. "No, she was outside this morning. I remember."

I was beginning to regret the plan I'd chosen. "Well, maybe she's just having a sleep. Come on, do you want some juice?"

Lucy followed me in reluctantly. I managed to get her to the piano to do her practice, and later to sit her in front of kids' TV. She didn't have any homework. But she kept going to the window and looking out, trying to see over the fence.

"Come on, Luce," I said, "let's go to my house."

Her eyes widened. "But Mummy says it's dirty."

Thanks a lot, Caroline, I thought. "No, it isn't. And I've got a new DVD you can watch."

"Which one?" she asked excitedly.

"Surprise, surprise," I said. I'd picked up a Disney she hadn't seen on the way to the school. The trick was to get her out of the house before either of the Rooneys got back. Fortunately she was now sufficiently distracted. I also mentioned that I had alphabet spaghetti for her tea, a foodstuff banned by Caroline.

At last we were out on the street. As we walked away, my heart was pounding like a drum.

Did I have the nerve to keep up this kind of pretense?

The phone rang at half past six.

"Matt, where's Lucy?" Caroline sounded anxious.

"Hello," I said, trying to lower the tension. "Nice to talk to you, too. Did you have a good day? She's here, of course."

My ex-wife wasn't to be pacified. "You know she's not meant to be round there during the week. Has she done her homework?"

"She didn't have any. She's done her piano." I tried to keep my voice as neutral as I could. "You sound uptight. What's the matter?"

"I'll tell you what the matter is. Happy's gone missing."

"What?"

"Did you see her when you were round here? Shami's going spare."

"No," I said, feigning sudden enlightenment. "Now you mention it, we didn't." I glanced at Lucy. She was engrossed in *Hercules*. "I thought she was inside."

"No, they left her in the garden this morning."

"Oh, right. I didn't notice."

"Look, it's probably better if you keep Lucy round there for another half hour. I don't want her to be upset by this."

"Okay."

"Have you got something she can eat?"

"Um, yeah."

"Something that isn't full of artificial preservatives and *E* numbers?"

"Yes."

"All right," Caroline said doubtfully. "I'll see you later."

"Look," I said, suddenly realizing I couldn't face the Rooneys, "you can come and get her, can't you? I'm actually trying to write something this evening."

"I'll believe that when I see it."

Cow.

I had the computer on when Caroline arrived, the screen showing a couple of lines of an unsolicited album review.

"Hello, sweetest little girl in the world," Caroline said, kissing Lucy. She was wearing a black skirt and a matching woolen cardigan that set off her bobbed dark hair. Black was apparently color of the day in the City.

"It's the God of the Underworld," our daughter said, pointing to the TV. "He's funny."

James Woods's voicing was indeed a cracker, but I had other things on my mind. Seeing the two of them together brought home how fragile they were; how easy it would be for the maniac who'd sliced up the dog to move on to them. At the same time, I felt a burning desire to share my burden with someone, to lighten the load that the bastard had saddled me with. But I restrained myself. Maybe if Caroline had been on her own I'd have summoned up the courage, but with Lucy there it was impossible.

"What's the matter with you?" my ex-wife said in the blunt manner she'd got used to taking with me over the years.

I shrugged. "Work. You know..."

"Lack of work, more like." Her eyes flared. "God, you're so indecisive, Matt. Why can't you just write a different book and sell it to a different publisher? Why do you have to take everything so personally? It's not their fault you wrote stuff they couldn't sell."

"Spoken like the caring soul you are," I said, unable to hold back. "Since when did you know anything about the publishing business?"

I realized too late that I'd given her an open goal.

"I'm an economist, stupid," she said, touching her temple. "It's what I do."

Lucy looked round from the sofa. "Mummy, Daddy, stop arguing," she said plaintively.

I felt something break inside me. It seemed that Caroline had a similar experience. We nodded to each other and declared a silent truce.

There was an uneasy silence while Lucy watched Hades get his comeuppance and I pretended to write about the new Laura Veirs album. Then they got their things together and headed downstairs.

I followed them, fear welling up inside me. "Do you want me to walk round with you?"

Caroline stared at me. "Don't be ridiculous."

"All right," I said, bending down to kiss Lucy. "See you in the morning, sweetie."

"Good night, Daddy," she said, glancing at each of us in turn. "It would be so nice if we could all sleep in the same house sometimes."

Both Caroline and I failed to come up with a response to that.

I watched them down the street as far as I could see them, and then went after them, skulking in the dark areas between the streetlights. They got home without incident. As I turned to go home, I saw an elderly man in Ruskin Park with his dog.

He glared at me as if I were a stalker.

The irony of that did not make me feel any better at all.

When I got back, I opened my e-mail program. I'd managed to put off doing that while Lucy was there, but now I had no excuse. I felt my stomach constrict as the receiving mail icon flashed. The process went on for some time.

When the chime went, I saw that I had a message with an attachment from 1612WD via another mail provider. The bastard. I now understood what he was calling himself, but I had no idea why. What was in the attachment? I downloaded a digital image. It showed me carrying the wrapped remains of Happy to the Volvo. Shit. He'd been there, judging by the angle and trees at the far side of the park. He must have had a camera with a seri-ously good zoom. I couldn't remember anyone taking pictures in the vicinity when I was loading the car.

I went back to the message.

It's me again, Matt. Thought you'd like to see one of my snaps from today. There are plenty more, some from inside Lucy's bedroom before you got there and others from Farn-borough. I don't think your ex-wife or her neighbors would be too happy if they saw them, let alone your daughter. She was very fond of the dog, wasn't she?

How the hell did he know all this? He must have been staking us out for weeks.

I've also got some e-mail addresses that I won't hesitate to forward the photos to if you start being uncooperative, Matt. I read on. He'd somehow managed to get hold of Caroline's company e-mail, as well as Jack's and Shami's at their places of employment. I don't imagine your ex-wife would be impressed if she found out that you'd disposed of the neighbors' dog. She'd take it as an indirect threat to Lucy and get her lawyers on to you straightaway. No visiting rights, no nothing. You get the picture? Sorry, that wasn't funny.

It wasn't, but he'd nailed me very successfully. The divorce had been a bad one, with Caroline wanting rid of me and me not wanting to put Lucy through the mangle. This would be just what Caroline needed to get me out of her life. But how did WD know? Or was he just guessing?

I'll be in touch again tomorrow, the message ended. That's when you'll be starting work for me. Get a good night's sleep.

I hit Reply.

Why are you calling yourself the White Devil? What's John

Webster's play of that name, first performed in 1612, got to do with anything? I clicked Send.

There was a chime soon afterward.

You got it eventually, Matt. I am the White Devil. Da-da. Cue doom-laden music. What's the play got to do with it? Come on, you can do better than that. But get some rest now or "Our sleeps are severed." Good night.

I sat back and looked up at the cracked ceiling. Jesus. This guy really knew how to get to me. "Our sleeps are severed"—*The White Devil,* act 2, scene 1; Brachiano divorcing Isabella, in Webster's great work of revenge and violent death. It was behind my novel *The Devil Murder,* the title being another quotation from the play. I'd studied Jacobean tragedy at college and been fascinated by it. There was a primitive inevitability to the plays that shook me—the mask of civilization was much flimsier and the seething bedlam beneath much closer than in Shakespeare, apart from *Titus Andronicus.* When I was searching for a plot to hang my third Sir Tertius novel on, I came on that of *The White Devil*—hypocrisy and corruption being justly punished. I even gave John Webster a small part. Most of the critics thought that was a neat touch. Some lunatic was taking his admiration too far.

Then I had another thought. In *The Devil Murder,* the villain, Lord Lucas of Merston, is done to death by the crazed father of a girl he has raped. The father happens to be a farmer and he kills the criminal by hacking him apart with a skinning knife. Sir Tertius finds the lord in the crucifix position, with his entrails hanging out.

Just like Happy's.

I put down the empty glass by my computer. The big slug of single malt had finally calmed me down. It had even brought a sense of perspective. This was all crazy. What was I doing, letting a nutter implicate me the way he had? It wasn't as if I was the one who'd killed Happy. It wasn't as if I'd extorted the five grand out of him. To nip this in the bud, all I needed to do was phone the police. They'd take some time to be convinced, but I would give them the money and show them where Happy's body was. I'd have a job explaining to Caroline and the Rooneys what I'd done, but I would think of a way. I had the e-mails, after all. Yes, that was it. I was putting a stop to this.

The phone rang before I got any further.

"Hello?" I said hesitantly, wondering if the White Devil had somehow discovered my ex-directory number.

"Matt, is that you?" My mother sounded perturbed.

"What is it, Fran?" I asked, the words coming out in a rush. "Are you all right?" If the bastard had done anything to her, I'd make him pay.

"Of course I'm all right, dear," she said, her voice softening. "You're the one who sounds worried."

That was typical of my mother. She could construct an entire mood around a few words. That was maybe why she was still a published author and I wasn't.

"Sorry. You know, problems with the writing…"

"Do you want to talk about it?" When I started out, I'd often spoken to Fran about the technicalities of fiction, but in recent years I'd kidded myself that I'd got beyond that stage. It would have been a good idea to get back to the basics with her, but I had other things on my mind tonight.

"No, it's all right. I'll sort it out." I remembered my initial fear. Could the Devil have got to her? "Is everything okay at home? No one's been…been bothering you?"

"Are you sure you're well, Matt?" she asked solicitously.

"Please, just answer the question."

I heard a sharp intake of breath. "As a matter of fact, you asked two questions." She paused to put me in my place. "Yes, everything is okay. No, no one's been bothering me. What's this about, Matt?"

"Nothing," I said, casting around for a get-out clause. "I saw something in the paper the other day about a prowler in your area."

"Really?" She didn't sound too bothered. "It wouldn't be the first time. Anyway, you know I always keep the doors and windows locked, and put the alarm on when I go to bed."

"Yes," I said, realizing that all I'd done was give her a reason to worry. Still, under the circumstances, it would be good if she took extra care.

"Anyway, I phoned to ask if you'd like come round at the weekend. Bring Sara, too."

I'd forgotten all about Sara. She was supposed to finish the story she'd been working on and come round to my place to spend the night.

"I'm...I'm not sure," I said. "I'll give you a ring. Good night."

The way Fran returned the greeting made it clear that she thought I was losing my grip.

Which was true.

Before I could move from the phone, I heard the key turn in the lock. Sara appeared, her brown hair tousled and her face lined. The furrows had been getting deeper in recent months. She worked too hard, and I knew I didn't always give her enough support.

"Hello, stranger," she said, dropping her bag. She peered at me. "What's the matter? You look like you've just seen a ghost."

"Um, no," I said, getting up and going over to kiss her. I'd been frantically trying to remember if I'd left anything around that would alert her to what had been going on. The screen saver was on the computer. I thought about switching the machine off, but that would only draw attention to it. I would shut it down normally when she was in the shower. She always headed straight for the bathroom after work.

"Hello, Sara," she said, giving me an encouraging smile. "It's lovely to see you. I've missed you so much."

I repeated the words, laughing. Sara had the ability to make anyone smile, not a quality widespread among journalists. It had helped her break some major stories.

"Sorry," I added. "I've had a hard day at the typeface."

Shit. Now she was on her way over to the screen.

"What have you been working on?" She looked at me hopefully. "Not the new novel."

I wasn't quick enough to dissemble. "Uh, no. Just some reviews."

The smile didn't fade. "Never mind. I'm sure it'll come together soon."

"Sara, my darling," I said, taking her arms. Her scent filled my nostrils. It took me back to the first time I'd met her. She'd walked up in a wave of perfume and I'd fallen head over heels in love on the spot. That had never happened to me before. Even more amazingly, she told me she'd had the same experience the first time she laid eyes on me across the crowded room. I shook my head to dispel the memory. "I…there's something I have to tell you." My serious tone made her move her head back to study me. I'd had it with the bastard I'd let into my life. I was going to share the burden. "Well, it's a bit weird. This morning I—"

My mobile rang. I raised my hands at her and went to my jacket pocket.

"Hello?"

"Matt, you will remember not to tell anyone about today, won't you?" The White Devil's voice was calm, almost cheerful. It had a neutral tone, as if it weren't really his—as if he was putting it on.

How did he know I was about to tell Sara?

"Matt, I know you're there. Speak!"

"Yes...I will remember that." I tried to smile at Sara as she went past me into the bathroom. I waited till the door had closed. "You bastard. Are you bugging me?"

There was a laugh that tailed off into a snarl. "What do you know about surveillance technology, Mr. Award-Winning Crime Novelist? As much as a sparrow can crap." The line went dead.

I sat down, my heart pounding. He was right. I didn't have a clue about modern surveillance hardware. He could have been beaming a camera down from a satellite for all I knew. The bastard had even found out my mobile number, though I guessed that wouldn't take either too much time or money. Shit. I was in this alone, after all. I couldn't risk anything happening to Lucy.

When Sara came out, I'd turned my computer off. I had my head in my hands.

"What's the matter?" she asked, clutching me to her warm body. "Who was that on the phone?"

"Just some tosser," I mumbled. Understatement of the millennium. Suddenly I remembered how close Sara and I had become over the past nine months. I was at the stage where I trusted her with everything. She was my savior; she could make anything better.

"Come to bed," she said, tugging at me gently, her cheeks red—they were always like that when she was aroused.

I followed her into the bedroom, the blood hot in my veins. But my head was filled with confused thoughts. Something was trying to make itself known.

"Come on," Sara said, tugging back the duvet. "I'll make you feel—"

The thought that had been nagging me burst to the surface.

"No!" I said, lunging forward.

"Well, well, Mr. Wells," Sara said, her smile slowly disappearing. "What have you been up to?"

She picked up the bundles of twenty-pound notes that I'd stuck under the covers when I brought Lucy round, and gave me a questioning stare.

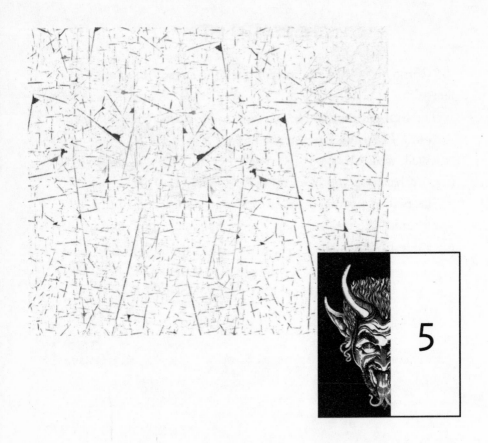

5

After what seemed like an eternity, Mrs. O'Grady, seventy-three and deeply wrinkled, finished arranging her bucket and mop in the cupboard off the sacristy. "Will that be all for tonight, Father Prendegast?" she asked.

"Yes, yes," the priest replied impatiently, his head with its large bald patch bowed over the papers on the table.

"Are you sure now?" Mrs. O'Grady had been doing the Wednesday night cleaning at St. Bartholomew's, West Kilburn, for more than thirty years and she prided herself on the solicitude that she afforded the men of God. The previous fathers had appreciated her, but this one was different. Although he'd been there for nearly ten years, she hardly felt that she knew him at all. He paid her little attention. She didn't like gossip, but she'd begun to believe what some of the other ladies said—that he'd come to their church under a cloud. There had been a scandal somewhere in the East End that was hushed up. She raised her head to the stained ceiling. Dear God, she thought, why can't your representatives on earth keep their hands to themselves?

Mrs. O'Grady took a step back when she realized Father Prendegast was glaring at her, as if he knew what was in her mind. She took her coat and hurried away, mumbling, "Good night to you, then." She stopped when she got outside and shivered. It wasn't cold—the last of the sun had spread in a red carpet over the western sky and its warmth was still in the air—but she felt a chill. There was something about that man, something she could almost smell. He was...he was dirty, a wrong 'un. She walked quickly down the gravel path, anxious to get back to her council flat and her little dog. She didn't notice the figure that rose up from behind one of the larger gravestones and moved silently toward the door of the church.

Norman Prendegast pushed his chair back and got up. At last the old cow had left him in peace. He selected a key from the ring on his belt and slotted it into the bottom drawer of an antique rolltop desk. He took the bottle of Jameson that one of the faithful had given him at Easter and broke the seal. The first few gulps did nothing, and then he began to feel the warmth rising from his belly. That was the stuff. He went back to the table and sat down again, setting the bottle on the accounts book he'd been trying to complete. He'd leave that chore to another night.

After he'd taken another long pull from the bottle, the priest fell into a reverie. Fifteen years he'd been in exile from his flock in Bethnal Green; fifteen years he'd been banned from even visiting them in his time off. It wasn't fair. He'd been everything a priest should be—unstinting in his efforts, a source of comfort to the faithful in times of loss and pain, a beacon of joy at weddings. His choir, his football and cricket teams, they'd won prizes. He swallowed again, but now the spirit tasted bitter as his grievances rose up around him like a demented chorus. You didn't do anything wrong. You were only offering them friendship. The boys loved you. The boys wanted you to touch them.

Father Prendegast heard a noise from the church. Mrs. O'Grady must have forgotten something. He stayed where he was. He didn't like the way she looked at him. She knew, he was sure of it. The hypocrites, the old harpies. They all knew about him, but they pretended they didn't. They pretended he was a normal priest rather than one who'd been given a last chance by the archbishop, and that only because the church couldn't face the shame. Five years in an isolated retreat in County Kerry and then this run-down hole. It was only full when the sinners came at Christmas and Easter. No one bothered to confess anything other than venial sins these days, anyway. They thought that meant they could forget the truly bad things they'd done. Hypocrites. Whited sepulchers. At least he'd confessed, though it had been required of him. Confessed and asked forgiveness. His conscience was clean, even if his desires still tormented him.

Norman Prendegast drank again. The bottle was still at his lips when the sacristy door opened, and then closed again.

"Who's that?" he demanded, his vision blurred. "Is it you, Mrs. O'Grady?"

The key turned in the lock.

"What's going on?" the priest said, his voice wavering. He tried to get the bottle out of sight. "This is a private room."

"Calm down, Father," said a low male voice. "I've just come for a little chat." The figure drew closer. "About old times."

There was something familiar about the voice, although the words were free of any recognizable accent.

"Who are you?" Father Prendegast asked, staring through the whisky-induced haze. "Do I know you?"

"Oh, yes," the man said. He was standing next to him now. "Don't you remember me?"

A gloved hand suddenly grabbed the priest's chin and forced his face round.

"Take a good look."

Prendegast blinked and tried to make out the features. The man was wearing a black cap, which he took off to reveal short blond hair. That meant nothing to him. But the features did. The small nose, the half smile on the pinched lips, but most of all the eyes—so brown that he could hardly distinguish between iris and pupil. Oh, sweet Jesus, was it really him, the one who'd brought him down? After all these years?

The intruder let go of his chin and laughed. "And my name is?"

The priest licked his lips and reached for the bottle. It was knocked off the table in a swift movement, smashing on the flagstones. The smell rose up to taunt him.

"What did you do that for?"

The hand was on him again, this time tightening on his throat. "What's my name, pederast?"

"Les...Leslie Dunn."

The grip loosened.

"Is the correct answer, Father. You win tonight's star prize." His attacker's face was close to his. "Ask me what it is, you pig."

"Please, I'll do anything…" He broke off as the pressure increased again. "Money…I've got…money."

"Is that right, Father Bugger of Boys?" There was another empty laugh. "Well, that's the one thing I don't need. Ask me what you've won."

"Ah...can't...can't breath... What...what have I won?"

He was pushed down onto the chair. Before the priest could resist, thick rope was being passed around his arms and upper body.

The face was up against his. He could smell mint on the breath of the altar boy he'd abused.

"You've won a first-class ticket on the midnight express to hell."

The last thing Father Norman Prendegast saw was a shining silver knife moving to and fro in front of his eyes.

The last thing he felt was a lancing agony from behind.

Detective Chief Inspector Karen Oaten, promoted to the Metropolitan Police's recently formed Violent Crimes Coordination Team in February, was standing in front of the altar of St. Bartholomew's. She was in white coveralls and bootees, the SOCOs crawling around her like a pack of hounds.

"Come on, Taff," she said, looking over her shoulder.

John Turner, wearing the same garb, came up the aisle slowly. His face was the same color as his protective suit. He had passed the inspector's exams and moved with his boss.

"I'll let you off," Oaten said in a low voice. "This is a bad one, right enough." The assistant commissioner responsible for the VCCT had made sure they got the case rather than the local division, and she'd arrived at the church just after one a.m. Even she had taken a deep breath when she saw what was on the altar.

The pathologist was still by the naked body. It was that of a flabby man in his fifties. He was lying on his chest over the altar, his legs and arms dangling down. A tall gold candlestick was on the ground, its top inserted between his buttocks.

"Who called it in?" the chief inspector asked.

"A Mrs. Brenda O'Grady," Turner replied, looking at his notebook. "She lives in a tower block down the road. She was in here doing the cleaning earlier tonight. Before she went to bed, she saw that the lights were still on and came to check. That's about all the sense I could get out of her. She saw the body."

"Does she know who it is?"

"She reckons it's the priest, Father Norman Prendegast, though she didn't look at him for long."

Karen Oaten nodded. "I'm not surprised." She turned to the front. "Let's go and see what the medic's got." She gave Turner a tight smile. "If you can handle it."

He returned the smile slackly. "I can handle it, guv." He owed Wild Oats plenty. She had insisted that he come with her to the Yard when she was singled out to join the new team. He still wasn't sure why he was there. Maybe it was because he never questioned her authority. The other blokes in the Eastern Homicide Division had never come to terms with being told what to do by a woman.

They picked their way past the SOCOs.

"Anything interesting?" Oaten asked.

One of the technicians, a bearded man, looked up and shrugged. "There are plenty of different fibers. It's too early to say if they'll give you any help. No bloody footprints or anything else obvious, I'm afraid."

They walked on up the steps to the altar. Other members of the team had already filmed and photographed the scene. The pathologist crouching down at the rear of the marble plinth was a short man with a protruding stomach whom they'd worked with before.

"Dr. Redrose," the chief inspector said. "What have you got for us?"

"Cause of death, a single, nonserrated blade wound to the heart," he said without looking up. "Delivered after the other wounds. I would hazard, none self-inflicted."

"Time of death?"

"Provisionally, between nine and eleven p.m."

"And the rest?"

"You know, Chief Inspector," the pathologist said, "this is a first."

"In what way?"

"In several ways. That's why it's so interesting." Redrose got to his feet. "First of all, you've got the ornate candlestick in his rectal passage." He inclined his head to the left. "If, as I suspect, that's its twin, then around thirty centimeters of gold is up there."

Turner pursed his lips. "Painful." Although he'd played rugby union until he left Wales ten years before, he still found the results of violence hard to take.

The medic glanced at him. "Painful doesn't even come close to describing what the poor devil went through."

"We think he was the priest," Oaten said.

"Ah. Sorry. The poor man of the cloth, then." He bent down. "Next, there's the eyes." He lifted up the head. "Take a look at that."

Turner steeled himself and went closer.

"Both removed with a sharp instrument," Redrose said. "You see here? Optic nerves cleanly severed."

"Where are they?" Oaten asked.

"Good question. They appear to have been taken as trophies, though you'll have to wait for the autopsy for confirmation. They might have been rammed down the throat."

"I see what you mean about it being a first," the chief inspector said. "I've seen bodies in churches before and I've seen mutilations, but not both together."

The pathologist stood up and gave them a triumphant grin. "I haven't finished." He lifted up the head again and pointed to the mouth.

"What is it?" Turner asked. "I can't see anything."

Karen Oaten leaned closer. "There's something projecting from the teeth." She raised a latex-covered finger. "See, Taff? It looks like a piece of paper in a clear plastic bag."

"Precisely," confirmed the medic.

"Can you get it out?" Oaten asked.

"You'll have to wait for the—"

"Let me rephrase that." She gave him a stony glare. "This is a particularly vicious murder. Time is of the essence if we're going to catch the killer. Please remove that piece of evidence."

"Very well, Chief Inspector. On your head be it." Redrose took a retractor from his bag and used it to open the dead man's jaws. A neatly folded square of paper about three centimeters across in the small bag fell onto the palm of Karen Oaten's hand. "Well caught, madam."

She ignored him, going over to the SOCO leader. "I need this opened and bagged," she said.

A few minutes later she and Turner were looking at an unfolded piece of white copy paper in a clear evidence bag. A line of words had been laser-printed on it.

"'What a mockery hath death made of thee,'" Oaten read aloud. She glanced at her sergeant. "What is that? The Bible?"

"Don't ask me," Turner replied, raising his shoulders. "I skipped chapel every time I could."

"We'll run it through the computer," the chief inspector said. "All that stuff's in digital form now."

"Sounds like someone really had it in for this Father Prende-gast," Turner said.

Karen Oaten looked back at the mutilated body on the altar. "I think we already knew that, Taff," she said, shaking her head at him slowly.

"Yeah," he said, feeling his face begin to glow, "I suppose we did."

The two heavily built men came over the ridge in the gloom, five meters between them. The last of the sun had disappeared into the clouds over the Atlantic and it was chilly on the moor—chilly enough for the hardiest walker to have headed back to the warmth of civilization hours ago. A damp wind was coming off the sea. Upland Devon was as unforgiving as ever.

"Anything, Rommel?" the man on the left said in a low voice.

"Fuck all, Geronimo," his companion grunted, checking the luminous compass on his right wrist. "According to the coordinates you worked out, we should have found him by now."

The first man looked around stealthily. He was wearing muddy camouflage fatigues. "To hell with this," he said, drawing his combat knife from the sheath on his belt. "I'm not having him do us again." The honed blade glinted in the light of the full moon that was rising in the east.

"Wolfe's never been caught, Geronimo." Rommel wiped moisture from his crew-cut hair. "Not by anyone."

"There's always a first time."

"And it's not tonight," came a voice from behind them.

The two men spun on their heels. Rommel's arm was grabbed and the knife chopped from it in a practiced karate move. He was jerked round to face Geronimo, a blade at his throat.

"Game over," said the assailant with a dry laugh. He released his captive and pushed him forward. "Christ, guys, I could hear you coming a mile off."

"Bollocks," Geronimo said, twisting his lips beneath a drooping mustache. "We took all the necessary precautions." He shone a torch on the ground between them.

Wolfe shrugged. "Okay, from five hundred meters, then." He glanced down at his victim. "You all right?"

Rommel nodded. "Take more than that to break any of my bones," he said, glaring at the taller man.

"Good. The Special Air Service is proud of you." Wolfe slipped his knife back into its sheath. "Well, slightly."

"Can we get back to the Land Rover now?" Geronimo asked.

Wolfe's expression grew more serious. "You must be joking. We're staying on the moor for another night. Don't worry. It's only a six-mile hike to the bivouac."

The other two exchanged glances and then grinned.

"Better get going, then," Rommel said, picking up his blade.

Wolfe nodded. "Good. I reckon you two are just about ready for our little jaunt to the big city."

They took a bearing and started walking northeast.

"How did you do it?" Geronimo asked after several minutes of rapid movement over the sparsely covered plateau. "How did you creep up on us?"

There was a long silence as their leader sniffed the wind. "I used all my experience and fieldcraft." He looked down a long valley, apparently sensing something in the dark. "And I had a purpose. You know that training ops like this are useless without a purpose."

"And the purpose is to track down the bastard who you reckon did for one of us," Rommel said.

"Correct. No one, repeat no one, fucks with an SAS sergeant, even if he's retired like Wellington was. Whoever it was is going to die in agony." Wolfe cocked an ear and raised his right arm. "They're down by the stream. Two of them. They must have got separated from their little friends."

Rommel and Geronimo drew closer.

"Exmoor pony for dinner again?" the latter asked, his voice level.

"Unless you've got a better idea," Wolfe replied.

The three men whose combat names had been chosen from warriors of old moved silently down the track in search of prey, their eyes reflecting the moon's cold light.

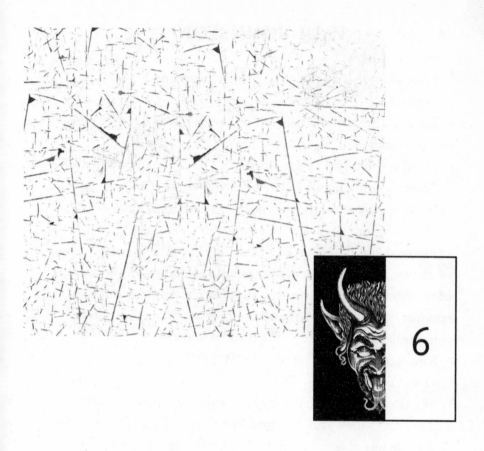

6

I looked at Sara, my lower jaw dropping. The five grand. What the hell was I going to tell her?

"I'm waiting, Matt," she said, her eyes locked on me. Sara had a disconcerting way of going from very loving to dead serious in a split second.

"Ah, right." I went over to the bed. "It's…it's money."

She raised an eyebrow. "Very funny. Is it yours?" She glanced down. "There must be thousands here."

"Um, five," I said, racking my brains for a credible explanation. "Five thousand."

"Five thousand pounds in cash?" Sara picked up one of the bundles and sniffed it. "What did you do? Rob a bank?"

"No, of course not. It's…it's a down payment."

"On what?"

I had it. "Actually," I said, sitting down beside her, "it's a bit embarrassing."

"Don't worry," she said with a laugh. "I love embarrassment."

"Bloody journalists," I said, receiving an elbow in my ribs. "Ow. Bastard journalists." I gave her a playful push.

"I'm waiting," she said, her expression serious again.

I looked her in the eye. I'd read how FBI agents were trained to do that, how it put them in a position of strength. "Well, I've been asked to ghostwrite the autobiography of a gangland enforcer." I'd also read somewhere that, if you're going to lie, you should keep as close to the truth as you can.

Sara seemed to have bought it. "Who?"

"I can't tell you that. I've been sworn to secrecy until the book's finished." I clenched my fists and raised them. "And you don't want to mess with this guy, know 'wot' I mean?"

A smile spread across her lips. "I might be prepared to pay for the information," she said, sliding a hand across my thigh. "Up front, know 'wot' I mean?"

"That is an atrocious attempt at Cockney."

She slapped my leg. "And yours was better?"

I started to collect the bundles.

"He paid you in cash?" she said, looking dubious again. "Did you sign a contract?"

"No. His is a cash business, innit?"

"All right," she said, after giving it some thought. "I won't tell the Inland Revenue." She grabbed my wrist. "But I want first option on any juicy bits, okay? The paper will pay well."

"I'll see," I said noncommittally. "That'll be up to the man himself."

Sara watched as I put the money in a holdall. "You'd better bank that tomorrow," she said, stretching her arms behind her head. "You know how unsafe this place is. You haven't even got an alarm."

I nodded. I knew only too well how unsafe my flat was. And how unsafe Lucy and Caroline were in our former family home. But the sight of the woman I loved waiting to be undressed on my bed drove away the fears. I brushed away the realization that my sparring with the lunatic and the disposal of Happy had aroused me, too. I didn't know what that said about my psychological condition.

Afterward Sara fell asleep quickly—she'd been away on assignments a lot recently. That left me on my own and anxiety gripped me again. What was I going to do about the White Devil? I wrestled with the problem for a long time.

The last time I looked at my watch, it was three-thirty. Sleep wasn't coming, and neither was anything like a plan of action.

Sara left first thing, after giving me a kiss and ruffling my hair. She was going to her place in Clapham to change for the office. I had a shower and got dressed, then headed off to pick up Lucy. I wasn't looking forward to seeing how she was taking Happy's disappearance.

As it turned out, I needn't have worried. Caroline and Shami had concocted a story that the dog had gone to dog hospital and that the dog doctors were taking care of her. My ex-wife told me that in a whispered conversation before she went to catch her train.

"Daddy?" Lucy said as we walked away from the house.

"Yes, sweetie?"

"Do you think Happy will come back from the dog hospital?"

I looked down at her freckled features and squeezed her hand. "Of course she will."

"It's just..." She paused and I heard a tiny sob.

"What is it, darling?" I said, bending down.

"It's just, Martin Swallow's dog got ill and he never...he never came home." Her eyes had filled with tears.

I gave her a hug and tried to comfort her. While I was telling her lies about Happy's imminent return, anger coursed through me. That bastard. He was already screwing up my daughter's life. What would happen when Caroline and Shami had to come clean about Happy having gone for good? One way or another, I was going to get back at him.

The rage was still in me when I got back to the flat. I'd only been in for a couple of minutes when the phone rang.

"'Morning, Matt." The White Devil's voice was jaunty. "Ready to start writing my life story?"

I swallowed hard and tried not to show any emotion. "I'm ready." It seemed that his proposition really was that I tell his story for him.

"Good. Turn on your computer. You'll find plenty of information. Read it and see what you think. Then do what you're good at. Don't worry, I don't want a biography. I want you to turn what I've done into the best crime story ever written. Add whatever you think is necessary, but don't take anything out. And make sure it's in the first person, okay? I, I, I." He gave a dry laugh. "I'm a reasonable man, Matt. Do me ten thousand words in a week and I'll send you another five grand. You'll get more information every day." He broke off. "And, Matt, remember the ground rule. Don't tell anyone." His voice was harsher. "You'll never know when I'm watching or when I'm listening.

Just like you'll never know if I decide to make a move on Lucy or anyone else you care about."

The line went dead. I hit 1471 and was told that the caller's number was unavailable. Shit. Then I realized that he'd used my restricted landline. How had he found that number?

I booted up my computer and checked my e-mails. As the Devil had said, there was a message from WD1578, with an attachment. 1578. I knew what he meant—1578 was taken as the date of John Webster's birth by many scholars. I copied the attached text to my hard disk and opened it.

Jesus. The guy—he didn't name his family—had been beaten regularly by his father and sodomized by his local priest. By the time he was nine, he was an accomplished shoplifter, fencing his loot to fund his collection of model tanks and soldiers. But that was only the beginning. When I got to the end, I discovered that he'd killed his old man by pushing him off the third floor of a partially completed building. He'd been twelve when he did that.

I felt the blood run cold in my veins.

A strange thing happened as I got down to work on the Devil's material. It was as if a curtain had been raised in my mind. For the past three months, I'd been clutching in the dark for a plot for my next novel. Suddenly it seemed that I could see things clearly, like at the beginning of a play. I could see the backdrop— Bethnal Green and its run-down tower blocks—and the characters had appeared on the stage: the pedophile priest, the bullying father, the quiet and loving mother. And in the center was the White Devil himself, small and devious, his spite and viciousness concealed.

And then I understood why he'd chosen to call himself that.

The White Devil was a play in which evil and guilt were hidden under the guise of courtly manners. White Devils were hypocrites, corrupt evil-doers lurking beneath layers of apparent probity. That was how the bastard had got away with the murder of his father. No one had suspected that the quiet altar boy could have stood up to a drunken laborer, let alone push him to his death.

I felt the quickening of breath I used to have when I hit on a plot that I knew I could turn into a decent book. It had been a couple of years since that had happened. Maybe Caroline was right. I'd constructed a comfort zone with my Albanian books, writing stuff that interested me and not much caring what readers might want. But this had the ring of credibility about it; this was cut from the rough fabric of life rather than the tissue of my imagination.

As happened when things were going well, I made fast progress. In the past, I'd thought about books for months before I started writing—wrangling about who was going to tell the story, what the relationships between the characters would be, what theme I wanted to tackle. But in the last Sir Tertius book, that had all come together without much advance planning. I'd just sat down, scribbled a few notes and started writing. That was also what happened with the Devil's story. By the time I went to pick up Lucy, I'd written the first chapter. It ended with the antihero I was calling Wayne Deakins (the initials WD being significant) knocking his father out in the living room. Before I left, I backed up what I'd written onto a diskette. Then it occurred to me that I should have copied all of the Devil's messages, too. I'd do that later.

Christ, was I really going to get a publishable novel out of the lunatic's life? Then I remembered how deep the Devil had his claws in me. He was obviously as mad as the avenging killers in Webster's play.

What chance did I have of exiting the final scene upright?

I had to think on my feet when I took Lucy back to Ferndene Road after school.

Shami Rooney was sitting in the front room next door. I knew she'd taken the day off work because of Happy. She stood up as soon as we opened the gate and came out.

"Matt?" she said, her voice taut. "Can I have a word?"

Before I could reply, she was on her way round. I took Lucy into the dining room and sat her at the piano.

"What's up?" I said over my shoulder. "Yes, practice the one about the crocodile, darling."

Shami beckoned me out into the hall.

"You were here during the day yesterday," she said, stating a fact rather than asking a question.

I managed to hold her gaze. "What do you mean?"

"Mrs. Stewart in number eight says she saw your Volvo when she was having her lunch. You know she always sits in the bow window looking out over the park."

My gut twisted as I remembered that detail. Mrs. Stewart was a sour-faced old widow who disapproved of anyone who didn't buy the *Daily Mail*. She particularly disapproved of people who got divorced, although I was the only one in my family she took that out on—apparently Caroline was guiltless in the matter. The reason she sat staring at Ruskin Park was so she could rush out and berate anyone who didn't clean up after their dog. Christ. I wondered how much she'd seen.

"Oh, yeah," I said, giving Shami a slack smile. "I did pop round. I was picking up some cases of books that I left in the attic." There was an element of truth in that. I was hoping that Caroline wouldn't go and check out my story, because the cases were all still there. I was getting better at lying to order, but there was still room for improvement.

"You didn't see Happy?" Shami asked. She was a decent woman, plump with a sweet face, and I didn't like what I was doing. Then again, if I told her what had really happened to her dog, she'd have a fit.

I shook my head. "No, I'm afraid I didn't. I thought she was inside."

The uncertain notes from the piano stopped.

"Daddy?" Lucy called. "Has Happy come back from the dog hospital?"

Shami and I exchanged glances, and then her eyes filled with tears. I touched her shoulder.

"Just a minute, sweetie," I said.

"I have to go," Shami said, swallowing a sob. "I need to stay by the phone. We've put ads in the papers." She hurried out.

I watched her leave, thinking that I'd better make sure Lucy didn't see the papers. I felt like a callous bastard. Then it struck me: maybe that was exactly what the Devil wanted.

I had to retain as much of my own nature as I could if I was going to survive this.

I went back to my place and logged on to my e-mail program. I wasn't surprised to see a message from the Devil, with another attachment.

Send me what you've got, Matt, I read.

I hit Reply and attached my text. I experienced what used to happen when I sent completed novels to my editor—brief sadness that my offspring had left home mixed with apprehension about what the recipient would think of it.

I leaned back in my chair, suddenly feeling exhausted. I was going round to Sara's when she finished work. I was desperate to see her, even though I couldn't share my burden. She'd brought me out of the depression that most writers live with often enough, her kindness and quick smile acting on me like a spell. She was my guiding light.

I stood up and headed for the kitchen—which wasn't more than an alcove—and made a pot of coffee. Then I sat down in front of the TV and turned on the news. I'd missed the national bulletin and the local London report was on. Normally I wouldn't have bothered watching yet another policy initiative by the mayor and more shots of beleaguered commuters. This time, when I got the gist of what was being presented, I made an exception.

A black female reporter was standing in front of a small Victorian Gothic building.

"…of St. Bartholomew's Catholic Church in West Kilburn. Detectives from the Metropolitan Police's elite Violent Crime Coordination Team were called to the scene not long after midnight. The murder victim underwent a horrific attack in the church. Detective Chief Inspector Karen Oaten made this statement."

The screen was filled by the face of a blond woman who managed to look stern and alluring simultaneously. "I can confirm that the dead man is Father Norman Prendegast."

The coffee I'd just swallowed shot back up my throat.

"At this time we do not know who his assailant was, but it is likely that he—or possibly she—fled the scene with a substantial amount of blood on his or her clothing. I am appealing to the public to help us locate this very dangerous criminal. Please contact your local police station or call my team." She gave a phone number. "All information will be treated in the strictest confidentiality."

The reporter came back on and wrapped the story up. I wasn't paying attention to her anymore. I was sweating heavily and my gut was coiled in a knot.

I knew the name Father Norman Prendegast. I'd typed it several times that day. It had been in the White Devil's notes. It was the name of the priest who had abused him—he'd originally been called O'Connell, but the Church had arranged a new identity.

I felt myself falling into the abyss faster than Lucifer in *Paradise Lost*.

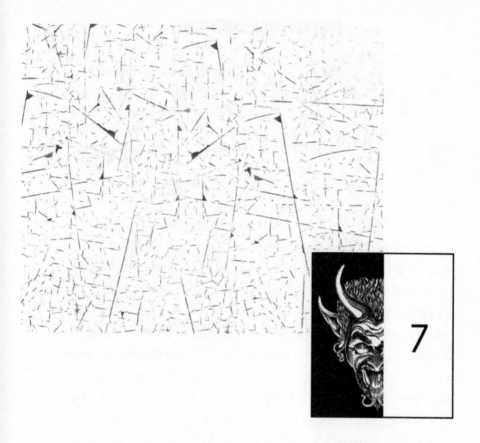

7

Eventually I got a grip. I kept telling myself not to be surprised. The White Devil had already shown himself to be a ruthless killer with Happy. The most worrying thing was the way he'd set things up. I was playing a game whose rules only he knew.

There was a chime from my computer—a new e-mail.

Facts Pertaining to the Murder of the Boy-Sodomizer Father Norman Prendegast.

One—a solid gold candlestick 1.6 meters in height was inserted into his fundament. Two—his eyes, which saw things they shouldn't have, were removed and taken to a safe place. Three—after he'd begged for mercy and whined that it wasn't his fault he liked boys, he was dispatched by a single stab wound to his black heart. Four—he was spread naked across the altar of the Mother Church that he'd defiled by his priesthood, as if he was buggering both it and, by extension, the corrupt leaders who turned a blind eye on his sins. Five—there was a quote from your favorite play about his person. "What a mockery…"

Are there bells ringing in your head, Matt?

There certainly were bells ringing in my head. This was getting beyond even the sickest of jokes. I got up, my knees jelly, and went over to the bookcase by the window where I kept my own first editions. I took out the second Sir Tertius novel, *The Devil Murder.* My hero had got himself involved with a bunch of demented Scots rebels led by a charlatan, who pretended he was descended from William Wallace. As history showed, rebels often ended up rebelling against one another. The murderous Rennie was set upon by his own followers after Sir Tertius revealed his lies. They performed a black mass in a ruined abbey and killed him by "skewering his fundament," putting out his eyes and driving a dagger through his heart. When he found out about the murder, my clever-dick hero spouted the line from *The White Devil* about death making a mockery of the victim.

What was going on? Did the White Devil want me to write his story or was he framing me for the murder of the priest?

I sent a message asking those questions to the last e-mail address. It bounced back with a fatal error, saying the account no longer existed.

The phone rang, making me jump.

"Matt."

Christ, he did have a camera on me. Or was he just guessing I'd be climbing the walls?

"What are you doing?" I shouted.

"What's your problem?" he replied mildly. "You've got an alibi for last night, haven't you?"

Sara. I might have known he'd have logged her presence.

"Yeah, that's true. But still…"

"Why am I using your modus operandi?" He gave a sardonic laugh that made the hairs on my neck stand. "Because I can. And because I genuinely like your books. But you should have written more with Sir Tertius. You disappointed a lot of your fans."

"I can't now, can I? I'm too busy writing your hideous story."

"Oh, you don't think it's hideous, Matt. You love it. I can tell that from the chapter you sent me. I'm really looking forward to the next one, where you describe what I did to that shit-eating priest. Don't disappoint me. You know how nasty I can get."

He cut the connection.

I put the phone down after wiping the receiver on my shirt. I felt so dirty that a ten-minute shower did nothing to shift the muck.

I was a murderer's accomplice, in thought if not in deed.

Later on, my inability to decide what to do disappeared faster than a wallet dropped in Leicester Square. After pacing up and down the confined space of my sitting room, I remembered the Devil's earlier messages. I needed to keep a record, so I copied them onto a diskette, and then found myself unsure what to do with it. If I'd been a character in a crime novel, I'd have deposited it with my solicitor, in an envelope bearing the words In the Event of My Death. But my dealings with solicitors over the divorce had made me swear never to have anything more to do with their breed. I could have hidden it somewhere in the flat. Then again, my attempt to hide the money had been a conspicuous failure. What about Sara? I didn't dare tell her anything about the Devil, but if I secreted the diskette somewhere at her place... Yes, that was a decent plan. I was going round there, anyway.

An hour later I was in Clapham. I went into her kitchen.

"Sara, my sweet?"

She was at the cooker, making an omelet. She gave me a mock suspicious look over her shoulder.

"You want something."

"Charming."

She laughed. "Only joking. It's just that men are so transparent."

I let that go. "Actually, you're right. Did you see the news tonight?"

"Is there a night when I don't see the news? I am the news." She cut the omelet neatly in two and flipped the pieces onto plates. "Here you are." We went over to the table.

"There was a murder," I said, pouring her a glass of Chinon Blanc.

"There were several murders. If you include Iraq and Palestine, there were dozens of murders."

"No, I mean in London."

Sara briefly held the salad she was transferring to her plate in midair. "Oh, the priest."

"That's the one." It had occurred to me that the Devil might have been messing me around. There hadn't been many details of what had been done to the victim on the news. Sara had plenty of contacts on the paper. "Do you think you could find out what happened to him?"

"Why?" Bluntness was a quality she said she'd inherited from her father, a Yorkshireman who used to run a farm. I hadn't met him and didn't want to.

"Because I write crime novels," I said, looking down at my plate.

"You revolting voyeur," she said, pretending to be shocked. "Not to mention thief. Can't you make up your own ways of killing people?"

This conversation was getting ironic beyond even my limits. "Ever heard of realism?" I asked innocently.

"You're asking a reporter if she knows about realism?"

I raised my hand. "All right, point taken." I gave her a placatory smile. "Is there anyone on the crime desk you can talk to?"

"The crime desk?" she said, laughing. "Is that how you think newspapers work these days? Everyone has their own workstation, a computer and a phone."

"Okay, do you know anyone on the crime workstation?"

"You're serious, aren't you? You want me to do your dirty work for you." She refilled her wineglass. "You're still a journalist, aren't you? Why can't you use your contacts?"

"Oh yeah. I'll phone up *Maximum* and talk to my mates there about murder. The death metal expert will be just the guy to ask."

"Ha-ha." She gave me a tight smile. "All right, I'll make a call. Do you mind if I finish eating first?"

I managed to disguise my impatience. After we'd cleared up, I sat down and feigned interest in a women's magazine of Sara's. She got the message and picked up the phone.

The *Daily Independent*'s crime correspondent was apparently called Jeremy. I got the impression that Sara didn't like him much—she kept making faces at me while she was listening.

"Prat," she said as she put the phone down. "He went to Eton. But I have to admit he's bloody good." She looked down at the shorthand notes she'd taken. "God, this is nasty. Are you sure you want to hear it?"

I nodded, realizing with a sinking feeling that my fears were about to be confirmed. As they were. Candlestick, eyes, heart wound, altar and paper in the mouth—they were all as the Devil had listed.

"The police have banned reporting about the piece of paper," Sara said, her forehead furrowed. "Apparently there's something written on it. They're not saying what."

The quotation from Webster. I wondered what the Met's finest minds would make of that.

"Matt?" Sara said, coming across to me. "What's the matter? You've gone pale."

I gave her a weak smile. "As you said, it's pretty nasty." Sara hadn't read the Sir Tertius novels as she didn't like anything set in the past, so she wouldn't make the connection with the modus operandi. "Thanks," I said, pulling her down and kissing her.

"That's all right," she said, grinning lasciviously. "You vulture."

That didn't come close to what I felt about myself. But I still succumbed to our mutual desires, even though the relief from my cares was only fleeting. Later, when she was asleep, I put the diskette with the Devil's e-mails inside her copy of my last Albanian novel. I was beginning to understand what I was up against. If anything happened to me, there was a reasonable chance she'd take out my books and look through them.

I slept for almost five hours. It was the deep and dreamless kind of sleep that doesn't make you feel you've rested at all. I woke up as the first gray fingers of dawn slipped under the blind in Sara's bedroom. She was still on her side, her breath regular and her eyes tightly closed. I didn't want to wake her, so I stayed where I was. It was time I started thinking about how to stand up to the Devil.

What did I have to go on? His first e-mails had shown that he'd read my books carefully. That suggested he was educated to a reasonable level. He'd followed up on John Webster, as well. But the material he'd sent me about his childhood, underprivileged and abused in the extreme, didn't sit easily with that. He obviously came from a poor East End family. I didn't think I had many readers with a background like that. Had he managed to pass some exams after his father's murder? Had he got to college? He hadn't given away much for me to track him down—no family name, no address or school. At least I knew the name of the priest who'd abused him.

I sat up in bed, moving slowly to avoid waking Sara. I had a lead. If I was lucky, I wouldn't even have to do much tracing myself. The tabloid reporters would be swarming over the body, looking for a motive for the murder. His real identity would come out soon enough. If I had the name of the church he was attached to in the East End, I'd be able to check the altar boys—there must have been records of them. I didn't know the Devil's age, but I could limit the number of names to the years that the priest was there. The TV news had said that he'd been ten years at St. Bartholomew's. He was in his fifties, so he couldn't have been more than twenty years at his previous church. I was on the bastard's trail.

Then I remembered the threat the Devil posed to Lucy, Sara and everyone else I knew. If he was still watching me the way he had been when I got rid of Happy, then heading off to Bethnal Green would be asking for trouble.

I slumped back down under the duvet. What else could I infer about my tormentor? He'd found out a lot about my movements, and those of Caroline and the neighbors—he'd obviously been watching the houses in Ferndene Road for some time in order to work out their routines. I had another flash of inspiration. Mrs. Stewart down the road. Maybe she'd noticed someone loitering in the park. The prospect of going to talk to the desiccated old bigot wasn't appealing, but it was a start. Even if he was watching me, the Devil couldn't really get uptight about me going down there. I could take Lucy with me and make the visit look like a family one. Christ. I reined myself in. What was I thinking of? Lucy was already in enough danger. I'd talk to Mrs. Stewart on my own.

What else? The guy obviously had a lot of spare time on his hands. He also had the wheels that he'd used to tail me to Farnborough, and a high-quality camera. Did he have money and therefore didn't need to work? Or was he paying people to watch me and the others? Neither of those thoughts made me feel good.

What about the White Devil's motives? Did he really want his story written up as a novel? There must be more to it than that. Why had he chosen me? Did he really like my books? Had he obtained some insights into my character from my writing? He had an uncanny ability to foresee how I would react. I had the distinct feeling he was using me as more than his paid scribe. Was he trying to tie me to his criminal activities?

So much for the bastard. The question now was, how to stand up to him? I had friends—my mates from the rugby club, other crime writers—who would help me out. But I couldn't risk Lucy by contacting them. Tell no one, the Devil had said. I'd seen what he'd done to Happy, and if he was the priest's killer, he was capable of anything.

No, I was still alone. But maybe, if he gave me more to go on, I could make use of my friends. Some of them were almost as crazy as he was and others had skills that would definitely be useful.

But not yet. I had to play for time.

I didn't manage to get back to sleep.

I made it to Caroline's in time to take Lucy down to school. We could have gone in the car, but I'd always loved the half hour we spent walking together. My daughter was in pigtails and she was inordinately proud of them. She seemed less concerned about Happy now. I'd heard from my ex-wife that Jack and Shami hadn't had any response to their appeals so far, and that they were both desperately unhappy. The Devil was ruining more lives than mine.

I found myself staring suspiciously at every male we passed. I tried to resist the temptation to keep looking round, but I took the opportunity to check if anyone was following us when we waited for the traffic lights to change. Unless he'd kitted himself out with a kid or kids in school uniform, there was no one out of the ordinary on the streets leading to Dulwich Village. Then the idea that the Devil was one of my fellow parents hit me. I dismissed it rapidly. I didn't know anyone who'd been brought up in the East End, let alone anyone who could have done that to the priest. Or did I? Maybe there really was no one I could trust. Except Sara. But she was the last person I wanted to bring into the limelight. The bastard already knew about her.

I said goodbye to Lucy and watched her get into line in the playground. When all the kids were inside, I headed back to Caroline's to pick up my car. And to talk to Mrs. Stewart. I wasn't looking forward to that, but I forced myself to come up with an approach that wouldn't raise her suspicions.

I saw her sitting in her front window as I approached. She turned and gave me a disapproving look, her eyebrows rising in surprise as I opened her gate and went to her door. There was the sound of several locks turning and bolts being undone.

"Good morning, Mrs. Stewart," I said cheerfully.

I could see she was struggling with how to address me. She knew only my first name and she obviously wasn't keen on using that.

"Lucy's father," she said at last. "Can I help you?"

"Matt," I said, unable to resist rubbing her nose in it.

She didn't respond and she didn't invite me in.

"Mrs. Stewart," I said, "I hope *you* can help me. I was wondering if you'd noticed a man with a camera in Ruskin Park. He'd have been there several times over the past few weeks."

She peered at me through thick, pink-rimmed glasses. "A man with a camera?" She thought about it, and then looked at me suspiciously. "Why do you want to know?"

I smiled in what I hoped was a suitably fatuous way. "Well, I've got this friend, Steve Jones is his name, and we had a bet." I saw her lips tighten. Either she recognized the name of the Sex Pistols' guitarist or she frowned on gambling. I guessed the latter. "He's a keen birdwatcher, you see, and he's been taking pictures of what Ruskin Park has to offer in the avian line. Anyway, I thought he was pulling my leg—I mean, why come here when there are so many larger parks in London? So he bet me that he was telling the truth and that he's so good at standing behind trees that I would never even see him. And I haven't." I smiled at her ingratiatingly. "But I was thinking, if you had, I could still win the bet. I mean, if you could tell me, if you saw him, of course, which trees he was hiding behind…"

I could tell she wasn't convinced by my story, but she wasn't able to stop herself showing off how observant she was.

"As a matter of fact, I have seen a man."

I felt my stomach clench.

"I don't remember where he was exactly, but I saw him at least three times." She leaned forward conspiratorially. "In fact, I thought about calling the police in case he was a stalker or a child molester. But I watched him through my binoculars. He never stayed long, just a few minutes in the morning and a few more in the late afternoon."

"Can you describe him?" I asked. "Just so I can be sure it's my friend."

"'Nondescript' is the best I can do," the old woman said, nodding as if that was how she'd expect any friend of mine to look. "He always wore a black coat and a woolen cap pulled low over his forehead. And, yes, he did have a camera."

"What kind of size was he?"

"Medium height, I would say. At best."

"Yes, that sounds like Steve," I said lamely. "Mrs. Stewart, you remember when I was round at our...at Caroline's house in the middle of the day earlier this week?"

"The day Happy went missing," she said, her eyes narrowing.

I nodded. "Did you happen to see him then?"

She shook her head. "No, I didn't." She started to close the door. "I was watching you and wondering what you were doing."

I gave her my story about shifting books. It didn't look like she was too convinced.

"Good day to you," she said, closing the door in my face.

I stood outside the black wooden panels and wondered exactly what she'd seen. Did she think I'd loaded Happy into the Volvo?

I walked away. All I'd learned was that the Devil, or someone working for him, had been in the park—something I already knew from the photograph. And that he—or his sidekick—wasn't very tall. Big deal. All I'd really done was make Mrs. Stewart suspicious, and perhaps draw her to the bastard's attention.

Too bad, I thought as I went back to the Volvo. I had other things on my mind.

In particular, the contents of the next e-mail attachment that I was sure was waiting for me back home.

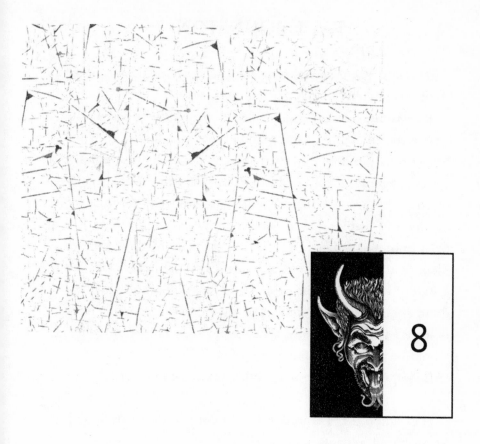

8

The man was standing at the window of his penthouse. Today the river looked even grayer than usual. It was amazing that salmon and other fish survived in that murk, he thought. In the past it had been much worse, though. He remembered the bodies floating downstream and being picked up by scavengers in Dickens's *Our Mutual Friend*. Back then, the Thames wasn't grey—it was dark brown with the untreated sewage that poured into it twenty-four hours a day. But in John Webster's time it had been better—there were millions fewer people living in London in the early seventeenth century. And yet, the filth that culminated in the Great Plague must have been disgusting. The river had always been a sewer, from the time the Romans built the first city. The river was an open drain and human beings were animals. He knew that better than anyone.

The White Devil thought about the notes he'd sent the writer that morning. He couldn't have said that they'd disturbed him. Nothing disturbed him anymore. He was immune, driven, dedicated only to his purpose. But he'd felt stirrings of something as he put the facts down. Not remorse or anything as feeble as that. Not even hate, though there had been enough of that in the past. It took him some time to identify the emotion, but he finally got it. Pride. He was proud of what he'd done, just as he'd been proud of what he'd done to his father. People like that deserved to die, they deserved to die in agony. They had done, and soon others would be going the same way.

It was why he'd been put on the surface of the earth.

"Les Dunn, Les Dunn. Les 'as done it again! Les 'as done it again! Pissed 'is pants. Crapped 'isself."

The words burned into him, even though they weren't true. Richard Brady had always picked on him, from the first day in Primary One. He was big, red-faced, and he had a mouth on him. His father was a lorry driver who brought him sweets and other things he stole from his loads. Richard Brady didn't even have to nick from the shops on the Roman Road like the rest of them. He came to school with his pockets full.

It was the last year of primary school now.

"Oy, Les! 'Ave you done doing it?"

The crowd of arse-lickers around Brady sniggered. When Les didn't answer, the bully walked quickly over to him.

"I didn't hear what you said," Brady yelled, cupping his ear.

Les felt himself start shaking, but he kept his lips together.

"Gone all quiet, 'ave we?" Brady grinned, and then grabbed Les's balls. "Still can't hear you." He squeezed harder.

Les's eyes were bulging. He took a deep breath and whispered two words. "You're…dead."

Brady leaned closer. "What?" Suddenly he was less sure of himself.

"I'm…going to…fuckin'…kill you."

The bully took a step back, his face less crimson than usual. He looked round the crowd that had gathered. "Yeah, I think 'e's done doing it," he said, taking his hand away.

His cronies stared at him as he walked off, then started shouting at Les again. But he didn't care. He knew he'd won. He'd discovered the power of words and how to wield it.

For the rest of that final term, Richard Brady kept his distance. He still joined in when the other boys made fun of Les, but he didn't instigate the bullying. It was as if he'd seen a small dog's teeth and lost the will to taunt it. He even waved at Les on the last day in the playground. He was moving to Watford in the summer holidays and he wouldn't be seeing any of his primary schoolmates again.

By that time, Les had become an expert at concealing himself and watching people covertly. He took up a position behind some rubbish bins when the Brady family was getting ready to move out of the terraced house in Gawber Street. They had five kids and so much stuff that it wouldn't all fit in Mr. Brady's lorry. He'd got a friend to bring another one. When they'd filled it, old man Brady shouted out the address to the other driver.

Les smiled as he wrote it down in his notebook.

Two weeks later, he used some of the money he'd got from the local fences to take the train up to Watford. He had found a map of the town in the library and made a copy showing the streets between the station and the Bradys' new place. It was a sultry day, the August sun hidden behind gray-white clouds that presaged rain. Les hid behind a battered Ford Cortina. In the early afternoon, the five kids appeared. Richard was the third by age and the only boy. He said something and all four of his sisters started shouting at him. Then they gathered together and walked away. Richard watched them leave, and then turned in the opposite direction. Les followed him, slinging the canvas bag he'd brought over his shoulder.

Richard Brady didn't seem to have made any new friends since he'd arrived. He mooched around on a street corner, but when none of the local boys paid any attention to him, he set off toward a patch of green at the end of a road. Les, keeping his distance, realized that it was a small wood. Beyond it could be seen recently harvested fields. There didn't seem to be anyone around. The heat was keeping people indoors, as well as making Richard Brady's armpits damp. Les sniffed. He could smell him.

Brady disappeared into the trees. As Les got closer, ducking behind the parked cars, he picked up another scent. Richard was smoking from behind a tree trunk. When he reached the edge of the wood, Les squatted down and opened the bag. After he'd pulled on gloves and equipped himself, he concealed the bag beneath a bush and started to crawl silently through the undergrowth. He could hear Brady singing some horrible Sham 69 song about going drinking. He stopped when he got behind the tree. Controlled his breathing. And started the countdown. Ten…nine… On three, he tossed one of the bricks he'd brought to the left. On one, he went round the right-hand side of the tree. Brady was on all fours, looking in the opposite direction.

Les clubbed him on the side of the head with the other brick. Brady lay moaning on the parched earth, blood coming from his ear. He wasn't completely out, but Les wasn't bothered. He unwound the rope and slung it over a sturdy branch about eight feet above ground level. Then he got Brady into a sitting position and fitted the noose he'd fashioned round his neck. Les had spent hours working on it, having found a diagram in a book of knots in the library. There was so much to learn in there.

When he had it tight, he started pulling. Richard Brady was a fat pig. It took Les a few minutes to get him into a standing position, but he'd been working hard on his fitness, building up his upper-body strength. By that time, the bully was coming round. Les kept hauling away, until Brady's feet were well above the ground. The boy started to choke, his face redder than ever. His eyes opened. When he saw Les, they got wider. They were already bloodshot. The tip of his tongue was caught between his front teeth. As Les finished securing the other end of the rope, blood dribbled down Brady's chin. He was biting through his tongue, making throaty noises that sounded like someone trying to be sick and not succeeding.

Les smiled up at him. He'd taken the precaution of tying his hands and legs, as he'd seen in *The Big Book of Executions*. He stepped close and brandished the smoldering cigarette he'd found in the dust.

"Smoking is very bad for you," he said, taking a drag. "Sorry, I can't hear you. Are you done choking? Not yet? That's all right, I can wait."

And he did. He waited the thirteen minutes and twenty seconds it took Richard Brady to die. Then he undid the ropes from his wrists and ankles and took them away, along with the two bricks—he dumped them in cleared ground near the station.

On the train back to Euston, Leslie Dunn couldn't stop smiling.

★ ★ ★

There was a small piece in the evening paper the next day about a boy found in a wood on the outskirts of Watford. The police didn't think it was suicide and their inquiries were continuing. But it never occurred to them to come down to the East End. A month later, Les was scanning the paper in the library. The coroner had pronounced an open verdict. He said he suspected that other boys may have been involved, but the police had been unable to make a breakthrough. Richard Brady's family was said to be distraught.

Les looked that word up in the *Oxford English Dictionary.*

"Ha!" He snorted before he could stop himself.

"Shoosh!" said the elderly librarian, the one with her gray hair in a ponytail. She'd taken the boy under her wing and looked very disappointed by his outburst.

"Who's John Webster?" Karen Oaten asked. She was sitting at her desk in the glass-partitioned office on the eighth floor of New Scotland Yard.

John Turner looked at his notebook. "He wrote plays, apparently. He was born around 1578 and he died around 1630. Here."

The chief inspector looked around. "What, in the Yard?"

"In London," Turner said, unamused. He'd spent the previous evening reading through the Penguin Classics volume of Jacobean tragedies. It was the first Penguin Classic he'd ever bought and he'd be charging it to expenses. "He was famous for two plays—*The Duchess of Malfi* and *The White Devil.*"

"Tell me the line in the victim's mouth was from the first one."

Turner shook his head. "Sorry, guv. 'What a mockery hath death made of thee' is line 125 from act 5, scene 4 of *The White Devil.*"

"Bollocks," Oaten exclaimed. "That's just what we need. A Satanist killing priests. The papers are already having a feeding frenzy." She indicated the pile of newsprint that she'd dumped on the floor next to her desk.

"Priests?" Turner said. "We've only got one."

"So far." The chief inspector leaned back in her chair. She was wearing one of the well-cut gray trouser suits she'd taken to since her promotion. "All right, what's the story of this play?"

Turner sat down opposite her and gave her a résumé of the action.

"So what you're saying is that a bunch of aristocrats go around slaughtering one another to get their own back?"

"Basically, yes, guv."

She ran her hand across her hair. "Is that what this is about? Revenge?"

Turner looked dubious. "Could be, I suppose."

"And who's the White Devil?"

"I'm a bit confused about that. There isn't a character with that name. According to the notes, White Devils are evil disguised, or hypocrites. So just about all the characters are White Devils."

Oaten gave him a frustrated look. "Is there a priest?"

"Yes, there is, actually. Monticelso. Well, he's a cardinal. And he ends up pope."

"Does he get murdered?" she asked hopefully.

Turner shrugged. "Sorry, he doesn't, guv."

The chief inspector held her hand out. "I'd better read the thing myself," she said. "What did you do at college, Taff?"

"What college?"

"Ah, sorry. I did sports science, so this is all going to be over. my head, too."

Turner was aware that Wild Oats had been a sportswoman. The word in the Eastern Homicide Division was that she'd played hockey for the England second team and that she'd been a useful high jumper. There had been plenty of belly laughs about that when she wasn't around. "You were a sportswoman, guv. Why did you join the force?" He fully expected to be told where to stick his question.

Instead, Oaten put down the book he'd handed her and chewed her bottom lip. "Because I like discipline, Taff. That's what I got from sport. I get it in the Met, too. Not the army-style rubbish that we did at the college in Hendon—marching up and down like a bunch of moronic squaddies. I mean the discipline of an investigation. Putting everything together in a logical fashion and catching the villain."

"And you reckon that reading a seventeenth-century play will help us catch this lunatic?"

Oaten sighed. "I'll take any help I can get." She looked down at the files that covered her desk. "The SOCOs haven't come up with anything that looks much good. No unusual clothing fibers, no blood apart from the victim's, thousands of fingerprints in the church—but you can be pretty sure our killer's aren't among them since the candlestick was clean. He had gloves on throughout, obviously. The autopsy confirmed Redrose's preliminary conclusions, and there was no sign of the eyes anywhere. The people who attended St. Bartholomew's haven't got a bad word to say about Father Prendegast. Now that he's dead, at least. But we got the feeling some of them didn't like him much, didn't we? He doesn't seem to have had any relatives or close friends. Devoted to the children of God, as Mrs. O'Grady said." She glanced up at him. "Are we getting anywhere with his previous...what's the word? Incumbency."

Turner laughed. "You mean his last job?" The laugh died when he saw the look on her face. "Well, he was in Ireland, in some kind of monastery."

"And before that?"

"Simmons and Pavlou are checking."

"Put rockets up their arses, will you?" Oaten turned back to her papers.

"Guv?" the inspector said nervously. "Do you think we've got a serial?"

The chief inspector raised her head wearily. "Do I *think* we've got a serial? Applying the discipline of the investigation, no, I don't. There isn't any evidence suggesting that. The experts told me the MO doesn't match any known pattern." She pursed her lips. "Applying my gut feeling, I'll put my pension on there being more killings, Taff. There will have been previous ones, too. No one carries out this kind of carefully planned and executed—excuse the pun—activity without having been there before." She bent her head again.

John Turner walked out of her office with a heavy heart. He had the feeling he wasn't going to be seeing Naomi and the kids much in the coming weeks. At least he didn't have to read any more old plays. What was the line he'd copied down? "See the corrupted use some make of books."

Dead right. He was glad he'd never made it past A levels.

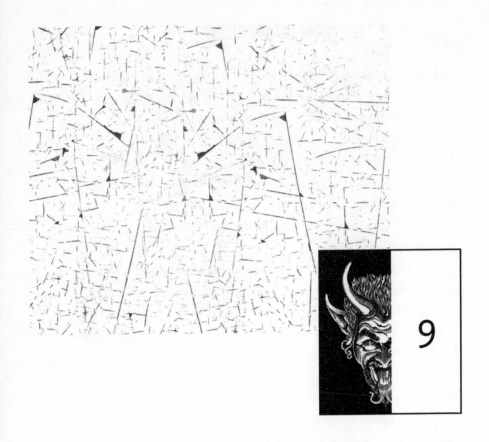

9

I pushed my chair back from the desk. My armpits were drenched and my stomach was in turmoil. The lunatic. He'd murdered the boy who'd bullied him at primary school. Not only that. At the age of twelve, he'd planned and carried out the killing with what seemed like a total lack of emotion. This guy could have had a great career as a hit man. Jesus, maybe that's what he was.

Thinking more about the text he'd sent me, I realized I could make it into a convincing narrative without too much difficulty. Not because it would be based on real life—I was convinced the murder had actually happened and didn't see the need of wasting time searching newspaper archives, especially when I didn't know the year it took place or whether the name Richard Brady was real—but because I found myself empathizing with the Devil. He'd suffered years of violence from his father, so he killed him. He'd been ridiculed and physically assaulted by the bully, so he hung him from a tree. He'd been abused by the priest, so he slaughtered him in his own church. And his adoption of the White Devil as an alias suggested that, like the Jacobean playwrights, he was obsessed with revenge. That was something I could relate to, not that it made me feel proud of myself.

Ever since I'd been cut loose by my publishers and my agent, resentment had been festering in me. In the early days after my double rejection, I'd come up with numerous schemes to get my own back—by pouring paint stripper over my agent Christian Fels's beloved vintage Bugatti, by sending an envelope full of shit to my editor Jeanie Young-Burke, by bad-mouthing them to everyone I knew, by showing up at other authors' launch parties and dousing with beer the critics like Alexander Drys and Lizzie Everhead, who'd knifed me. In the event, all I'd managed was the article in the newspaper bitching about the callousness of modern publishing. The following day, a crime writer who'd never liked me much sent an e-mail consisting of two words: *Sad git.*

Vengeance, retribution, the avenging angel—there was something attractive about those ideas, something that seemed right. Perhaps because the Old Testament concept of an eye for an eye underpinned our concepts of justice, of crime and punishment, but perhaps also because revenging yourself on someone was an ethical act. An injustice had been perpetrated and there was nothing inappropriate about exacting due recompense. Everyone had heard of the wronged wives who cut up their husband's Savile Row suits, buried their CD collections or broadcast tapes in the local pub of the adulterers cavorting with their lovers.

They became popular heroines, women who'd taken a deserved pound of flesh. The desire for vengeance was hardwired into the human psyche. The question was, how far did you take it? How many laws were you prepared to break? In my case, the answer to the second question was a pathetic none. The Devil was clearly situated at the opposite end of the scale.

But that didn't mean the emotions I felt were any less strong. I didn't want to kill Christian or Jeanie, but I'd happily have humiliated them or made them weep. How different was I from my tormentor? I thought of Robert Louis Stevenson's *Dr. Jekyll and Mr. Hyde*—two sides of the same man, the evil "hidden" beneath the good. Or Joseph Conrad's "secret sharer"—the doppelganger, a reflection of yourself that you struggle to come to terms with. Was that why the Devil had chosen me? Was he so smart? Nothing he'd done up till now contradicted such a conclusion. He'd read my books—Sir Tertius in the violent stew of a London enthused by revenge tragedy, Zog Hadzhi in the vendetta-stricken badlands of Albania. He'd also read my article. The bastard knew me better than I did myself. He may even have understood my fascination with revenge before I found myself in the position of wanting it.

Sickened by the realization that I was driven by the same urges as the murderer, I hammered out a couple of thousand words about the death of the bully. When I reread it, I saw that I'd given the narrator/murderer, Wayne Deakins, a psychological profile based as much on my own as on the one I'd inferred the Devil possessed. Bloody hell. He was pulling my strings as if I were a marionette.

By three o'clock in the afternoon, I'd had enough. I walked down to the village and went into the newsagent's, planning to read the paper while I was waiting for Lucy. I couldn't miss the tabloid headlines. Dead Priest Was Pedophile, Shame of Church Cover-Up, Murder Victim Was Pervert. I bought a selection of tabloids and broadsheets, and found a bench in Dulwich Park.

The consensus was that the Catholic Church had spirited Father Prendegast away from his church in the East End of London in May 1979, when complaints were made about his conduct by some altar and choirboys. He'd been sent to a remote monastery in western Ireland and given a new identity. The Church had taken out injunctions against all the papers, threatening to sue if the dead man's former name was published. Its line was that the boys and their families needed to be protected from "unwanted intrusion into their privacy." The tabloids weren't cowed any longer. They'd gone ahead and printed the priest's real name of Patrick O'Connell and the name of his church—St. Peter's in Bonner Street. They also had interviews, no doubt paid for, with two boys, now in their late thirties, who claimed that Father Pat, as he'd encouraged them to call him, had fondled them, taken off their clothes and submitted them to repeated sexual abuse. They expressed horror that he'd been given a new identity and another job by the Church. The archbishop wasn't commenting, and neither were the police. They were the only ones who'd shut up shop. Everyone from MPs to Anglican bishops had got in on the act, condemning the Catholic Church and demanding that it put its house in order. Lawyers, no doubt in private rubbing their hands with glee at the prospect of juicy compensation cases, were also to the fore.

I looked up at the sky, pale blue dotted with cotton-wool clouds, and worked through what this meant for me. I now knew where the priest had worked, and the names of two of his victims. It wouldn't be difficult to find out the names of other boys who had attended St. Peter's. In fact, it would be very easy.

I wondered if the White Devil was indirectly challenging me to discover who he was. He must have known that the priest's background would come out. Was he relying on the fact that I would be too frightened for Lucy and Sara to take any steps? I lowered my eyes and looked around. Apart from some women with buggies and toddlers, there was no one in the vicinity. But the Devil—or someone working for him—could be watching from the bushes, waiting for me to make a wrong move. I wasn't prepared to do that, especially now that I was about to have Lucy with me.

But later? Maybe I would try to contact the men who'd been interviewed. One of them ran a tool shop in Carlisle now, while the other had a fruit and vegetable stall on the Roman Road— Harry Winder was his name. Then I had a thought that made me sit up. Could he be the Devil? Or could Andrew Lough, the hardware man in the north? I examined their photographs. Winder was tall, thickset and balding, a family man with four children, while Lough was in a wheelchair suffering from early-onset multiple sclerosis. Neither of them were likely candidates, though I couldn't rule them out. In any case, they would probably remember the names of other boys.

My mobile phone rang. No number was displayed on the screen.

"Hello, Matt." It was the White Devil. "Enjoying the papers?"

"Where are you?" I said, standing up and turning round 360 degrees. I could see no one speaking on a phone.

"Wouldn't you like to know?" He chuckled, but there was no warmth in his voice. "So now you know about the good father's dirty past. What are you going to do? Dash off down the Roman and talk to Harry Winder? Ring up Andy Lough? I didn't know he had MS. Still, he always was a bit of a tosser."

Bastard. He was way ahead of me.

"Matt? You've gone all quiet."

"What do you want?"

"Oh, just passing the time of day. Have you written up the bully episode?"

"Yes. I'll send it to you later."

"You *are* doing well. Another chapter and you'll be in line for the next cash payment."

"I don't want your filthy money."

"Oh, yes, you do." The Devil's tone hardened. "That's our agreement, remember?" He gave a dry laugh. "Besides, you never know. You might catch me when I deliver it."

"What the fuck are you playing at?" I shouted, getting a sharp look from a woman with a small girl. I lowered my voice. "Are you trying to frame me? Did you have to kill the priest the way you did?"

"That was a token of my admiration for your books," he replied smoothly. "You shouldn't go putting ideas in people's heads, Matt. Yes, you're right to be concerned. One anonymous call to Scotland Yard and you become suspect number one."

"Oh, bollocks," I said, trying to play tough. "Who's going to believe that a crime novelist would go around murdering people the way he does in his books? Not even the police are that thick."

"Don't panic, Matt. Remember, you've got an alibi." He paused. "Of course, you could have hired someone else to do your dirty work. That happens in your books, too."

"Screw you," I said under my breath.

"Careful," the Devil replied, his tone sharp again. "Your alibi would disappear if I decided to make a move on Sara."

I felt the hairs rise on the back of my neck. "You—" I broke off when I realized the danger of provoking him further.

"Now, go off like a good daddy and pick up Lucy, Matt. I'm looking forward to the piece you've written. I know you're enjoying this project. It's right up your street, isn't it?"

I didn't answer.

"Isn't it?"

"I suppose I have an interest in revenge, if that's what you mean."

"That's what I mean, all right, Matt. You're no different from me. Oh, in case you were thinking of it, don't bother checking up on my background in the East End." He laughed. "Priests aren't the only people who can get new identities. And priests aren't the only people who die in agony for their sins."

He rang off.

I shivered. The threat was clear. I was no nearer to him than when he'd first contacted me. But, as he'd just shown, he was very close to me and the ones I loved. Then an alternative meaning of his last words struck me. Jesus, was he lining up to murder someone else? Was he going to use another of the methods from my novels?

I didn't know what to do.

Someone tapped me on the shoulder when I was in the playground waiting for Lucy. I whipped my head round, my eyes wide.

"Christ, Matt, what's up?"

"Sorry, mate." I slapped my friend Dave Cummings on the arm. "Don't go creeping up on people." I nodded to Ginny, who was hanging back as if she didn't want to intrude. Her face was pale, but her eyes were fixed on her husband with a mixture of boredom and dislike. I'd begun to wonder how their marriage survived.

He eyed me dubiously. "Are you all right? You don't look too good."

"Not enough sleep," I said, yawning.

Dave grinned. He was a Yorkshireman, of medium height but heavily built. His nose had been broken so many times that the surgeons could do nothing but shape it into a ragged slalom. He used to be a useful scrum-half with a turn of speed that brought us a lot of scores. "New book on the go?"

"Yeah," I replied listlessly.

"Got a contract?"

"Not yet."

"You should get a real job, mate." He ran his hand over his thick brown hair.

All the time I'd known him, he'd worn it short at the front and long at the back in the much-mocked mullet style—he said he'd missed his chance when he was young.

"What, like yours?" Dave was an ex-paratrooper. He had a reputation for barely restrained ferocity on the field and his club nickname was Psycho. He was equally forceful in his business. He ran a demolition company and took great pleasure in operating the machines himself whenever he could.

"What's wrong with my line of work?" he said, squaring up to me with mock aggression. "At least I don't sit around making things up all day."

I wished that was what I was engaged in at present. "What are you doing here, anyway? Have you knocked down every old building south of the river?"

He gave me another manic grin. "No. I gave myself the afternoon off. I'm taking Tom go-karting."

"Don't get behind the controls yourself, you lunatic."

He laughed and slapped his gut. He'd given up playing around the same time I had. "I wish I could."

The bell rang and the sound of children's voices started to rise to a crescendo.

"Are you sure you're all right, Matt?" Dave said, looking at me with concern.

I nodded and concentrated on finding Lucy. "Of course I am."

"Here, Tom!" he shouted, waving to his crew-cut eight-year-old. He nudged me in the ribs. "Let me know if there's anything I can do," he said, smiling at Lucy. "I mean it."

I bent down to kiss my daughter. Over her head I watched Dave wait for Ginny and their daughter, Annie, with ill-concealed impatience. I felt my eyes sting. That was the problem. I couldn't tell Psycho or anyone else about the bastard who was haunting me in case he turned on them and theirs.

Lucy chattered away as we walked back to Ferndene Road, but I found it difficult to follow what she was saying. I was thinking about the Devil and how to get to him before he killed again. He'd made it clear that he'd changed his name. Of course, that could have been a lie to put me off his trail, but I didn't think so. He'd shown how careful he was at planning and carrying out his crimes. It wasn't hard to believe that he had covered himself by assuming another identity. How did you go about doing that? I wasn't sure. The old crime-novel staple was obtaining a replacement birth certificate for someone of similar age who had died young. But I had the feeling that was less secure than it used to be now that records were computerized. In which case, it came down to the standard solution to all problems. Money. The Devil didn't seem to work, or he could afford to hire sidekicks. Was he rich? If so, how had he got there from being a fatherless teenager in Bethnal Green? People who had wealth were often in the public eye, one way or another.

"—and then I fainted."

"What, sweetie?"

Lucy was smiling at me. "I said, and then I fainted."

"What?" I stopped walking and squatted down beside her. "When?"

"Silly daddy," she said, squealing with laughter. "I got you, I got you. I could see you weren't listening."

I grabbed her round the waist, feeling how delicate and vulnerable her body was. "Very funny. What do you want for tea?"

She stared at me. "We already talked about that. You said I could have sausages."

I nodded, trying to hide my confusion. "Ha, got you back," I said, tickling her.

She pushed me off, giggling, and we completed the walk.

Jesus. I was even starting to lose it in front of my daughter. There was going to be a reckoning for the bastard who was doing this to me.

The Hereward in Greenwich was one of the roughest pubs in the area. Its regulars wanted it that way. They were never disturbed by tourists who'd been to the Cutty Sark or the Maritime Museum, by the rich kids who'd bought flats in the Georgian houses or even by slumming students from Goldsmith's. The Hereward had a seriously bad reputation and the police hardly ever organized raids. It was frequented by the local lowlife, encouraged by an ex-con landlord who had his fingers in numerous illegal pies.

The three men watching the pub knew all that. One of them had been inside a few times, dressed in raggedy-arsed jeans and a porkpie hat. He'd been taken for a hardman and left alone with his drink. The regulars weren't stupid. He was indeed as hard as they came.

"Target has exited," Rommel said from the corner opposite. Now he was dressed in a leather bomber jacket, a woolen cap over his short hair and dark glasses shading his eyes. He spoke into a hands-free microphone and watched as a thirty-year-old man with dirty shoulder-length dreadlocks stumbled down the steps.

His two colleagues were in a pale blue Orion with a hundred-and-thirty-thousand miles on the clock. They'd picked it up from a dealer in Neasden, who asked no questions when they paid cash and gave what he was sure were a false name and address.

"Okay," said the man in the passenger seat. "We've got him." He pulled on gloves and nodded to the driver. Both of them were wearing black woolen hats and sunglasses. "Let's go, Geronimo."

The car moved forward smoothly, then ground to a halt five yards in front of the skinny man in dirty jeans and denim jacket. He was clearly the worse for several drinks, his gait unsteady.

"Oy—" he gasped, as he was grabbed from behind by the Orion's passenger. That was all he managed. A hand tightened over his mouth and he was thrown into the backseat.

Meanwhile Rommel had crossed the road quickly. He went up to the double doors of the Hereward, taking from inside his jacket a half-meter steel bar which he slid through the handles in case anyone had seen what had happened. He smiled when he felt the door shudder. As they'd suspected, their man had friends who watched his back.

He ran to the car and got in beside the driver, who pulled out in front of a bus and drove rapidly away.

From the rear seat, Wolfe looked back for several minutes. "Okay, we're clear. Take channel one." They'd worked out several escape routes in case of pursuit, but it seemed his team had been too good for the opposition, as he'd suspected it would be. He turned to the quivering figure beside him. His hands had been cuffed behind his back and a strip of duct tape stuck over his mouth.

"Easy as nicking ice cream from a kid," said Rommel, grinning.

"You'll be wondering what's going on, Terry," Wolfe said, his voice low. "Here's a clue. Jimmy Tanner."

The captive's acne-scarred face turned even paler.

"You're going to tell us everything you know about him and all the people he spoke to in that shithole." His tone was menacing now. "Or I'll rip your balls off one by one and one and put them in a toad-in-the-hole." He smiled. "Which you'll eat for your tea."

Terence Smail, alcoholic, small-time drug dealer and pimp, looked like he was about to throw up. When he failed to do that, he fainted.

Sara was working late at the paper, so I was on my own that evening. I sent the chapter I'd written to the Devil's last e-mail address and waited for a reply. None came. Jesus, was he in the middle of slaughtering someone else who had done him harm? I went on to the Internet and did a search for "changing your identity." There were dozens of sites offering new names and documents for fees ranging from paltry (for photocopied fake documents) to very expensive (supposedly for "the real thing"— these people had no sense of irony). I wondered if he'd used one of them. I doubted it. He'd have gone for a more secure way. He wouldn't have been able to trust that his changed identity was safe on the Web. I was sure he'd have found another method. Maybe he had criminal connections. East End gangsters? I didn't want to get involved with them, and, anyway, he'd find out soon enough if someone was snooping around. I couldn't risk it.

But what was the alternative? Wait for the next victim to appear on the news?

I couldn't come up with anything else, so I drank half a bottle of single malt and passed out in front of the television.

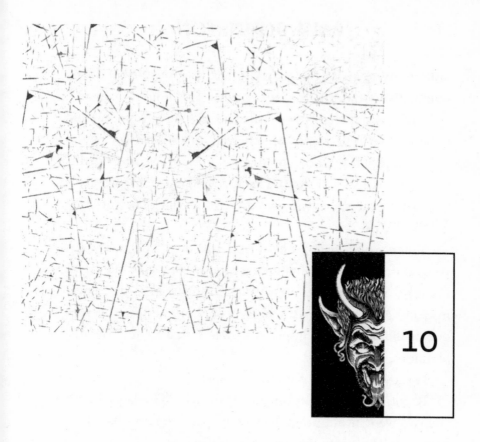

10

Karen Oaten stormed down the corridor to the VCCT office, her cheeks red and her heart pounding. She had just spent a very uncomfortable half hour with the assistant commissioner. He had set the team up as his personal fiefdom, dispensing with the normal chain of command. He wanted to know how it was that the newspapers had found out about Father Prendegast's previous identity before the Met. It was a good question, one to which she would also like an answer.

"Simmons!" she shouted as she banged open the door. "Pavlou! My office." She glanced round at John Turner, who was trying to hide behind his computer. "You, too, Taff."

The chief inspector slammed the door when her three subordinates were inside. She didn't bother dropping the blind. She wanted the rest of the team to see what was about to happen.

"Right, you useless tossers," she said, glaring at Simmons and Pavlou. "I've just had my arse chewed up and spat out by the AC. That means I'm now looking for arses for my own lunch."

"Excuse me, guv," D.S. Paul Pavlou said politely. He was half-Cypriot, his face permanently covered by a thick layer of black stubble. "We—"

"Shut it, you piece of shit!" Oaten yelled. "I'll tell you when you can open your kebab-stinking mouth." Her eyes moved on to Morry Simmons. He was pasty-faced and in his forties, a permanent detective sergeant who was only on the team because one of the other chief inspectors owed him a favor. "Try me, Simmons, just try me."

He showed no sign of wanting to speak.

"Right," Oaten said, glancing at Turner. "The last I heard, you two were investigating the victim's past. You now have permission to explain to me why you screwed up."

Neither Simmons nor Pavlou was inclined to answer.

"Open it!" Oaten shouted.

Pavlou glanced at his colleague. "Well, guv, we got as far as the bishop who had responsibility for St Bartholomew's. He told us about the monastery in Ireland. I called, but no one there knew anything about Father Prendegast."

The chief inspector was shaking her head. "It didn't occur to you to ask me if you could go over there and ask in person?"

Simmons's eyes opened wide. "What, you would have signed off on that?"

"This is the Violent Crime Coordination Team, not some local nick. Of course I'd have signed off on it." She looked at each of them. "Or at least, I'd have sent someone with more than half a dozen brain cells over there." She picked up one of the tabloids that was lying on her desk. "Now I don't have to. The press has done your job for you. 'In an astonishing twist,'" she read, "'we can reveal that murder victim Father Norman Prendegast was a pederast given a new identity by the Catholic Church. Blah blah real name Father Patrick O'Connell, blah blah St. Peter's, Bonner Street, Bethnal Green, blah blah former choirboys Harry Winder and Andrew Lough, blah blah subjected to repulsive sexual practices.'" Oaten glared at Simmons and Pavlou. "And how do you think the papers got hold of this?"

"Oh, that's obvious, guv," Simmons said, a grin splitting his sallow face. "They chucked money at anyone they could find."

"Wrong!" the chief inspector shouted, crumpling the newspaper up and throwing it accurately at his chest. "They did what you wankers are supposed to do. They asked questions, and when people stonewalled them, they kept on asking."

"But they went to Ireland," Pavlou said, pointing at a picture of the monastery where the dead man had been hidden away.

Oaten groaned. "We've already been over that, you pillock. This isn't about who goes where, it's about so-called detectives who don't know their arse from their armpit." She shot a glance at Turner. "Help us out here, Taff. What do we do next?"

"Um, interview Winder and Lough. Find out who else might have been abused by the victim. Talk to other people who attended St. Peter's back in the late seventies and early eighties."

The chief inspector was nodding. "Thank God someone around here knows his job."

Pavlou stepped forward, his expression keen. "I'd be happy to go up to the northeast to interview Lough."

"I bet you would," Karen Oaten replied mordantly. "The question is, am I happy to risk another cock-up by letting you go?" She rubbed her forehead. "All right, contact the locals and get them to bring Lough in for questioning. At least that should keep the press off him till you get there." She turned to Simmons. "You get down to Bethnal Green and talk to this Harry Winder. Remind him that, even if he's sold his story to some rag, he has to come clean with us. Think you can manage that?"

The two sergeants nodded unhappily.

"Get going then!" She raised a hand at Turner. "Not you, Taff." She waited till the door closed behind the others. "Morons. So, what are you working on?"

"Right now Chief Inspector Hardy's got me—"

"Never mind Hardy, you're reporting only to me from now on. There are too many people busy building their own little empires in this team." She gave a hollow laugh. "If you can't beat them… Okay, let's have it."

Turner nodded. "Right, guv. I was looking at the modus operandi."

Oaten sat back in her chair. "And?"

"Well, it seems to me there's some kind of message in it." He flipped open his notebook. "Candlestick up him, sprawled over the altar, eyes removed, the quotation in the mouth…"

"Go on."

"The wound to the backside suggests sexual abuse, doesn't it?"

"Mmm."

"And the naked body over the altar makes it pretty obvious that the killer doesn't think much of the Catholic Church."

"What about the eyes?"

"Well, could the priest have seen things that the killer is ashamed of or that he regards as his own?"

"Possibly linked to the abuse carried out on him by the dead man?"

Turner nodded. "It seems reasonable to assume that the killer knew Prendegast, or rather O'Connell. And, yeah, that he was abused by him."

"So we need to start collecting alibis for the night of the murder from all the choirboys and such like that we find." Oaten smiled at him. "Good, Taff. What about the quotation in his mouth, though? How did it go again? 'What a—'"

"'—mockery hath death made of thee.' I was hoping you weren't going to ask me about that." Turner looked at his notes again. "Maybe the killer was just making a general point about how the priest has got his comeuppance."

"Or maybe there's more to it than that."

Turner shrugged.

"All right, go on working on that, but I want you to keep an eye on Simmons and Pavlou, too. And, don't worry, I'll keep D.C.I. Hardy off your back."

After he'd left, Karen Oaten pushed the newspapers from her desk and opened a file. In it were her own notes about the case. She was impressed that Taff Turner had gone the same direction as she had. But she, too, was uncertain about the quote from Webster's *The White Devil,* so she'd arranged a meeting at the university later in the day with a specialist in Jacobean literature. All Oaten knew about John Webster came from the movie *Shakespeare in Love*—he was the teenage slimebag who had dropped a mouse down Gwyneth Paltrow's dress, and squealed on her and the playwright. He was a nasty piece of work, but that wasn't what was giving her butterflies in her stomach. She'd seen killings as elaborate as this before. In every case the murderer had gone on to strike again—and soon.

It was why she'd joined the Met. What she'd told John Turner wasn't the whole story. She wished she could forget, but every time she started on a murder case, she thought of her childhood friend Christy Baker. They'd been inseparable from primary through to senior school in St. Albans, they'd shared everything and competed against each other at netball, hockey and athletics without ever falling out. Then, one December night when they were fifteen, Christy had disappeared on her way home from Karen's. It was only a five-minute walk, but she hadn't made it. Her naked and mutilated body was found ten miles away in a ditch. The killer, a deliveryman, was eventually caught, but not before he'd claimed seven more victims.

Karen Oaten didn't think of herself as being in the job for revenge, but deep down she knew that she wanted to catch as many sick bastards as she could. She had no sympathy for them. She'd seen what Christy's family had gone through; she'd been there herself. It was worse than anyone could imagine.

She twitched her head and came back to the present, wondering what scenes of horror lay in store for her team in the days and weeks ahead.

Evelyn Merton looked out of her kitchen window. The garden to the rear of the bungalow on the outskirts of Chelmsford was full of spring blooms. And so it should have been. She spent hours working in the flower beds and rock garden. Since her beloved brother, Gilbert, had died two years ago, she'd had to take on lawn duties, as well. At least they weren't too strenuous at this time of year, and the mower with powered wheels that she'd bought was a great help. Evelyn smiled as she saw a robin engaged in noisy combat as he defended his territory from another of his kind. Nature was full of hostility as well as beauty. She'd known that throughout her life, especially after she'd started teaching primary children.

It was so long ago, but she could remember many of the children that had passed through her hands. Of course, when she'd left college in the late fifties, everything had been very different. Although she'd grown up in the comfortable suburb of Chigwell, she chose to work in the underprivileged East End. The children of the poor were dressed in faded, patched clothes that had been handed down from older siblings. They were skinny, their faces wan. The National Health Service was gradually making a difference, but she still saw children with their legs bent by rickets and their complexions ruined by smallpox. At least, back then, they had understood discipline. The last years of her service in Bethnal Green had been marred by persistent bad behavior, particularly among the boys. She had been forced to take stern measures, even though teachers were no longer permitted to employ corporal punishment.

Miss Merton made herself a cup of milky tea and took it into the sitting room. Rajah, her blue Persian, opened an eye as she came in then went back to sleep, purring gently. He was old now and occasionally made a mess on the carpets but, once he'd had his nose rubbed in it, he behaved himself again. Before she settled into her armchair, Evelyn looked up at the class photographs she had hung above the television. There were rows and rows of eleven-year-olds, some of them serious but many grinning cheekily at the camera. The parents were to blame. The parents and the government. There was no discipline in society anymore. If it continued like this, she thought as she turned on the TV, there would be rioting in the streets.

The doorbell rang, provoking a sigh from Evelyn Merton. She enjoyed the morning talk shows, particularly the ones where feckless people were made to see the error of their ways.

A youngish man was standing outside, a blue cap on his head.

"'Mornin'," he said in a bold way that immediately put Evelyn's back up.

"Can I help you?" she asked coldly.

"Gas," he said, smiling to reveal gleaming and unnaturally pointed white teeth. "Come to read the meter." He looked at a clipboard. "Merton, is it?"

"*Miss* Merton. Very well, follow me." Evelyn stopped and turned as she was halfway down the hall. "Show me some identification, please."

The man closed the door and dropped the snib. He held the clipboard out to her. It was then that she realized he was wearing latex gloves. Surprised, she looked down at the board and took a heavy blow to her left temple.

She grunted, and then felt herself being dragged over the carpet to the main bedroom.

"Quiet, bitch," the man hissed between tight lips.

"Wha...what do you...want?" Evelyn asked. "No...no money in the house."

She grunted as she was pulled onto the bed. She could feel ropes being tightened around her wrists.

"No...no," she said, but she could hear that her voice was faint.

Then she felt ropes on her skin. They were tightened and her legs were opened. Looking up, she realized that her wrists and ankles had been tied to the bedposts.

"No..." she said, fear making her bladder empty.

"Oh, she's a dirty old woman," the man said with a sharp laugh. "She's going to have to lie in her own muck." He took his hat off and opened the bag he'd been carrying.

Evelyn Merton watched as he zipped a white plastic suit over his clothes, then put what looked like a surgical cap over his short fair hair.

"Scream if you like, *Miss* Merton," he said, emphasizing her title as if it were a swear word. "But the problem with living in a bungalow is that your neighbors aren't very likely to hear you, especially above the racket from your television." He smiled. "Besides, Mrs. Smith in number thirty-three is out shopping and Mr. Humboldt in number thirty-seven has been in hospital for the past ten days. Not that you've bothered to visit him, have you, you poisonous old toad?"

Evelyn started to sob, her eyes blurred by tears. She'd read often enough in the *Mail* about elderly women being assaulted in their own homes, but she'd never believed it would happen to her. Perhaps she could reason with the man. There was something about him that was familiar, but her throbbing head couldn't make sense of it. Something about him...

Her assailant sat down on the bed near her face and leaned over. "I imagine you'd like to know what's going on, Miss Merton," he said, his voice steady. He had a neutral accent, but to her experienced ear there was a trace of Cockney in it. "Don't worry, I'll fill you in." He gave a laugh that made her blood run cold. "But first, I'm going to shut you up. I used to have to listen to you enough." He grabbed her face, thumb and fingers pressing hard into her cheeks. She was forced to open her mouth and a cloth of some sort was stuffed into it. She panicked as she was forced to breathe through her nose, and struggled in her bonds.

"Calm down, you old cow," he said, the East End tones more evident. "Calm down and take your punishment like a...well, like a stinking old woman."

Evelyn's mind was filled with flashes from the past. *Take your punishment like a man.* That had been one of her catchphrases as a teacher. In the first part of her career, she'd applied the cane liberally. Later on, she'd been forced to come up with more imaginative forms of chastisement for the boys who had threatened her authority—and it was always boys. The girls had seemed to see sense when they encountered a worthy opponent and kept their heads down. Insolent faces cascaded through her thoughts: vicious, calculating little hooligans; ne'er-do-wells who'd begun smoking before they were ten and sworn like troopers…

"Mmm!" she said with a feeble groan. "Mmm!" She felt a blade close to her skin, slicing though her clothes.

"Yes, Miss Merton," the man said, this time his voice high-pitched like one of her pupils'. "Yes, yes, yes."

Evelyn closed her eyes as her outer and undergarments were cut apart and tugged from beneath her. No man had ever seen her entirely naked, not even Gilbert. When he had started coming to her bed not long after their mother died, she'd always kept the light off. She cringed in shame, feeling the soggy bedspread beneath her loins. Then her eyes sprang apart when she felt latex-covered fingers probe inside her.

"Well, well," the man said, bending over her midriff. "We all thought you were a virgin, but it seems that someone's been here." He gave her a lascivious grin. "Or did you use a cucumber?" Then a knowing expression spread across his smooth features. "Silly me," he said, following her eyes to the photograph on the bedside table. "I forgot. Mr. Gilbert. I remember your brother from sports days. He used to time the races." He laughed, a cold and pitiless sound that chilled her blood. "And call us 'dirty little tinkers.' You and your brother were the dirty ones, weren't you, Miss Merton? Still, nothing wrong with keeping it in the family. I had a very close relationship with my mother, too, you know. Then again, I was adopted."

Suddenly the knife, a large blade that could have been a soldier's, was in front of her eyes. She whimpered through the gag.

"No, Miss Merton, it's too late to say you're sorry." The man brought his face close to hers. "You hurt me, Miss Merton. You hurt me a lot. Do you remember?"

She shook her head, trying to keep her eyes off his.

"Let me help you. My name's Leslie Dunn. Mean anything to you?"

Evelyn closed her eyes. No, she thought desperately, it can't be him. Not the weasel-faced Les Dunn, the boy who used to look at her in the most impudent way, as if she had no right to discipline him.

"I can see it does. Nice to see you again." The man laughed. "Not." He ran his eyes over her body. "I always thought you'd look disgusting without any clothes on and I was right."

Then the blade was at her face again. "Let me remind you what you did to me so that you understand why I'm exacting retribution."

She moaned again.

He ignored her. "You made me stand in the corner with one leg raised for a whole lesson, do you remember? Because I put my hand up at the wrong time. You made me crawl around on all fours like a dog for a day because you thought I'd made a barking noise. It wasn't me, it was Richard Brady." He gave another empty laugh. "He paid the price a long time ago. And you ridiculed me in front of all the kids, not once, not twice, but hundreds of times." He stood up and started walking around the room in the heavy-footed way that Evelyn had always had. "'Leslie Dunn,'" he said in a high-pitched voice, "'if your parents weren't drunken idiots, you'd know that behavior like yours is unacceptable in polite society. Leslie Dunn, if you can't come to school with clean clothes, then don't come at all. Leslie Dunn, your writing is like a brainless chimpanzee's.'" He fixed his eyes on her. "And so on. You didn't really think you could get away with treating people like that, did you, Miss Brother-fucking Merton?" He slapped her hard on the cheek. "Did you?"

She was so terrified that she couldn't take her eyes off him. She watched as he went out of the bedroom, to return a short time later with a furry blue object dangling from one hand.

"Aaanng!" she exclaimed, trying to scream. Rajah was thrown at her, landing on her bare chest. She could feel his blood, sticky and warm, on her skin.

"I hate cats," said the man she'd taught. "Now, Miss Merton, it's time I told you what I'm going to do to you."

As Leslie Dunn's words cut into her brain, Evelyn felt a wave of heat flush through her veins. She didn't deserve this. It was years ago. She'd turned out plenty of good pupils, plenty of children who would have gone on to benefit society. No, she didn't deserve this. She'd been a good Catholic.

But, as the knife penetrated her, she acknowledged her sins. Cruelty, pride, hatred—not to mention what she had done with Gilbert for decades. Deep down, she knew she deserved everything she got.

And for her there would be no absolution.

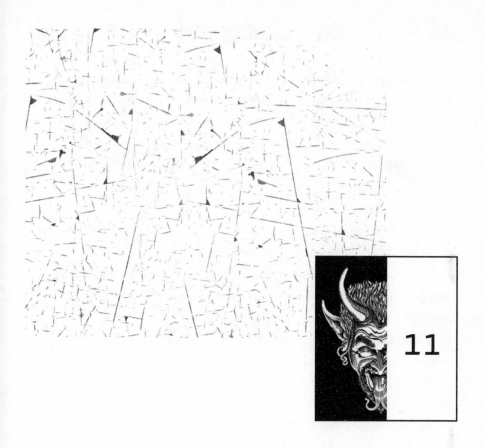

11

I spent the next day writing up the notes the White Devil had
sent me that morning. They were chilling. I hoped for a moment
that he was breaking out into fiction writing, but I had the firm
feeling he wasn't. At least this wasn't a contemporary killing,
though that didn't make it any better for the wretched vagrant
he claimed to have killed a couple of years after he'd left senior
school. I'd written plenty of violent scenes in my novels, but this
was worse than any of them. The man was clubbed to the
ground and kicked to death with steel-capped boots. At least that
hadn't happened in any of my books.

I picked up Lucy and took her home, helping her to make a
papier-mâché model of Edinburgh Castle for a project on

medieval fortifications. Then I came back to my place. Sara arrived unannounced. I was rereading the text I'd sent the Devil and only just managed to clear the screen before she let herself in. I wasn't proud of how I'd enhanced the revolting material. Writing "I felt the rib cage shatter under my boot" brought it home even more.

"Hi, my love," I said, getting up to kiss her. "I've missed you."

After a few moments, she pushed me away gently. "Steady on, tiger. I've been tramping the streets all day."

That meant she'd been dashing around in taxis paid for by the newspaper, but I resisted the temptation to say that. She looked worn out and pretty dejected.

"Have you seen the news?" she asked, turning on the TV. "Bloody Jeremy's over in Belfast covering that huge bank robbery."

"No, I haven't." I sat down beside her on the sofa. "Did you get a juicy story to cover in his place?"

She shook her head. "I wouldn't say 'juicy' was the right word, Matt. Poor old woman."

My stomach constricted. "What happened?" I asked, trying to keep my voice level.

"Retired teacher out in Chelmsford," Sara said, kicking off her shoes. "Fortunately the police wouldn't let us in." Her hand was on my arm, suddenly squeezing it hard. "Can you believe it? One of her arms was severed."

"What?" This time I was unable to hide my surprise.

"Severed," Sara repeated. "It seems the killer took it away." She swallowed. "After he cut her throat."

"Jesus," I whispered. My heart was thundering. "What was she, the victim?"

"What do you mean?" Sara's eyes flared. "She was a defenseless old lady."

"No, I mean what did she used to do?"

Sara relaxed slightly. "Oh, I get you. She was a primary schoolteacher."

"In Chelmsford?" I asked hopefully.

"No, somewhere in the East End." Her eyes were on me. "Are you all right?"

"Um…yes." I picked up my mug of tea and emptied it. What game was the Devil playing with me? Or was there more than one of his kind out there?

Sara got up. "I think we must have missed it," she said, turning off the television. "You can be sure it'll be on the ten o'clock news." She headed for the bathroom.

I booted up my computer and logged on to my e-mail program. There was a message from WDChelm. I opened it, my heart pounding.

Matt! I read. You must be pretty pissed off with me, giving you that out-of-date stuff this morning. Sorry, I couldn't resist. You're not the only one who can mislead his readers. Means you'll have to rewrite the chapter using the latest facts. No doubt your girlfriend Sara will be able to help you with them. Ha! I bought myself an extra day. Don't have to pay you the next advance yet! See if you can catch me when I do. Greetings from hell, your very own (White) Devil.

This was getting worse and worse. Now I'd have to pick Sara's brains about the murder. I'd try to disguise my interest by claiming it was that of a professional crime writer.

I quickly put together a bowl of pasta with bacon and onion, and managed to spend the first half of the meal talking about other things. Then, after she'd sunk a couple of glasses of Sicilian red, I made my move.

"So, your murder case," I said, filling her glass. "Want to talk about it?"

Sara gave me a suspicious look. "You want to incorporate it in your next book, do you?" She lit a cigarette. "Bloody scavenger." She smiled wearily.

I shrugged. "It's a job like any other."

She laughed, blowing out smoke. "Not many jobs give you the luxury of taking your kid to school, then sitting around at home all day."

"A perfect description of my life," I said, handing her an ashtray. "Are you going to tell me or not? I can tell you're dying to."

"Wait for the TV news," she said, playing hardball.

I moved into flattery mode. "You know much more than the BBC's going to come out with."

She looked away. "I wish I didn't, Matt. I really wish I didn't."

I hadn't ever seen her so reluctant to talk. Like most journalists, she was a great one for regaling people with her latest scoops.

"All right," she said, reaching for her laptop and turning it on. "Evelyn Louise Merton, age seventy-five. At least, that's the police's assumption." She looked at me ruefully. "They're having to wait for her dental records to be sure of the ID as there's no next of kin and her face is too battered for the neighbors to recognize. Lived at 35 Summerhill Drive, Chelmsford. Worked in East London schools from 1958 until 1990. Last place of work, St. Pius's School, Roman Road, Bethnal—"

"She was a Catholic?"

Sara stared at me. "Oh, I see what you mean. Yeah, I suppose she was if she taught at a place with that name." She hit the keys for a few moments and nodded. "Good spot, Mr. Detective."

I tried to smile, without much success.

"Lived on her own, with her cat, which—by the way—was also slaughtered by the murderer." She shook her head.

I tried to pull her close, but she resisted, her eyes flaring.

"Leave me alone!" she shouted. "How can you write about this sort of thing for fun?"

I felt my cheeks redden. Sara occasionally lost her grip, but not like this. The murder of the old woman had obviously got to her. "Hey…" I said, reaching out my arms.

"Tell me," she insisted, leaning away. "Tell me why you do it, Matt."

"I suppose…I suppose crime novels are a way of coming to terms with the violence of the world, a way of mediating between the reader and the abyss."

"Bullshit," she said, gulping down wine. "They're a way of making a quick buck by pandering to people's worst instincts."

"And what you do is any better?"

"At least it's true," she retorted.

I bit my tongue. Having a discussion with a journalist about the nature of truth wasn't a particularly enticing prospect. Anyway, the last person I wanted to piss off right now was the woman I loved.

"What are the police saying?" I asked after a long silence.

"Not much. The crime hacks reckon there's more evidence, but the Met is keeping quiet about it."

"The Met? What are they doing out in Essex?"

"Apparently the Violent Crime Coordination Team was called in." She caught my gaze. "Because of some similarities with that priest murder in West Kilburn."

Jesus. Was the Devil getting careless, or was he playing games with the police as well as me?

"Here it is," Sara said. She'd turned the TV back on and was increasing the volume.

We listened as a woman reporter of Asian descent ran through the story. She had less to say than Sara, but at the end of her piece there was an excerpt from the police statement. The tough but attractive face of D.C.I. Karen Oaten, whom I'd seen filmed outside St. Bartholomew's, came up on the screen.

"...and anyone who can pass on any information about this truly awful crime should not hesitate to contact us or any police station," she said.

Sara had picked up her phone. She rang her colleague who was on duty and asked if anything was breaking. She listened, her eyes wide, and I tried to pick up what was being said.

"What is it?" I asked when she finished.

"I can't believe this," Sara said, taking another pull of wine. "During the autopsy, they found a small plastic bag in the victim's...in her vagina. There was a piece of paper in it, with some words printed. The police aren't saying what they were."

I slumped down on the sofa. I didn't know what the message was, but I was pretty sure where it came from.

John Webster's *The White Devil,* unless I was very much mistaken.

Sara left in a cab for the paper. Her editor wanted the story updated before it went to press. Although I'd have preferred that she stayed, now I had the chance to think through what had happened. It wasn't just the way the Devil had screwed with me. It wasn't even the horrific death suffered by the former school-teacher. No, what was really getting to me was the modus operandi. The cunning bastard. He'd suckered me again. Now I was potentially in even deeper shit. Because in the third Sir

Tertius novel, *The Revenger's Comedy*, I had described how a character had his right arm severed before his throat was cut.

I hadn't meant the book to be the last of the series—in fact, I still had faint hopes of resurrecting my "dashing, desperately attractive detective" (as a female critic on the Internet had described him)—but I'd gradually lost interest in him and the period. Perhaps it was because of the levels of violence in the 1620s, or at least in my 1620s. I'd never exactly been a shrinking violet in that field. After *The Silence of the Lambs* and Patricia Cornwell's lurid tales, the bar for fictional excess was raised high and that didn't bother me. But Sir Tertius's last adventure was worse than the others. It had taken him to Oxford, where he'd got caught up in a grotesque game of "kill the yokel" between the students of two colleges. The lead villain ended up being killed by a butcher, whose son had been torn apart by a specially trained pack of hunting hounds. Not only had the evil huntmaster's arm been removed, horn still clasped in the fingers, but his private parts had been hacked off and a page from the Old Testament inserted in the cavity. The verses about "an eye for an eye" were on the page. I'd subsequently been verbally abused by a female crime writer at a conference who thought, like Sara, that I was using violence without justification.

My mobile rang. There was no number on the screen.

"What do you want?" I said tersely.

"Matt, Matt," said the White Devil. "I'm ringing to satisfy your curiosity."

"What about?" I asked, trying to disguise my interest.

"Did the good Sara fill you in on the murder?"

"Yes."

"And has she heard about the calling card I left?"

I couldn't hold myself back any longer. "You're fucking sick,"

I shouted. "Why did you kill the old woman, for Christ's sake? No one deserves to die like that."

"Oh, yes, they do," he said, his voice steely. "People who sin have to pay the price, not only in the next world."

I grabbed my notepad. "Did you know her, then?"

He gave a hollow laugh. "Don't go on a fishing trip, Matt. I'll tell you what I want you to know. The rest is for you to find out."

I swallowed hard. "All right, what line of Webster's did you use this time?"

"Very smart," he said ironically. "Act 5, scene 6, lines 73 to 75."

I fumbled through my copy. "You sick bastard," I said when I found the lines. "'Gentle madam, Seem to consent, only persuade him teach the way to death; let him die first.'" I dropped the book. "The victim was one of your teachers, wasn't she?"

"Bingo."

I looked at the lines again. "But what's the bit about letting him die first in aid of?"

"Didn't you hear that the bitch had a brother?"

"No."

"Well, she did. I discovered he'd been fucking her." A cold, metallic laugh. "Not only that, he used to treat us kids like shit at the sports day every year. He paid for that. You see, her brother died in July 2003. He was electrocuted by a faulty plug when he switched on his lawn mower. Accidental death, according to the coroner." He paused. "But it wasn't an accident."

"What?" I felt as if I'd just stepped off a cliff. "You mean…you mean you killed him?"

"I thank you, I thank you." The humor left his voice. "Why are you surprised, Matt? You already know how seriously I take my work."

"I can find you," I said, forgetting the danger for a moment.

"Yes, you can go through the school registers and find out all the boys Miss One-Arm Merton taught. You can triangulate that list with the dates you work out from Father Bugger O'Connell, and you can start to track me down." He gave what sounded like a hiss. "Go on, then, Matt. But you'd better hurry. The police are going to be after you soon, even if I don't steer them toward your books."

"I'm going to stop you."

"Be my guest. But remember I can kill Lucy and Sara and your mother before you even get close. Have you got the balls?" He sniggered. "Good night, Mr. Fictional Crime Expert."

He cut the connection.

I rammed the phone between the cushions of the sofa and let out a yell of frustration.

The blond-haired man was sitting in front of a bank of screens. Behind him, the lights from St. Katharine's Dock across the river shone through the blinds he'd partially closed. He had a martini with a maraschino cherry floating in it on the desk beside him. Despite the air-conditioning, the smell of the Sobranie Black Russians that he'd been smoking since he came back from Chelmsford was strong. He sipped from the tall-stemmed glass, getting the familiar rush from the almost neat gin.

The White Devil touched the pad of the control panel and zoomed in on the scene in Matt Wells's sitting room. Good. The writer was hammering away at the keyboard, no doubt writing up the chapter about the latest killing. Soon there would be a whole novel about his exploits, a veritable Book of Death. But Matt Wells wouldn't get any profit from it.

He went over to the gold-plated stereo system and slotted in the CD he had shoplifted in the City after he'd got back from Chelmsford. The skills he'd acquired as a boy had never left him. Robert Johnson started singing "Me and the Devil Blues." Humming along, he remembered what he'd done after he'd taken off the old bitch's arm—the one that she'd used to slap him countless times, even though she wasn't meant to. It was in his collection, along with the jar containing Father Bugger's eyes.

The Devil laughed. He was death, he was hell, he was a demon far worse than any from the fervid imagination of Hieronymus Bosch. He was insuperable, Lucifer rising, the very breath of the Apocalypse—and Matt Wells was his minion.

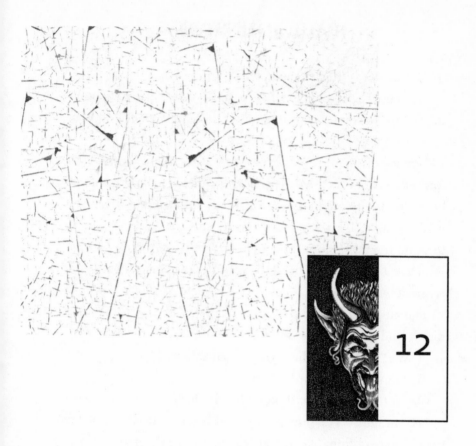

12

Karen Oaten stood on the viewing ramp overlooking the autopsy room. Beside her, John Turner was visibly struggling to keep his breakfast down. The pathologist and his assistants were working on the incomplete body of Evelyn Merton for the second time, at Oaten's request.

"Doesn't get any better, does it, Taff?" the chief inspector said, her face only slightly less pale than his.

"I can't...I can't believe that someone could do this to an old lady."

Oaten nodded. "That's not the worst of it. According to Redrose, the perpetrator showed considerable skill in amputating the arm. Which means he must have had practice."

"A butcher?" Turner suggested.

"Certainly a possibility, but we're not exactly narrowing down the field. There must be thousands of them in Greater London."

"A surgeon?"

"Plenty of them, too." She looked at the scene below. The former teacher's corpse was no longer covered in blood as it had been the day before in the house in Chelmsford, but it was still hard to take. "Anyway, we'll never find the killer by going through the professions. He could be a butcher, a cook, an ex-soldier, a farmer… We need to work the evidence. That's why we're down here."

The inspector glanced at her. "What is it you think they didn't find the first time round?"

"I want to know if there was sexual activity."

Turner swallowed hard. "Jesus."

Oaten nudged him with her elbow. "Bring me up to speed."

"Right, guv." The sergeant opened his notebook. "I put the people you got from D.C.I. Hardy's unit on the street in Chelmsford, working with the locals. So far they haven't found anyone who saw a suspicious individual in the vicinity yesterday. We've also started looking at the victim's background. Not much to go on. She was a retired primary schoolteacher. No close friends or relatives. The neighbor says she used to live with her brother. He died in a gardening accident two years ago."

"She worked in the East End, didn't she?"

Turner nodded. "Bethnal Green. At a Catholic school."

"Not far from where Father Prendegast, aka Father O'Connell, messed around with little boys."

"The second quotation from that play makes it clear enough that it's the same killer."

Karen Oaten's brow was furrowed. "Someone who was taught

by Miss Merton and went to church at St. Peter's. How are those lists of boys coming?"

"We're getting there. Lewis and Allen are already checking alibis. Simmons and Pavlou are going to help them."

"They're also going to find out what kind of person the victim was, whether she was popular or not, aren't they?"

"That's what I told them."

Oaten jerked her head away as the pathologist inserted an instrument between Evelyn Merton's legs. "Thanks for doing that, Taff. I think they take it better from you. I'm not exactly their idea of a caring, sharing boss."

Turner shrugged. "No problem, guv. They're okay really, just a bit old-fashioned."

"A bit out of line, to be precise," she said. "But I've learned that diplomacy is sometimes the best way to play things." She blinked as a loud voice came through the speaker set into the ceiling.

"Chief Inspector?" The pathologist was looking through the glass at her, speaking into a hanging microphone. "It's very hard to be sure, but there are contusions in the vagina that may well not have been made when the message was inserted."

Oaten leaned forward to the microphone in front of her and switched it on. "No semen?"

"Not that I can identify at this stage." The medic's voice was dry and mechanical. "As you can imagine, there are several fluids. We've taken swabs for analysis."

Turner looked at the chief inspector. Her lips were pressed tightly together and her hands were gripping the wooden shelf beneath the window. "Guv? Are you all right?"

She turned to him slowly, her eyes widening. "No, Taff, I'm not fucking all right. Some bastard cut an old woman's arm off, cut her throat and then maybe molested her." She started walking out of the mortuary. "I'm going to get the scum who did this if it's the last thing I do." She glanced back at him. "And if I have the chance, I'm going to make him hurt."

Turner caught up with her. "Careful, guv," he said in a low voice. "You sound like you're turning into one of those people in the play. A revenger."

Karen Oaten kept her eyes off him. "Revenge is a powerful motive, Taff. That's what's driving our killer, I'm sure of it. If we want to catch him before he slaughters everyone who ever wronged him, we have to get inside his head. I'll see you later."

"Where are you going?" he called after her.

"I had an appointment with an expert in Jacobean tragedy yesterday, remember?" she said over her shoulder. "Had to postpone because of what happened in Chelmsford. But now, after the second quotation, it's even more pressing."

The chief inspector strode toward her car, trying to blink away the sight of the schoolteacher's mutilated body. The man—she was sure it was a male—who killed her had left his calling card in the poor woman's most private place. She'd sworn an oath back there in the morgue to catch him, and she felt the power of her words burning in her veins.

If she had to go to hell to catch this devil, she would gladly do so.

I finished the rewrite of my tormentor's latest chapter and sent it off to him at four in the morning. That meant, at least in theory, that he might be delivering the next payment any time. I tried to sit up and watch the road below from a gap between the curtains, but it wasn't long before I fell into a blood-dripping, demon-filled dream. When I awoke with a start, I saw it was daylight. Shit. I ran downstairs. There was no package on the mat. Panting with relief, I went slowly back upstairs to my flat.

I wanted to get the newspapers to find out the latest on the Chelmsford murder, but I couldn't leave the house in case he showed up. I thought about it. Even if I did catch him, what did I think I was going to be able to do? Take on the man who had killed at least four people? With what? My Swiss Army knife? I realized I was trembling. I remembered the Devil's taunts. I was a crime writer who was now deeply involved in real-life crime. He was right. I couldn't cope. Then I thought of Lucy. I had to protect her. What would my life be worth if something happened to my beautiful little girl? And Sara? Could I live with her being hurt?

It was Saturday. By nine o'clock it was warm, the birds in the gardens between the houses making a colossal amount of noise. The usual arrangement was that Caroline had Lucy on Saturdays and I had her on Sundays. That suited me. I could wait for the Devil's delivery. I logged on to my e-mail program. There was no message from him. What did that mean? Was he on his way here or was he tearing some other poor soul to pieces?

I dressed quickly, not taking a shower or shaving so that I could keep an eye on the road. The usual laid-back activities of a Saturday morning were going on—men wandering off to get the papers, with small children running around them; couples walking their dogs; families loading up people carriers for ex-peditions to the country. No one or nothing out of the ordinary. The postman came along the street with his buggy. I knew him. He dropped a couple of bills through the flap and continued on his way. Nothing else happened.

I unplugged my laptop and brought it over to the window, keeping the Internet connection attached. If I couldn't go out to get the papers, I could at least check their Web sites. I wished I hadn't. The details about the old woman's murder, especially in the tabloids, were horrific. I went to the *Daily Independent* and found Sara's story. She was co-credited with a colleague. Apparently there had been a late-night press conference at which Detective Chief Inspector Karen Oaten ("tight-lipped and barely controlling her outrage") had described the modus operandi. But there had been no mention of the quotation from *The White Devil*. Either the bastard had lied about that, or the police were keeping it quiet. If the latter was the case, they might as well not have bothered. The tabloids were already linking the murders and splashing the words "serial" and "killer" about their copy liberally. At least no one had spotted the similarities to the murders in my novels. There hadn't even been any e-mails to me from fans. So much for my presence in the public imagination.

I was stuffing a piece of stale bread into my mouth when my mobile rang.

"Mmm?" I answered.

"What kind of telephone manner is that, Matt?" It was the Devil. "Eating breakfast on the hoof is bad for your digestion."

I got the mouthful down. "What do you want?"

"A bit of politeness would be nice," he said, his voice hardening.

"You didn't send me any notes this morning. I thought this was my day off."

There was a hollow laugh. "Very likely. You're busy looking out for me."

How did he know that? He must have some kind of bug or camera in my place.

"Aren't you?"

"Um, yeah, I am," I said weakly. "Well, you did tell me you'd be bringing the money."

"Yes, I did, didn't I? But I didn't tell you exactly when I'd be doing that, did I? Could be today, could be tomorrow. Who knows?" His tone got sharper. "If I were you, Matt, I'd keep a closer eye on your daughter than on the street. Who knows what dangers your ex-wife might inadvertently expose her to?"

The line went dead.

A wave of panic crashed over me. I grabbed my mobile, wallet and keys, pulled on my leather jacket and ran out of the house. Getting into the Volvo, I drove at speed down to Dulwich Village. I knew Caroline's routine. She always took Lucy to the local café for breakfast. Then they went for a walk in the park before Lucy's ballet class at midday. If I was lucky, they'd still be eating. I parked round the corner and walked toward the café.

Before I got there, I realized two things. The first was that the Devil had very successfully got me out of the house so he could make his delivery unnoticed. The second was that I was about to be engulfed in a firestorm. Caroline was very jealous of the time she spent with Lucy. She'd made it clear on numerous occasions that my presence, even accidental, was not to be tolerated. I stopped outside the newsagent's and decided to keep my distance. I bought a copy of one of the broadsheets that I hadn't checked on the Internet and opened it, loitering behind a lamppost twenty meters from the café.

Ten minutes later, Caroline and Lucy came out. My daughter was dressed in a pink anorak and skirt with white tights, while my ex-wife was wearing the torn jeans and baggy sweater that she affected at weekends—trying to look as unlike a City high-flier as she could, as I'd pointed out before the divorce at the cost of a serious ear-bashing. They set off toward College Road.

I followed them at what I thought was a discreet distance, the newspaper flapping in front of me like a sail buffeted by the breeze. When they turned into the park, I gave them a minute and then went in. I watched as Lucy ran ahead. She loved the boating lake and its birds. Caroline didn't make any effort to keep up with her. She knew that Lucy was careful. But she didn't know about the White Devil. I felt a pang of guilt. I should have found a way to tell her. Then I remembered how dangerous the bastard was.

Caroline sat down on a bench near the water and studied her paper. I moved along the line of bushes behind her with my eyes on Lucy. She was crouching down and throwing bread to the birds. The park was quite busy with couples, children, dogs, buggies. It didn't seem like a place where the Devil could get to Lucy.

I looked to my left and watched a skinny man in his thirties limping past. His clothes were ragged and dirty, his hair unkempt. Probably a junkie who'd spent the night in the undergrowth. Turning back, I couldn't see Lucy. Shit. Caroline was still reading her paper on the bench. I ran behind her, resisting the urge to shout my daughter's name. The ducks and seagulls that had gathered around the bread she'd scattered made noises of outrage and flapped their wings as I went through them. Where was she?

I couldn't keep quiet any longer.

"Lucy!" I yelled. "Lucy, where are you?" I looked around frantically. Caroline had got up, alarm on her face. "Lucy, come to Daddy! Lucy!" I ran to the trees that were set back from the lake. A young couple with a Labrador were walking there. "Have you seen a little girl, pink anorak and skirt?" I demanded.

They stepped back at the fervor of my tone, and then looked at each other.

"Yes," the woman said, raising an arm. "Over there."

"Thanks," I gasped.

"She was with a man, yeah?" the guy said.

"What?" I started to run in the direction the woman had indicated. "What did he look like?" I shouted over my shoulder. They both shrugged.

The last tree in the row was an ancient oak, its trunk thick and gnarled.

"Lucy!" I shouted desperately. "Lucy!"

"Matt!" Caroline screamed, about fifty yards to my rear. "Where is she?"

And then Lucy stepped out from behind the oak. I almost pissed myself as the tension left me. She was walking toward me, a baseball cap I'd never seen before on her head and a small leather bag in her right hand.

"Lucy!" So close to her, my voice was too loud. It scared her, tears springing up in her eyes. "Are you all right, darling?"

"Yes, Daddy, of course I'm all right," she said in the painstaking tone she took when she thought she'd been unjustly accused.

"Where did you get that hat?" I asked, clutching her to me. It was red, with a cartoon character on the front. Jesus. It was the Tasmanian Devil, the cartoon one with the oversize jaws that arrived in a miniature whirlwind. The crazy bastard.

"This is for you, Daddy," she said, wriggling out of my arms and handing me the black leather man's handbag.

"What's going on?" Caroline said, trying to catch her breath. "What are you doing here, Matt?"

I gave her a glare to shut her up. "Where did you get the hat and the bag, sweetie?"

"Mr. White gave them to me," she said, no trace of fear in her voice or face.

"Mr. White?" my ex-wife said, staring at Lucy. "We don't know any Mr. White."

"Daddy does." My daughter pointed to the bag. "Mr. White said I was to give Daddy the bag and I could keep the cap."

I tried to get my pounding heart under control.

"Who is this Mr.—"

I held my hand up at Caroline. "What did Mr. White look like, Lucy?"

She laughed. "Silly daddy. Mr. White's your friend. He said so. You must know what he looks like."

I glanced at Caroline. Her face was suffused with crimson, a sure sign that anger was about to erupt. "Just tell me what he looked like," I said, kneeling down in front of Lucy. "So I'm sure it's the right person."

My daughter gave me a curious look and then laughed again. "All right, silly daddy. Mr. White's got long black hair." She pouted. "And a mouse."

"What?" Caroline and I said in unison.

"I said, he's got a mouse." Lucy burst out in peals of laughter. "Don't you remember the story we used to read? About the boy who wouldn't say 'mustache'? So he said his daddy had a mouse under his nose."

I stood up again, ignoring the tirade that Caroline had started. Long black hair and a mustache—it sounded like the kind of disguise you could buy in any joke shop. Still, I'd get Lucy to do a drawing of him tomorrow.

"Are you even listening to me, Matt?" my ex-wife said, pushing me in the chest. "What the hell's going on? What's in that bag?"

I looked down at the object in my hands. The money. It had to be the money. I couldn't open it in front of Caroline and Lucy.

"Oh, it's…it's some CDs I lent the guy. I…I met him in the pub and we got talking. We both like Americana." I felt my cheeks redden. I could tell that Caroline didn't believe me, but she wasn't prepared to make even more of a scene in front of Lucy.

"Yeah," she said under her breath. "Like you have a friend called Mr. White. I suppose he's a fan of that awful movie *Reservoir Dogs* like you." She squatted down. "Lucy, you know you shouldn't talk to people you don't know, or take things from them."

My daughter got tearful again. "But he knows Daddy," she said, giving me a heartbreaking look. "He said so. And Daddy knows him."

"It's all right, sweetie," I said, patting her head.

"What the hell are you doing down here, anyway, Matt?" Caroline said as she stood up. "You know the rules. Saturday is my day with Lucy." Her eyes widened. "Were you following us?"

"No, of course not," I said, glancing away. The couple I'd spoken to were watching us anxiously. I waved to show that things were okay, but they didn't look convinced.

"You better not have been," my ex-wife said, taking Lucy's hand. "You don't want that piece of rubbish, darling," she added, flicking the cap onto the grass.

Lucy raised her head and put on the haughty look that she'd inherited from Caroline. I could tell that she wanted the Tasmanian Devil cap. I picked it up and watched them leave. I wasn't planning on giving it back to her, though. I was planning on jamming it down the madman's throat. I couldn't believe he'd taken the risk of talking to Lucy. He must have seen how close I was.

If he'd wanted to ram home the message that I was totally powerless to resist him, he couldn't have chosen a better way.

★ ★ ★

The three men were standing around Terry Smail. He was hanging upside down from a joist in an abandoned warehouse. His captors had all taken off their caps and sunglasses, revealing close-cropped hair and scarred faces.

"I don't know," jabbered their naked victim. "Aah! I didn't know Jimmy well. I…I don't know who he drank with."

The man in charge shook his head. His lips were only a couple of inches from Terry's inverted ear. "You know that isn't true. Do you want us to take you down again?"

Smail squealed and jerked his head forward. The sight of the red patch that was his groin made him shake violently, but his wrists were behind his back and the movements did nothing but give him more pain from the chain round his ankles.

"What we did to you the last time was only the start," Wolfe said, grabbing him by the shoulders. "After all, your wedding tackle's still intact."

Rommel and Geronimo laughed harshly.

"So far," continued Wolfe. "Next time we won't just be removing your pubes with this high-tech instrument." He held up the rusty and blood-spattered painter's scraper. "Sorry we couldn't find anything cleaner." His glance cut off the others' guffaws. "It's very simple, Terry." His eyes, dark as coal, the pupils unnaturally black, met the hanging man's. "Either you spill your guts or we spill them." He paused, watching Smail's mouth open and close. "Tell me who Jimmy Tanner drank with."

"I…oh fuckin' hell, it hurts. All right, all right, I'll tell you. Just let me down."

The team leader gave him another thirty seconds in the air, then nodded to his colleagues. The chain was loosened and the captive dumped unceremoniously on the rough floor.

"We're listening, Terry," Wolfe said. "Talk and we'll let you go."

Smail looked at him disbelievingly, and then sobbed as he took in the bloody mess of his ankles. The chain had almost cut through to the bones.

"Jimmy Tanner drank with...?"

"Oh, Christ, I can't. They'll kill me."

"And we won't?"

"All right, all right. Jimmy, he didn't much drink with anyone. He got vicious when he'd had a skin-full and we'd seen what he could do. He broke Big Mikey's arm like it was a stick." Terry Smail glanced at the three men around him. "Oh, I get it. You're like him. You're SAS like he said he used to be, ain't you?"

"Keep talking," said the leader, raising the scraper.

The captive gulped. "It must've been about six months ago. These two blokes turned up at the Hereward. We all reckoned they was dodgy, but they got talking to Knives, the landlord. I reckon money changed hands. Anyway, Knives introduces them to Jimmy and soon they're getting on like a house on fire. I heard...I heard they wanted Jimmy to show them things." He looked at his captors again. "The kind of things you people do."

"What were their names?"

"I dunno. Aah-ee!" Smail tried to swing away from the rusty blade that was being dragged down his chest. "Corky. That's all I know. One of them was called Corky. I dunno nothing about the other one."

"And they used to drink with Jimmy till when?"

"Till about six weeks ago. When he...when he stopped coming. What's this all about? What's happened to Jimmy?"

Wolfe shook his head. "That's what you're going to tell us, Terry."

"I...I dunno." Smail's eyes moved around frantically. "Honest I don't."

Wolfe pulled the scraper back. "Describe the men."

Terry let out a long sigh of relief. "Um, the one called Corky was nothing special. Not too tall. He had a crappy beard that had bits of food in it and he always wore a woolly hat." He broke off and looked up at the men. "Like you guys. His nose looked like it'd been flattened by a brick and his eyes were all bloodshot. He was a pisshead, I reckon, even though he only ever drank mineral water."

"And the man with no name?"

"He was smaller than me. He always wore a baseball cap, red, with some cartoon character on it. He had this shitty long hair, black, in kinda rat's tails. Oh, yeah, and he had these weird teeth. Pointed. Looked like he was a fuckin' vampire. That's what we used to call him. Count Dracula." He let out a string of feeble, cracked laughs, and then stopped when he saw the three men's faces. "That's all I know. Honest. Can I go now?"

Wolfe stood up and looked at his companions. "Oh, you can go all right." He leaned over the naked man. "You can go on the express elevator to hell. But first you're going to tell us what you're holding back. Who is the man with the pointed teeth? We want to meet him very badly." He tossed the scraper to Geronimo.

Terence Smail's screams echoed round the empty building. The seagulls outside took up a keening chant that obscured his travails from every passerby.

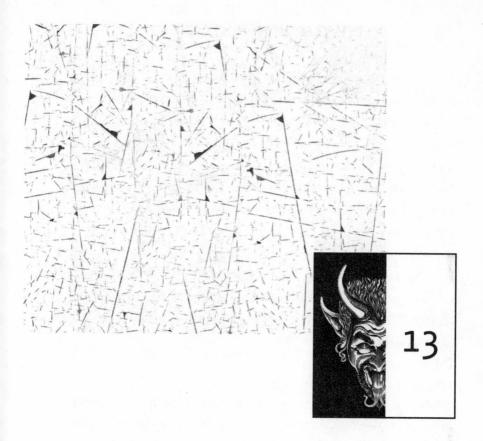

13

I went back to the Volvo and drove home, having placed the leather bag unopened on the front passenger seat. I felt even more intensely the mixture of rage and impotence that had weighed me down since the Devil first got his claws into me. But there was another emotion now. I tried to resist it because I knew he had planted it in me and was assiduously cultivating it—the desire for revenge. He had spoken to Lucy, he'd touched her. I was going to make him pay. He'd been studying me; he knew how my mind worked even though he'd never met me. But why did he want me to go after him? Did he have some weird kind of death wish, or was he sure that he could keep me at a distance?

I parked outside my place and went inside, the bag under my

jacket. For some reason I didn't want anyone to see me carrying it. As I was climbing the stairs, I understood why not. It was blood money, tainted by the deaths of the Devil's victims. What was I going to do with it? Hide it in the loft? The money was another part of my tormentor's plan that I didn't understand. He'd made me his slave by threatening Lucy and everyone else I loved. He didn't need to pay me. Did that betray a psychological weakness, that he had to pay for attention? Or was there something more subtle in his thinking?

I checked my e-mails. There was one from Sara, saying that she was tied up with the story and would ring me when she could. There was also one from my mother, and it made my heart pound again.

Dearest,

I hope this finds you well. I know we spoke on the phone the other day, but I wanted to get in touch and I feel more comfortable writing—you understand how writers are, defter by pen and keyboard than by tongue (that could be taken as rude!). You sounded troubled when I called you. I know that your problems with publishers and agents have been getting to you. Don't let the bastards grind you down! You just have to get on with the next book and prove them wrong. I know you can do it!

Now, something else. Have you been following the news recently? I'm sure you will have been. Those two murders in the headlines. Have you noticed how similar they are to two of the killings in your books? I looked up the particular passages. The priest in Kilburn seems to have been done as per pages 257 to 264 of *The Devil Murder*. And the poor woman in Chelmsford had her arm severed, just like the vile Blakeston in *The Revenger's Comedy*, pages 325 to 331. Isn't that extraordinary? Obviously a coincidence, but rather a chilling one. Have you had any of your fans pointing it out?

Anyway, don't worry. I won't bring it to the attention of the police!

Must get on with *Elvira and Tiffany Go to the Beach*. Give my love to Lucy (and the opposite to Caroline—sorry, only joking!).

With fondest love,

Fran

"Jesus," I said under my breath. "Thanks a lot for that, Mother."

Then my mobile rang. There was no number on the screen.

"Hello, Matt. What—"

"You fucking piece of shit!" I shouted. "What were you doing talking to Lucy? How dare you touch her? I'm going to—"

"You're going to what?" the Devil answered, his voice steely. "Find me? Catch me? Kill me? Oh, yes, please, Matt. That would be so much fun. You see, I have this enormous death wish." His laugh was as far from humorous as I could imagine. "Just calm down. What makes you so sure that I was Mr. White? I might have dozens of helpers, hundreds for all you know. Do you really think I would take a risk like that myself?"

I kept silent. I had the feeling that he was quite capable of getting a kick from a stunt like that, but I had no way of knowing how many people were working for him.

"Anyway, be a good little writer and open the bag now, will you?"

I held the phone between my shoulder and ear, and reached across for it. I could see the bundles of twenty-pounds notes before the zip was fully open.

"All right?" the Devil asked.

"There seems to be another five thousand," I said, emptying the bag.

He laughed, this time more warmly. "I don't think you've got everything I put in for you. Look in the side pocket."

I felt a stab of concern. What else had the calculating son of a bitch sent me? I pulled the button on the small pocket open. Christ. What was it? I put my fingers in carefully and felt a wiry substance. Taking it out, I saw a mass of brown and white hairs.

"Good man," said the Devil. "Do you know what they are?"

I swallowed the bitter liquid that had rushed up my throat. "Hair," I said faintly.

"That's right, Matt. Pubic hair."

My fingers sprang apart before I could control myself and the hairs tumbled to the floor.

"A mixture of Bugger O'Connell's and the cow Merton's. Dear me, Matt. What are they doing in your flat? How suspicious. You'd better get rid of them. Of course, there's plenty more where they came from. I can sprinkle them outside your place, I can hide them anywhere I like inside. What do you think of that?"

"Screw you," I said in a defeated voice.

"I look forward to it. Oh, by the way, I thought it was pretty funny that your mother was the first to connect the killings to your books. Wow, you really are getting yourself exposed. Now, if you'll excuse me, I have to go and visit an old enemy." He grunted—a revolting, degenerate sound. "It's time to bury the hatchet, or something along those lines. No rest for the wicked. You'll be getting my notes tomorrow morning. Sorry if they mess up your day with Lucy, but I'm sure Caroline will be happy to have extra time with her. Hey, Matt, she really has got a temper on her, hasn't she?" He laughed one last time and hung up.

I let the phone drop to the floor. Jesus Christ Almighty. The Devil was all over me like the Black Death. He must have hacked into my e-mail program to have read my mother's message. I looked around my sitting room suspiciously. Had he installed a camera? If so, what were the chances of me finding it? Even assuming I did, if I put it out of action that might provoke him to even worse horrors. He probably had my landline tapped and a scanner on my mobile, too. Why not go the whole hog? Had he put a transmitter on the Volvo? In my shoes?

Then I remembered what he'd said about Caroline. Did that prove he'd been Mr. White after all, or had he just been observing? Maybe an accomplice had told him about Caroline's screaming fit.

I put my head between my knees. None of that was important now. The bastard was on his way to kill someone else, that much was obvious. What I had no way of knowing was who that person was. Even if I'd taken Lucy, Caroline, Fran and Sara to the police for protection and admitted everything I knew, there would be no way they could stop the murder of someone else.

For too long I'd luxuriated in the power of life and death over the characters in my novels. I'd never thought how it would feel to have such power over real people. But the White Devil had. If I was to stand any chance of playing his game, I needed to understand his callousness.

I didn't know if my imagination could reach such depths of depravity.

"Thanks for being so flexible," Karen Oaten said to the auburn-haired woman sitting opposite her—although she was of average height, her thinness made her seem taller than she was. They were in the café in the basement of a large bookshop on Gower Street. "I didn't expect you'd be able to see me on a Saturday."

"That's all right. I work seven days a week. My partner, Shaz, is forever pestering me to take more breaks." Lizzie Everhead smiled. "She'll be pleased to know I've given in at last, Chief Inspector."

That was a direct-enough statement of the academic's sexuality to someone she'd only just met, Oaten thought. She'd been going to ask her to call her by her first name, but now she decided against it. Too much informality was never a good idea in a murder case, even if this angle was unlikely to pay off. What did she really imagine she was going to find out from this literally blue-stockinged lecturer?

"It's pretty much a working break, isn't it, Doctor?" she said, stirring sugar into her coffee. The literature expert was drinking hot water with a slice of lemon.

"Please, call me Lizzie." The woman laughed. "I love what I do. This isn't what I call work. Sitting on exam boards and the like is torture, but not this." She tied her legs in knots, contriving to wrap her foot around her calf as well as crossing her knees. "So, how can I help..." She looked at Oaten's card. "Karen?"

Oaten felt spots of red on her cheeks. She'd never felt completely at ease with lesbians, even though her own sex life had never been better than deeply average. There had been no shortage of opportunities for same-sex relationships at college, but she'd thrown herself into a series of hopeless affairs with married men and gormless students. For some years, her vibrator had been her only source of release. If only she had the time to find herself a decent man—even a half-decent one would do.

"Er, yes," she said, coming back to herself. "I gather you're an expert in Jacobean tragedy."

"That's right," Lizzie Everhead said, inclining her head. She had unusually large eyes, the irises a deep blue shade. "Among other things. What do you need to know?"

Karen straightened her back. "I must warn you that the information I'm about to impart is highly confidential."

"Ooh, how exciting!" said the doctor, rubbing her hands. She took in the look on the chief inspector's face. "Sorry. Of course. I understand. I won't tell anyone." She smiled. "Not even Shaz."

"I'll be the one in trouble if the press gets wind of this, not you," Oaten said. "As long as you understand that."

The academic nodded and leaned closer. "Fire away."

"Right." The chief inspector lowered her voice. "I imagine you'll have heard about the murders of the priest in Kilburn and the old lady in Chelmsford."

Lizzie Everhead looked blank. "No, I don't read the papers or listen to the news. Radio 3 is my cup of…" She glanced down at the table. "…hot water." She saw how serious Oaten's expression was. "Sorry. Tell me."

So the D.C.I. did, leaving out only one detail. There was a strange kind of gratification in seeing the face of the distinguished scholar of violent tragedy go paler than a sheet when confronted with real-life violence.

"How utterly awful," Lizzie said, taking an ironed handkerchief from her bag and dabbing her lips. "Unbelievable."

"There's more," Karen said, and told her about the quotations that had been found in the bodies.

The academic sat back and fanned her face with the tissue. "I'm…I'm speechless. A very…a very unusual condition for me, I can tell you." She drank from her cup and dabbed her lips again. "Lines from Webster's *White Devil?* Hidden in the mouth and the…" She left the sentence unfinished. "I'm…I'm at a loss."

Karen Oaten leaned even closer, her face more composed than it had been when she'd described the bodies. "Lizzie, you have to think. Is there any reason why the murderer would have left those particular lines from that particular play?"

Lizzie Everhead sat perfectly still for several minutes before she spoke. "Are you familiar with the concept of revenge, Karen?"

"I have run into it occasionally in my line of work," Oaten replied dryly.

"No, I'm talking about revenge as in revenge tragedy. For the playwrights and audiences of the early seventeenth century, revenge wasn't just a personal motivation or a way of restoring family honor. It was much more than that. It was a recasting of the traditional concept of justice, the Old Testament dictum of an eye for an eye and—"

"A tooth for a tooth," Karen completed. "I remember that from religious studies at school."

"Mmm," Lizzie Everhead acknowledged. "You see, it was a time when people were beginning to doubt the old certainties. Bear in mind that a Catholic king, the Scottish James VI, had been foisted on England after the death of the Protestant Good Queen Bess. And James's son Charles drove the country to division and ended up by paying with his head. So we can see in revenge tragedy the first shoots of revolutionary thinking— that the King is not all-powerful and that a different kind of justice, one more attuned to free-thinking human beings, might apply."

Karen Oaten looked confused. "What's that got to do with the murders?"

"Well, for one thing, you said both the victims were Catholics."

"That's right."

"I'm interested by that. You see, Jacobean tragedy tended to use foreign settings such as Italy and Spain. Catholic countries that were regarded as having more bloodthirsty customs, particularly concerning personal and family honor."

"I understand there were quite a few plays of this kind. Why has the killer or killers chosen *The White Devil?*"

Lizzie gave an impatient smile. "I was coming to that. White Devils are hypocrites, people who hide their true base nature beneath a layer of respectability. Could that apply to either of your victims? It sounds like the priest was a prime example of a White Devil."

Karen nodded. "We're looking into the ex-schoolteacher, too."

"Maybe she was harsh. Or maybe she had some family secret."

"Maybe," Karen said noncommittally. "What about the lines themselves?"

"Right. 'What a mockery hath death made of thee.' That is spoken by Flamineo the revenger, when he sees the ghost of his dead master, Brachiano. Flamineo himself is soon punished for his misdeeds. He describes his life as 'a black charnel,' that is, if you like, a mortuary. The point is, sin is repaid by death. There's a strong parallel with the Catholic vision of damnation, of eternal suffering in Hell."

"You mean for the person who seeks revenge?" Oaten said, her forehead furrowed. "As if the killer knows he's going to die and suffer torment."

"Exactly. I would guess that he or—I suppose there's at least a small possibility—she was brought up a Catholic."

The chief inspector made a note. "What about the other line—'Only persuade him teach the way to death; let him die first'?"

Lizzie stroked her chin with long fingers. "That is spoken by

Zanche, the handmaid of Vittoria, Flamineo's sister. It's probably fair to say that the latter pair are the greatest of the White Devils alluded to by the title. Vittoria is little more than a high-class whore who connives in the murder of both her husbands. Here, she and Flamineo, the second husband Brachiano's supposedly loyal servant, are plotting against each other, despite the fact that they supposedly love each other."

"So sin outweighs even family ties?"

The academic nodded. "Yes. But I can't take it any further than that. Unless the dead woman had a husband who predeceased her."

Karen shook her head. "She had a brother, though."

Lizzie caught her eye. "Interesting. There's a strong under-current of incest in *The White Devil,* as in many plays of the time."

"How is that going to help me catch the killer?"

"I can't say. But it's certainly possible that incest is an impor-tant element in this whole ghastly affair....oh!" The doctor sat back in her chair and unraveled her legs. "How absolutely ex-traordinary!"

"What?" Karen said, her curiosity piqued.

Lizzie Everhead held up the delicate fingers of her left hand, as if she had plucked something out of the air. "I'll have to check the texts, but there's a contemporary crime novelist who's written a series set in the 1620s. How very strange."

"What?" the chief inspector said in exasperation.

"Well, one of my other fields of expertise is crime fiction," Lizzie said, looking back at Karen. "This writer—his name is Matt Stone—has a detective-hero called Sir Tertius Greville. I'm almost certain there's a murder similar to your priest's in one of the books, and the removal of an arm in another."

Karen Oaten stood up. She'd already bought *Blood, Lust and*

Gender, Dr. Everhead's study of revenge tragedy. "Thanks very much for your help," she said. "You wouldn't happen to know where the crime section is?"

The academic nodded. "I'll show you the way," she said with a crooked smile.

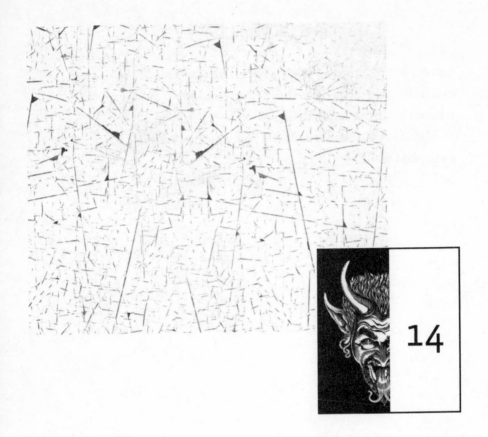

14

Dr. Bernard Keane looked at his gold Cartier watch. It was nearly
two-thirty. He seldom allowed his Saturday clinic to overrun, as
he liked to spend the afternoon with his horses, but in this patient's
case he'd been prepared to make an exception. The man's address
in Docklands was exclusive. He knew a politician with a flat in
the renovated building—the man, a terrible snob if truth be
told—had whispered to him that he'd paid more than two million
for it. So Mr. John Webster was obviously a major player and a
welcome addition to his list. He'd understood fully his prospec-
tive patient's request for complete privacy—in particular, that his
address shouldn't be entered into the practice records.

The doctor got up from his mahogany desk and opened the

gauze curtains. Harley Street. When he'd started off as a newly qualified general practitioner in the run-down East End, he'd never imagined that he would achieve his ambition. The increase in demand for slimming therapies—the public's absurd desire for the perfect body—had enabled him to specialize in that area. He had developed his own treatment, cobbled together from various well-known books, and, to his amazement, it had worked—no doubt because he stressed discipline. The simple fact was that people responded well to discipline, even when they had to apply it themselves.

The bell rang. Dr. Keane went to answer the door himself. He'd let his petite but well-stacked receptionist, Marianne, leave. It wouldn't be long before he had her over his desk, as he'd done with all her predecessors. There was an underlying coarseness to her that he knew he could manipulate.

"Dr. Keane?" the man on the landing asked. He was of medium height and build, in early middle age and in no apparent need of a slimming regime. That didn't matter. People often had ludicrously inaccurate ideas about their appearance.

"Mr. Webster, I presume," the doctor said with a practiced laugh.

The man smiled back at him. He was wearing a well-cut pin-striped suit and a Homburg hat on top of long black hair. He also had a drooping mustache. His hands were sheathed in black kid gloves. Bernard Keane wondered about his profession. He was probably one of those computer whiz kids who had made a mint.

"Do come in," the doctor said, closing the door behind him. "You can leave your bag out here."

"No, I'll keep hold of it," Mr. Webster replied. The bag was like the large, rectangular ones that pilots carry. "Thank you," he said, lowering himself into the leather armchair he'd been ushered toward.

Keane sat down across the desk from him. "So, what can I do for you?" he asked, his eyes on the man. There was something about him that made him feel faintly uneasy. He'd once been stalked by a female patient who used all her wiles to trap him in an inappropriate sexual relationship. That had cost him a lot of money. This Mr. Webster was making his antennae twitch.

"You don't recognize me?" the man said.

"I...no, should I?" The doctor felt that he was being tested and he didn't like it.

"No." Mr. Webster smiled again, showing perfect white teeth that Keane saw had been capped at great expense. The canines were curiously pointed. "In fact, I'm pleased you don't." He opened his bag and took out a thick gray file. "Would you indulge me by taking a look at this?" he asked politely, stepping round the desk and standing beside the doctor.

As soon as Keane saw the name on the file, he knew he was in trouble. He reached for the phone, and then let out a scream that was quickly cut off as a gag was stuffed into his mouth. Staring in horror at the knife that had pinned his right hand to the desk in a flash, he scarcely felt the rope that was run round his chest, securing him to the revolving chair. Soon there were ropes on his ankles and left forearm, as well.

Mr. Webster turned the chair toward him, grinning as Keane tried to scream again. The movement had made the knife blade cut laterally through his hand.

"Oh, sorry, how thoughtless of me." The man laughed harshly. "Then again, *thoughtless* is a word that could be applied to you, couldn't it, Dr. Keane?"

He tried to speak. He wanted to explain himself, make

excuses, beg for forgiveness, but the gag was still in his mouth, a strip of tape now over his lips.

"You remember her, don't you?" Mr. Webster said, taking off his gloves.

With a spasm of horror, the doctor saw that his assailant was wearing latex surgical gloves beneath. Oh, God, what did he intend to do? What was going on?

"Catherine Dunn. Date of birth March 21, 1947. Address, 14 Marlin Court, Bethnal Green. Telephone, none." The man bent over him and he caught the smell of expensive aftershave and aromatic tobacco. "Attended your surgery on March 12, 1983, complaining of stomach pains." He turned a page. "See, here are your notes. 'Patient is clearly undernourished. Given advice about diet. No follow-up required.'" Webster grabbed his cheeks and pressed hard. The doctor felt like his eyes were about to pop out. "No follow-up required," his captor repeated.

Webster stepped back and took off his hat. Then he gripped his hair at the top of his forehead and peeled it back. Beneath the wig was short fair hair, almost certainly peroxide. The mustache was pulled away next. "Now do you recognize me, Doctor?"

Keane had already suspected the worst. Although the hair and build were different, the unwavering brown eyes were the same. It was the youth who had stormed into his surgery, screaming about how his mother had died in agony of stomach cancer, how it was Keane's fault and how he was going to pay for it. If his partner, a former army medic, hadn't intervened, he might have been made to pay for it there and then. But the young man had been dragged out, shouting and swearing. He said he'd be back, but he'd never showed up. He'd always been lurking in Keane's mind, though, even years after he moved from Bethnal Green.

The rage in his eyes, the savagery in him—the doctor had never seen anything like it.

He closed his eyes, the pain in his hand worsening.

"Not crying, are you, Doctor?" Webster said, his tone mocking.

Webster. His name wasn't Webster. It was Dunn. Lance? Leslie? That was it, Leslie Dunn. Keane remembered treating him for measles when he was younger. He had a black eye and his nose had been broken. The father, no doubt. Not that he'd reported it to the police or social services. Families like that were drunken and feckless. There was no point in trying to improve their lives.

His captor leaned close again. "You're probably wondering why Leslie Dunn didn't bother you again. Well, I'll tell you. You took my mother away from me, you destroyed my life back then. But if I'd hurt you, what would have happened? I'd have been caught, sent to a young offenders' institution, had the shit kicked out of me. I didn't fancy that at all." His smile was pitiless, as cold as the heart of an iceberg. "Besides, I reckoned you wouldn't forget me." He glanced around the expensively decorated room. "Even in the middle of all this conspicuous wealth." He looked back at Keane. "I was right, wasn't I?"

The doctor nodded slowly. The boy had been too ignorant to launch a medical negligence suit, but the guilt had always been there, lurking like a malevolent spider in the most inaccessible part of his mind. If only he'd been brought up a Catholic, like the trembling, dispirited woman who had come to him for help all those years ago. He'd have been able to confess his sin and get on with his life. But it didn't matter now. He was sure he was at the end of his road.

Keane watched as the man who'd called himself Webster

stripped off his suit and shirt. Beneath them he was wearing a white coverall with a hood like the ones used by scenes-of-crime officers on the TV. He dug deeper into his bag and brought out an oilskin bundle. Clearing the desk with a backhand sweep of his arm, he unrolled the oilskin. Gleaming surgical instruments were lodged in pockets. They ranged from needle-thin probes to a large bone-saw.

"Nnngg!" Keane moaned, pulling on his bonds. The pain in his hand didn't bother him now. He was consumed by fear of what was to come.

"Take your punishment like a man," Dunn said, laughing emptily. He picked up a scalpel. "Now, where shall I begin? Oh, I know. You failed to diagnose a case of advanced stomach cancer. You didn't even bother to order the most basic of tests. Have you any idea how much pain my mother was in?" He pulled open the doctor's striped shirt and caught his eye. "For someone who specializes in dieting, you don't set a very good example, do you?" He ran the scalpel down the support girdle Keane wore and pulled it apart. "The pain my mother suffered was like this."

The doctor jerked back in the chair as his stomach was pierced, almost swallowing the gag.

"And like this."

Another stabbing pain.

"And like this."

Again and again he tried to scream, breathing desperately through his nose. He was in agony, his eyes blurred by tears. The thrusting and cutting continued. He had no idea how many wounds had been made. The pain was almost unbearable, but he didn't pass out.

At last Dunn stood up and tossed the bloody scalpel onto the desk. "Take a look," he said, wrenching the doctor's head down.

Keane was horrified at the damage that had been done to his abdomen despite the pain he was in.

"Come in," he heard Dunn say. Turning slightly, he saw a figure approaching. He couldn't make out the face.

"We're just getting to the good bit." Dunn's face was close to his again. "Take this thought with you to the eternal furnace, you fucking murderer," he said. "We're going to rape your wife and daughter before we cut them apart. Then we're going to slaughter your horses and feed their guts to your dogs, before we finish them off, too."

The last thing that Bernard Keane saw though his remaining eye was the carving knife in Leslie Dunn's right hand and the bone-saw in his left.

Before his world dissolved in a welter of crimson, he wondered who his killer's accomplice might be. He was an only child when his mother had died....

As soon as I saw the TV news after the Saturday sport, I knew it had to be the White Devil. A Harley Street doctor murdered in what was described as "the most gruesome fashion"—it was just his style. I called Sara on her mobile and asked her if she'd heard anything about it. She told me that Jeremy, the crime correspondent, was back from Belfast and that he was covering the killing. She'd been sent to a climate-change conference in Cambridge after the environment correspondent called in sick. She didn't think she'd be back till late, so we arranged that I'd go round to her place on Sunday evening. I told her I loved her and she repeated the words, though she sounded distracted.

I sat at my desk wondering what to do. If the bastard had killed the doctor in a way copied from one of my books, it wouldn't be long before someone made the connection my mother had and contacted the police. If they confiscated my computer and examined the hard disk, they'd find the chapters I'd written for the Devil. They'd also find his e-mails to me, but the different addresses he'd used meant that they could easily say I'd written them myself. Then there was the money. If the police found it, I'd have a lot of explaining to do. I had to get rid of it. But how? My tormentor was watching me, he was listening to me. Whatever I did, he'd know. And then what would happen to Lucy and the others?

Jesus. I was a writer. I used my imagination every day of my life. I had to be able to come up with a plan. I sat with my head in my hands for a long time, but nothing happened. I needed to kick-start my brain. When inspiration didn't appear during the writing process, I used to put on my headphones and listen to loud music. It was worth a try. I looked through my CD collection and settled on Richmond Fontaine's *Post to Wire*. My mind filled with images of deserted truck stops and dusty motels, but then the plangent vocals and weeping guitar lines brought the clarity I was after. Things began to come together.

I decided that, whatever I did, it had to be in the open. If the Devil really was watching me all the time, I couldn't do anything that would raise his suspicions. So I got all the bundles of twenties together and put them in a kit bag from my rugby days. Then I put it in the bottom of my wardrobe. While I was bending down there, I hastily transferred the bundles to a hunting jacket my mother had given my for some reason best known to herself—I'd never hunted anything in my life. It had numerous large pockets for the carcasses of dead game. I kept the lights low in the bedroom, hoping that the Devil couldn't see what I was up to. If he could, I reckoned he'd be on the phone soon enough to ask what I thought I was doing.

I went back into the sitting room and booted up my computer. I transferred all the e-mails to and from the Devil, plus the chapters I'd written, to diskettes. They would be going in my hunting jacket, too. The difficult part was what to do with the computer itself. I had a plan. Going into the kitchen, I made myself a mug of coffee and then went back to my desk. Looking as nonchalant as I could, I put the mug down beside the laptop. Then I started to type. Given that the bastard seemed to be able to hack into any file I opened, I wrote up my thoughts on the Harley Street killing. That would impress him. At least he hadn't called—so far.

I picked up my mug and drank, pulling my mouth back with a yelp as if I'd scalded my lips and depositing the coffee all over the keyboard.

"Shit!" I yelled.

As I'd hoped, the machine reacted badly. After a few moments the screen went blank, a grinding noise started and the smell of burning filled my nostrils. I pulled out the mains connection and sat there swearing.

After what I thought was long enough, I picked up my mobile and called my rugby league friend Roger van Zandt, who was a computer expert.

"Hi, Rog," I said. "You okay?"

"Down the Duck. Why aren't you here, Wellsy? Shagging again?" He laughed. I could hear raucous sounds in the background. "Dave wants to know if your friend from the newspaper is a page three girl."

Excellent. Two birds with one stone. "Tell Dave I'm coming down there to sort him out. Hey, Dodger, can you have a look at my laptop? I just managed to pour a mug of coffee over it."

"You jackass. Yeah, all right. Bring it with you. And prepare to get very drunk."

I cut the connection. So far so good. I put the computer in a heavy-duty plastic bag and then went into my bedroom, not bothering to turn on the light. I slipped the diskettes into my hunting jacket and then put it on. I also pulled on a pair of trainers I hadn't used for months. If I was lucky, there wouldn't be a bug in them. I took off my watch and threw it onto the bed. Making sure my mobile stayed on the desk, I picked up my keys and left the flat.

I felt like the Michelin Man in my money-inflated jacket, but I was hoping it would be taken for one of those puffer things that skiers wear. Walking at medium pace down the streets to the Village, I kept my eyes and ears open. I couldn't see anyone on my tail. Then again, the Devil wouldn't need to bother. He probably knew exactly where I was going.

The Duck was as packed as it always gets on a Saturday. I spotted Rog and Dave in the far corner. They were with Andrew Jackson, an American guy from the rugby club. The next hour passed in the standard way—talk about the state of the league game, whinging about kids, mockery about wives and girl-friends. Sara had made it clear from the start that she didn't want to meet my male friends. The problem was, that made them think she was a snooty bitch, as Rog so pleasantly put it.

Then Dave turned to me and stroked his boxer's nose.

"So what about these murders then, Mr. Crime Writer?"

"Oh yeah," said Andy Jackson. He was tall, heavily built and fair-haired. A chef by profession, he'd come to the U.K. ten years back to get married to a woman from Croydon. They'd got divorced a year later, but he'd never got home again. He found an undemanding restaurant to work in and spent the rest of his time in the pub or playing rugby league. "They must be giving you some ideas, man."

I shrugged and swallowed lager. "I don't need ideas." I tapped my head. "I've got a wonderfully healthy imagination, Slash." We called him that because of the way he took the legs away from opposition players—nothing to do with the Guns N' Roses guitarist.

"Screw you," he replied with a grin. "I remember you telling me you read the papers every day for stuff."

Rog, a curly-haired and deceptively thin former center who used to put in heavy tackles, was giving me a thoughtful look. "Didn't you have someone killed in a church with something up his arse in one of your books, Matt?"

Shit. I went on the offensive. "So?" I said, glancing around the pub. Everyone else seemed to be involved in their own conversations and there was no one obviously watching me. "You think people read my books and carry out copycat murders?"

The three of them sat back, surprised by my vehemence.

"Of course not," Andy said. "Take it easy."

I let my shoulders drop. "Sorry. Bad day at the typeface." I handed the bag with my computer to Rog. "See what you can do with this."

"Okay," he said doubtfully. "But if liquid's got to the hard disk, I'll have to replace it."

That was what I was hoping. I nodded, my expression fake unhappy. "Whatever it takes. No hurry. I've got my old one in the loft."

"He's got an old one in the loft," Andy said in an attempt at a Bela Lugosi accent. "In the east wing."

"Pete Satterthwaite's the only person I know with a house big enough to have wings," I said.

Rog laughed. "Bonehead? He's also got all sorts of skeletons in his cupboards."

We talked a bit about the team's former main sponsor, who was balder than the baldest coot. Then we got on to the inadequacies of the current Great Britain Test team, until Dave got up to take a leak. I let him go ahead, then followed him. I'd kept my jacket on despite the heat in the pub. Now came the tricky bit. Dave was my closest friend, in as much as writers have close friends. I trusted him, but would he trust me?

Inside the toilet, I waited until a pisshead fumbled with his buttons and left. Then I beckoned to Dave.

"What's up, Matt?" he said, one hand on his member. When he'd finished, he followed me into the only crapper. "People will talk," he said with a grin.

"Listen, Psycho," I said, my voice low. "I want you to keep something for me." I pulled a plastic bag out of a pocket and started filling it with the bundles of banknotes.

Dave whistled. "Jesus, have you been robbing banks?"

"Wanker. No, I got paid in cash for a job. I'll tell you about it later. I don't want Caroline to find out about it or she'll be on my back for maintenance, even though she earns a fortune. Can you keep it for me?"

Dave stared down at the bag. "How much is it?"

"Ten grand."

"Bloody hell! Why can't you put it in a deposit account?"

"I will. But not yet." I touched my nose with my forefinger. "I've got my reasons."

Dave shrugged. "All right. I'll stick it under the floorboards."

"One more thing," I said, grabbing his arm. "I don't want the other guys to see it. Can you stuff it down your shirt?"

"What?" He looked at the bulky bag. "There isn't room for my belly in this shirt."

Fortunately he had kept on his loose parka. After a lot of

fiddling, we managed to secrete the money and the backup diskettes down his back and front. Then I stuffed my own pockets with all the toilet paper I could find so that my jacket kept its former shape.

"Are you all right?" Dave said, rubbing his chin.

"I'll explain everything later."

When we got back to the table, the other two looked up at us.

"I don't think buggery's permitted in the head here," Andy said with a wide grin.

"Sod off," Dave said, provoking a gale of laughter.

It was only as I was buying the next round that I realized what I'd done. I'd brought my best mates into the Devil's field of fire.

That betrayal made me feel lower on the evolutionary scale than an earthworm.

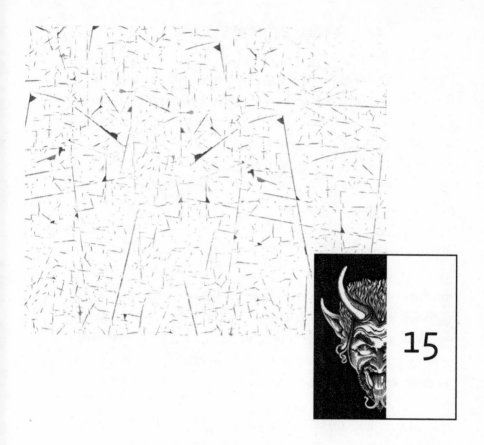

15

John Turner stood in his white coveralls and bootees, trying to get his breathing under control. The body had been found by a doctor on the floor below who'd come up to borrow a journal. That man had had a lucky escape.

The inspector opened the gauze curtains and looked down at Harley Street. Ordinary people were going about their ordinary lives, black cabs passing and foreign teenagers shouting at one another. Why did he have to put up with scenes of horror like this on a more or less daily basis? He knew the answer well enough. His father had been a copper, ending up as a desk sergeant in central Cardiff, and his grandfather had walked the beat, too. It was in his blood. He froze, conscious again of the torn body to his right. It was bad enough, but what lay on the floor beyond had gone beyond anything he'd ever experienced. Even the most degenerate horror film scriptwriter would have struggled to come up with anything as horrendous as that.

Karen Oaten looked up at him from where she was squatting by the severed head. "Come on, Taff. It's got to be done." She turned to the pathologist, Redrose, who was at her side. "Well?"

"It's Bernard Keane, all right," the potbellied medic said, shaking his head. "I knew him from one of our charity committees. This is appalling." He returned her gaze. "Jesus, someone will have to tell his wife."

"She's on her way," Oaten said. "Don't worry, I can handle that. You're sure it's him, though? I don't want to put her through identifying him formally until the undertakers have been to work on him." She shook her head. "They'll have their work cut out."

"I'm sure it's him, Chief Inspector." The pathologist got to his feet unsteadily.

Oaten gave him a few moments. "What about the cause of death?"

"Take your pick. Shock or loss of blood." Redrose moved over to the chair where the victim's body lay sprawled. "Judging by the lack of blood spray, I'd say that the head was removed post-mortem. Conversely, these wounds, or at least many of them, were inflicted while Bernard...Dr. Keane was still breathing. My initial examination indicates that the stomach has been cut out." He looked at Oaten and then at Turner. "There's a clear plastic packet inside the abdominal cavity."

Turner's hand moved to his mouth before he could stop it.

"Take it out," the chief inspector instructed the pathologist.

"I should really wait for the postmor—" Redrose broke off

when he saw her expression. "Very well." He picked up a pair of tweezers from his bag and, pulling up his mask and bending over the opened midriff, carefully removed a flat, square object.

"There's a piece of paper in it," Turner said, catching his superior's eye. "It's him again."

She nodded solemnly. "I think we'd all already come to that conclusion, Taff." She called over the senior SOCO. "Get the contents out and check the bag for prints."

"That really ought to be done in the lab," the technician said.

Oaten gave him a severe look. "Just do what I say, will you? Inspector Turner will be your witness if anyone questions procedure." She turned back to Redrose. "Time of death?"

He glanced at his notes. "A rough calculation from the temperature readings would be between six and eight hours ago."

"So between two and four this afternoon," Turner said. "I'll go and check the receptionist's computer."

"Here you are, ma'am," the SOCO said, handing her a larger plastic evidence bag with an unfolded piece of A4 paper in it. "I mean, guv."

Karen Oaten read aloud the cutout fragments of newsprint that had been stuck on the sheet. "'Like the wild Irish, I'll ne'er think thee dead Till I can play at football with thy head.'"

"Good God," the pathologist said. "The monster's making jokes about it."

"I think I can guess where this came from," Oaten said. "In fact, I've got a copy of the text in my bag outside."

Turner came back into the consulting room. "Guv, it's him all right. I couldn't get past the receptionist's password, but she kept a handwritten register, as well. Two-thirty, last patient— Mr. John Webster."

The chief inspector held up the quotation to him. "This killer thinks he's funny," she said, glaring at everyone in the room. "Well, I'm not bloody laughing."

She and Turner spent another hour there, and then the doctor's remains were removed to the morgue. They took off their coveralls outside and looked around the reception area. It was expensively furnished, a couple of good modernist paintings on the walls.

Morry Simmons appeared at the door. "Guv? We've got him."

"What?" Oaten turned to him, her eyes wide.

"Well, there's two of them, actually." Simmons looked at both of them, the usual slack smile on his lips. "I mean, we've got them on the CCTV."

"You tosser," Turner said.

"Oh, you thought I meant we'd caught…sorry." Simmons was suddenly unable to look either of them in the eye.

"All right, Morry," the chief inspector said wearily. "Show us."

He led them down to the building supervisor's office in the basement. The man hadn't been on duty at the time of the murder—he only worked until one o'clock on Saturdays—but the closed-circuit system ran continuously. He'd rewound the tape to 2:29 and found a single man in a suit entering the building. At nine minutes past three another figure, this one dressed in overalls, went to the lift. At 3:17, the two emerged from the lift together and exited by the main door.

"Can you print these images off?" Oaten asked.

The supervisor shook his head.

"Okay, we'll be taking the tape, anyway." She waved him away. "You can wait outside."

The three detectives gazed up at the screen that was fixed to the wall above the desk.

"Run it again, Morry," the chief inspector ordered.

After fiddling with the controls, Simmons managed that. They watched as two men of medium height appeared in the corridor.

"Freeze it there," Oaten said. She craned up at the screen. "Both of them are carrying bags—one of them presumably containing the tools they used to cut the victim up. I'm assuming the other contains his stomach."

Morry Simmons, who hadn't seen the body, shivered.

"The guy on the left's in disguise, surely," Turner said. "That long hair and mustache are about thirty years out of date."

"And the hat's about a hundred years out of date," the D.C.I. added. "But it obscures his eyes effectively. Expensive-looking suit." She turned her gaze on the second figure. "I'd say this one works out. Does that beard look real to you?"

"No," answered Turner at the same time as Simmons said, "Yes."

"No, Morry," Karen Oaten said patiently. "It isn't real. The baseball cap doesn't help, I admit."

Simmons tried to redeem himself. "Workman's overalls."

"Without any helpful company name on them, as far as I can see," the chief inspector said. She stepped back. "Right, Morry, start knocking on doors. Find out if anyone saw this pair going in or coming out in the midafternoon. Take Pavlou with you." She watched the sergeant leave. "And try not to screw up," she called after him. "Taff, you'd better get the tape to the photo lab. Get them to make the clearest hard copies they can."

They left the basement together.

"I'll see you back at the Yard then, guv," Turner said, glancing at his watch. "No sleep tonight."

"Not till a lot later, at least," Oaten said, giving him a wave.

After he'd gone, she took the lift back up to the top floor and reclaimed the plastic bag of books she'd left there.

She was about to start going through the text of *The White Devil* when she had a better idea. She took out her mobile and found a number in the memory.

"Lizzie, this is—"

"Karen," completed the academic. "I recognized your voice. Did you forget something?"

"Um, no. Look, I shouldn't really be doing this on the phone, but I'm pressed for time. Does this mean anything to you?" She read out the words she'd copied into her notebook from the sheet in the plastic bag.

"Oh, yes," Lizzie Everhead said cheerfully. "It's good old John Webster again."

"I thought it might be," Oaten said dryly. "From the same play?"

"Bingo. Let me just check the reference." There was the sound of pages turning. "Yes, I thought so. It's act 4, scene 1. Lines 136 to 7. This is Francisco speaking about his enemy Brachiano. Francisco's the good avenger, if you like." There was a brief pause. "Crikey, I'd forgotten that. The next line's in Latin— *'Flectere si nequeo superos, Acheronta movebo.'* I don't suppose you know Latin, Karen?"

"You don't suppose correctly."

The academic giggled. "It's a quotation from Virgil. Rough translation—if I can't get the powers above to help me, I'll appeal to those of the underworld. Rather appropriate for a White Devil, wouldn't you say?"

The chief inspector wasn't impressed by Lizzie's jocularity. "I know you don't listen to the news, but there's been another murder."

"Oh, dammit." The academic sounded suitably chastened. "I'm terribly sorry."

"It's okay. I need something else from you, Lizzie. That crime author you mentioned. Matt Stone? Has he written a scene where someone gets their stomach removed and their head cut off?"

There was silence on the line.

"Lizzie?"

"Are you...are you saying that's what's happened?" Her voice was suddenly brittle, that of a little girl.

"Just answer the question," Oaten said impatiently.

"Let me think...oh, my God, there is such a scene. It's in his last novel, *Red Sun Over Durres*. A member of the Albanian mafia who betrays his boss has exactly that punishment meted out to him. Then his stomach is fed to the pigs."

"Christ," Karen said before she could stop herself. "This writer guy is seriously sick."

"Not as sick as the person you're trying to catch," Lizzie observed.

"True," the chief inspector agreed. "Thanks for the help. I'll be in touch."

She closed her phone and looked down at the bag of books that she'd bought. She was beginning to think it was well past time she had a conversation with this Matt Stone.

The first thing she would be asking was, where was he between 2:29 and 3:17 p.m. today?

My guts were in turmoil when I got back from the pub. Not because of the lager, though there had been enough of that, but because of what the White Devil might have had waiting for me.

I noticed there were three missed calls on my mobile, no numbers given. He'd been after me, all right. Did that mean he, or an accomplice, might not have been on my tail? Before I could think that through, the landline rang.

"Yeah?" I said, making myself sound even more pissed than I was.

"Well, Matt," said the Devil. There was a faint hint of concern in his voice. "Did you have a good evening?"

Had the bastard or one of his sidekicks been watching me in the pub? Maybe not. I decided it was time I stood up to him. "What do you care?"

He gave a laugh that made me shudder. "Oh, I care, Matt. I care very much. Almost as much as you care for Lucy and Sara." He let the words sink in. "Now, turn on your computer."

He didn't seem to know what had happened to the laptop. That made me feel better.

"I presume you've got a backup," he added, dashing my hopes.

"You piece of shit," I said, keeping on the offensive. It wasn't just the lager. Seeing my mates had made me realize that I wasn't alone, though I'd never forgive myself if anything happened to them. "I know about that Harley Street doctor."

"Do you?" the Devil asked, his tone ironic. "Do you really? Tell me how he died then, smart-arse."

I couldn't answer that. All I was sure of was that he would have copied one of the killings in my books.

"Here's a clue," he said. "The character called Emzer in *Red Sun Over Durres.*"

I had to cast my mind back. It was the last book I'd published, but most authors I knew looked ahead to their next project and I was no different, even though I hadn't had a next project until very recently. It's surprisingly difficult to recall details of your previous novels. But in Emzer's case I had no problem. It was one of my most excessive deaths. Jesus.

"You…you stabbed him over and over and cut out his stomach while he was still alive? Then…then you cut off his head? Was that the 'gruesome manner' referred to on the television?"

"Precisely." The Devil sounded very pleased with himself. "And what message do you think I left inside him?"

My mind was all over the place. I couldn't think of a single line from Webster.

"Clue. What's the most popular sport in the world?"

"Football," I answered, without hesitation. Then it came to me. "Like the wild Irish, I'll never think thee dead Till I can play at football with thy head." I had a friend from Dublin at college. He wasn't impressed by those lines, claiming that it was the Lowland Scots who used to kick their enemies' heads around the town squares. "You're fucking sick!" I shouted down the phone. "You're out of your mind!"

There was a long silence, and then he started to speak in a low, menacing voice. "On the contrary, Matt Wells, also known as Stone. I'm in perfect mental and physical health, and I know exactly what I'm doing."

"Well, piss off and leave me alone. If you're so clever, why do you need a useless writer like me to tell your story?" As the words left my mouth, I had flashes of my daughter and my lover, and realized the danger I was putting them in.

The Devil laughed. "You're not useless, my friend. You're just out of synch with the market. That's why you should be grateful to me for giving you the story that will put you on the bestseller list."

"But you're framing me for the murders."

"Am I? You've got alibis, haven't you? Oh, no, I forgot. You were on your own all afternoon today, weren't you? What a pity."

He laughed again. "We're in this together, Matt. When will you realize that? We're two of a kind. You're driven by hatred and the desire for revenge just like I am. Soon I'll make that crystal clear to you. Now, get out your old computer and check your e-mails. I've sent you my notes about the latest victim. If you work all night, you'll be able to spend tomorrow with Lucy after all."

The line went dead. I hit 1471 but, as usual, the number was restricted. Shit. How did my tormentor know that I had a second laptop? I thought back to the phone conversation. How much had he given away? Very little. Perhaps he hadn't been spying on me when I'd stashed the money and diskettes in my jacket. Perhaps he didn't know about my meeting the lads. Suddenly I felt better. Then I remembered what he'd done to the doctor and felt the new vigor drain out of me. What chance did I have of beating him? He was always several steps ahead of me. And what did he mean about making how similar we were crystal clear to me? I had a bad feeling about that.

I went up to the loft and dug out the box with my old laptop in it. After I'd plugged it in and downloaded the updated mail system, I clicked on his message. It was as he'd said. The tabloids would have a field day if they found out these details. Then I thought about the motive. The Devil didn't specifically say why he'd chosen the victim, but there were hints that he was responsible for the death of a loved one. It was pretty thin. If everyone who had a loved one let down by the National Health Service took lethal revenge, there wouldn't be many doctors left alive.

I sat back and looked up at the cracks in the ceiling. He was taunting me, I knew it. He was giving me enough information to start tracking him down. There was the school, the church and now the doctor—the likelihood was that he'd once practiced in the East End. Of course, getting hold of the records wasn't straightforward for an ordinary citizen. Files like that were confidential, and I suspected that the onslaught of journalists after the first two killings would have made the local education authority and the Catholic Church very reluctant to part with information, just as the health authority would be now.

Then it struck me. The Devil himself had given me the means to find out about his background. He'd given me ten thousand pounds. That would be enough to buy anything I needed from bureaucrats on the take. I swallowed the laugh in case he was watching. The irony was enjoyable—until I realized that he had deliberately provided me with funds. He wanted me to find him, if only to prove how alike we were. I wasn't sure if I had the nerve to meet him head-on.

I spent the next four hours writing the chapter on the latest killing. I felt worryingly comfortable taking on the voice of the killer. I had to make some of it up, such as how the White Devil, Wayne Deakins, got in and out of the building unobserved. I presumed that Harley Street clinics had security cameras, so I resorted to a disguise. The first one that came to mind was the long black hair and droopy mustache that the Devil or his sidekick had used in the park with Lucy. After I'd edited the text, I replied to the Devil's message and sent the chapter as an attachment. Then, after transferring them to diskette, I deleted the messages. I knew an expert would find them on the hard drive, but at least I was buying myself some time. I put the diskette in a sealed plastic bag and hid it in a packet of cornflakes. Again, a thorough search would reveal it, but I didn't think the police would get on to me so quickly—as long as I did what the Devil asked.

I tried to get some sleep, but the birds had already started their predawn racket. Anyway, I had too much on my mind.

At last I was beginning to put together a plan to send the Devil back where he came from.

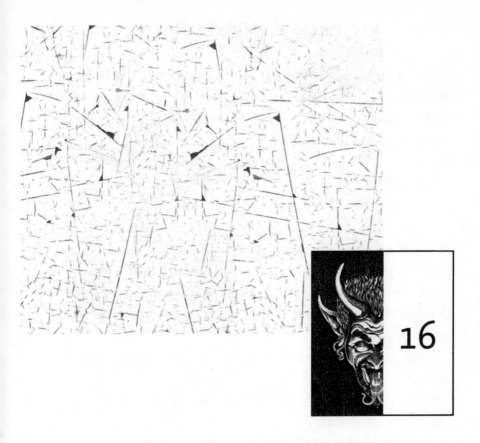

16

D.C.I. Karen Oaten stood in front of her team at the Yard, her eyes bulging.

"Right, you tossers!" she shouted. "Who was it? Who spoke to the journalist from this piece of shit?" She held up a garishly colored tabloid. "I've just had the commissioner himself on the phone." She leaned toward the detectives and watched with satisfaction as they moved back as one. "I don't like being told that I run a leaky ship, and I particularly don't like being told that my job is on the line." She tossed the newspaper away. "So here's how it is. If my job's on the line, then so are yours. Are you getting me? All your jobs." She moved her eyes around them slowly. "We're chasing what could be the worst serial killer in years. He's running rings round us. That's why we're all in here on a Sunday. This isn't the time to be protecting someone who's taking tabloid money." She turned to her office. "You know what you have to do. I want the squealer in my office by 6:00 p.m. today." She started to walk. "Inspector Turner, in here."

The gathering broke up.

"Yes, guv?" the Welshman said as he came in.

"Close the door," the chief inspector said, waiting till he'd done so. "Sorry, Taff. Nothing personal. I had to put the boot in. Someone's taking the piss big-time. How do you think the doctor's family feels, having the fact that his head was cut off and his stomach removed rammed down their...well, you know what I mean."

Turner nodded. "We'd have had to come out with it sooner or later."

Oaten's eyes flashed. "Yes, but not the morning after he was killed, for Christ's sake."

"I know who it was," the inspector said, glancing over his shoulder. The blinds were closed.

"Tell me, Taff."

"I'd rather wait to see if he...the person comes forward or if anyone else shops him," he said, keeping his eyes off her. "That way your grip on the team will be stronger."

Oaten frowned as she thought about it. "Yes, true enough. But if no one appears by six, you tell me, okay?"

"Okay."

"Right," she said, sitting down behind her desk. "I've got a meeting with the A.C. in half an hour. Help me go through everything we've got. I can't afford any more cock-ups."

Turner sat down opposite her and pulled out his notebook. "The initial knocking on doors didn't get us much—only one old woman who thought she'd seen a man in a suit and a hat walk into the victim's building around the time we have from the camera. As if we needed confirmation of that."

"And she didn't see if he arrived on foot or whatever?"

"Nope. We'll be checking again, but people will be away for the weekend and it may be we don't get anything more till they come back."

The chief inspector sighed. "Despite nationwide television and radio requests for witnesses to come forward."

Turner shrugged. "We've got the pair of them on film, anyway. Not that the hard copies we've printed off are much use, considering the men are obviously in disguise."

Oaten looked at the file on her desk. "The other guy's about the same size as the one in the suit. Maybe they're brothers."

"In arms?"

"Ha-ha. The question is, which one's the killer? Or do they both get involved?" She grimaced as she swallowed coffee from a plastic cup. "The overalls worn by the bearded one could belong to any workman in the city." Oaten turned a page. "The postmortem confirmed what the doc told us at the scene. And the SOCOs didn't come up with much."

"The two men must have had a change of clothes in their bags. They'd have been spattered with blood. The trail stops in the reception area. They obviously changed there."

Karen Oaten was shaking her head. "No fingerprints, no suggestive fibers or other physical evidence. Just like the other scenes." She glanced across at him. "They're certainly careful."

"And they're working to a plan," Turner added.

"We're taking the motive as revenge since the lines from the play push us in that direction. But we've got three long lists of names to collate and investigate—from the church records, the school rolls and, now, from Dr. Keane's patient register when he was in Bethnal Green."

"The team will start pulling in people today, including the ones we've already spoken to. They know that anyone whose alibis for the three killings don't check or who are suspicious in any other way are to be held for us to question." Turner's voice was downbeat. "These people are smart, guv. They aren't going to have left anything obvious."

Oaten nodded. "But we have to check it all, don't we?"

"What about the writer?" the inspector asked, inclining his head toward the piles of novels on his boss's desk. "He could be involved, couldn't he?"

"I doubt it. He spends his days at a computer making murders up, not committing them. But there are too many coincidences with the MOs to ignore him." She gave her subordinate a tight smile. "And we don't like coincidences in our business, do we?"

Turner was stroking his unshaven cheek. "No, we don't. What are you going to do about him, guv?"

Oaten started tapping on her keyboard. "The problem is, Matt Stone is a pseudonym. I've been on his Web site, but I can't get the agent and publisher on the contacts page to answer the phone to find out his real name. No one in that industry answers the phone out of office hours, apparently. So I'm going to send him an e-mail asking him to get in touch."

Turner raised an eyebrow. "That's a bit risky, isn't it? If he is involved, he'll scarper."

"Yes, he will," the chief inspector replied. "Then we'll know." She looked round at him. "The most likely result is that he doesn't answer. He'll probably be away for the weekend. People like him usually are." She finished typing. "There it goes, anyway."

John Turner stood up. "Guv?"

"Christ, Taff, you look like even more of a streak of misery than you usually do."

"Yeah, well, lack of sleep, you know. Look, as you pointed out to the team, the time between the murders is getting shorter. There's going to be another one soon."

Oaten nodded slowly. "I reckon there is."

"But we haven't got a clue who the victim will be."

"No."

Turner closed his notebook with a snap. "Don't you ever get frustrated by this job?"

Karen Oaten straightened her back. "Of course I do. That's why I swore to myself that I'm going to catch this animal—or animals, plural, as they now are." Her chin jutted forward. "You've got to stay hungry, Taff. Otherwise the beasts in the jungle out there will rip you to shreds."

The inspector headed out. Not for the first time, his boss's determination made him worry more about the effect it might have on her than on the people she was hunting.

I spent the day with Lucy. It wasn't a great success. I was tired and she was fretting about Happy—there had been shouting and crying from the neighbors' the previous night. The dog's name had been heard frequently. So much had happened that I'd almost forgotten the Devil's first demonstration of his power. I had a couple of flashes of the horrible scene on my daughter's bed and felt like a total scumbag for having got her involved. But what choice did I have? I couldn't have left Happy's carcass where it was.

Maybe taking Lucy to the South Bank didn't help. There was a showing of *Monsieur Hulot's Holiday* at the National Film

Theatre and I thought she'd like Jacques Tati's crazy behavior. She laughed a few times, but was generally subdued. Maybe she didn't like the fact that it was a black-and-white movie. Afterward we just stood on Waterloo Bridge and watched the water flow by.

I went straight to Sara's after I'd dropped Lucy off back home. She was just in, having been at the newspaper. We kissed and I instantly felt better.

"How are you doing?" I asked when we'd settled on her sofa with a bottle of cava.

"Not great," she said. "I thought I was going to be able to sleep late this morning, but I got sent off to a church in Potter's Bar. The priest declared he was gay during the week and there were all these demonstrators with placards saying Gay Clergy Get Lost and No Buggers in Church. Can you believe it?"

"Not as bad as your lot," I said. "The pope thinks homosexuality's abhorrent, doesn't he? How many millions in compensation have been paid out to the victims of abuse by priests?"

"Whoa, Matt," she said, her eyes bulging. They were bloodshot and there were dark rings around them. "I may be a lapsed Catholic, but I'm still a member of the church. You should respect that."

"Sorry," I said, my face reddening. "I was only messing around."

"Yes," she said, gulping wine. "That's your problem, isn't it? You spend your life making up stories and living in your little protected pocket in Herne Hill. Some of us have to deal with the real world." She emptied her glass.

I refilled it and gradually the atmosphere lightened.

"Look, I'm sorry," she said. "You'll have to cut me some slack. I've been having a hard time at work recently."

"The murders?" I said, putting my arm round her.

She nodded, but didn't reply. I managed to get her talking by telling her about Monsieur Hulot's idiocies—we'd seen *Traffic* a few months back. But her heart wasn't in it and, after a quick meal, she went off to bed. I kissed her good-night, but I knew there was no point in joining her. Her body language made it clear that making love was off the menu. Sometimes she was hard to get to, and I'd learned to leave her be on those occasions. She always came round eventually. At the beginning of our relationship, I had been needy. My father had just been killed and she'd helped me through that. Lately it had begun to seem like she was the vulnerable one. It was just as well I hadn't told her about the White Devil.

I spent the rest of the evening reading the Sunday papers and listening to the only band Sara had any time for—the Grateful Dead. I didn't find out anything about the murder of Dr. Keane that the Devil hadn't already told me. It seemed that my suspicions about there being a security camera at the scene had been right. Two men were being sought, one with the long hair and mustache that sounded very like the man Lucy had seen in the park, and another with a beard. At least I now had confirmation of my suspicion that the Devil had at least one accomplice. Eventually I turned off the stereo and went to the bedroom, but I didn't get undressed. The expression on Sara's sleeping face was tranquil. She'd obviously conquered her demons, so I decided not to disturb her.

I went out of the house quietly and drove back to my flat, reflecting on how far off the mark Sara was. The "protected pocket" she thought I lived in had been infiltrated by a savage killer, who was doing his best to incriminate me. If I wasn't careful, she'd be in as much danger from him as Lucy, my mother and even Caroline were.

That thought chilled me to the bones.

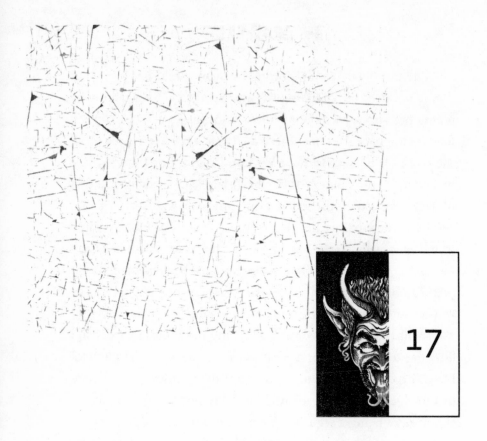

17

It was nearly three in the morning. The Hereward in Green-wich, lock-in long over, was chained up and deserted when the Orion came round the corner, Geronimo at the wheel. It took only a few seconds to deliver Terry Smail back to his local. The team took pursuit precautions after they left, but it was soon clear that no one was on their tail.

Sitting in the front passenger seat, Wolfe allowed himself to relax a fraction. They had obtained more than he'd expected from the fourth-division lowlife. It seemed that the man named Corky wasn't the main player—the one with the pointed teeth was in charge. Smail came out with that when Rommel had taken a screwdriver to his kneecaps. Apparently, one time the slimebag had tried to ingratiate himself with Jimmy Tanner and his new friends, only to be told in a seriously menacing way by the nameless man to leave them alone. It seemed hard to believe that the old soldier could have been taken by a pair of wide-boys, no matter how good they were, but the drink had really got to him—he'd hardly recognized Wolfe the last time they met, even though they'd served together in the SAS for more than five years.

Smail had kept the best till last. Wolfe knew that would be the way. That was why they had moved on to their captive's groin after damaging his knees beyond repair. Just before he passed out, Terry revealed where the bearded man called Corky lived. By squeezing him they'd find Count Dracula and they'd put a stake through his black heart—after they'd heard him tell them what had happened to Jimmy.

They were on their way to Forest Hill now.

I wasn't in the mood for any more of the White Devil's games when I got back from Sara's, so I didn't check my e-mails. If the bastard wanted me badly enough, he'd call me up when he saw that I'd returned. As it turned out, I was allowed a break. Although it took some time to come, I eventually dropped into a deep and surprisingly untroubled sleep.

Next morning I walked Lucy to school as usual. She was still subdued. Apparently the neighbors had been shouting at each other again. I tried to comfort her, but I was aware that I wasn't doing a very good job.

When I got back, I made coffee and ate a couple of pieces of toast. Then, reluctantly, I booted up my reserve laptop. First I checked the main newspaper sites. There was plenty of speculation about the doctor's murder, all the correspondents being positive that a serial killer one tabloid had dubbed "the New Ripper" had struck again, even though this time he hadn't been on his own. At least they'd got that much right. The rest of their reporting had about as much substance as the worst scenes in my novels.

I logged on to my e-mail program. To my surprise, there was no message from the Devil. To my dismay, there was one via my Web site from k.oaten@met.police.uk. That was all I needed. I leaned back in my chair and worked out my choices. I could get in touch with the sternly attractive female D.C.I. I'd seen on the TV—either telling her everything I knew or dissembling as best I could; or I could keep my head down. She obviously didn't know my real name, but it wouldn't be long till she discovered it. All she had to do was contact my ex-editor or agent. I could get out of London, but then I'd be leaving Lucy and the others at the mercy of the Devil. I could hardly gather together my daughter, Sara, my mother, Caroline and all of my friends and their families, and spirit them away. No, there was nothing else for it. I had to talk to Karen Oaten in order to get her off my case—but I couldn't tell her anything about my tormentor. Did I have it in me to lie to a senior police officer? I would soon find out.

I picked up the phone and dialed the mobile number given in her e-mail.

"Oaten," she answered crisply.

"Um, hello, my name's Matt Wells. You sent me a message."

"Matt Wells?" She sounded puzzled.

I was pleased that I'd put her on the back foot. "Also known as Matt Stone."

"Oh, yes. Thanks very much for getting in touch, Mr. Stone…Mr. Wells. I'd very much like to talk to you." Her tone had turned insistent.

"You mean now?"

"If that's all right. We can come to you."

"Hold on a minute." I looked around the flat. It was in a mess, but that wasn't what was bothering me. The Devil was probably watching and listening. If I volunteered to meet the police-woman elsewhere, he might think that I was spilling my guts about him. I couldn't risk that. "Sure, all right." I gave her the address. She said she'd be round in under half an hour and hung up.

I spent the time saving to diskette and then deleting the last messages to and from the Devil. I didn't imagine she'd be turning up with a warrant to search the place. If she did, I was stuffed—unless I got rid of the laptop, which would immediately raise her suspicions as I'd obviously read her e-mail. No, I'd have to brazen things out. I tried to think myself into the minds of my two fic-tional investigators. How would Sir Tertius and Zog have prepared for an interrogation? With total lack of concern in the former case and deep foreboding in the latter. Neither was much help to me.

When the bell rang, I made myself walk downstairs at a lei-surely pace. The woman I opened the door to was accompanied by a burly man in a crumpled blue suit. She was tall and well proportioned, with the look of an ex-athlete who'd kept in shape. Her blond hair was pulled back, emphasizing features that were more striking in real life than on TV.

"Mr. Wells?" she asked. "I suppose I should use your real name."

I nodded. "Hello." I gave her what I hoped wasn't too ex-pansive a smile. "And I suppose I should see some ID."

She opened her wallet to display her warrant card, her col-league doing the same.

"This is Detective Inspector Turner," Oaten said. "We won't take up much of your time."

I led them upstairs, my heart racing. These people clearly knew what they were about. I felt like a total amateur, despite my theoretical knowledge of police procedure.

"Not working?" the chief inspector asked, glancing at the dark screen of my laptop.

"Thinking," I said, tapping my head. "Unfortunately, writers never get even a minute off."

They both looked at me dubiously.

I ushered them to the sofa. "Coffee? Tea?"

"No, thanks," Oaten replied. "We're rather busy, as you'll no doubt appreciate."

"How do you mean?" I said, playing dumb.

"Mr. Wells, I imagine you're aware of the recent murders in and around London," the chief inspector said. Her colleague took out a notebook and pen.

"I've seen the news," I replied, raising my shoulders. I had to be careful here.

The Devil had told me plenty of details that hadn't been made public.

Oaten leaned forward, long fingers splayed on the black fabric of her trousers. "Mr. Wells, has it struck you that there are certain similarities with certain murders in your novels?"

I kept my eyes on her. "I had begun to wonder. Though the reports haven't gone into enough detail for me to take the links too seriously." I hoped I was playing the scene with sufficient cool.

The chief inspector pursed her lips. "What if I were to tell you that the murders of Father Norman Prendegast, Miss Evelyn Merton and Dr. Bernard Keane were almost exact replicas of those in three of your books?" She turned to her colleague and he read out the titles and page references.

I felt their eyes on me, cold and unwavering. My lower jaw

dropped in what I wanted to look like astonishment. "What?" I said weakly. "You can't be serious."

Oaten stood up and took a position in front of me, one leg in front of the other like a boxer preparing to fight. "We're serious, all right, Mr. Wells. I need to know where you were on the following dates and times." She raised her hand and the man, who had also got to his feet, read from his notebook.

I tried to look intimidated—which wasn't difficult—and opened my diary. "Um, on the first, I was here. With my girl-friend. Last Friday I was here, working. On Saturday afternoon I was here." My stomach was in turmoil. "Both times, on my own." I stared up at them.

"Did you know any of the victims?" the inspector asked. He had a Welsh accent.

"Of course not."

Karen Oaten was still standing over me. "Mr. Wells, you're familiar with a seventeenth-century play called *The White Devil*." It was a statement rather than a question.

"Yes, I am. I studied English literature at university."

"And you used the dramatist John Webster as a minor char-acter in your novel *The Devil Murder*." The chief inspector glanced at her colleague and they sat down again.

"You've read my books?" I said, unable to conce l the novelist's pleasure at finding readers even in a nightmare situa-tion like this one.

"As much of them as I had to," Oaten replied with a grimace. "This is strictly confidential. The killer left a quotation from *The White Devil* in each victim."

"*In* each victim?" I said, sounding horrified.

She nodded. "I'll spare you the details. Why do you think he—or she—would do such a thing?"

I remembered that the Devil may have been watching and listening. "I…I really don't know."

"Come on, you can do better than that," the Welshman said, glaring at me.

"Well, if I had to hazard a guess, I'd say it was something to do with revenge. That's one of the main features of Jacobean tragedy."

"So I understand," Oaten said. "I've been talking to Dr. Lizzie Everhead. You know her, I believe."

I stifled a groan. Lizzie Everhead was the academic who had laid into me in public. She'd accused me of everything from historical inaccuracy to callous brutality.

"Yes," I said, keeping my tone neutral. "I've bumped into her at crime-writing conferences."

"And," continued the chief inspector, "since you knew none of the victims, you would have no motive for revenging yourself on them."

"Certainly not," I said, laying on the outrage with a trowel.

She ignored that. "Mr. Wells, I presume your fans communicate with you via your Web site, as I did. Have any of them shown…unusual tendencies?"

"A lot of them." I tried to lighten the atmosphere by smiling. "Some want to be my best friend, or more than that. I always keep them at arm's length. Some want me to write more books in my first series and some want me to help them get published. But, as far as I can tell, none of them is homicidal." I imagined the Devil listening to the lie and laughing.

Karen Oaten looked at my laptop. "Would you mind if we checked your correspondence?"

I bit my lip, aware of how suspicious they were about to become. "I'm afraid I managed to pour coffee over my main computer. I've given it to a friend who's an expert. I hope he can salvage the files. That one's my old laptop. It's been in the attic for the past three years so there's nothing recent on it—apart from your e-mail." I was going to ask them if they had a warrant, but managed to stop myself in time. I needed to be as cooperative as possible, without antagonizing the Devil.

"Never mind," the chief inspector said, to my surprise. "We can always ask your Web site provider to give us access. I presume you have no objection."

I tried to keep calm. "No."

"We'll need your girlfriend's name and contact details," the Welshman said.

I gave them to him, feeling bad about dumping Sara in the shit. On the other hand, she'd probably be happy to get a potential story angle. "She's a journalist on the *Daily Independent*," I added. That didn't seem to impress them.

"You'll be doing yourself a favor if you don't tell her we're coming," Turner said, giving me a hard look.

Oaten got up again. "I think we've taken enough of your time for now, Mr. Wells. Thank you for being so—" She broke off as her mobile rang. She listened for over a minute, her expression getting more and more grave.

"Guv?" the inspector said when she'd finished.

Karen Oaten was paying no attention to him. Her eyes were locked on mine, her gaze unyielding. "Mr. Wells, do you know a man called Alexander Drys?"

A deep foreboding washed over me. "I don't know him in person," I said. "He's a literary critic." I didn't add that he'd given me a string of vicious reviews and that I'd have happily ripped his balls off if he'd ever had the nerve to show up at a literary function.

"I see," Oaten said, turning on her heel and heading for the door.

"What's happened?" I asked desperately.

"Watch the news," the chief inspector said over her shoulder. "We'll be in touch." That sounded more like a threat than anything else.

I heard the street door close behind them and then their car move away at speed. I had the distinct feeling that the Devil had upped the stakes once again.

"Just put the tray down and get out of here, girl," Alexander Drys had said to the maid.

He was in the drawing room of his house on Cheyne Walk in Chelsea, preparing to take morning coffee. He'd always hated interruptions, especially when he was preparing to write his monthly roundup of reviews for the magazine. If he'd been honest with himself—a rare event—he would have admitted that his temper had always been quick. He'd been spoiled from the earliest age. His father, a London Greek shipping magnate, was generous though rarely in the house, while his mother, a former model, was always present during the holidays to look after his every need. Along with the staff, of course.

Drys looked at the meager selection of fancy cakes on the tray. He would have to do something about the girl. She was Portuguese and hardly knew a word of English. He should never have listened to his butler, who was probably screwing her. The situation was particularly bad on Mondays, when all the other servants had the day off.

He got up from the Louis XVI chaise longue and moved his twenty-stone body to the window. The river was sparkling in the afternoon sunlight, its normal sludgy tone transformed. The plebs were driving across Albert Bridge in their hundreds, off to their worthless jobs or to the shops. At least there were no kids to be seen. Thank God he'd remained single—not that there had ever been any chance of him getting married, despite his father's insistence that the dynasty be continued. Alexander Drys had no interest in shipping and no desire to share the house with a wife, never mind mewling brats. Particularly not when he could ring up Madame Ostrovka any time he wanted and take advantage of her endless supply of blonds from the former Soviet Union. "Fuck 'em and chuck 'em," that was the motto he'd been regaling his cronies at the club with for decades.

No, the only thing that interested him was dissecting crime novels. He blamed Sir Arthur Conan Doyle. He'd come across *The Dancing Men* in an anthology at school back in the fifties, and had been instantly hooked. After he'd finished reading English at Cambridge (an undistinguished third, but no one remembered that), he used his connections and family wealth to obtain reviewing positions on numerous publications. True, he was less in evidence now than in his heyday during the eighties—Thatcherite contempt for frivolous writing having been very much to his taste—but a notice from him could still make or, more often, break a novelist's career. Not that he cared about that. If you wrote fiction, you deserved criticism. That was one reason why he'd never attempted it himself. Well, that and a lamentable lack of application. Anything longer than eight-hundred words was a real challenge.

Drys went back to the chaise longue and ate the five dainties quickly. After a cup of Earl Grey, he turned to the piles of books that he'd lined up on the Persian carpet. They were in four tiers. The one on the left consisted of books that he hadn't even opened—either he knew the author wasn't one who would interest him or he disliked the publisher. The next was made up of books of which he'd read ten pages and then given up. The third pile was of books he'd read through and decided to put the knife into—this was what his readers expected, indeed, desired. The fourth and smallest consisted of books that he would praise. Not excessively, and certainly not without caveats. The fact that the publishers of those novels had wined and dined him was neither here nor here.

Alexander Drys raised his head. He'd heard a noise at the rear of the house, a strange noise—something between a thud and a crack. What on earth was that stupid girl doing? He reached over to the art deco coffee table and rang the brass bell, a seventeenth-century piece from his ancestors' island of Psara. When she didn't appear, he hauled himself to his feet and went to the door.

Two men in gray boiler suits and protective helmets were standing on the landing outside.

"Wha—"

Drys fell back into the drawing room when he was struck hard in the face, landing with a crash. His vision was clouded, but he felt himself being dragged across the parquet. For a while he lost his sense of time. When he regained his senses, he found himself sitting with his legs apart, his arms stretched to opposite ends of the coffee table. He tried to move his hands. They had been tied to the table legs.

"What…what's going on?" he gasped, blinking.

The man who squatted down in front of him was of medium height. He was wearing a mask, one of those sold by novelty shops—but instead of President Bush or Tony Blair, this one had a strangely blank expression, the artificial skin very pale.

"Who…who are you?" Drys asked, glancing round at the other man. He was wearing an identical mask. "There's no money in the house."

The man in front of him laughed, a horrible sound. "Oh, we don't want money, Alex. You don't mind if I call you Alex, do you? Alexander makes me think of the ancient hero, and let's face it, you're not exactly from that mold."

Drys tried to control his wobbling chins. "How dare you?" he said in the voice he used with the servants. "I'm—"

"A vicious piece of shit who ruins people's lives," the masked man completed.

Drys watched as he opened a large leather bag and took out two things. The first was a blue cardboard folder, which he laid on the table. The second caused his armpits to be drenched with sweat. It was a large, stainless-steel chef's knife.

"Wha—"

The man raised his hand.

Drys noticed that it was sheathed in latex. That made his heart beat even faster.

"Now, Mr. Renowned Literary Critic, I'm going to read some of your deathless prose out to you." The man's voice was curiously accentless, as if he'd been to too many elocution lessons. He gave another mirthless laugh. "This is a game, you see. The rules are simple. I read you three pieces. Then you tell me who the author in question is. All the pieces concern the same person. If you get it right, we'll walk away. If you get it wrong, well—" he picked up the knife and angled it against the light "—you could do with losing some weight."

Drys tried to speak, but found he couldn't. This was madness. They couldn't be serious. This sort of thing didn't happen to people in his position. He felt a sudden need to empty his bladder. He managed to hold its contents in, but only just.

"Extract one," said the man in the mask, opening the folder. "'This novel is a farrago of unlikely plot twists, superficial char-

acters and a completely unbelievable social milieu. The protago-
nist is one of the most unsympathetic, if not downright obnox-
ious, investigators to have appeared in recent times.'"

His breathing shallow, Drys tried to think. Over the years he'd
written so many reviews, both stand-alones and shorter ones in
the roundups, that he couldn't possibly remember whose book
these words applied to. He panicked and tried to wrench his hands
out of their bonds. He saw the man in front of him nod to his
companion. A rope came round his neck and was tightened. He
felt his eyes spring wide open and his tongue swell in his mouth.

"Bad critic," the man with the file said, the brown eyes behind
the mask steady. "Don't try that again. Let him breathe, Watson."

The pressure loosened on Drys's throat. He panted air into
his lungs.

"Extract two. 'The crime genre is replete with superbly
realized private eyes and policemen. Who would willingly part
with their money to grind through a tediously recounted investigation carried out by this grubby and bungling detective?'"

Another surge of panic gripped Drys. He struggled to think
who that could have applied to. So many third-rate writers of
crime fiction had been published, some of them unaccountably
winning prizes and being feted by critics with less discrimina-
tion than he had. The words were vaguely familiar—he couldn't
have referred to too many heroes as "grubby"—but still he
couldn't place them. He stared beseechingly at his captor.

"Please, I—"

"Memory not up to scratch?" the masked man said mock-
ingly. "Never mind. You've got one more chance." He laid his
fingers on the knife. "Before it's time for me to start chopping."

This time Drys couldn't control himself. He sat with his face
burning as warm liquid soaked his trousers.

"Bad, bad critic," scolded his tormentor, shaking his head. "That's an expensive piece of furniture, isn't it?" He turned to the next page and started to read aloud. "'This book is enough to make any right-thinking reader despair. The supposed hero is a dissolute rake who extracts sexual favors from his female clients in lieu of payment. The violence is crude and unjustified, and the historical references defective. Why do people write books like this?'"

Drys sat back in the rapidly cooling puddle he had made and tried to restrain a smile. He had remembered; he knew who the writer was. Thank God, he would soon be seeing the last of these imbeciles. Then a frightening thought struck him. What if the man behind the mask was the author himself? He kept his expression as composed as he could.

"Well, Mr. Esteemed Literary Arbiter?" asked the man, leaning forward.

"Matt Stone," Drys said, his tone patronizing. "Now, will you kindly get out of my house?"

"Matt Stone," mused the man in front of him, picking up the knife. "Very good, Mr. Drys." He gave a disturbing laugh. "But not good enough. You see, Matt Stone is a pen name. I need the author's real name. Sorry, didn't I make that clear?"

Alexander Drys tried to scream, but a rag was stuffed into his mouth before any sound came out. He had no idea what Matt Stone's real name was. He'd never concerned himself with the mainly talentless fools whose books he read. His eyes opened wide as he saw the man with the knife bend over his right hand. The other man was pulling hard on the rope round Drys's neck, keeping his body upright. He felt unjustly done by. Was he really going to suffer for such an insignificant writer? There were others whose careers he had completely ruined, even one who had committed suicide.

"Matt *Wells* is his name," the man said, looking at him with empty eyes. "Think about how hurtful your words were while I'm cutting."

The critic felt the blade slice into his skin and prayed for mercy to the God he'd ignored all his life.

It didn't come.

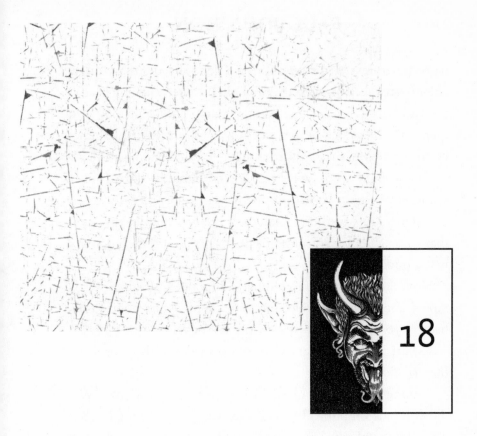

18

I didn't have to wait for the evening news to find out what had happened to Alexander Drys. My mobile rang a quarter of an hour before I left to pick up Lucy.

"Matt."

"What have you done, you bastard?" I yelled.

The Devil paused, "A little more caution, my friend." His voice still friendly. "I know the police have been to see you. How do you know they haven't got you under surveillance?"

I went to the front window. I couldn't see anything out of the ordinary. "Look, you murdering maniac," I said, lowering my voice. "Tell me what you did to Drys."

"All right. First I cut off his hands—the ones that typed those nasty, unfair reviews of your books. Then I sliced out his tongue and inserted it in his rectum. After all, he'd been licking his rich friends' arses for years. He was wriggling and squirming a lot then, so his head was beaten to a pulp with a ball-peen hammer. No more vicious thoughts from that perverted brain, eh, Matt?"

I'd collapsed onto the sofa as he recounted the horrors like a schoolboy proudly reciting a poem.

"Matt? Are you there? Don't tell me you're unhappy about that shitbag's less-than-pleasant death. I know how much you hated him."

How did he know? How long had he been bugging me? I'd ranted about Drys to Sara, but not recently. The poor bastard hadn't even bothered to review my last novel.

"Matt? At least congratulate me on ridding the world of a literary bloodsucker."

"You're out of your mind," I finally managed to say. "Why did you pick on him? He couldn't have done anything to you." Then I remembered what he'd said—hands, tongue, hammer to skull—and my stomach constricted even tighter. "Christ, that was what happened to one of the villains in the first Sir Tertius novel."

"*The Italian Tragedy,* that's right." The Devil gave an easy laugh. "Hey, Matt, we're friends, aren't we? I've got to the end of my own death list, so now I've started on yours."

My blood ran cold. "What do you mean?"

"Don't play dumb. And don't worry. You've got the perfect alibi. The police were round at your place when Drys got his." He sniggered. "Of course, you could have hired someone to kill him." He gave an even nastier laugh. "You could have hired me." The line went dead.

I threw the phone down in despair. What did he mean by *my*

death list? Jesus, was he going to wipe out everyone I'd ever expressed a negative feeling about? If that was the case, there were going to be a lot of dead people in the publishing business—editors, agents, publicity girls, marketing people, fellow novelists whose success I resented, booksellers who hadn't chosen my books for their three-for-two promotions...

The Devil couldn't be serious.

D.C.I. Karen Oaten and D.I. John Turner were standing in Alexander Drys's drawing room. They were kitted out in white coveralls and bootees.

"Hell's teeth," the inspector said, looking away from the abomination on the chaise longue.

"Steady, Taff," said his superior, bending over the naked dead man's blood-spattered face. She glanced at the pathologist. "You say his tongue's been removed. Has anything been inserted into the mouth?"

Redrose shook his head. "I expected that question. No, there's no plastic bag with a line of poetry or whatever in it."

"Nowhere about his person?"

"Nowhere. The only thing that's been inserted is his tongue into his—"

"Yes, you mentioned that." Oaten glanced at the white-faced Turner. "Any idea why?"

"I just collect the severed body parts," the pathologist said, inclining his head toward the table where the critic's severed hands lay in clear plastic bags. They were like grotesque ornaments, the palms downward and the fingers tensed like a piano player's. "It's for you people to work out what goes on in the monster's mind."

"Thanks a lot," the chief inspector said ironically.

Redrose looked up at her. "All right, if you want my provisional opinion, it's the same killer as in the previous three murders. The hands were removed with a modicum of expertise, but nothing to suggest that the perpetrator had medical or even butcher's training. The tongue was pulled outward with what the marks on top and bottom suggest was a pair of pliers and cut off with a very sharp, nonserrated blade." He turned to the smashed remains of the head. "As for the skull, it was shattered with a large number of blows from a relatively compact, rounded instrument—my guess is one of those hammers, what are they called?"

"Ball-peen," Turner said, his eyes still averted.

"That's the ticket," the pathologist said approvingly. "Into DIY are we, Inspector? All right, here's my psychological analysis, for what it's worth. I'd say the hands being removed has an obvious link with the man's job—he was a literary critic who wrote for a living, wasn't he? The tongue in the rectal passage is a bit more obscure. Was he a sexual deviant?"

Oaten shrugged. "We haven't got that far yet. The blows to the head that killed him interest me. The previous killings were carried out with what you described in your reports as 'controlled brutality.' So was this one, apart from the head. Why was it smashed up the way it was?"

"Maybe he was struggling with his assailant," Turner suggested.

"No, the victim was restrained," said the pathologist, pointing to rope burns on the stumps of the arms.

"So it was in cold blood," the chief inspector said. She moved over to the lead SOCO. "Anything interesting?"

"Two people, like at the doctor's. Looks like they changed their clothes on the landing after the murder. There are no traces, at least not so far, on the staircase or around the rear window where they gained access by cutting out a pane."

"No sign of a plastic bag with a message?"

The man raised his shoulders and looked around the room. "Not yet. Then again, there are a lot of books in here." The shelves that covered three of the walls rose to the ceiling and were all full.

Karen Oaten swung her gaze across the thousands of volumes. The SOCO team leader was smart. Even though there was no message in the body, it was possible, given the victim's profession, that one had been left in a book. "Get one of your lot to run an eye over the books in here," she said to the technician. "I'm particularly interested in anything by John Webster or Matt Stone."

The SOCO nodded.

Oaten's mobile rang. Her heart sank when she heard the commissioner's less-than-dulcet tones. She brought him up to speed with the investigation.

"D.C.I. Oaten, I've been talking to the A.C.," he said. "We feel you're underresourced. D.C.I. Hardy's team will be joining yours. You'll retain operational command, but I don't want any pissing about. Share what you know and cooperate with each other. This lunatic is making us look like incompetents. If there are more murders, it'll be very hard to keep you in place." The connection was cut.

The chief inspector stood staring at her phone. She had mixed feelings. Hardy's people helping out would be useful, but she didn't want that nicotine-stained tosser breathing down her neck. As for the threat of being kicked off the case, that only made her more determined to find the killers. Anyone who thought she was going to allow her career to be stalled by a pair of bloodthirsty savages—no doubt male—would find out how wrong they were. She was a woman in the Met. What she'd gone through to get where she was made catching these lunatics look like a pissing contest—and she'd won the last of those she'd undertaken by using a hand-operated pump to hit the ceiling during her leaving party from her previous job. There was something nagging her about her time in East London. Something—

"Guv?" John Turner was standing at the far end of the room. "The SOCOs are all snowed under. I'll have a look for that wanker Wells's, I mean, Stone's, books myself."

Oaten went over. "What have you got against him?" She'd found the novelist rather alluring, not that she'd let it show.

"I told you in the car," he said, staring up at the rows of books. "There's something wrong about him. He's hiding things."

The chief inspector laughed. "Everyone hides things from us, Taff. We're coppers, remember?"

Turner wasn't listening. "They're in alphabetical order," he said triumphantly. "This shouldn't take long." He went to the left-hand wall by the window. "Over here," he said, beckoning to the photographer. "One of the books is sticking out."

Oaten joined him and waited for the photos to be taken, blinking as the flash discharged. "*The Italian Tragedy.* That was his first book, as I remember." She removed the hardback volume carefully and opened it. There was a press release inside proclaiming "the debut of an immense new talent in crimewriting." She ran the pages past her latex-covered thumb. A flicker of red caught her eye. She went back to the page, her heart suddenly racing.

"Spot on, Taff," she said in a low voice. "There's a bit underlined in red. 'Of all deaths, the violent death is best,'" she read. Then she took in the preceding passage. "Our friend Wells has his investigator Sir Tertius talking to an actor, who quotes that line from a Webster play." She looked up at her subordinate. "Guess which one. *The White Devil.*"

Turner had his mobile phone in his hand. "I'll have him picked up."

Oaten shook her head. "You're forgetting something." She turned to the pathologist. "What were your parameters for the time of death again, Doctor?"

"Between 10:00 and 12:00, I'd hazard."

The chief inspector turned back to the Welshman. "Remember where we were between half ten and half eleven?"

"Shit," he said, putting his phone back in his pocket. "He could have an accomplice."

"You mean two." Oaten nodded. "Yes, he could. But hauling him in and questioning him is hardly likely to get him to own up—not if he's the kind of calculating bastard behind murders like this one and the others."

"But we *can* keep an eye on him," Turner said.

"Oh, yes," she replied. "We can certainly do that. In fact, some of Hardy's people can take that job off our hands. The teams are amalgamating." She saw the dismay on his face. "Don't worry, I'm still in charge. For the time being, at least." She moved away. "Come on," she said over her shoulder. "Our lot here know what they're doing. We've got the people who knew the previous victims to check out."

"We'll soon have a list of people who knew this guy, too."

Oaten nodded. "The problem is, I have a feeling that Alexander Drys doesn't have anything to do with the others."

Turner gave her a long-suffering look. "Which leaves us where?"

"Stuffed, if we don't get a shift on."

They stripped off their coveralls in the hall. Before they left, a female detective sergeant told them that the Portuguese maid had given a statement via an interpreter. She hadn't seen who'd grabbed her from behind and tied her up in the cloakroom. If she hadn't happened to keep a penknife in her pocket on her mother's strict instructions—you could never trust British men—she'd probably still have been in there and the alarm wouldn't have been raised. As it was, it had taken her more than an hour to saw through the ropes with the blunt blade.

Oaten and Turner left the house with their eyes down. Four murders and still they hadn't had a single decent break. They'd been doing everything by the book. Surely something had to give soon.

I went round to Sara's after I'd finished supervising Lucy. Caroline gave me the usual cold stare when I said goodbye. Part of me wanted to say that it would be better for our daughter if we could be friends, but another, more damaged part told me that would have been a complete waste of time. Caroline had no time for me, especially now that I wasn't earning from my writing. She'd always taken a dim view of people who didn't contribute to the wealth of nations. If she'd known the danger I'd put Lucy and her in, she'd have taken the carving knife to me.

Sara wasn't there when I got to her flat. I called her on her mobile and she said she was on the train. She sounded lively. When she came in, there was a strange smile on her lips. I went to greet her, putting my arm round her shoulders and trying to kiss her. She moved her face and I hit cheek.

"What happened, babe?" I asked, going to the fridge to get a bottle of wine. "Did you get promoted or something?"

She didn't reply, heading into the bedroom to change out of her work clothes.

She returned a few minutes later in tracksuit bottoms and a red T-shirt with Che Guevara's head on it.

"No, Matt," she said, giving me a curious look. "Nothing like that."

"Want to tell me about it?" I asked, sitting down on the sofa beside her and handing her a glass.

"It's no big deal. The excitements of a national newspaper. Not." She ran her hand across her hair and laughed. "I'm seriously considering a change of career."

I was surprised by that. Ever since I'd known her—it was about a year since we'd literally bumped into each other at a publisher's party, her glass of red drenching my shirt—Sara had seemed as committed to her job as anyone I'd known. She lived for news stories, happily inhaling the high-octane fuel that drove newspapers and thriving on it. Which reminded me.

"You're not on the Drys murder, are you?"

The glass stopped on its way to her lips. I saw her eyelashes quiver for a couple of moments. "The Drys murder?" she repeated. "Oh, the literary critic. No, Jeremy's doing that." She turned to me, her expression suddenly serious. "Did you know him?"

"Not in person. Don't you remember? I moaned about him once or twice. As an example of the kind of journalist who hides away from the real world—he never went to any crime-fiction events—and writes hurtful things about people at long range."

Sara looked at me thoughtfully. "Oh, yes, now I remember. You said he gave you some stinking reviews."

"Me and plenty of other crime novelists."

"Just as well," she said, emptying her glass. "At least you won't be the police's number-one suspect."

"No," I said. Then I remembered that I'd given the detectives her contact numbers. For some reason I held back from asking her if they'd been in touch. I reckoned she'd tell me if they had and I didn't want to ruin her evening if they hadn't yet.

As it turned out, the evening was a nonevent, anyway. Sara said her stomach was giving her grief and retired to bed early. It wasn't the first time she'd been distant with me recently. No doubt I hadn't been paying her enough attention since the Devil appeared.

After watching the news, which told me less than I already knew about Drys's murder, I checked on her. She was asleep, but she clearly wasn't at rest. Her lips were twitching and her legs moving. Maybe journalist's burnout was getting to her earlier than it did with most hacks. I left quietly and drove home.

It was while I was between Clapham and Herne Hill that I came to the decision. To hell with the White Devil and all his works. I wasn't going to take any more of his shit. It was time I stood up to him like a man, not like a crime writer.

I spent the next two hours thinking, refining the plan I'd come up with the previous night and covering as many bases as I could. Then I fell into a sleep haunted by the ghosts of mutilated victims and the screams of abused children. They gradually faded and I found myself dreaming about revenge. There was a lot of blood.

When I woke the next morning, I knew I'd made the right choice. I would fight the Devil with his own weapons, and my revenge would be greater than his. It was the only way.

Otherwise he would take me down to the underworld with him.

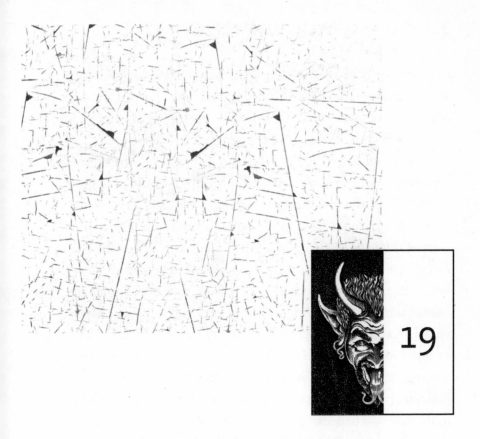

19

The White Devil stood in front of the bank of screens in his penthouse by the Thames. The water was leaden-gray with a hint of fecal brown, seagulls scavenging over it like white-feathered demons. It was a river of the underworld, the dark walled buildings on the other side the houses of the living dead; a scene Hieronymus Bosch could have conjured up, a triumph of death as good as Pieter Bruegel's. He let out a sigh. Life couldn't get any better.

The Devil looked down at the leather-bound volume that lay on the Georgian table he'd bought for the dining area. Earlier, he'd pasted in the pages Matt had written. But he was looking at the page at the front. *The Death List* was the book's title and a register of names prefaced the narrative, in two columns. On the left were people's names, among them Billy Dunn, Richard Brady, Father Patrick O'Connell, Evelyn Merton, Gilbert Merton, Bernard Keane, Alexander Drys—these, the ones he'd already killed, had a red cross against them. There were others as yet untouched by the human blood he'd used as ink—Christian Fels, Jeanie Young-Burke, Lucy Emilia Wells, Caroline Zerb, Fran Wells, and more. Including, of course, Matt Wells.

As the city came slowly to life that morning, the Devil considered the man he had picked out to work for him. He could easily have written his own story; he didn't need the fool Matt Wells. But he did need a fall guy. A crime writer—a drone who made his living from trying and failing to imagine other people's pain—was the perfect choice. Crime novelists. What did they know? How many of them had committed a crime worse than scoring a small amount of dope or speeding? How many of them had felt another human being's life drain away, their eyes flutter as the last darkness came down, their limbs shake in the dance of death? Hypocrites, frauds, White Devils. They were worse than he was. At least he had reasons for what he was doing.

The Devil went back to the bank of screens on the rear wall. There had been an unusually determined look on Matt's face when he came back from his girlfriend's earlier on. That was interesting. Could he be stiffening the sinew, summoning up the blood? Could he be going to offer a challenge? That would be a bonus. Not that it would do the writer any good. He would soon be screaming for mercy.

As the literary critic had done. Drys had been a pitiful victim, begging for sympathy while he still had his tongue, offering money, works of art, everything he had. Maybe that was why the Devil's partner hadn't been able to hold back with the hammer. For God's sake, man, he'd thought as he watched the blows. At least die with some dignity. Underlining the Webster quotation in Matt Wells's first novel had been a nice touch. He wondered if the police had found it yet.

His partner had performed well during the head-smashing— this time there had been no choking back the vomit. The Devil had hoped that the experience of participating in the doctor's death would bring familiarity, and he'd been right.

He ran his eye down the list. If he was going to slaughter them all, he needed to stick to the plan he'd worked out in such detail and memorized. He didn't need a print version, but he'd sent one as a hidden attachment to one of the e-mails received by Matt Wells from the various Internet cafés he used—when the police found that, the crime writer would have nowhere to hide. Then he'd destroyed all his hard copies and diskettes. He no longer needed them.

He sat back and looked at the book's contents page again. The column on the right listed his nameless victims, those he'd learned his trade on—the homeless, the junkies and the whores. He'd referred to them by where he found them— Charing Cross Road, Embankment, Beak Street... Nine of them. They had been his basic training after his father and the bully. No one had even noticed that they'd gone—into the canals and building sites, the car scrapyards and the foundations of the new roads that continuously appeared around London. Here today, gone to hell tomorrow, and nobody cared. The city was a graveyard, a realm of the dead, while people pre- tended they didn't know. That was changing. There was hysteria in the air now, after the four murders he'd let them find out about.

The White Devil pointed the TV handset and selected one of the twenty-four-hour news channels. He didn't hear anything further about the Drys murder. Then an item came on that made him flinch for the first time since he was a kid.

"…outside the Hereward public house in Greenwich, where the horrific discovery was made. A passerby returning from a late-night party saw stray dogs trying to get into three packing cases that had been left at the pub's door. He saw the severed limbs and head, as well as the torso, of a male. Even more shocking was the fact that he knew the man. The Metropolitan Police has not confirmed the victim's identity yet, but we understand that next of kin have been informed and that his name is Terence Smail, aged thirty, a regular of the Hereward. No witnesses have come forward and detectives suspect there may be a gangland connection…"

The White Devil got hold of himself, using the breathing techniques that Jimmy Tanner had taught him. This couldn't be a coincidence. Terence Smail. Terry—he remembered the pathetic specimen who'd hung around the pub. Had he heard anything of what had passed between the Devil, Corky and Tanner? Could he have passed that on to the people who'd killed him? Obviously someone had made an example of him, but who was the example for? It could be, as the reporter said, that he'd fallen foul of one of the numerous criminal operations that used the pub. But what if Jimmy Tanner had mentioned that he was instructing someone to an ex-comrade in the SAS? What if someone had found out Jimmy was missing and was looking for him? Those guys were lethal; they didn't take prisoners— even the wasted sot Jimmy had been dangerous enough. It could be that he and Corky were in the deepest shit.

The Devil realized he would have to speed up the plan and get away sooner than he'd expected. He glanced at the names. The next victim caught his eye, a person whose life was measured in hours and minutes. Looking up, he caught sight of himself in the ornate Victorian mirror he'd hung beyond the table and laughed.

"'If the devil Did ever take good shape,'" he declaimed, "'Behold his picture.'"

John Webster's play, act 3, scene 2. The long-dead Jacobean was an outstanding dramatist. What would he have made of the way his lines were being used in modern London? Would he have approved of the appropriate punishment of offences? Of course he would.

The White Devil walked to his dressing room to prepare for his next entry.

I got up early the next morning and, assuming that the Devil was watching, made a pretense of being half asleep, stumbling about like a pisshead. I deliberately didn't boot up my laptop. No doubt there was another load of notes from him to write up. They could wait. I had more pressing things to do. I dug out my lamentably unwashed running kit and set off for Brockwell Park in the early dawn light. My knee gave me gip, but I could bear it. At last I had a purpose in life.

I got to the southern end of the park, my lungs heaving, and spotted the phone box I remembered from walks with Lucy in her buggy. I hoped it was still in working order. Opening the door, I was blasted by the reek of stale urine. I looked around and saw no one except a couple of other middle-aged men bringing forward their heart attacks by jogging far too fast. I had to take the chance that the Devil and his people weren't on my tail. Or D.C.I. Oaten's mob.

Taking out the phone card I always kept in my wallet for emergencies, I made the first of my planned calls.

"Hello?" My mother sounded wide-awake but cautious.

"It's me," I said, my mouth close to the receiver. "I haven't got much time. I need you to do something that's going to surprise you. I want you to go to Heathrow without delay. Book yourself on the first available flight to any destination in Europe. Take your mobile phone with you. Don't answer it the first time it rings. If it rings four times and then stops, it'll be me. Pick it up the next time it rings, okay? And don't tell me where you are."

"What on earth—"

"Don't interrupt, Fran," I said firmly. "You're in great danger. I can't tell you about it. But you'll be fine if you do what I tell you. You're always on about how you need a holiday. Well, this is your chance. I'll be in touch. Promise me you'll do this. For me." I was ladling on the loving-son treatment, not that it was difficult. I was terrified that the Devil would get his hands on her.

"Well, all right, Matt," she said doubtfully. "I'll get going as soon as I can."

"Good. I'll be in touch. Have a fine time." I terminated the call. My mother was strong-willed, but she knew when to listen to other people. She had plenty of money and traveled abroad on her own often enough, always with British Airways. One down.

I rang the next number on my list.

Dave Cummings answered his mobile on the second ring. I could hear kids' voices in the background.

"It's Matt. Listen, I'm in a lot of trouble and I need your help."

"Thought you might be, lad," he said with typical Yorkshire bluntness. "What do you want me to do with the money?"

"Nothing," I replied. I'd decided to ignore the Devil's cash.

If I used even a small amount of it, I'd be complicit with him. "Keep it hidden, and the diskettes somewhere else. Look, I need several favors. First of all, can you pick Lucy up after school?"

"No problem."

"Then take her back to your place."

"Ditto."

"Then take her and all of your lot off to your cottage in the country till you hear from me."

"What? The wife, as well?"

"The wife, the dog, everyone."

There was a pause. "What's this about, Matt?"

"Lucy's in danger. So's anyone who knows me. I need a bit of time to sort this out, and I need to know Lucy and all of you are safe."

"Lowlife?"

"Very low."

"I want to help."

I'd known he would offer support without hesitation. "Look, Psycho, do this today. I'll need more help later on." I went through the same mobile contact procedure as with my mother. "All right?"

"Aye, all right. Keep cool, Matt. Remember, you've got friends."

"Thanks, Dave." I rang off. I knew I could rely on him, but not even he could beat the Devil—at least, not on his own.

Next on the list was Roger van Zandt. He took longer to answer his phone. Being divorced, childless and self-employed, he had no reason to get up early—apart from his computers and the dioramas of Second World War battles that he filled his house with.

"Rog? It's Matt."

"What the hell do you—"

"It's an emergency."

"It'd better be, Wellsy." He sounded like he wanted to take my head off. No doubt he'd downed a pint too many last night. "If it's about your laptop, I'm still working on it. You really messed—"

"Forget the laptop, Dodger. What do you know about surveillance systems? Or rather, about how to disable them?"

"What? Are you sober?"

"Yes!" I shouted. "Listen to me. I'm in danger and so is everyone who knows me. That includes you. Get out of your flat and go into the West End. Find a security-system supplier and pick his brains about how to locate and disable pinhole cameras, listening devices, whatever. Okay? Have you got money?"

"I've got plenty of credit on my cards."

"Good. Get whatever you need and I'll pay you back. Whatever you do, don't go back home. I'll contact you." I set up the four-ring procedure again. "Look, Rog, I'm really sorry—"

"Forget it, Matt. This is why we're mates, isn't it? Ooh, I've just come over all excited."

"Calm down," I said, touched by his eagerness, but also concerned by it. "I'm not joking. You really are in danger. I'll tell you about it later, okay?"

I rang off. So far, so good. Next number.

"Andy?"

"Hey, man." Andrew Jackson's New Jersey tones blasted out of the earpiece. "Bit early for a social call, isn't it?" He moved his mouth away from the receiver. "It's all right, doll. I won't be a minute."

I might have known. He was a serial shagger. "I'm afraid you will be a minute, Slash," I said. "This is serious." I made it clear to him how much shit we were in.

"You've been careless, haven't you, Wellsy? Never mind. I'll sort things out for you."

I'd been hoping he'd say that. If ever a man answered the description of "muscle for hire" it was Andy. Apart from sex, there had been nothing he enjoyed more than mowing down opposition players on both sides of the Atlantic—first as a strongside linebacker back home and then as a lethal prop for the Bisons.

"Can you get off work?"

"Screw work. The restaurant's been half empty for weeks. Tell me what you need."

I gave him the name and address I wanted him to keep an eye on, and then set up the same mobile contact as the others. Before I hung up, I heard him telling his bird to hop it. The man was a star.

That left three people to consider. One was my ex-wife. I'd thought about Caroline for some time. If I gave her any hint of what I was up against, she'd go straight to the police. I'd already decided that was a waste of time. They couldn't protect my friends and family, at least not until they were sure I wasn't involved in the murders. It wasn't fair that I was going to take Lucy from her, but I'd try to square it with her later.

The second and much more important person was Sara. I'd thought about warning her, but I was worried that her journalist's nose for a good story would lead her into danger. I knew she usually worked with a photographer who was a judo black belt. I didn't feel good about it, but I'd have to hope that he would keep the Devil at bay until I came up with a better plan.

That left one person—me. I knew I was probably under permanent surveillance by both the Devil and the police. That meant I had a very limited range of options. I'd made a list of people the lunatic was most likely to attack on my behalf. Two stood out. Andy Jackson was covering one of them. I had to do what I could for the other.

I made one more phone call and, with difficulty, set up a meeting. Then I ran back home, making myself appear even more knackered than I was. I showered and dressed, and went round to the former family home. That was a nightmare. I had to dissemble to Caroline that everything was normal, and then I had to walk Lucy down to school, wondering all the time if I would ever see her again. It wasn't that I didn't trust Dave. He'd sacrifice himself for my daughter, I was sure of that. It was myself I was worried about. What chance did I stand taking on the White Devil?

"Bye, Daddy," Lucy said.

"Bye, sweetest," I said, trying to keep my voice steady. "Remember, I've got a meeting this afternoon. Dave will take you home with Tom."

"I remember," she said solemnly. Then she turned and walked into her classroom.

I felt something break inside me, but it was too late to do anything about it. I had made my choices, thrown my dice, crossed my Rubicon.

The question was, would I be coming back?

John Turner walked into his superior's office. "'Morning, guv." He looked over his shoulder. "Is it right what I'm hearing? You packed Morry Simmons off to Traffic?"

The chief inspector nodded. "What did you think I was going to do? Keep him on the team after he owned up to selling the story to the press?"

"Yes, but we're seriously undermanned...I mean, short-staffed..."

Oaten didn't notice the gender correction. "We'll survive," she said.

"Hope so," the Welshman muttered.

"Let's get cracking," Oaten said from behind a heap of files. "We have a list of seventy-three boys who attended Father Prendegast/O'Connell's church, were taught by Miss Merton and were registered with Doctor Keane."

"That's right, guv," John Turner said from the other side of her desk. He looked at his notebook. "Five are dead. Sixty-two have alibis that check for at least two of the murders."

"And six we can't find." The chief inspector ran a hand across her hair. "In addition to that, we have dozens of people who knew Alexander Drys, most of them members of what they like to call high society. Hardy's people are checking them, but, frankly, I don't think there's a direct link to the previous victims."

"Despite the fact that the killer appears to be the same person?" Turner shook his head. "Cold-hearted bastard, using the victim's blood to underline that bit in Wells's book."

Oaten leaned back in her chair and stared up at the ceiling. "Yes, there's Matt Wells, too. Anything interesting on him?"

"We caught up with his girlfriend this morning. She confirmed his alibi for the priest's murder. For what that's worth."

The chief inspector's eyes met his. "Meaning?"

"She's a typical journalist. She seemed to be more interested in the murders than her man."

"Do you think he told her to expect us?"

"She said not. Again, for what that's worth."

"The modus squares with Wells's book, too," Karen Oaten said.

"Yes, it does." There was excitement in the Welshman's voice. Oaten looked unconvinced. "There's more?" she asked.

Turner nodded and scowled. "Hardy's guys who're on surveillance say that Wells had an early-morning run today. He went round Brockwell Park while they stopped for breakfast. Tossers. Then he walked his daughter to school and went back to his place. They say he's still there."

Karen Oaten examined the notes she'd made. "Let's leave Wells out of this for the time being. We can't link him to the first three murders. Obviously he had motive for the Drys killing—you saw the reviews the victim wrote of his books— but he has the perfect alibi. From us. We need to concentrate on the six missing men from the list. Run through the names again, will you, Taff?"

"John Marriott, Peter Jones, Leslie Dunn, Adam O'Riley, Luke Towne and Nicholas Cork."

"What have we got on them?"

"Marriott was a seaman, last seen in 1996. His family haven't heard from him since, but they reckon he's shacked up with a woman in Brazil. He jumped ship there."

"Forget him for the time being."

"Jones and Towne both had problems with alcohol. They were inside for burglary, separate incidents, in the nineties. Their families think they'll be on the streets. If they're alive."

"I can't see alkies being capable of these murders, can you?"

The Welshman shrugged. "Not really. That leaves Dunn, O'Riley and Cork. O'Riley's got form for Grievous Bodily Harm. But he has a drug problem. As well as being as thick as two short planks, according to his school report."

"Not too likely it's him, then."

"So we're down to Dunn and Cork. They're the most interesting ones, too. Cork seems to have been the violent type. His sister says he used to beat up his parents as soon as he got big enough. They haven't heard from him for years and they're happy about that. According to the school reports, Dunn was a pain in the arse. He was also bullied. His father was killed in an accident on a building site when the boy was twelve. His mother died of cancer when he was seventeen. Later, he worked in a call center. The personnel manager there thinks he went to work in a bank afterward, but doesn't remember which one. We're still checking that." Turner stared across at his superior. "What is it, guv?"

Oaten raised a hand, her face creased in thought. "Hackney," she said.

"What about it?"

"Remember that case we worked before we transferred here? The guy whose belly was ripped open, the wife who was a lawyer and the baby? We never found the killer."

John Turner's jaw dropped. "Christ. He was a bank manager, wasn't he? Do you think there's a link?"

She nodded. "Maybe. There was no message left about his person, but maybe he was a dress rehearsal before the killer got on to his real agenda. Check the file and get on to the branch he worked at. If Leslie Dunn was employed there, he might well be our man."

Turner was on his way to the door. "It could be Cork's working with him," he said over his shoulder.

"Could be." Oaten stood up as he left. She slapped her forehead hard. She should have made the connection before. Hackney. She'd hated working in the area, but it had been the making of her career with its high drug-related crime rate and plentiful murders. Except that she'd managed to overlook what might turn out to be the crucial link. Then she sat down again slowly, her expression grim. They were still nowhere near cracking the case. Even if Dunn did turn out to have worked for the murdered bank manager, they still had to find him. She found his file among the pile on her desk. It seemed that none of his school contemporaries had seen him since he left at sixteen.

That was about as cold a trail as you could get.

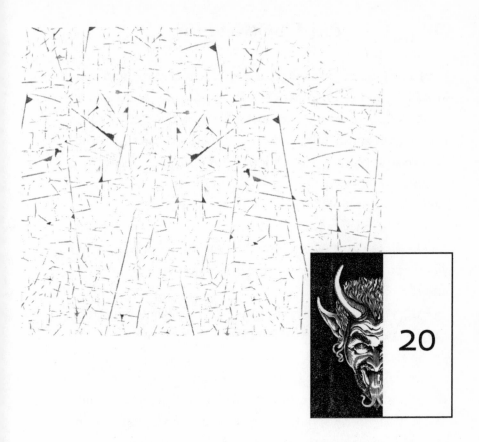

20

I spotted the cops after I'd got dressed. I was wearing my leather jacket, black shirt and trousers, and Dr. Martens—standard male crimewriter's garb. The cops were in a blue Rover about fifty yards down the street. I hadn't seen them in the morning when I went running. Maybe they weren't on shift then. I hoped they hadn't spotted me making the phone calls. That would have piqued Karen Oaten's curiosity. I thought about her for a moment. There was something about her, even though she was potentially an enemy thanks to the Devil.

I left the flat, looking as nonchalant as I could about the men on my tail. They were welcome to follow me now. I walked down to Herne Hill station and bought a travel card. I spotted a guy in a crumpled parka getting on the carriage behind mine. I paid him no further attention. At Victoria, I took the Tube up to Tottenham Court Road and walked to the nearby square where Sixth Sense Ltd., my former publishers, had their office.

"I've an appointment with Jeanie Young-Burke," I said to the attractive, raven-haired young woman at reception. I'd never seen her before. The rapid turnover of receptionists had always struck me. Presumably they were driven up the wall by would-be novelists trying to do a sales job on their magnum opus, or by previously published writers like me desperately trying to get back into the business.

"Ah, yes, Mr. Stone." She gave me a brilliant smile. "My name's Mandy. I've been looking forward to meeting you. I love the Sir Tertius books."

I was taken aback by her friendliness and we got talking. Like all the postuniversity recruits, she wanted to become an editor. The way she spoke about writing, not just mine, suggested that she would make a pretty good one. Our conversation was interrupted by a courier and I sat down. I was still surprised that my former editor had agreed to see me. Then again, I had told her a very large lie.

A tall, solemn young man wearing round glasses came through the security door. "Mr. Stone? Matt?"

I stood up and shook his hand. "And you are?"

"Oh, I'm sorry," he said, blushing. He looked like he wasn't long out of primary school. "Reggie Hampton. I'm Jeanie's assistant."

"Right," I said, following him through the door. My ex-editor went through staff even quicker than the front desk. There were rumors that, since her divorce, she used them for bedroom as well as office services. "How do you find it here?"

"Fascinating," he said, flashing me a toothy smile. "I want to be an editor myself."

I refrained from pointing out to him that the attrition rate of editors was almost as high as that of subalterns on the Somme—unless they found a copper-bottomed bestseller sharpish. Then again, what did I know about bestsellers?

Reggie left me at Jeanie's workstation. It was separated from the rest of the open-plan office by glass panels, indicating her seniority. I'd lost touch with her job title. It seemed to change every few months. The last one I remembered was associate publisher, but no doubt that was out of date.

My former editor waved me to a seat in front of her desk. She was on the phone. I soon realized she was telling some unlucky agent how little she appreciated being sent a book that she described as "terribly substandard." She'd probably used a similar phrase about my last contracted tome.

"Matt!" she said, putting the phone down and extending a well-manicured hand. She didn't get up. Jeanie Young-Burke was in her late forties, but she looked older. Her make-up was applied skillfully enough, but it couldn't completely hide the lines that twenty-five years in publishing had given her. "What a surprise!"

"Hello, Jeanie." I tried not to stare at the publicity photo of her latest prodigy—a stunning former model who had written, or at least put her name to, a novel about murders in the rag trade.

"Nice to see you, too. Prospering, I presume?"

"Darling, everything's wonderful," she replied, putting a piece of chewing gum between her scarlet lips. She'd given up smoking a couple of years back, but it seemed she always needed something in her mouth. "So sorry we couldn't publish any more of your lovely Zog books. The market just didn't seem to like them."

I tried to look nonchalant as Reggie arrived with a tray of coffee.

"Thank you," Jeanie said, fluttering her eyelashes at him. "Sweet boy," she whispered after he'd left. "He's got a first from Oxford, you know."

"I'm sure that'll do him a lot of good in this business."

That made her raise an eyebrow. "Bitterness is a most unendearing trait, you know, Matt." She poured me a cup of coffee. "Now, tell me all about this new project of yours. It sounds very exciting." She gave me an arch smile. "Especially since you've parted company with Christian Fels. I never liked doing business with him."

I had a flash of my former agent and hoped that the Devil hadn't got to him yet, even though I despised him. "Well, these things work for a while and then they lose their momentum. My fault as much as anyone's."

"How very magnanimous of you," Jeanie said, not looking too convinced. "So, this book you've written…"

"Right," I said, taking a deep breath. "It's provisionally called *The Death List* and—"

"Excellent title," she interrupted, making a note.

"—it's a revenge story."

"Excellent, again. Readers love revenge tales. All that vicarious violence they'd like to visit on their spouses, their bosses, their family…"

"Quite," I said, taken aback by her fervor. I hadn't accounted for that in my plan. "Um, it's based on a true story, actually."

"Brilliant," she exclaimed. "Publicity will love that." She looked up when I failed to continue. "Matt?"

"Nothing," I said. I'd experienced a sudden loss of confidence in my strategy. Then I remembered Lucy's face in the playground and persevered. "Actually, Jeanie, do you mind if we pop round the corner to that café where you like to talk in private?" I glanced out at the people in the office. "It's a bit sensitive."

Jeanie gave me a dubious look before enlightenment flooded her face. "Oh, the true-story bit, you mean." She looked at her watch, a diamond number that she'd been given by one of her biggest successes. "Well...all right. I've got the editorial meeting in forty minutes...."

"Great," I said, standing up. "I won't need that long."

She collected her coat and voluminous handbag, and then led me out. "I'll be back in time for the meeting, Reggie," she trilled.

I followed her through the office, smiling at Mandy when we got to reception.

I steeled myself as we cleared the security door and went out onto the street. It was now or never.

"Jeanie?" I said, crowding close to her. "Look at this." I jabbed the Luger that my father had obtained in Hamburg after the war into her side, giving her just a glimpse of the barrel in my pocket. It wasn't in working order, but she wasn't to know that. "Don't make a sound," I hissed.

She seemed to get the message. We walked round the square and onto Charing Cross Road. I hadn't seen the policeman who'd been tailing me. If he was still around, I hoped he hadn't noticed anything amiss. I hailed the first cab that passed and bundled Jeanie in the back.

"Heathrow," I said to the driver. "And could we have some privacy, please?" He closed the glass partition and switched off the microphone.

"What the fuck are you playing at, Matt?" Jeanie demanded, her eyes wide.

"The gun is still pointing at you," I said, my hand in my pocket. "But I'll leave it alone if you listen to what I have to say. All right?" I waited for her to nod. "But you have to understand that Lucy, the woman I love and everyone else I know are in mortal danger. If you make a fuss, I won't hesitate to silence you. You know how important my daughter is to me."

My ex-editor stared at me, and then relaxed slightly. "It's a pity you didn't get some of that passion into your writing, Matt," she said with heavy irony. "All right, tell me."

So I did. Without going into all the details, but giving her enough to persuade her how serious I was. I also told her that she would have first option on the book I would write based on my experiences. The latter seemed to convince her to play along, even though she was unimpressed with my earlier lie about having already produced a manuscript.

"So let me get this straight," she said, raising an eyebrow. "You want me to take the first plane that I can to a European desti-nation of my choice and hide out there until you give me the all clear to come back." She shook her head. "This is madness. What about my work? Can't I contact the office?"

"Call them once from a payphone in the airport and tell them your mother's been taken seriously ill. That's it, unless you want to risk being located. This guy is an expert. Don't answer your phone unless it rings four times first, okay? And don't tell anyone where you are, including me." I turned the screw. "You remember what happened to that poor woman, Miss Merton, in Essex?"

She shivered. Like many people in publishing who dealt with violent material, she had a weak stomach about the real thing.

"You say that this White Devil is behind Alexander Drys's murder, too?"

I nodded. I might have known that she'd be more concerned by what had happened to someone in the business. "He cut off Drys's hands and tongue, and then stuck the latter up his backside."

Jeanie looked aghast for a second but quickly rallied. "He always was an arse-licker," she said, looking at me warily. "He didn't much like your books, did he?"

"That's the point," I said in exasperation. "I'm being drawn into this. If I can beat the Devil, we'll have the book of the century."

"You'd better be right, darling." She gave me a crooked smile. "Otherwise I'll have your guts for garters."

I stayed with her all the way to Terminal One. I would have liked to make sure she checked in, but, as with my mother, I didn't want to know where she ended up going in case the Devil was to wring it out of me.

"Call me this afternoon," Jeanie said imperiously as she got out. "And, just to be clear, you're paying for all this."

I shrugged and smiled at her. Since she'd dropped me, I'd gone through the full cycle of resenting her, of hating her, of wanting to strangle her. Now I'd remembered that I actually rather liked her.

But, as the taxi drove back to central London, I put my former, and perhaps future, editor out of my mind. I had a hell of a lot to do before I could sit down to write a book.

The priority was keeping Lucy, Sara, my mother, my friends and myself alive.

Christian Fels, Eton and Trinity College, Oxford, literary agent to the rich, famous and prodigiously talented, pushed the chair back from his desk and looked out over his garden. He'd been in the Highgate mansion for twenty years now, ever since the first of his million-selling authors hit the jackpot. Single, gay and approaching retirement, he'd cut back his list recently in order to concentrate on his biggest earners. It was a shame, really. Some of the authors he'd had to let go were more talented than the bestsellers, but anyone who knew anything about publishing was aware that talent only got you so far. Down in the flower beds beyond the fifty-yard expanse of lawn, his gardener, a most accommodating young Bosnian, was busy weeding, his backside raised in a way that was deliberately provocative. Delicious youth!

Fels went to the dresser and poured himself a cup of Darjeeling. He stared at his reflection in the rococo mirror and checked that the long strands of hair were still plastered over his bald skull. There had been a footballer famous for such a hairstyle, but he couldn't remember his name. One of the other top agents had sold his memoirs. He patted his cheeks to bring the color up in them. He was doing well for sixty-four. People often complimented him on his appearance, though he knew that most of them only did it because they wanted something out of him. He tightened the knot of his silk tie. It had cost him more than five hundred pounds. He treated himself to a tie like that every time he completed a deal. It wouldn't be long before he bought another.

He went back to his desk. Another hour and he would have finished vetting the complex American contract for one of his children's authors—hardcover and mass-market editions, audio and film rights, product endorsements. The deal would add a wing to his third villa, the one on the Côte D'Azur. He wasn't sure if he would be taking Vlado there with him when summer came. There were plenty more like him in the South of France, those ones tanned and lean from water sports. Variety was the spice of life.

The doorbell rang when he'd only got through another three clauses.

"Bloody hell!" Fels muttered, throwing down his Mont Blanc fountain pen. It was probably one of the juniors from the agency. He'd told his colleagues often enough to leave him alone in the mornings, but the idiots always found something they couldn't handle without his expert input.

He went downstairs, wishing not for the first time that he'd installed one of the agency secretaries in his house. But no, that would have made grabbing Vlado less straightforward.

Looking at the security screen, he made out a shortish man wearing a cap. He had turned away from the door. Some kind of courier, he presumed—he was carrying a box. Perhaps it contained the long-overdue script from the most tiresome of his female authors; tiresome, but extremely high-earning. He pressed the button and watched the door swing open.

"Mr. Fels?" the man said in a curiously accentless voice. He sounded like a BBC newsreader from the 1950s.

"The same. Is that for me?"

"Yes," the man said. "And so is this."

Christian Fels only saw the short black truncheon the instant before it crashed onto his left temple. He toppled backward onto the carpeted hall and lay motionless, his eyes misting over. He was aware of the front door closing, then of his body being dragged into the dining room. It was when he was being lifted onto the table that he realized he had more than one assailant.

"Wha—" His voice sounded far away, as if it were coming

from a megaphone on the other side of the city. "What...what d'you want?"

The man who had hit him leaned over. Fels realized that he had put on a mask, one that hugged the contours of his face. It made him look like a ghost, but it had the desired effect—he couldn't remember anything about his face.

"Christian William Niall Leconbury Fels," the man said, giving a dry laugh. "A handy moniker, I'll say!" He looked across to his companion, who was wearing a similar mask and did not speak. "Known in the literary world as 'the Barracuda.'" He laughed again. "Not very flattering, is it?"

Fels came back to a higher level of consciousness. "Get...get out of my house, you...you criminals. My gardener's out the back. All I have to do is—"

"Shout and your balls will be cut off," his attacker said, jabbing something sharp into the flesh of Fels's thigh. "Message received?"

"Ye...yes."

"Good. Now, I imagine you want to know what's in the box." The man lifted up the brown cardboard package. It was about a foot across.

Fels tried to raise his hands and realized that they were bound.

"I tell you what, I'll open it for you." The man ran the knife along the seal and put his latex-covered hands inside. "Do you know what these are?" he asked, lifting a pile of books out.

Christian Fels blinked away the blood from his left eye. He saw books, books with jackets that were vaguely familiar to him. He tried to make out the titles and the author's name. *The Revenger's Comedy*. Matt Stone. *Tirana Blues*. He knew these books and the man who wrote them.

"Yes, that's right," the man said, bending low over his face so that the smell of mint was pungent in Fels's nostrils. "They're by one of your authors, or should I say ex-authors?"

"Matt...Matt Stone," he stammered. He remembered the fellow, of course. Average talent, if truth were told, but an unusually vivid imagination. He'd done a couple of crime novels set in Albania, hadn't he? There was no way they were ever going to sell well, even though he himself had screwed a more than generous advance out of the publishers.

"Matt Stone," the man in the mask confirmed. "Also known as Wells. Do you know what you're going to do with these books, Christian? You don't mind if I call you Christian, do you? Though behaving like a barracuda is hardly very Christian, is it?" The man let out a laugh that suggested unfathomable depths of depravity. "I'll tell you." He paused to ratchet up the tension. "You're going to eat them. Every last page of them. Not forgetting the jackets."

Fels choked before anything had been stuffed into his mouth. "What?" he gasped. "Why?"

The man looked at him with cold, dark eyes. "Because you consumed Matt Wells's career. Now you can consume his books." He tore out some pages and rammed them into the agent's mouth.

"Aaaach!" Fels groaned, unable to scream, and unable to chew or swallow. "Nnnnggmmm!"

Then something very strange happened. The man and his accomplice suddenly moved away from him. He twisted his head round, frantically trying to spit out the semisodden paper. A tall, fair-haired man in a tracksuit top was standing at the door, a spade in his hand. He wasn't Vlado.

"Well, now, what have we here?" the man asked in a strong American accent. "I think I can hear Klaxons," he said, cupping his hand to his ear. "I can definitely hear Klaxons."

Fels could hear them, too. Oh, blessed relief! He would reward his good-looking savior handsomely.

"No, no, you're not going anywhere, shitheads," the American said, moving to block the two intruders' passage to the door.

"You're making a mistake," the man in the mask said, his voice icy. "Let us past."

"Screw you, pal," the big man said, brandishing the spade.

"Dolt," the attacker said. There was a flash of highly polished metal and the sickening sound of flesh being punctured.

Christian Fels managed to spit the mass of pulp from his mouth. He twisted his head round as far as it would go, strands of his hair dangling over his face like jellyfish tentacles. He was in time to see the two men in caps turning toward the rear of the house.

"Vlado!" he said with a gasp.

"Never mind bloody Vlado," said the American. He'd collapsed against the wall, his eyes fixed on the haft of the knife that was protruding from his upper chest. "What about Andrew Jackson?"

As his rescuer's golden locks fell forward, Fels swooned clean away.

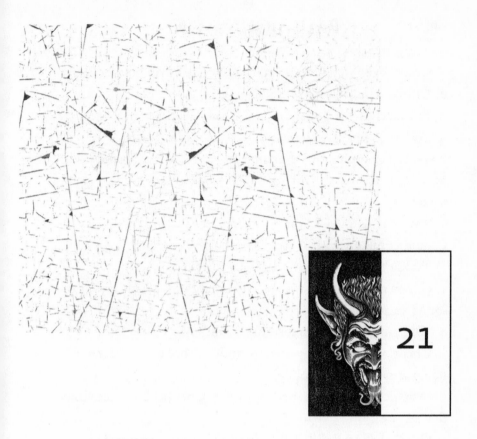

21

I called Andy's mobile from a public phone on Oxford Street and let it ring four times. Then I hung up and pressed Redial.

"Hello?"

The male voice was familiar, but there was something wrong about it.

"Andy?" I said in a low voice.

"Who is this, please?"

I clocked the Welsh tones. They belonged to D.I. Turner. I cut the connection quickly. What the hell was going on? Before I could think further, my mobile rang. I wondered if it was the detective, having recognized my voice. I'd given his superior my number.

"Hello?" I said cautiously.

"Matt Wells." The Devil's voice was colder than I'd ever heard it. "You just made a very big mistake."

The hairs on the back of my neck rose. "What do you mean?"

"What do I mean?" he shouted. I'd never heard him so fierce. It was as if an even more terrifying monster had burst from inside him. "That man at Christian Fels's house was one of your friends."

"At Christian Fels's house?" I repeated. Playing dumb was all I could come up with. "You were there?"

"Don't fuck with me!" the Devil shrieked.

"I don't know what you're talking about," I said, trying to sound surprised.

"Big guy, fair hair, American accent."

Christ, what had happened to Andy? What was the detective doing answering his mobile?

"I've no idea. Maybe he was one of Christian's people from the agency."

"No!" the Devil yelled. "Andrew Jackson is his name. Do you think I'm a fool? I've had your house under surveillance for months. I know everyone who comes and goes. Listen to me. If you play games with me, your daughter will be the next to scream her life away."

Jesus. The phone was shaking in my hand. "What...what did you do to Christian?" I'd hated my former agent since he cut me loose, but I didn't want him hurt—that was why I'd sent Andy up there. Christ. "What did you do to Andy?"

"You'll find out. I'm expecting a chapter from you about Drys's killing. Make sure I have it by tonight. This conversation is over."

I stood on the street with my fists clenched, lines of shoppers flowing past me. What had happened to Christian and Andy? I had to find out. I called D.C.I. Oaten's mobile from the public phone.

"Yes?" she answered curtly.

"This is Matt Wells."

"Mr. Wells." She sounded both surprised and relieved. "Where are you?" Her question was good news. I'd obviously lost the police tail. "I very much need to talk to you."

"What happened to Christian Fels and Andrew Jackson?" I demanded.

"Where are you?" she repeated, her tone hardening. "I'll send a car."

There was no way I was going to get caught up with the police. I needed freedom of movement if I was going to deal with the Devil. "Never mind that," I said firmly. "Tell me what happened. Was Fels attacked?"

"Why do you think that?" She wasn't giving an inch.

I banged the receiver against the glass. "Stop playing games!" I shouted, only realizing after the words came out that I was parroting what the Devil had said. "I'm not telling you where I am, but I need to know what happened to Christian and Andy."

"Mr. Wells, I know that you're keeping information from us. I can arrest you for obstructing an inquiry."

"Only if you can find me. Listen, there are things I can tell you about the murders, but I'm not coming in. People are in danger. Tell me what happened to Christian and Andy, then I'll cooperate."

Oaten gave that some thought. "I have to tell you that you are a potential suspect in the murders, Mr. Wells. I can't make deals with you."

I needed to sweeten her. "All right." I gave her the names of my Internet provider and my Web site operator. "I'm sure you

can get a warrant to access my incoming and outgoing e-mails."
I took a deep breath. "They prove that the killer has been in
contact with me and that I've been replying to him."

"What? You really are in an ocean of trouble. I strongly advise
you to surrender yourself."

"No chance. Come on, Karen," I said, deciding that familiarity couldn't make the situation worse. "Cut the crap. I need
to protect my family and friends, can't you understand that? You
know I'm not the murderer. I was sitting in the same room as
you were when Drys was killed."

There was a long pause. "I repeat, I'm making no deals with
you, Matt." At least she was responding to my informality.
"Christian Fels was attacked in his house by two masked men.
Andrew Jackson interrupted them as they were stuffing pages
from your novels into Mr. Fels's mouth. He has a knife wound
to his upper chest that the paramedics say is not life-threaten-
ing. He's been taken to the Whittington Hospital. Mr. Fels has
a head wound, but it isn't too serious. He's…how can I put it?
Screaming blue murder?"

I laughed, the relief that Andy and Christian were okay
breaking the tension that had been building up all day. "I'll bet
he is." My ex-agent's fuse was notoriously short.

"He hasn't been very complimentary about you," Oaten
added. "No doubt because he thinks you were behind the
attack."

"Tell him I sent Andy Jackson to keep an eye on him."

"Not good enough," she said, her voice hardening again.
"This is a multiple-murder inquiry. Members of the public are
not entitled to take the law into their own hands. Why didn't
you tell us that Fels was going to be attacked?"

"Because I didn't know. You'll understand when you see the

e-mails. This guy has got a hold on me. He's stringing me along. I can't risk antagonizing him."

"I think your friend Mr. Jackson just did," she said dryly. "Matt, if you're in as much danger as I think you are, you have to come in. We can protect you and anyone else he's threatening."

I wished I could believe that, but there wasn't time. The Devil was on the loose and he was angry. I had to move my plans ahead. "Got to go, Karen. Don't bother calling my mobile. I know you can locate me by it."

"Wait," she said hurriedly. "There's a cost to what you're doing. Mr. Fels's gardener had his neck broken when the assailants left. Think about it, Matt. Innocent victims?"

My stomach constricted. I couldn't come up with anything to say, so I hung up and dialed Dave Cummings's mobile.

"Hallo!" he shouted above a lot of machine noise.

"It's Matt."

"Hang on," he said. The noise reduced in volume. "Just disposing of a derelict factory. What's up, mate?"

"Forget demolition," I said. "The shit's hit the fan. You need to get out to the cottage as soon as you can. I'll meet you at the school in an hour." I hung up.

Before I left Oxford Street, I went into a phone shop and bought a pay-as-you-go mobile, insisting that they give me one with a fully charged battery. I saw a cab stop and pushed a tourist out of the way. He yelled at me in some Romance language, which made the cabbie laugh. I scowled at him, told him where to go and got my new phone into commission. The first person I called was Roger van Zandt.

"Where are you, Rog?"

"Baker Street," he said. "I've got the gear you wanted."

It was no good to me now. The police would definitely be watching my flat so I couldn't go back there.

"All right," I said. "You know that Internet café we met at about a month ago? Don't say the name."

"You what?"

"I'll explain later. You know the one I mean?"

"'Course. Are you all right, Matt?"

"I'll meet you there at the number you used to wear on your back. Get it?" Rog used to be a center on the rugby team and his number was four.

"Bloody hell, you're being mysterious. Okay."

I rang off and watched the boats on the gray-brown river as we crossed Waterloo Bridge. The Devil was somewhere in the city. He knew it as well as I did, as well as John Webster had done back in the seventeenth century. But where was he? Could he already be on his way to Lucy's school?

I told the cabbie to hurry up and was greeted with more laughter. For a moment I wished I was in a foreign capital where taxi drivers didn't care about the speed limit. That made me think of my mother and Jeanie. They should both have been abroad by now. I would call them later from a public phone to make sure.

I rang Dave again. "Where are you?"

"Denmark Hill. Should be there in under ten minutes."

"Okay. Same here." I rang off and had a thought. If the Devil had a legion of helpers, maybe Dave's cottage wasn't safe.

As I paid off the cabbie, I saw Dave's large four-by-four pull up outside the school.

Looking around and seeing no sign of anyone suspicious, I went over to him. "Thanks for dropping everything."

"No worries. It's only a two-hundred-grand contract." He

grinned. "I can always use that ten grand you gave me as partial restitution."

I glared at him. "Don't even think about it."

He slapped me on the back. "Joke, you pillock. Right, what are we doing?"

"Pulling Lucy and your pair out of their classes. We'll tell the teachers that there's been a family emergency."

"What, in both our families?"

I shrugged. "Why not?"

"Okay. Then what?"

"Get home and pick up Ginny." I grabbed his arm. "Listen, Dave, it's not safe for you to go to your cottage. The bastard may have been watching you."

There was a flash of anger in his eyes. "Is that right? Fucker."

A cleaner who was passing us in the playground tutted her disapproval.

"Don't worry," he said, with a grin. "I'll think of something. Better if you don't know, eh?"

I nodded. He was way ahead of me. In the same spirit, I decided it was better if he didn't know what had happened to Andy. I gave him my new mobile number.

"Just one thing, Matt," he said, his tone more serious. "Does Caroline know about this?"

"Not yet," I replied, avoiding his eyes. He was aiding and abetting the abduction of a child without her mother's permission. I couldn't tell my ex-wife till Dave was well clear of his home.

"It's okay," he said, giving me a thump on the shoulder. "I trust you."

As we headed into the school to interrupt classes, I heard him mutter, "Christ knows why."

★ ★ ★

Karen Oaten watched as the mortuary attendants removed the body of the gardener. Christian Fels had identified him as Vlado Petrovic, a Bosnian national whose papers were in order. Judging by the way Fels's eyes had dampened when he saw the body, he'd had more than employer-employee relations with the unfortunate immigrant.

Fels had been treated by a paramedic, having refused to go to hospital. There was a bandage round his head, thin strands of hair hanging over it like those on a cheap Halloween mask.

"Have you arrested that lunatic Wells yet, Inspector?" he said, glaring at her.

"Chief Inspector," Oaten corrected. She'd always had a problem with bullies like Fels. "We're working on it. Although, by your own admission, Mr. Wells is taller than either of your attackers." She gave him a tight smile. "And he provided a bodyguard for you."

"Is that what he's saying?" Fels scoffed. "I always knew that man was a waste of my time. If he wasn't behind the attack, why did those masked maniacs try to make me eat his books?"

"Good question."

The literary agent stared at her. "Well?" he demanded.

"*I* ask the questions," she said. "*You* answer them."

Fels took a step back, and then retreated farther into his sumptuously furnished drawing room. "Have a seat, Chief Inspector," he said, flapping his hand at the leather armchairs.

"No, thanks," Oaten said. "Taff!" she called through the open door.

The inspector appeared. "Yes, guv?"

"Have you got any more questions for Mr. Fels?"

"No, he's given us a provisional statement."

"All right." Karen Oaten turned from examining a row of plastic-covered first editions. "Tell me, Mr. Fels, why did you part company with Matt Wells?"

The agent gave her an exasperated glare. "What has that to do with what happened here today?"

"Allow me to be the judge of that, please."

Fels found her gaze too piercing for comfort. "Oh, very well. The simple answer is that I wasn't making enough money from him."

"And the more complicated one?"

The agent hesitated. "Well, to tell you the truth, I rather liked the fellow at first. He was smart and engaging when I took him on. Then he became obsessed by the ludicrous idea of setting a crime series in Albania. I told him it wouldn't sell, but he didn't listen. I don't think he's the man he was. I heard that his ex-wife rode roughshod over him in the divorce. Since then he's been full of self-pity and resentment." He gave Oaten a crooked smile. "Neither of which qualities is exactly marketable."

For some reason the chief inspector found herself wanting to stick up for Matt Wells. She restrained herself. "Very well," she said, moving to the door. "We'll be in touch to take your formal statement, Mr. Fels. Uniformed officers will patrol the area until further notice."

"You mean my assailants might come back?" Fels said, his face suddenly even paler than it had been.

Oaten struggled not to smile. The vain old snob seemed to care only about his own skin. "Oh, probably not," she said, deliberately refusing to give him any more substantial comfort. Maybe that would teach him some humility.

When she and Turner got to the Volvo, she extended her hand for the keys. "I'll drive. You can bring me up to speed on what the rest of the team's been up to." The plan for the day had been a concerted effort to track down Leslie Dunn and Nicholas Cork, the two most suspicious missing men from the lists that had been compiled. The attack on Fels had distracted her from that.

"The last I heard," Turner said, "Pavlou was on his way to the bank in Hackney. D.C.I. Hardy's people are following up on Drys's circle of friends and family, though there isn't much of the latter. They're mostly dead or in Greece."

"They're a dead end, as well," the chief inspector said morosely, accelerating down Highgate Road. "He was killed because of his connection with Matt Wells—the bad reviews."

Turner looked at her, his face a picture of confusion. "Excuse me, guv, but what's going on with Wells? Since he's refusing to come in, we have to treat him as a suspect, don't we?"

Oaten bit her lip. "In theory, yes. I think I believe him when he says his family and other contacts are in danger. He did send his friend to protect Fels, after all. And he put me on to his Internet people. When we've read his e-mails, we should have a clearer idea of what's going on."

The inspector was peering at his notes. "What are you going to do about Hardy's people who managed to lose him today?"

"Same as I did with Morry Simmons," she said, overtaking a bus.

"We need them, guv," Turner protested.

"So does Traffic," she said, inclining her head toward a van that was parked illegally. Her phone rang. She tossed it across to her colleague. "Answer that, will you?"

"Turner." He glanced at her. "She's got her hands full. Tell me, Paul." He listened, his lips forming into a smile as he scribbled notes. "Okay, nice one. We'll see you back at the Yard." He dropped the phone onto his lap.

"What's Pavlou got?" Oaten asked impatiently.

"Leslie Dunn," the inspector answered, the smile turning into a grin. "He worked at the Savings Trust Bank in Hackney for a year, then was fired by the manager—our murder victim Steven Newton—for persistent disobedience and for, quote, 'an unsatisfactory attitude toward customers.'"

"So we've got a motive for that murder."

"Yep." Turner gave her a triumphant look. "That's not all. One of the tellers heard a rumor that Pavlou has just checked out. The bastard won the lottery in September 2001. Nine and a half million quid."

The chief inspector glanced at him. "Meaning he could hire killers or get himself trained up and equipped."

"Mmm."

"Why aren't you smiling anymore?"

The Welshman closed his notebook. "Because the trail stops there. Dunn requested the privacy-protection option." He looked out at the pedestrians on the streets of Camden Town. "Since then he seems to have disappeared off the face of the earth."

Karen Oaten gripped the wheel hard. "With all that money, he wouldn't have had any problem getting a new identity." She braked hard as the lights changed. "Shit."

The chief inspector's phone rang again. Turner listened, and then cut the connection.

"That was D.C.I. Hardy. One, he's extremely pissed off that you got the A.C. to transfer his guys out."

"Tough."

"And two, there's been a report about Nicholas Cork."

Oaten slipped dexterously past a people-carrier laden with kids. "Spit it out, Taff."

"A badly smashed-up and partially decomposed body was found on the rocks in northern Cornwall last September. There was a video-club card bearing the name N. Cork in a pocket."

The chief inspector thought for a couple of seconds. "Have we got dental records for him?"

Turner flicked through the pages of his notebook. "Sorry, don't know, guv," he said finally.

"Bloody well find out, then!" Oaten shouted. "Until we're sure the body's his, Cork is still a suspect for Dunn's accomplice."

"Guv?" the inspector asked as they crossed Euston Road. "I can see why Dunn killed the people that he knew, but why would he be after Matt Wells's circle? What's in it for him?"

"Good question, Taff," Oaten said, her face less tense. "Maybe the e-mails will answer that."

"I've got another question," the Welshman said. "That murder down in Greenwich last night?"

The D.C.I. nodded. "Petty criminal with form, cut up into several pieces, boxed up and left outside his local?"

"That's the one. Are we sure it isn't connected with our killer?"

Karen Oaten turned her head to him briefly. "Sure? We aren't sure about anything in this case, Taff. But there was no plastic bag with a quotation from John Webster and no apparent links to Bethnal Green or Matt Wells, so I'm leaving it to the team down there. For the time being, at least."

Turner looked doubtful. "I don't know, guv. Another mutilation job just after Drys and the others? I don't like it."

"Neither do I. That's why we'll be getting regular updates from the Southern Homicide Division. But we've got enough on our plates as it is."

The inspector nodded, his expression pained. He'd had difficulty eating for days.

22

The look that Lucy gave me as Dave drove away almost broke my heart. She had been very surprised when I took her out of class. Fortunately her teacher, Mrs. Maggs, was a fan of my books and let us go without asking any awkward questions. Lucy seemed to accept that Dave and his family were taking her on a mystery tour, only asking about her mummy at the last moment. I told her that Caroline knew all about it and would see her later. I was getting good at lying—too good.

I caught the bus to Brixton after walking around the back streets of Dulwich Village for a while. If anyone was on my tail, they were doing a very good job of concealing themselves. The café I'd arranged to meet Rog at was called the Vital Spark. It was off Coldharbour Lane and, despite its name, wasn't well lit. That was just what I wanted. We took our coffees to a deserted back corner.

Rog held up a large plastic bag. "Here's your stuff," he said, searching in the pockets of his brown corduroy jacket. "And here's the receipt."

I swallowed hard when I saw the amount. Maybe I would have to use the Devil's money after all. "Look, Dodger," I said, booting up a computer, "the situation's changed." I took in his bewildered expression. I was going to have to come clean, but I wanted him to have the chance to opt out. Rog wasn't as much of a hard man as Dave and Andy. On the team, he used to weave and sidestep his way round opposition players rather than trample over them. He could put in the hard tackles when it counted, even though, off the pitch, he spent almost as much time on his own as I did—gluing and painting models of tanks and aircraft in his case, rather than pretending to write. "Listen, here's where I am."

I filled him in about the White Devil's activities. His face went from confusion to amazement to horror, and finally to what was unmistakably anger. Then I told him what had happened to Andy. This was the crunch moment. There hadn't been any point in telling Dave—he was in whatever happened and knowing Andy had been hurt wouldn't have changed anything for him. With Rog, I wasn't sure.

"Bastards," he said in a low voice. "I'll fucking have them."

I put my hand on his arm. "This isn't a run in the park. The Devil's killed at least eight people and I reckon it could be more."

He stuck his chest out. "Let him and his sidekick have a go, then. They owe us for what they did to Andy. You sure he's going to be all right?"

"As sure as I can be without speaking to him. Maybe we'll manage to do that later." I nodded at the screen. "Now we've got work to do. Set me up with a new e-mail account, will you?" I watched as his fingers sped across the keys. In a few minutes I had another identity, *SirZog1*. Then I logged on to my own account, wondering if the police had obtained access to it yet, and printed out the latest e-mail from the Devil.

"Jesus Christ," Rog said, shaking his head as he read it. "Did he really do all that to the poor sod Drys? Why?"

"Apparently because he gave me some bad reviews."

"You're joking."

"Afraid not. He's trying to implicate me, and at the same time get me to write his bloody story. I remember reading that some serial killers feel the need for immortality."

Rog was staring at me. "But if he wants you to write his story, why's he trying to frame you? You won't be able to do much from a jail cell."

"Ah, that's where he's smart," I said, looking over the document. The Devil's notes about the murder of the critic were as detailed as ever, but it was up to me to turn them into a readable story. "He's getting me to write his achievements up every day."

"You'll have a holiday tomorrow, then," Rog said, nudging me in the ribs.

"Why?"

"He didn't manage to kill that Fels bloke, did he?"

I stopped typing. "Jesus."

"What?"

"That may mean he has a go at someone else to make up for it." I ran out of the café and located the nearest pay phone. First I called my mother's mobile, letting it ring four times. She picked up when I rang again.

"Hello?" She sounded a bit querulous.

"It's me. Are you all right? Don't tell me where you are!"

There was a pause. "Oh, I see. Yes…I'm all right."

"Good flight?"

"Um, yes."

"What's the matter? Don't worry, everyone else is fine." She didn't know Andy, so I didn't tell her about him. She hated Christian Fels because of what she regarded as his betrayal of me, but now wasn't the time to mention that—especially given that his gardener had been murdered.

"Oh," she said hesitantly. "That's good."

"Hotel okay?"

"Yes. Look, Matt, I've got to go." Suddenly she was speaking quickly. "I love you, darling." Then she hung up.

I stood in the booth, peering at the phone. My mother had always had a tendency to distraction, but this was worse than usual. I supposed she was upset by what I was putting her through, but I couldn't remember the last time she'd addressed me as "darling."

Wolfe and Rommel were in the front of the Orion, parked about fifty yards from the house in Forest Hill. According to the now dismembered Terry Smail, this was the home of the man called Corky—the man who had been with Jimmy Tanner in the pub. The street was pretty run-down and there was rubbish strewn around many of the houses' small front gardens.

There was a squelch from the walkie-talkie on Wolfe's lap.

"Receiving?"

"Got you, Geronimo. Advise." Their comrade was standing at the bus stop that was just beyond the house. He'd been there for nearly an hour.

"Still no movement inside. Curtains remain drawn."

"All right, get back here. Out."

Wolfe glanced at Rommel as if he expected him to object. "We can see well enough from here. Geronimo's too obvious where he is."

Rommel's expression remained blank as Geronimo opened the back door.

"Cheer up, wanker," Geronimo said. "The scum will be back soon."

"Better be," Rommel said with a scowl. "I'm going to hurt him."

Wolfe nudged him with his elbow. "Steady. We're all going to hurt him once we find out what happened to Jimmy. But he's not the main man. We need him to lead us to the bastard with the pointed teeth, so no lethal force till I say so."

Rommel looked round at Geronimo and their eyes met. They'd been in similar situations often enough and they knew not to argue with Wolfe.

"It seems we're not the only ones chopping people up," their leader said, turning the page of the *Daily Independent*. He read out parts of the story about the murders of a priest, a retired schoolteacher, a doctor and a newspaper critic.

"And the coppers think it's the same guy?" Rommel said, glaring at a small boy who had stopped his bicycle at the window. The boy departed at speed.

"Looks like it," Wolfe replied. "And this journalist thinks the body at the Hereward is connected, too."

Geronimo laughed. "Shows how much journalists know."

They sat in silence as the afternoon drew on. Geronimo and Rommel started talking about old times, their eyes still fixed on the street and the house. Wolfe let them rattle on. He didn't care about the past—all that mattered to him was finding out what had happened to his brother-in-arms Jimmy Tanner. Jimmy had saved his life on more than one occasion and he owed him.

"...and then that Iraqi came out of the bunker with his AK47 pointed straight at Dave," said Geronimo.

"...and Dave just grinned at him," said Rommel.

"...and emptied a magazine into him before he could move," Geronimo said with a harsh laugh.

Wolfe looked over his shoulder. "Names," he said in a low voice. "We don't use real names out of barracks."

"Shit," Geronimo said, dropping his gaze. "Sorry, boss. Patton—Patton was the one who shot the towel-head."

Wolfe nodded. "That's right, Patton. Good soldier—nerves of steel and smart with it. Shame he left the regiment."

"Shame he was pushed, you mean," Rommel said bitterly.

"Yeah, well, he sometimes got a bit too clever for his own good," said Geronimo. He kept his eyes off Wolfe. The boss had been instrumental in easing their old comrade Dave Cummings out because he had become a bit of a loose cannon. That didn't mean that Geronimo and Rommel hadn't kept in touch with Dave, though. He'd been a good mate of Jimmy Tanner's, too.

"Motorbike approaching from rear," Rommel said, lowering himself in his seat. "Reducing speed. Could be our man."

Wolfe dropped lower, too, his eyes fixed on the road. "Okay, get ready. If he stops outside the house, we'll take him as he gets off the bike."

Rommel started the Orion's engine. At the same moment the motorbike came level with them. The rider, kitted out in leathers and wearing a black helmet with an opaque visor, turned his head toward the car. Suddenly he revved the engine and moved off rapidly down the street, forcing a woman with a child to jump out of the way.

"Go!" Wolfe yelled. He was slammed back in his seat as Rommel hit the accelerator.

"Shit, the bastard spotted us straight off," Geronimo said from the rear.

"Don't worry." Wolfe watched as the motorbike took a right turn, the rider's knee close to the asphalt. "He can run, but he can't hide from us."

The next number I called was Karen Oaten's. She was in a meeting, but she must have walked out—I heard the other voices fade and then disappear.

"Matt, I'm glad you got in touch. Listen, we think we know who the Devil is."

I felt relief flood through me. "Who?"

"That's the problem. He seems to have changed identity in the past four years. We're trying to track down his new name."

The anxiety came back with a vengeance. "So you haven't got any way of stopping him."

"I'm afraid not. At least, not yet."

"Jesus. I think he might make another attempt today."

"To kill?" Her voice was tense. "Why?"

"Because he failed with Christian Fels."

"Don't worry, we've got people at his house."

"I don't think he'll be dumb enough to try there again, Karen. I've taken steps to protect my family and my ex-editor. But there are plenty of others he could target."

"Give me names and addresses," she said quickly.

I admired her professionalism. I told her where Sara and Caroline were to be found. Then I reeled off several names at my former publishers, including the owner. I went through friends I had in the crime-writing world—authors, journalists, booksellers and dealers, collectors, anyone I could think of. I couldn't remember all their addresses, but I knew the localities. I didn't mention my friends, though. I needed them to remain unknown to the police.

"It's going to need a lot of manpower," I said.

"Yes, it is." For a moment she sounded uncertain. "I'll do what I can. I can't promise we'll be able to cover everyone." She paused. "Matt. It's important that you come in. You can help us."

"Have you read the e-mails yet?"

"No, the warrant's on its way as we speak."

"When you've read them, you'll understand why I'm doing this. Listen, I want to ask you a favor, Karen."

She gave a wry laugh. "I hardly think you're in a position to—"

"You know I am," I interrupted. "At least until you can track me down—and that would be a waste of your precious manpower. Listen, I want you to promise not to put a trace on my mobile phone. The Devil might do something horrendous if he can't get through to me. Will you do that?"

There was a long silence. "I'm going to pretend I didn't hear that. Still, it may be that in all the rush here your phone gets forgotten for an hour or two."

"Thanks, Karen. I appreciate it."

"Yes, well, you owe me now. I'll be expecting payment very soon, Matt. In the meantime, have you ever met or do you have any knowledge of a man by the name of Terence—Terry— Smail?"

"No," I said. "Never heard of him."

"You'd better be telling the truth."

The phone went dead. Who the hell was Terry Smail? I wondered as I turned on my old mobile and went back into the café. I got down to writing the latest chapter while Rog tried to hack into the British Airways system to find out where my mother had gone. I wasn't happy about how she'd sounded on the phone. I was halfway through when my old mobile phone rang.

It was the Devil and he had company.

Caroline Zerb had walked out of the bank in Cornhill at precisely 1:00 p.m. She had just completed a meeting with her staff about an important section in the monthly *Far East Economic Review*, and she felt an even greater need than usual to get out of the office for lunch. Her ex-husband thought she stayed at her desk to eat her wholemeal sandwiches, but, as with so many other things, he was way off target. She was dedicated to her job, but she was also capable of taking time for herself. She'd found that she worked much better in the afternoon when she took an hour off.

As usual she crossed Southwark Bridge, looking toward the preposterous shape of Tower Bridge and feeling completely at ease with the world. She was at the hub of world business, her expertise giving her power and influence that very few people had. No wonder Matt hadn't been able to understand her after she went into the City. What did he know about power and influence? He'd once claimed that he had the power of life and death over the characters in his novels, but Caroline knew that was nothing compared to daily meetings with international financiers who wanted to hear your point of view. Fiction was a waste of time. She only ever read books on economics and history.

And yet, she thought as she walked along the riverbank past Shakespeare's Globe, there had always been something different about Matt. She had fallen head over heels in love with him at university. She could scarcely believe it when the hero of the rugby league team paid attention to a bluestocking virgin. And she'd continued to love him when Lucy, beautiful Lucy, was born and his books began to make him relatively well known.

Caroline watched as a balloon floated away high above the river. Their relationship had begun to change when Matt got himself so involved with that ridiculous Albanian series. Everyone he knew told him it would end in tears, but he wouldn't listen. Her mother told her that you had to allow the people you loved to make their own mistakes, that was part of life. Maybe, but the problem was that, by then, she had begun to fall out of love with Matt. There was no other man. She had neither the time nor the inclination for that. All she felt was boredom with his ranting and his deluded self-importance—as if anyone really cared what a crime novelist thought about anything.

Ah, Matt, she thought, approaching a bench. There was a man in overalls and a baseball cap pulled low sitting at the far end. It was still good to see her former husband with Lucy every day, even though she found it hard to give him more than a few civil words. And he had appeared to be happier. The woman, Sara, seemed to be good for him, even if she did have a curious glint in her eyes—the typical grasping look of the newshound. But in the past few days he'd been strange, nervous, as if he was hiding something. He'd have to get a grip on himself if he didn't want what remained of his writing career to disappear downstream like the empty soft drink cans in the Thames.

She moved into the center of the bench as another man came

to sit down. He was wearing a puffer jacket that was surely far too hot for the day, the hood of a gray sweatshirt over his head. If it hadn't been for the wispy mustache, she'd have taken him for a girl.

Caroline started to eat one of her organic cheddar sandwiches. She watched tourists laughing as they took photos of one another and found herself thinking about her life. How happy was she really? She had a job she loved, a child she adored, and yet, there was something missing. She'd been thinking about it a lot recently. Perhaps the neighbors' dog disappearing and the effect that was having on Shami and Jack was the reason. She knew the absence of a man wasn't the problem. She could bed any of the young lions in the company without doing more than winking at them, but the fact was, she didn't miss sex. It had been good with Matt. Apart from Lucy, that was one of the main reasons she had stuck with him as long as she had. No, what she had realized was missing was adventure, the unexpected, a sudden break from the rhythms of everyday life.

She shook her head and told herself not to be so flighty. She had work to do and her lunch break was almost over. It was when she was crumpling up her sandwich bag that she saw the man on her right lean forward and look intensely at the other guy to her left.

It was almost as if he was giving the hooded man some kind of signal.

The White Devil took a step back from the blindfolded and gagged captive tied to the chair. He smiled at the masked figure behind, who gave him a blank look in return. He would have to be careful with his partner. He hadn't expected such devotion to violence and the act of killing so suddenly. That could lead to a dangerous lack of caution.

The Devil glanced around the lock-up garage. It was in Deptford, in a lane that was overlooked by the high rear wall of a Victorian factory—that property was listed for demolition and no one except junkies and half-blind drunks had set foot in it for years. It was good for privacy, as was the fact that the people who used the other garages shared his studied lack of concern about what went on in the vicinity.

It had been easy enough to snatch their latest victim. No one had noticed the transfer to the battered white van that now took up half of the space—the garage was a double one, the wall having been knocked through. There was plenty of room for the upcoming fun and games.

The person on the chair let out a high-pitched moan. The Devil moved over quickly and delivered a hard slap to the left cheek.

"Be quiet, you piece of shit," he said, bending closer. "Noise means pain, you understand?"

The trembling captive nodded slowly.

"That's all it needs," the Devil said to his partner. "Now you try." He watched as the masked figure gave the prisoner a full-blooded punch that almost knocked the chair over. "Good," he said, smiling. "Looks like you aren't fond of this one."

"No, I'm not."

The Devil stepped back and started laying out his tools on the workbench. Maybe he'd made the right decision in locating his partner after all. Being confronted by the realities of murder had seemed initially to knock the stomach from the figure in the mask. He hoped that the procedure they were about to undertake—his most ambitious yet—would be the making of his Dr. Watson. It had better be. After all, he wasn't in this purely for himself.

As he fingered the glinting steel instruments, he thought of what he'd achieved so far. The murder of that bastard Newton from the bank in Hackney had been a trial run. At that stage, he wasn't sure himself that he could carry out what he wanted to. He hadn't taken his partner on that excursion, nor on those of the priest or the old bitch who used to teach him. But when the Devil saw that all was going to plan, it had been safe to appear as a double act at the doctor's and the fat critic's.

He scowled and put the scalpel down carefully on the table. Everything had been fine until this morning, when the writer had started to fight back and the body parts had been found outside the Hereward. Could there be a connection? The Devil originally hadn't been sure that Matt Wells had it in him, for all the macho posturing he showed at bookshop events and literary festivals. Most writers were nothing more than drunks who propped up the nearest bar they could find and boasted about their sales, always inflating them, and their film deals, which hardly ever made it to any screen. They were liars and hypocrites, every last one of them.

But Matt Wells had actually had the nerve to stand up to him. He'd sent that American muscleman to protect Christian Fels. The Devil had been so enraged about being deflected from his plan for the agent that he had taken it out on the innocent gardener. His partner hadn't turned away at the sound of the neck cracking. It was the first time the Devil had killed in that way. Jimmy Tanner had trained him well. It was a pity the former SAS guy had become so unreliable from the booze. He lay in the foundations of a bridge outside Bromley, silenced forever after the insertion of a combat knife between his fifth and sixth ribs. That had been as good an end to the Devil's apprenticeship as he could have thought of, as well as being an appropriate death for a man who had been a state-sponsored assassin. Was it possible that someone—Matt Wells?—had found out about his meetings with Tanner? Even if he had, the Devil and his partner would kill everyone on the expanded death list before he could locate them.

That bastard Wells. He had actually taken steps to protect the people he thought would be targets. The Devil grinned. That wouldn't do the fool any good. It would be a long time before anyone caught up with them. And even if that happened, there would be a container-load of pain to endure.

"Right," he said to the hooded figure. "It's time we got started." He watched as their captive tensed. Obviously the effect of the punch was wearing off. Good. The Devil wanted his victim to be aware of what was coming.

Pain was what it was all about, pain and horror. After this killing, the writer would understand that no one he'd ever met was safe. Then they would see how he reacted to real pressure.

The Devil selected a couple of instruments, nodded to his partner and walked over to the prisoner. He removed the blindfold and was gratified by the sight of two damp and terrified eyes. They implored him for mercy, but they also seemed to contain the knowledge that none would be forthcoming.

Then he had a thought. Why not up the pressure on Matt Wells right now? He handed the scalpel and probe to his partner and took his mobile from his pocket.

The smile that spread across his face as he started to speak made his victim whimper and moan.

23

I was finishing the chapter about Alexander Drys when my old mobile rang. My heart skipped a couple of beats. I had to hope that D.C.I. Oaten was being true to her word and hadn't put a trace on the phone.

"I suppose you think you've been very clever, Matt." The Devil's voice was worryingly confident.

I moved away from Rog, who was still trying to get into the British Airways system. "What do you mean?"

"I know what you've been up to, my friend. I have to say I'm very disappointed." His tone was mocking and I had a bad feeling about what was about to happen. But it was too late to retreat.

"Like I give a fuck what you feel," I said, provoking a grin from the guy in a beanie hat at the till. I went outside. "You think you're so clever, but you're not the only person with a functioning brain."

There was a pause. "Is that right, Matt?" His voice was now ice cold. "Have a listen to this."

I heard what sounded like a slap and then a muffled groan followed by choking, high-pitched screams. Jesus, who did the bastard have?

"Recognize the voice?"

I kept quiet, too shocked to hazard a guess.

"I asked you a question," the Devil said, almost shouting.

"I don't know!" I yelled back.

He laughed. "You think you're so clever, Mr. Award-Winning Crime Novelist. Well, I'm not going to tell you who I'm about to torture and kill. How does that make you feel?"

"Sick," I said, turning away from a pair of laughing children who'd entered the café. "Look, take me instead. If you let the person you've got go, I'll hand myself over to you."

There was another laugh, this one filled with terrible malevolence. "No, no, it isn't time for you to suffer pain, Matt. It will be soon enough. In the meantime, be sure that someone you spoke to earlier today is about to die in agony."

I was so shocked that I almost cried out.

"I hope you haven't been talking to that bitch detective," the Devil continued. "Because people you talk to have recently acquired a substantially reduced life expectancy. You're making this a war between you and me, Matt."

"Come on!" I shouted. "Let's finish it now, man to man."

"Man to man?" he sneered. "I'm not even sure you are a man yet. You're a writer, a fraudster, someone who lives from making things up. That isn't my definition of a man."

I heard the whimpering of the victim in the background.

"Please," I begged, "don't hurt any of my family. Or my friends."

For a few moments I thought I'd got to him. Then he laughed again. "It's too late for that, Matt. And where's my chapter? If I don't have it soon, you'll be mourning someone a lot closer to you than Alexander Drys." He gave me a new e-mail address and then cut the connection.

I ran to the public phone and called Dave Cummings.

"Matt, what's going on, lad?" His voice was normal.

Relief flooded through me. "Is Lucy okay? Are all of you okay?"

"'Course she is, mate. And so are we. Ginny's taking it well, apart from a bit of whining early on. We're...well, never mind what we're doing. Don't want you working out where we are, do we? What's up?"

"Nothing," I said, not wanting to alarm him. "Listen, are you in range of a mobile phone supplier?"

"Aye, I suppose so."

"Get a new one, pay-as-you-go, and text the number to me with it." I gave him my new mobile number. "Turn off your old one."

"Got you. He might be scanning us. Need any help?"

"No, mate. Just look after Luce and your lot. I'll be in touch."

"Get the bastard," Dave said. "Though I'd really like to do that myself."

"Yeah, Psycho, I know you would. Got to go." I signed off, having decided that talking to Lucy would just make her anxious. Then I called D.C.I. Oaten.

"Karen? It's Matt Wells. Have you got everyone I listed under protection?"

"Almost everyone," she replied. "What's happened?"

"I just had the Devil on the phone. He's got someone I know. He says he's about to kill whomever it is."

"Where's your daughter?" she said, her voice clipped.

"She's safe."

"Not as safe as she would be under police protection. Listen, Matt, I've been reading the e-mails between you and this White Devil. You've got nothing to worry about. Why don't you come in and help us?"

I wasn't sure that I believed her. Someone as devious as this killer could have set up the various accounts and sent messages to himself. I reckoned she still had me down as a suspect.

She changed tack. "You realize that you're obstructing an investigation, maintaining contact with a multiple murder suspect and—"

That made me sure I couldn't trust her. "Never mind that," I interrupted. "Who haven't you been able to locate?" I heard her ask the Welshman for a list.

"Right. You said you've taken steps to protect your mother and your editor, Ms. Young-Burke. We've spoken to your girl-friend, Sara Robbins. She's on a story in Oxford, but she's with a photographer. She's going to ring us before she separates from him. We haven't actually been able to speak to your wife, but one of her colleagues assured us that she was in the company building. He thought she was in a meeting because her mobile phone had been turned off. I've left messages for her to call me."

Caroline hadn't been my top priority since I'd put off telling her about what I'd done with Lucy.

"Other than that, we've got people at your publishers. Most of the staff there are accounted for."

"Most of them?" I asked.

"What, Taff?" she shouted. "Oh. Apparently some of them went out with an author. They were going on to a theater matinee, and then to dinner. We'll catch up with them."

"Okay," I said dubiously. "What about my author friends?"

"Well, you can hardly expect us to send people out all over the country. We've notified the local forces and they'll do what they deem necessary. I have to assume that your Devil is London-based. Essex is as far as he's gone from the capital."

"So far. All right." I had a question for her. I'd seen a report in one of the papers in the café about the murder in Greenwich and she'd asked me about the dead man. "Is Terence Smail part of this?"

There was a pause. "No connection has been established yet. Were you being straight with me? The name means nothing to you?"

"I told you, no. Okay, that's it."

"Aren't you going to give me your new contact number, Matt?"

I thought about it. "Sorry, no. I need to keep on the move. Thanks for what you're doing, Karen." I hung up, imagining the look on her face and glad that I wasn't within range of her muscular physique.

Back in the café, Rog was still hammering away at the keyboard and cursing under his breath. A pencil was stuck through his salt-and-pepper curls.

"No luck?" I asked.

"Getting there, but it's slow." He glanced at me. "Of course, only a solid-gold superstar like me could have got even this far."

I left him to it and finished the Drys chapter. Before I sent it to my tormentor, I tried to imagine who his latest victim could be. My mother had sounded strange on the phone, but it couldn't have been her. She was a fighter; she wouldn't have allowed herself to be held captive and pretend otherwise. Caroline? No, she was bound to be still in the office, as Oaten said. Who the hell did he have? Christ, they hadn't accounted for everyone from Sixth Sense.

I went back out to the public phone and called Jeanie Young-Burke's mobile, using the agreed method.

"Hello!" she shouted above a lot of background noise.

"It's Matt."

"Darling, how sweet of you to call." I tried to get a word in, but not before she'd let slip where she was. "Paris is a delight. I've found the most charming little bistro and I'm surrounded by divine Frenchmen. This was such a good idea of yours."

I raised my eyes to the pale blue sky. Trust Jeanie to fall on her feet. "In case you're worrying, the police are keeping an eye on everyone I know at your office."

"Oh, don't bother about them," she said with a shrieking laugh. "They know how to look after themselves."

"Really?" I said, struck by her naiveté. "Don't call any of them, remember? I'll let you know when you can come back."

"Fine, darling. Frankly, I don't know if I ever want to come back." There was a trill of laughter, and then she cut the connection.

Before I went inside, I called Sara. Her mobile rang for a long time. When she finally replied, she sounded out of breath.

"Hi, it's me," I said, catching the noise of a train in the background.

"Oh. Matt." She sounded surprised.

"Are you still in Oxford?"

"What? Oh, yes. We'll be heading back soon."

"I'm sorry about all this."

"It's okay. I want the exclusive, though."

I laughed. "Typical bloody journo. You'll remember to talk to the police before you get back to the Smoke?"

"Of course," she said bitterly. "I'm really looking forward to having a cop outside my flat tonight."

I wasn't sure where I was going to be later on, but Sara's place wasn't an option, given said cop. "I'll see if I can make it," I lied.

"Don't bother. They've got you under guard, too, haven't they?"

"Um, yeah. Okay, I'll talk to you later. Love you." I rang off, feeling less than proud of myself for not telling her I'd eluded the surveillance.

I was becoming as duplicitous as the White Devil. The fact that he was bringing me down to his level made me even more determined to nail the bastard.

Before he nailed someone I cared for.

John Turner was driving the unmarked Volvo at speed behind a police car with its lights flashing and siren blaring. It was early evening and the commuter traffic was pulling aside to let them past. Beside him, D.C.I. Oaten was gripping her seat belt with one hand, her mobile in the other.

"No, Paul!" she shouted. "Don't let the SOCOs start yet. I want to see the scene myself first. We'll be there—" She broke off and glanced at her colleague. "How long?"

The inspector was watching the car in front like a hawk as it tore along Upper Thames Street toward London Bridge. "Five minutes max," he said. "The uniformed boys have cordoned off Southwark Cathedral and the Borough Market."

"In five," Oaten concluded, letting the phone drop to her lap. "Jesus, Taff, this is getting way out of control."

Turner's expression was grim. "Hardy's people shouldn't have let Wells give them the slip. He's in this up to his elbows. What about the guy who was cut up in Greenwich? Could he be linked to the other killings?"

Oaten chewed her lip. "If he is, God knows how. I hope Hardy can find out, but I'm not too confident. Of course, it could be that the killer's trying to distract us." She looked out at the lights on the river—leisure boats full of people having a good time, tourists taking in the sights and sounds of "olde" London Town, seagulls swooping down to investigate bits of rubbish. Most people lived normal lives, unperturbed by the horrors in the newspapers. Why the hell wasn't she one of them? She knew the answer. Because she had a particular talent. She could spot a villain at long range. All her experience was telling her that Matt Wells wasn't dirty, but she couldn't be sure. The fact that she felt the unmistakable signs of physical attraction toward him wasn't helping.

"We'll see," she said noncommittally.

"Does the A.C. know you've been talking to Wells, guv?" her subordinate asked.

"Drop it, Taff," she ordered. "The less you know about that the better."

There was an uneasy silence in the car until Turner pulled up beside Paul Pavlou. The D.S. was standing at the eastern entrance to Borough Market.

"Good evening, guv, sir," he said. "It's over here."

Karen Oaten and the inspector followed him under a police line and down the sloping street. A crowd of onlookers had gathered, their necks straining as they tried to see what was in the large wheeled rubbish bin. A middle-aged man with a slack jaw was standing next to D.S. Simmons.

"What's Morry doing here?" Turner said under his breath.

"I reinstated him," Oaten said. "You were right. We need all the hands we can get."

"I don't suppose he'll be running to the press again after the strip you tore off him."

"No, neither do I. He paid the money he got over to the Police Benevolence Fund. Voluntarily, of course."

"'Evening, guv," Simmons said, his tie done up and his hair less chaotic than usual. "This is Alfred Andrews. He found the—" The sergeant inclined his head to the bin. "He saw the—"

"Oh, for God's sake," the chief inspector said, pulling on a pair of gloves and nodding to the SOCOs who were standing by. "Get a provisional statement, Taff."

They went to the bin, one photographer holding a videocam and another flashing away with a digital camera. As Oaten got closer, she saw what had attracted the cleaner's attention. Two hands, the fingers long and delicate, were protruding from the almost closed lid of the bin, as if someone had tried unsuccessfully to clamber out. Even more striking than the hands was what had been done to them. The ends of the digits were smeared by blackening blood, like those of a child who'd been playing with finger paints. When she leaned into the lights that had been set up, Oaten saw that all ten fingernails were missing, and the tissue beneath badly damaged. She took a deep breath. The bastard had pulled out the victim's fingernails, but she had a feeling that was just the start.

She took a step back and watched as the lid was lifted and propped up.

Behind her, a voice said, "Delightful."

She turned to meet the steady gaze of the pathologist Redrose.

Together they advanced to the rim of the rectangular steel structure. It must have been emptied recently as there wasn't much in it. Only a human body. Oaten told herself to get a grip. She found herself hoping like hell it wasn't someone close to Matt Wells. Could the White Devil really have got to one of them?

The naked victim was in a kneeling position, the forearms over the edge and the fair-haired head bent forward to touch the inside of the bin. The chief inspector tried to make out the features, but it was impossible.

"Let's push the body back," Redrose said to his assistants. Photographs were taken first. After they'd handled the torso carefully, the movement showing that rigor mortis hadn't set in yet, he looked downward. "Male," he said. "And young—under thirty, I'd say. My God. Lift me up." His assistants obliged. After a short examination, he signaled that he be lowered back down.

"Well?" Karen Oaten said, having taken in the gaping wounds to the face, throat and chest.

"This is preliminary, of course," the doctor said, "but it looks to me like the poor man's been savagely bitten. His nose is missing, as is a substantial section of the front of the neck. His nipples have also been bitten off."

Oaten peered back into the bin. "There isn't much blood in there. Obviously he was assaulted elsewhere."

"Yes. We'll have to get him out of here." Redrose looked round. "Ah, good, they've got the tent up. I'll be able to carry out a more detailed exam there."

"Want to have a guess at the cause of death?"

"Not really. But I'll say shock or loss of blood for the time being."

"Okay. Let me know if you find anything on the body or—"

"In its orifices." The medic gave her a tight smile. "I haven't much doubt it's your killer again."

Oaten went back to Turner. "What have you got?"

"Not much. The market had been closed for a couple of hours when he started his cleaning rounds. Mr. Andrews saw the bin being emptied around six-thirty, so the body was deposited after that. He didn't see anything happen around the bin, but he did notice a white van drive off at some stage. He isn't sure when." The Welshman shrugged. "He doesn't wear a watch."

"It should all be on film," the chief inspector said, pointing at the security cameras hanging from the eaves.

"I've already sent Pavlou off to get the tapes."

"Good. Any other witnesses?"

"Morry and a couple of the others are canvassing the crowd and the neighboring shops. Nothing yet." Turner shrugged. "You know what it's like in a busy street."

"Everyone minding their own business. We'll put an appeal for information out on the ten o'clock news. We may get lucky and find a passing driver who had a perfect view of the killers' faces."

"You're assuming it's the two of them again?"

"It would have been difficult for one person to get the body into the bin."

"Perhaps they had it wrapped in something that they took with them."

Oaten nodded. "Good thinking. But more interesting is why the hands were left out. It's like they wanted the body to be found quickly."

"Chief Inspector?"

Redrose was standing at the door of the white incident tent, a mask pushed down around his neck. There was something in his hand. As she got closer, taking rapid steps, Oaten saw that it was a small, clear plastic bag.

"Don't worry," he said. "It's been photographed. It was in his mouth."

Inside the tent, the victim lay stretched out on an open black body bag. He was a tall young man, she now realized. She wondered what connection he had to Wells, if there was one at all. She beckoned the SOCO team leader forward. The folded sheet of paper was removed and smoothed out, then inserted in an evidence bag. It was laser-printed.

"'Far be it from my thoughts to seek revenge,'" Oaten read.

"That *White Devil* play again?" Turner said from behind her.

"Probably. What's the lunatic saying now? That revenge isn't anything to do with this killing?"

"I have more," Redrose said proudly, holding out a clamp with a crumpled and stained piece of card in it. "Here, I can straighten it." He applied another clamp.

"Where was this?" the chief inspector asked.

"In his rectal passage."

"Jesus," Turner said with a scowl.

"Reginald Hampton," Oaten read. "Editorial assistant." She looked at her subordinate. "He worked for Sixth Sense Ltd. They're Matt Wells's publishers."

The inspector's expression grew even sterner. "I told you, guv. That guy's all wrong."

Karen Oaten returned his stare. "Maybe," she said, stepping out into the street.

The crowd had begun to thin, people dispersing to the pub to discuss the day's unexpected highpoint. They didn't yet know that the same killer and his accomplice had struck again, though they probably suspected it. The idea of the frenzy that would create in the media made the chief inspector feel almost as disgusted as the condition of the victim had.

Maybe she was getting soft, but she was going to catch the degenerates who did this.

No matter what it did to her.

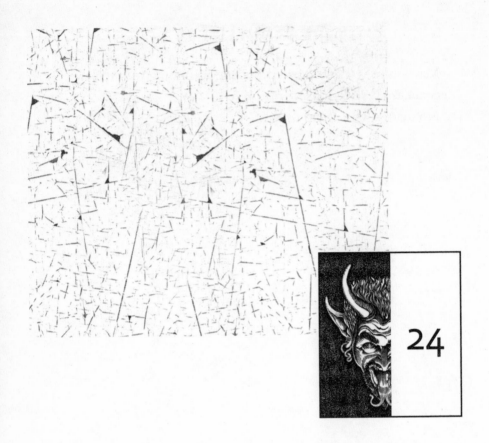

24

Rog finally cracked the British Airways entry codes. I watched in mounting panic as he went through the day's flights. My mother's name wasn't on any of them. I'd called her mobile number earlier, but it had been turned off. That was very unlike her. She'd taken a while to get used to modern technology, but now she was a great fan. As far as I knew, she never shut down her phone. As soon as Rog confirmed that she hadn't left Heathrow from BA in Terminal One, I ran outside and called Karen Oaten.

"I'm busy, Matt," she said wearily.

"My mother," I said, the words tumbling out. "I think the Devil may have got her."

"What? Why?"

I explained the situation.

"I don't know," she said, moving away from other people who were talking loudly. "I think he's been otherwise engaged."

"What?"

"Matt, do you know someone at your publishers called Reginald Hampton?"

I had a brief flash of the tall apprentice editor who'd taken me to Jeanie that morning and felt my stomach somersault. "Yes. What's happened to him?"

There was a pause. "I shouldn't be telling you this. It looks like the White Devil has killed him."

My knees went weak and I leaned against the side of the phone booth. "Oh, my God. But that's ridiculous. I only met Reggie for a couple of minutes this morning." I gulped down the bitter liquid that had risen up my throat. "How…how do you know it was the Devil?"

She was almost whispering. "He left one of his messages. Something about it being far from his thoughts to seek revenge."

I took a deep breath. "It's him, all right. Was Reggie…what was done to him?"

"Horrific things. I've told you enough, Matt. You really need to come in. I can't cover for you much longer." She paused. "What do you want me to do about your mother?"

I felt a wave of hopelessness crash over me. No doubt the modus operandi was tied to one of my books, making me even more of a hot suspect. Anyway, what could the police do? They hadn't been able to protect the innocent editorial assistant. "Nothing," I said. "This is all down to me and I have to sort it myself."

"Matt, at least give me your number!"

I prepared to hang up. "No."

"Hold on," she said urgently. "Your wife finally got in touch. Apparently she'd been kept late by some Japanese bankers. She was very upset, wanted to know where your daughter was…"

"I'll call her. Bye, Karen."

"Wait," she said, lowering her voice. "I shouldn't be telling you this, either, but maybe it'll help you find the animal before he gets to you and your daughter."

"What is it?"

"He won the lottery in 2001. Nine and a half million pounds. The thing is, he took the privacy option and hasn't been seen since. Presumably he's changed his name."

"What was his original name?"

She hesitated. "Leslie Dunn," she said, and then the line went dead.

The name made me shiver. Was this really the fiend who'd been tormenting me? Suddenly he felt closer, even though he obviously called himself something else now. I struggled to get a grip on myself.

I stayed at the phone and made a call to Caroline's mobile.

"Matt!" she screamed when I identified myself. "Where's Lucy? What the hell's going on? There's a policeman outside the front door and another one outside yours."

"Calm down," I said, realizing how inadequate that must have sounded. "What did the police tell you?"

"Some woman detective—Oates?"

"Oaten."

"Whatever. She said you were caught up in a murder investigation. You fucking idiot! What have you done? Where's Lucy?"

"She's safe. She's with…friends. Caroline, you'll have to trust me on this. It's for the best. She's in danger. We all are."

"Because of some lunacy of yours? What have you done? Got yourself involved with some stupid gangsters? Jesus, you really are pathetic."

I wasn't going to argue with her. "Caro, do what the police tell you and sit tight. Lucy's fine. I'll be in touch." I replaced the receiver, aware of the level of abuse that would be being cast in my direction.

Back inside the café, I called my mother's number again. I felt an explosion of relief when she answered.

"Fran, what happened? Why was your phone off?"

"Oh, I was tired, Matt. Had a sleep." She sounded a bit bewildered.

"Everything all right?"

"Yes, it is. Let me sleep again now, darling."

To my surprise, she hung up. And she'd called me "darling" again. Maybe she'd been overindulging in the local firewater, wherever she was.

I went back inside and pulled Rog off the BA system. "What do you know about the National Lottery?"

"Not a lot." He gave me a crooked grin. "I've heard that it's got one of the toughest antihacking systems of them all."

"Fancy trying to break in?"

The grin widened. "Do squirrels eat their nuts in winter?"

I gave him the name. Was the man who'd been called Leslie Dunn really the Devil? Suddenly I felt closer to him, even though I knew I probably wasn't. But if there was one person who could track him down in cyberspace, it was my friend the Dodger.

I watched him as his fingers danced across the keys and began to feel useless. I was allowing the situation to get away from me. What was needed was action. I decided to turn my old mobile on for a minute to see if I had any messages. That turned out to be a good move. There was a text from Andy Jackson. Can't stay in this shit-hole any longer. Getting out tonight. Call me, I read.

I shared the news with Rog as I turned off the phone.

"That means he can't be too badly hurt," he said, his eyes on the screen.

"Maybe. But you know Slash. He played most of one game with a broken arm, remember?"

"Nutter." He glanced at me. "Look, I won't be able to get far on this machine. I need something with more memory. Back home I've got—"

"—the White Devil potentially watching you."

"Oh, yeah. Where are we going to spend the night, then?"

It didn't take me long to come up with the answer. "At Peter Satterthwaite's."

Rog stopped typing and turned to me, his eyes wide. "Bonehead? You can't be serious."

"Oh, yes I can. Anyway, what are you complaining about? He'll have all the computers you need. Come on."

"Are you sure this is a good idea?" he said, clearing the screen.

"Have you got a better one? He's one person the Devil is unlikely to be watching."

Rog grinned. "Plus he's got a security system that Houdini couldn't get past."

"Exactly." I sent Andy a message telling him to meet us there and to turn off his phone. "Let's go."

I paid the guy at the till, giving him a tenner tip and asking him to forget we'd ever been there. He nodded and smiled knowingly. Out on the street, I hailed a cab and told him the destination I wanted.

On the way to Blackheath, I thought about what I was doing.

Was I out of my mind taking on the Devil? Reggie Hampton had already paid for the few words he'd exchanged with me. I told myself that Christian Fels would have died if I hadn't sent Andy up to Highgate, but that didn't make me feel much better. I'd taken all the steps I could to protect my people, but now the lunatic was selecting innocent victims.

The cabbie dropped us at the end of a gated street on the north side of the Heath. "Ponces," he muttered as he drove off. I didn't blame him. This was rich man's alley in spades.

The uniformed guy in the sentry-box eyed us up. "Can I help you?" he asked, his tone unwelcoming in the extreme.

"Yes," I said. "We're visiting Peter Satterthwaite."

"Wait a moment." He picked up his phone.

I'd decided against calling Bonehead in advance. He'd probably have told me where to stick my head. I was relying on his well-known curiosity to get us inside.

"Your names?" the guard asked.

"Matt Wells and Roger van Zandt."

He spoke them into the phone with painstaking care and no little distaste. No doubt most visitors to the place looked classier than we did. I was relieved to see disappointment in his expression.

"All right," the gorilla said, pressing a button. "It's the house at the end."

"We know that, pillock," Rog said under his breath. He might have spent his spare time making models like a geeky kid, but he had a hard streak. Now he wasn't playing league anymore, I wondered how he was using that up.

We walked down the wide street. The houses on either side were large and detached, a range of this year's BMWs and Mercedes in the driveways. The curtains were open in most rooms, the residents showing off their antique furniture and modern art works to one another. They didn't just rely on the goon at the gate for protection. There were alarm boxes on every front wall. Except Bonehead's. His system was on another level, in every sense.

The heavy black door opened as we walked up the drive.

"Well, blow my dick and send me to heaven," said the tall, thin figure silhouetted in the light. "I never expected you guys would have the nerve to show up here again."

"Hello, Boney," Rog said, keeping his distance.

"Dodger, Wellsy." Peter Satterthwaite was in his midforties. He'd made a fortune when he was young, selling cheap but reliable computers. He moved in exalted circles in the City, but he'd never lost his native Lancastrian accent. "What do you wankers want?"

I laughed. Bonehead had never been one for civility. He'd grown up on an estate in Skelmersdale, which had made him as tough as nails. He was also a homosexual at total ease with his sexuality. He'd shaved his head long before it became the fashion for every man embarrassed about losing his hair.

"I've managed to screw up massively," I said. "I really need your help."

He stared at me belligerently. "After what you guys did to me? You've got a bloody nerve." One of the few things that had kept him going as a kid had been his love for rugby league. He'd spent most of the cash he nicked or made from stolen goods on attending games at Wigan. After he made his millions, he invested in the South London Bison. Unfortunately some of our teammates didn't have it in them to take money from someone they referred to behind his back as "a nancy poof," so he was voted off the board after a year.

I shrugged. "You know that wasn't down to Rog and me."

"Is that right?" he said, doubt written all over his face. Then he looked at me inquisitively. "What is this trouble you've got yourself into?" I knew he wouldn't be able to resist asking.

"Can we come in?" I asked. "It's a bit chilly out here."

Bonehead thought about it and then led us inside. We'd been to the place before for a club dinner, but since then he'd added even more outrageous furniture and over-the-top paintings. In the spacious hall, there was a yellow velvet-covered chair with a back high enough to accommodate a giraffe. On the wall above was what I took to be a Lucien Freud original. No one else could have done the drooping breasts and floppy genitalia with such gusto.

"You on your own?" I said, as we followed him into a room furnished only with multicolored leather poufs.

"What's it to you?"

"Just asking."

"As a matter of fact, I am," he said, throwing us bottles of lager from a fridge concealed in a wooden cabinet. "So, dickheads, tell me why you're here."

I did that, not giving him all the details about the Devil, but enough to get him interested.

"Jesus, Wellsy," he said when I'd finished. "Are you sure this isn't the plot of your latest novel?"

"I'm sure, all right. Dave Cummings has taken my kid and his family into hiding. The police are doing their best to protect everyone else I know, but the bastard's way ahead of them."

"I hope you didn't tell them about me," Bonehead said, suddenly anxious.

I shook my head. Actually, I'd forgotten him—he'd never been a particularly close friend and, since the rupture at the Bison, we hadn't seen much of each other. Now I remembered that he kept a large stock of illegal substances in the house.

"Good," he said, emptying his beer and opening another. "What do you need?"

I glanced at Rog. "A high-powered computer?"

"No problem."

"A couple of beds for the night?"

Bonehead laughed. "I could put you both in a double."

"Piss off," said Rog, glaring at him.

"Oh, you'd rather share with me, would you, Dodger?"

"Thanks, Pete," I said, draining my beer. "I don't suppose you've got anything to eat?"

There was a buzz from a box on the wall by the door.

"That'll probably be Andy Jackson," I said as he walked over to it.

"Looks like you'll be three in the bed, then," Bonehead said with a wicked smile. "Let him in," he said to the gorilla at the gate.

"The computer?" Rog asked.

"Upstairs, second door on the right. The password's *Arse69*."

Rog departed, shaking his head.

"Right, Wellsy," Bonehead said, grinning wickedly as he tossed me another beer. "How are we going to catch this Devil of yours?"

I wasn't sure whether Peter Satterthwaite was up to nailing a multiple murderer, but he scared the hell out of me.

The White Devil was sitting in front of the bank of screens. There had been no sign of Matt Wells since the morning. He'd checked the tapes. The camera he'd planted above the street door showed a couple of men—obviously police—slumped in a

Rover outside. What had the writer been saying to the authorities? Was he hatching some scheme with that hard-faced blond bitch?

The Devil laughed. They could try their worst. He wasn't frightened of them.

After all, he and his partner had managed to dump a naked body in a rubbish bin in full view of people during the evening rush hour. It was all down to observation. Corky had watched the Borough Market at the end of many days' trading and he knew exactly when the cleaners came on duty. The white van looked no different from hundreds that the traders and their customers used every day for deliveries. They'd abandoned it in Streatham, after changing into ordinary casual clothes in the back and taking their overalls with them in holdalls. They'd split up immediately and he'd gone a roundabout route by bus to return home. His partner had done the same.

Picking up the fool from the publishers had been easy enough. He'd discovered who worked for Matt Wells's ex-editor by watching the building in the early evening. Jeanie Young-Burke often left work late, and in recent weeks she'd usually been accompanied by a tall young man with no chin. Matt Wells had obviously warned Young-Burke off as there had been no sign of her that night—the writer would pay dearly for that—but he hadn't thought to do the same for her assistant and current sex slave. When young Reginald had gone off for lunch with an author and some women from the publishers, the Devil had got him into the van by calling him, having obtained his mobile number from the helpful young woman on the switchboard, and telling him that Jeanie had a surprise for him in the street behind the restaurant. He fell for that immediately.

How he'd begged when they went to work on him. He

offered money—apparently his daddy was a merchant banker—he offered his mother's jewelry, he even offered a cottage in Wales. The Devil had laughed then bitten off his nose. His partner joined in, tearing the nipples off with relish. The Devil finished the upper-class fool off by sinking his teeth into his neck. The dentist who'd been paid handsomely to sharpen his canines had done a good job; he'd also agreed to delete the relevant records from his filing system—for an additional fee, of course. Not that it mattered. He'd used a false name.

The Devil got up and went to the extensive drinks cabinet. He poured himself a glass of neat Bombay gin and carefully tipped a single drop of Martini into it. It was time to celebrate. This was turning into even more fun than he'd thought it would be. Matt Wells was fighting back. He'd deactivated his mobile phone, thus rendering himself untraceable. He wasn't using his car with the bug the Devil had placed under the chassis. And he'd done what he thought was enough to protect his nearest and dearest. It would be fascinating to see what he did next. Would the writer have the nerve to come after him? If he did, it would bring things to an explosive climax.

One of his mobile phones rang.

"It's me." Corky was out of breath and sounded rattled, his motorbike engine also audible.

"What is it?"

"Trouble. Three guys in an Orion waiting in my street. They're about fifty yards behind me, stuck in traffic."

"Police?"

"Not sure. They looked harder than that."

"Villains?"

"Could be. But they remind me more of Jimmy Tanner." The engine revs rose. "Got to go." The connection was cut.

The Devil got his breathing under control. The Hereward had turned out to be a bad choice. Someone had passed on information, no doubt the fool Smail who had been cut apart. Could Corky have let something slip to him? No, he wasn't that stupid, even though he sometimes looked as if he'd been drinking again.

He dismissed the thought and laughed. Ever since he'd won the lottery he had felt invincible. That had been proof that the world was his—if someone like him could win nine and a half million quid of ordinary people's money, anything was possible. No, whoever was on Corky's tail wouldn't get to the Devil in time.

His next victim had only a few hours to live.

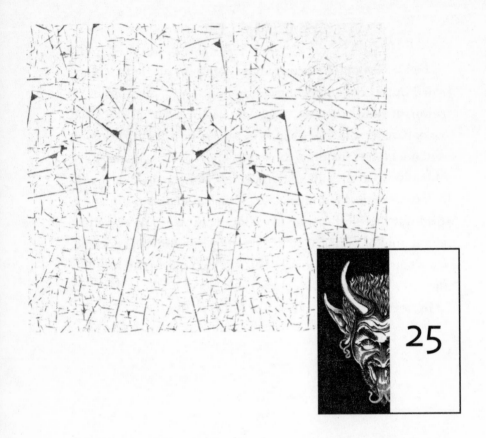

25

I woke up in the ridiculously comfortable bed that Bonehead had directed me to. He'd proudly announced that he had nine spare bedrooms, so Andy, Rog and I didn't have to share after all. That was a relief. I'd been on several rugby tours with those guys, and though they were my mates, I never wanted to spend another night in the same room as them. Rog snored like a walrus, while Andy suffered from nightmares that seemed to involve him taking on the Germans at Omaha Beach single-handed. One time when we'd had to share a double bed, he'd hit me so hard that I thought the bruise round my eye would never fade. It scared the shit out of the guy who was marking me on the pitch the next day, though.

I took a shower, dressed and went down the corridor to find the others.

"'Morning, Andy," I said, drawing gold-embroidered curtains and looking out over a huge expanse of lawn. "How are you feeling?" Last night he'd been a bit woozy from the drugs he'd been given in hospital.

"I'll survive, man," he said, touching the dressing on his upper chest gingerly. "God knows how, but the blade missed the lot— heart, lungs and major arteries. I've always been a lucky son of a bitch." His expression darkened. "I'm going to get that little fuck in the mask."

"No, you're not. He's mine."

He laughed. "Like you could take anyone out. You're a winger, a flyboy. Did you spend the night screwing Bonehead?"

I put my finger to my lips. All we needed now was to be turfed out of our temporary refuge. Andy wasn't really a homophobe and he hadn't voted against the Bisons' one-time benefactor, but he could scarcely be classed as one of nature's diplomats.

"Come on, then," he said, pulling on a dressing gown. "I'm starving." He headed off downstairs.

I put my head round Rog's door. He was at the computer, his bed undisturbed. "Jesus, have you been at it all night, Dodger?" I asked

He glanced round and nodded, his eyes ringed in black.

"Any luck?"

"Sort of."

I went over and looked at the heaps of printouts. The pages were covered in numbers. I picked one up. "Manston Invest- ment Bank, British Virgin Islands?"

"Yup." Rog pushed his chair back and stretched his arms. "I'll tell you something, Matt. This guy's bloody smart."

"You're tracing him via his financial transactions?"

He nodded. "Starting off was easy enough. Leslie Dunn paid the check that was made out to him into an ordinary account. I tracked it down pretty quickly." He thrust a printout at me. "You see the deposit? Nine and a half million, September 24, 2001."

"You hacked into the bank's system?"

He shrugged. "Piece of piss. The thing is, he soon started shifting his newfound wealth all over the place. Mainly offshore accounts. Now they really are tricky to get into, but…well, you know how good I am."

I slapped him on the back, harder than he expected.

"Ow, that hurt."

"Get on with it."

He turned back to the screen. "There are deposits in Jersey, in the British Virgin Islands, in various dodgy South American countries, even in Cuba." His head dropped. "The problem is, the accounts are all code-numbered in the databases. No names appear anywhere." He grunted. "So that people like me can't find out how much has been squirreled away by bent politicians, rock stars and supposedly honest businessmen like Boney."

"What about the National Lottery system?"

Rog bit his lip. "I've had several goes at that. It really is a bastard."

I squeezed his shoulder. "Come on, you need to eat and sleep. You can try again later."

We went downstairs and found Bonehead and Andy shouting abuse at each other across the kitchen table.

"—and my old dad knows more about bloody cooking than you ever will, you Yankee—"

"Boys, boys," I said, raising my arms. "We're all friends here, aren't we?"

"Oh yeah," Andy muttered.

I glared at him. "In case it's escaped your notice, you're eating this man's bacon and sausages. At least hold off putting the boot into him till you've finished breakfast."

Our host grinned combatively. "I don't need you to fight my battles for me, Matt."

"I know you don't," I said, sitting down next to him. "But I might be needing you to do that for *me*." I glanced at the other two. "We've got to get this guy before he tracks me down. If he gets me, then Lucy, Sara, Dave, his family, maybe you are next. Are you with me?"

The three of them took less than a second to respond positively, with a worrying amount of enthusiasm.

"What do you want me to do?" Bonehead asked, lighting a cigarette and blowing the smoke at Andy.

"Can you take a look at the financial trail Rog has found? You know about that kind of stuff. Maybe we can find the Devil's new name that way. That'll free Rog up to concentrate on the lottery archive."

"Why?" Andy asked, looking puzzled. "Won't the bastard's old name be the only one in there?"

"That's right," Rog said wearily. "But even people who request privacy are asked to give a forwarding address so that they can be passed messages. It's amazing how many friends and relatives lottery winners suddenly find they have."

"Yeah, but surely this guy would just have given a fake one," Andy said.

I shrugged. "Maybe. But you never know. He might have had a long-lost cousin he always fancied. It's worth a try, anyway." I looked at Rog. "After you've had a kip."

He shook his head and poured himself more coffee. "Nah,

I'm okay. I want to get this finished. To tell you the truth, I'm a bit worried about Dave."

Bonehead laughed. "You're worried about Psycho Cummings? You must be joking."

Rog grinned. "The poor bloke will be in hell. He's shacked up somewhere with Ginny the Sour and kids, not to mention Wellsy's Lucy, and he's not allowed to play with his demolition machines. He'll be going round the bend."

That provoked a round of laughter. Ginny Cummings had never been popular with the lads. Then again, I don't suppose Caroline had been, either. That was one reason why I hadn't been bothered about not introducing them to Sara. It was a rule of life that most people learned too late—whatever they might pretend, lovers and mates rarely get on.

I went out to the hall and called my mother on Pete's line. She had her phone turned off again. I needed to have a serious conversation with her about that. Before I could get back to the kitchen, my mobile rang.

"Matt, you all right?"

"Hiya, Dave. We were just talking about you."

"All good, I hope." He paused. "Who's we?"

I told him where I was and in whose company. "Christ, good thought, lad," Dave said. "Bonehead'll look after you. And he's got such a lovely complexion."

"Shut up, you idiot. How's Lucy?"

"Fine. She's been asking after you."

I didn't have it in me to talk to my little girl. I wanted to keep her as far from the Devil's filth as I could. "Tell her I've had to go on a trip, with her mother, and that we'll be back soon." I hated to get Lucy's hopes up about Caroline and me, but it was the only way I could think of to keep her happy.

"Um, Matt?"

It was obvious that Dave wanted something. "Spit it out."

"The thing is, I've got a big job on today. Old house in Orpington. It's worth a lot of money."

"Can't you get your guys to do it without you?" I asked, my heart sinking.

"Not really, mate. They're headless chickens." Dave was like a terrier—he always got his way in the end.

I thought about it. I couldn't see how the Devil could have tracked Dave. "All right," I said reluctantly. "But be careful you aren't followed back from the job, yeah? And remember not to use your old mobile again."

There was silence on the line.

"Tell me you haven't used it, Dave," I said, my heart well and truly sunk.

"Sorry, Matt. I had to check my messages. Some of them were to do with the job today."

I closed my eyes. What had he done? Could the Devil have been monitoring him out of London? On balance, it was pretty improbable. "All right," I said. "Just don't use it again. Take care."

"Aye, you too. What are you doing?"

"Need-to-know basis only, Dave," I said, and cut the connection.

Back in the kitchen, Andy and Bonehead were back at each other's throats, this time about the relative merits of gridiron and rugby league.

"Have you eaten enough, Slash?" I demanded. "Only, if you don't mind, I'd quite like to get moving."

Andy's face immediately took on a serious look. "Okay, man. What are we going to do?"

"Are you up to this?" I said, peering at his chest.

"Sure I am. Maybe I should change my dressing, though. The nice nurse with the big jugs told me that cleanliness was next to—"

"You'll find a full medical kit in the bathroom off my bedroom," Pete interjected.

Andy got up from the table. "Cream for hemorrhoids and stuff like that?"

Bonehead managed to restrain himself. "Where are you going?" he asked me.

"It's probably better if neither of you know," I said, helping myself to the single remaining sausage. "You've got my new mobile number, Rog. Ring me on that if you find anything hot."

They both looked at me doubtfully, and then nodded.

"Here," Pete said, tossing me a key. "You'll see the Grand Cherokee at the side of the house. If you put so much as a scratch on it, I'll break your legs."

"You and whose army?"

He raised his middle finger.

I left them at the table, Rog pouring himself yet more coffee. If we hadn't been up against a murderous bastard like the Devil, I'd almost have enjoyed the camaraderie that had been largely missing from my life since I stopped playing league. As it was, I just felt scared that I'd involved my mates in something they'd probably live to regret. If they lived.

I met Andy in the hall. He'd obviously raided Bonehead's wardrobe, having kitted himself out in a red-white-and-blue sweater. It suited him nationally but not stylistically, though I didn't bother pointing that out.

"Neat wheels," he said as we got into the big Jeep. "Shame about the color." Bonehead had chosen a seriously vile shade of puce.

I drove to the gate and waited for another sour-faced goon to raise it for us.

"So, are you going to tell me where we're going?" Andy said, holding the seat belt off his injured chest.

"Okay. We're going to university."

"Come again?" Andy was a great guy, but he'd only been at a catering school and he never read anything except the tabloid with the most tits and bums. "What good will I be to you at that kind of place?"

"Wait and see, big man," I said, directing the Jeep toward the city center. I hoped Pete had paid his congestion charge because I was planning on parking at Waterloo.

When we got there, Andy grimaced as he stood up.

"Are you in pain?" I asked as we headed out of the multi-storey.

"Nothing a few beers won't sort."

"Forget it," I said sternly. "You're off the booze till I say otherwise."

We walked toward the bridge. I knew exactly where I was going. I'd been there before. King's College London had a building on the south side of the river. A seminar room on the third floor had been the scene of one of my worst humiliations as a writer.

We walked through crowds of students. It looked like we were in luck. A lecture had obviously just ended. After the last young man emerged, the woman I wanted to speak to followed. She had the same frizzy auburn hair and loose garments that I remembered.

"Dr. Everhead," I said, trying to sound less nervous than I was. This woman had made me squirm in front of rows of people. She was also a world authority on Jacobean tragedy. I wanted to pick her brains, as well as to warn her about the Devil.

The lecturer's jaw dropped. Her face went whiter than a wedding dress. For a moment I thought she was going to faint, an unlikely reaction from a battle-hardened feminist. Then she turned and headed at speed for the stairs. I managed to dart in front of her.

"Don't worry, I'm not going to lay into you. You were perfectly entitled to attack my books."

That didn't seem to comfort her much. She was looking anxiously to either side of me. Fortunately the corridor was empty, apart from Andy. His bulk wouldn't have been particularly reassuring to her.

"Matt Stone," she said, her voice surprisingly faint. "What…what are you doing here?"

"I'd like to talk to you."

She looked at her watch. "I have a lecture in…oh, all right. My office is round here." She walked away, looking over her shoulder. "Who's your friend?"

I introduced Andy. He gave her a wide grin, which didn't impress her. It had always been clear that Lizzie Everhead preferred women, both as crime writers and as human beings. She ushered us into a small office that was crammed with books and papers, and then stood by the open door. I could see that she was still nervous.

"I…I've been talking to the police," she said, folding her arms defensively.

"Oh, yes?" I wasn't sure how to take that.

"A Detective Chief Inspector Oaten."

"Karen. I know her."

That seemed to surprise her. "Do you? She's been consulting me about those awful murders."

Now I got it. Oaten must have been asking her about the references to *The White Devil*. "The Webster quotations?"

The academic's eyes sprang wide open. "You know about those?"

I nodded. "Karen Oaten's been talking to me, too."

Lizzie Everhead looked down the corridor, the tension in her face easing when she heard voices outside. She turned back to us. "Put that down, please," she said to Andy, who had picked up a dark-colored wooden object.

"What is it?" he asked.

She raised her eyes to the ceiling. "If you must know, it's a seventeenth-century dildo."

I glared at Andy to head off the inevitable wisecrack, and then looked back at her. "So you know that the killer's been copying murders in my novels?"

She nodded, her expression anxious again. "Have you…have you any idea why?"

I shrugged. "I was going to ask you that."

Lizzie Everhead looked puzzled. "Me? Why should I be able to give an opinion?"

"You're an expert on both Webster and crime fiction," I said, smiling to put her at ease. "Even though you don't think much of mine."

"Neither did Alexander Drys," she said sharply. "And look what happened to him."

"Were you a friend of his?"

She shook her head. "Don't be ridiculous. He was a terrible bigot. But he didn't deserve to die that way."

"Of course he didn't."

"Exactly what is it that you want from me?" she said, a mixture of irritation and curiosity in her voice.

"Do you honestly think I'm involved in these murders?"

She looked at me dubiously. "I…I don't know. I suppose not."

"There's a vote of confidence for you, man," Andy said ironically.

I tried to ignore him. "Dr. Everhead, I really need your help. Can you see any pattern in the quotations?"

She thought about that and then shook her head. "Apart from the obvious one of revenge, no. I take it you didn't know the first three victims."

"'Course he didn't, lady," Andy said, stepping forward.

Lizzie Everhead dodged him and moved out into the corridor. "I think you'd better leave now," she said firmly.

She obviously didn't have anything more to say. We headed out. As I passed her, I said, "I don't want to scare you, but D.C.I. Oaten's been organizing protection for people who might be targets. Maybe you should ask her about that."

I could tell Lizzie Everhead was frightened, but she was trying not to show it. "I'm in frequent touch with New Scotland Yard," she said. "Goodbye."

"Well, thanks a lot," I said to Andy as we went down the stairs. "That was a massive success."

"Aw, come on, man. She needed shaking up a bit. In fact, she obviously needed—"

"That's enough, you moron." It had just occurred to me that Karen Oaten might be very interested to hear that I'd paid Lizzie Everhead a visit.

I had the distinct feeling that the academic was on the line to her right now.

John Turner was sitting in D.C.I. Oaten's office, ticking off the notes that he had made. "The CCTV images from Borough Market aren't much help," he said. "They show a pair of men of medium height in overalls with caps pulled low over their faces. It's pretty obvious they knew where the cameras were. It's impossible to distinguish their features. It looks like one had a mustache, but you know how blurred those pictures are. They got out of a white van, registration P692 MDG, and carried a large object in dark-colored wrapping to the bin. Unfortunately, the open lid obscured what they did then."

"But they were obviously removing the wrapping and arranging the body," Karen Oaten said. "They then went back to the van with the wrapping and drove off."

Turner nodded. "And the van was found in a back street in Streatham at 10:35 p.m. The SOCOs haven't found a single usable print on it."

"No witnesses, of course."

The inspector shook his head. "What about the autopsy, guv?"

Oaten picked up a gray file. "Redrose found that the bites to the face and neck were made by a person whose canine teeth appear to have been sharpened."

"What?"

"And that the nipples were bitten off by a different individual, someone with normal teeth."

"Dental records are no use to us."

"Not until we have someone in custody to check the bites against." The chief inspector looked out of the window. Dark clouds were blotting out the sun.

"What about the quotation?" Turner asked.

"I spoke to Lizzie Everhead last night. She didn't have much to say, only that it suggests the victim wasn't so closely linked to the general pattern of revenge."

"What reason would these lunatics have to take revenge on a twenty-six-year-old publisher's assistant, anyway?" the Welshman demanded in frustration. "All the friends and colleagues we've spoken to said that he was a decent guy with no vices and no dodgy friends."

Oaten grunted. "No vices apart from screwing his boss."

"His boss who conveniently disappeared yesterday."

"Calm down, John. She's not involved in this. Matt Wells told her to lie low."

"Yes, Matt Wells," the inspector said, standing up. "Everything seems to lead back to him. The attachments say '*I severed her arm*,' '*I cut off his head*' and so on. That means it's him, surely."

Oaten stared at him. She didn't think he was right. She didn't know much about novels, but she reckoned that writing one in the voice of a killer didn't mean the author was automatically one him- or herself. Besides, there was a charm about Wells that she was pretty sure wasn't an act. Still, the fact remained that Matt had to be brought in. But he was smart. He'd been keeping his head down. What if Taff was right? What if Matt Wells really was the Devil and he was taking the piss out of her? All her instincts told her that he wasn't a callous killer, but his involvement with the murders was undeniable.

"What about the MO?" Turner asked.

"There was a mutilated body found in a garbage container in Matt Stone's *Tirana Blues*," the D.C.I. said, avoiding the Welshman's gaze.

The phone on her desk rang.

"Oaten." She listened, her stomach tightening like a vice. "What? Oh, no! Where? We're on our way."

"What is it, guv?" Turner asked as she headed for the door.

"Lizzie Everhead," she said, her face pale and her expression grim. "She's been found dead in her office. Apparently it's a real mess."

They passed quickly through the main office, each shouting orders to subordinates.

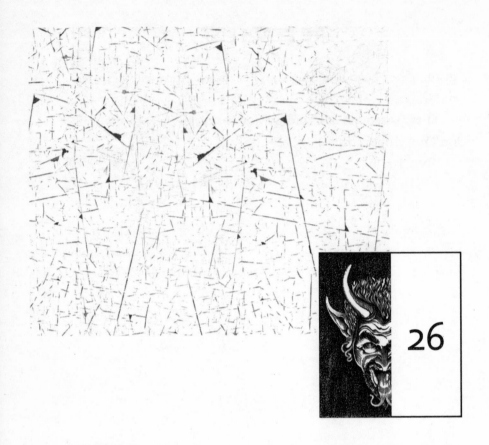

26

"Now what?" Andy said as I drove the Jeep out of the car park.

"I've got some calls to make." I spotted a payphone on Waterloo Road and pulled in.

The first person I rang was my mother. Her phone was still turned off. I felt stirrings of major concern. She'd sounded different both times I'd talked to her, and it wasn't like her to forget to turn her phone on. But what could I do? Rog was busy enough tracking down the Devil. I had to assume she'd either got on a BA flight from Terminal 4 or had broken the habit of a lifetime and used another airline.

I called Sara. Again, it took her a long time to answer.

"Hi," I said. "Are you all right?"

"Sure," she replied. "You?"

"Surviving."

"I see there was another murder last night."

"You're not covering it, are you?"

"No, Jeremy's having the time of his life, the ghoul."

I looked round as a police car raced up the street, its lights flashing and its siren wailing. "Is everything okay at your place?"

"Yeah. Apart from the neighbors asking what the copper was doing outside. I told them I was involved in a pedophilia case. That shut the nosy bastards up. Look, Matt, I've got to go. Will I see you later?"

"I doubt it. It's better if I keep clear of my known haunts."

"Oh, well, keep in touch." She cut the connection before I could tell her I loved her.

I took a deep breath and rang Caroline's number. Another police car went past at high speed. I had to shout to make myself heard.

"Where is she?" My ex-wife's voice was as near to a scream as she could allow herself in the office. "You've no right to keep Lucy from me."

"Lucy's safe," I said. "Are *you* all right?"

Stupid question.

"Of course I'm not all right. I've got a policeman at the door, my ex-husband has abducted my child and the CEO just called an unscheduled meeting."

"I'll take that as yes, then," I said, ringing off. I had enough on my plate without Caroline twisting the knife.

"That looked like fun," Andy said as I got back into the Jeep.

I scowled at him and drove off.

"Let me guess," he said, unabashed. "We're going back to Bonehead's."

"Wrong. We're going to the supermarket first. You're cooking that mixed grill you're always boasting about for lunch."

"Now you're talking," Andy said, his hands on his belly. "I was beginning to feel a bit hungry."

As I drove past the Elephant and Castle, I saw an ambulance coming toward us with its lights flashing.

Something bad had obviously just happened at Waterloo.

Oaten and Turner dipped under the cordon outside the university building by Waterloo Bridge. There were weeping students standing in groups, their arms round each other as they waited to be interviewed. Paul Pavlou and Morry Simmons were talking to some of them. Despite the university authorities' reluctance, the entire place had been evacuated so that it could be searched from top to bottom. One call from the commissioner to the vice chancellor had sufficed.

The SOCOs were standing by on the third floor. In front of them stood Dr Redrose, already kitted out in coveralls.

"We must stop meeting like this, Chief Inspector," he said with an uneven smile.

"I'm not in the mood for humor," Oaten replied, taking a set of coveralls from a SOCO. After she'd put on bootees and gloves and pulled the hood over her hair, she went through the partially open door, the photographers at her shoulder. She went over to the window. It was on the west side of the building, looking down over the relentless bridge traffic. One lane on the nearside had been closed by the police vehicles. She steeled herself to take in what had been done to Lizzie Everhead.

"My word," Redrose said from her side. That counted as a display of emotion from him. "It would appear the victim has been...has been nailed to her desk." He got down on his knees and inspected the underside of the piece of furniture. "The nails must be at least six inches long. The ends have been bent to prevent the poor woman pulling away."

"It looks like a chisel has been driven into the base of her skull," Oaten said, examining the black plastic handle and the base of the blade that was surrounded by the academic's tousled hair.

"Quite," said the pathologist, back on his feet. He looked more closely. "The chisel in question has a particularly long blade. The end of it is embedded in the desk."

Karen Oaten was taking deep breaths. "That...that would have required considerable strength."

Redrose bent nearer. "Not necessarily. The handle of the tool has been struck by a blunt instrument—I'd guess, the hammer that was used to drive the nails home."

The chief inspector cursed herself for her inattention. She'd known the dead woman and her gruesome end was hard to take. "There's a fair amount of blood from the wounds in her hands," she said quietly.

The pathologist nodded. "I'm afraid she was alive when the nails pierced them. She was kept alive long enough for her to suffer terrible pain."

"Christ, what a maniac. Any sign of a message?"

"Not at first glance," Redrose said, leaning in. "She appears to be fully clothed. I'll have to get her on the mortuary table to explore her...well, you know what I mean."

The chief inspector squatted down. "There's something under her left hand."

"You're right. I can see the edge of a small plastic bag. It doesn't appear to be perforated by the nail. I think we can remove it."

Karen Oaten watched as photographs were taken and then the

chief SOCO eased the bag out using tweezers. "I need to see the contents now," she said.

More photos were taken, then the bag was opened and the folded paper inside removed.

The SOCO opened it out. As on previous occasions, the words were in laser print. They read, "My tragedy must have some idle mirth in't." But this time there was more. "Now your expert is gone, I'll help you. *The White Devil,* act 4, scene 1, line 118. Ha-ha."

Oaten felt herself consumed by cold fury. She would not be mocked by a villain, especially not by one who had just killed someone she'd liked. Again, guilt struck her like a blow to the heart. She should have arranged for Lizzie Everhead to be protected. It had never occurred to her that the Devil would take out someone peripheral to the investigation. After Reginald Hampton's murder, how could she have been so stupid?

"Guv?" John Turner was at her shoulder. "Are you all right?" He took her arm and led her out into the corridor. "Better let the doc and the SOCOs do their jobs now, eh?" He took out a paper handkerchief and handed it to her. She turned to the wall and hurriedly dabbed her eyes.

"How did no one hear the banging as he hammered in the nails?" she said angrily.

"Apparently there have been workmen in all week," the inspector said, stepping closer. "Listen to this. I've had a quick look at the CCTV tape from a camera in the entrance hall." He paused to make sure she was paying attention. "Guv, Matt Wells was here this morning between 11:04 and 11:17." He glanced at his notebook. "The body was found at 11:27 by two of her students."

Oaten felt her eyes open wide. "Matt Wells? He was here?"

"Yes. With that guy Andrew Jackson, the one who was injured at the Fels place yesterday. Apparently he discharged himself from the hospital last night."

The chief inspector was struggling to take it in. Matt Wells. Could it have been Wells who'd nailed poor Lizzie to her desk? Or had it been the heavily built American? There was something wrong here, she felt that immediately. Yes, that was it. The two figures caught by the cameras at Dr. Keane's and at the Borough Market were of medium height. Both Wells and the American were bigger than that, the latter substantially so. Did that mean there were four killers out there? She clenched her fists and twitched her head. This needed careful thought. But in the meantime, it was indisputable that Matt Wells had been here this morning. Why?

"We've got to pick him up," Turner said. "I'll give the order. Will you tell the media?"

Oaten nodded slowly. She'd cut the novelist far too much slack. It was time she pulled him in. If her superiors found out about the contacts she'd had with him, she'd be finished.

But if he was the one who'd murdered Lizzie Everhead, she'd tear him apart with her own hands—and to hell with her career.

We found Peter Satterthwaite and Rog sitting in the former's study. He hadn't shown us it last night. It was large and furnished with leather office chairs and several wide desks, all with computers on them.

"Shit, Boney," Andy said, his arms full with bags of meat, "why'd'you need so many computers?"

"I sometimes bring my staff here," Pete said. "You know, Andy? Work. Remember what that is?"

"Go screw yourself," the American said, grinning. "I'm about to cook your lunch. Where's your grill?"

"Out the back, in the first shed." Bonehead waved me over. "Here, look at this, Matt. I've found out all sorts of interesting stuff about your Devil."

He waved a thick sheaf of printouts at me. I peered at one and could make absolutely nothing of it. "Explain, please."

He grinned. "You can't even understand the simplest bank details? No wonder you're so poor. All right, here's the simpleton's version. This guy is either very smart or he's got some very smart advisers."

"Or both."

"True. The bottom line is that over the last four years he's increased the value of his investments to just under thirty-three million U.S. dollars."

"Bloody hell. How did he manage that?"

"Do you really want to know?"

I raised my hands. "No. Has he broken any laws?"

"Theoretically not." Bonehead gave a toothy smile. "Well, no more than I have. You've got to understand, Matt—when you've got a decent wedge, it's dead easy to make it bigger. All it takes is a bit of nerve—"

"I think we can assume the Devil's got that in lorry-loads."

"And the right advice."

"Ditto." I straightened up. "So he's got plenty of cash to spend on surveillance equipment, vehicles, sidekicks, whatever?"

"Definitely." Pete held out another heap of paper. "He's withdrawn more than three million quid from various U.K. accounts over the past twelve months."

I felt a quiver of excitement. "You've hacked into banks in this country? So you must have his account details. His name and address."

Bonehead grimaced. "Sorry, mate. The kind of bank he deals

with has levels of security that your average commercial outfit doesn't bother with. All I've got is another list of numbers."

"No way of getting more than that?"

He raised his shoulders. "I'm talking to a guy I know. He's even more of a computer whiz kid than the Dodger." He laughed as Rog flashed him V-signs with both hands. "He's calling me back before the end of the day."

I went over to the other operating computer. "Any luck with the National Lottery?"

Rog's chin jutted forward. "Sort of."

"Which means?"

"Well, I'm almost in," he said, his fingers still moving over the keys. "But I reckon there's a time limit. I might get blown out when I log on because I'll need some time to orientate myself. If that happens, I won't be able to get back in. Don't worry, I can get round it. I'm almost there."

I squeezed his arm. I was touched by how much my friends were doing for me. I hoped I'd have done the same for them, but I was always more of a loner. Most writers were, as were most rugby wingers, league and union. It wasn't a characteristic I was particularly proud of.

I rang Dave. As usual, there was a deafening sound of machinery when he answered.

"Hallo, lad," he said, cutting the revs. "What's up?"

"Nothing much. Are you okay?"

"Champion. The roof'll be coming down any minute."

"I'm very happy for you. Dave, send me a text message before you leave in case I need you."

"Right you are. Cheers."

I went out to the back terrace. Andy was standing there engulfed in smoke.

"Oh, man," he said, "this charcoal's sodden. Still, nothing can resist the flaming hands of Aaaandrew Jaaaackson."

"That'll be right." I looked at the array of raw food he'd laid out on a table. Steaks, chops, sausages, corn on the cob.

"Something's missing," he said.

"Fifty other guests?" I suggested.

"No, you asshole. The beer."

"Uh-uh, no booze till we catch the—"

"Matt!" Bonehead's voice was loud and urgent. "Get in here now!"

I gave Andy a puzzled look and ran back to the study. I found Peter and Rog staring at the TV screen.

"I just heard the headlines," Bonehead said. "There's been another murder. At Waterloo."

I felt the hairs on my neck rise. Jesus. The police cars and the ambulance I'd seen. They must have been heading there.

"This is it," Rog said.

The newsreader's heavily made-up face was somber. "We're getting reports of a murder near Waterloo Station," she said. "Over to our correspondent at the scene, Roy Meltcher."

I watched as a man in an anorak spoke to camera. Behind him was a police cordon and a crowd of people. I immediately recognized the building. It was the university block that Andy and I had visited. I began to get a very bad feeling.

"Yes, Fay, you join me outside King's College London's facility just south of Waterloo Bridge. Shortly before noon today, students discovered the body of a female lecturer on the third floor. Police are not releasing the woman's name, but I can reveal that she was in the English Literature department."

Jesus.

The anchor cut in. "Roy, I gather there are fears that this is the latest in the series of murders that some are attributing to the so-called New Ripper."

The reporter was nodding. "Yes, Fay, that is the indication we're getting. Details of the murder are not being given yet, but I understand that there are links to the other killings. In a sensational development, Detective Chief Inspector Karen Oaten of the VCCT made this statement."

The picture cut to what was clearly a lecture room.

Karen was standing next to the stern Welshman. "We are very anxious to talk to two men who were seen in the building between 11:00 and 11:30 this morning," she said.

I froze as photographs of me and Andy came up on the screen. Mine was from a book jacket, while my friend's had obviously been taken in the hospital yesterday.

"They are Matthew John Wells, age thirty-eight, a crime novelist who uses the name Matt Stone, and Andrew Krieger Jackson, an American age thirty-seven. Mr. Wells lives in Herne Hill, while Mr. Jackson's home is in Catford, South London. Anyone who has seen either man in the last twenty-four hours should call this number—" she read it out "—or contact their local police station. All information will be treated with the strictest confidentiality." Karen Oaten was looking even more determined than I'd seen her before. "This is a particularly horrible crime. It is essential that members of the public do not approach these men. The likelihood is that they are highly dangerous."

The reporter was back on the screen. "So there you are, Fay. Although the police are refusing to confirm that Mr. Wells and Mr. Jackson can be linked to the earlier murders, it seems reasonable to draw that conclusion." He signed off.

"Shit," I said as Rog turned down the volume. I glanced at him and Bonehead. "Who's going to tell Slash?"

Rog got up and left the room.

"It's bollocks, isn't it, Matt?" Peter said, his eyes locked on mine. "This is your chance to be totally straight with me."

"It's bollocks," I repeated slowly, my body numb.

He slapped me on the back. "I knew it was. Now, wake up. We've got to catch this arsehole before the cops get to you."

Rog came back with Andy, who looked dazed.

"What is this?" he asked.

"This is us being framed by the Devil," I said. "He must have been on our tail."

"How could he have been?" Bonehead said. "No one knows you're here. Keep your wits about you, mate."

He was right. The Devil was the ultimate planner. He must have targeted Lizzie Everhead earlier—I was sure she was the victim—and we'd been unlucky enough to walk in a few minutes before him and get picked up by the CCTV.

"All right, what do we do?" Andy said, looking round at all three of us. "I'll turn myself in if that'll buy you time, Matt."

I could have wept, but I knew that wouldn't have impressed any of them.

"Thanks, mate, but there's no point in doing that. It's me they want, not you." I glanced at Roger. "Are you into the lottery site?"

"Any minute now."

"Well, go for it. In the meantime, I'm going to check my e-mails. I've got a feeling the bastard will have been in touch." Before I sat down in front of a screen, I ran my eyes round them. "Peter, Rog, you guys can walk away from this thing right now. So can you, Andy. I'm prepared to find this piece of shit on my own."

They all spoke together, a mixture of "Forget it," "No

chance" and "Get outta here," the last from Andy. Again, I was touched, but I made sure I didn't show it. Ex-rugby league players only cry when they've had a bellyful of ale.

"Whoah!" Andy yelled, peering at the cloud of smoke outside. "My ribs!" He departed at speed.

"Thanks, guys," I said quietly, logging on to my new e-mail identity. As I thought, the Devil had sent what he always referred to as notes. They didn't make for pleasant reading. The bastard had obviously sent them before he'd seen the news, so at least I was spared mockery from him about that. But that was small comfort. He'd gone back to mimicking murders in my books. In *Tirana Blues,* the first Zog novel, an Albanian politician is found nailed to the table with a chisel rammed into the base of his skull to sever his spinal cord. Jesus. Oaten would be even more convinced I was guilty when she discovered that similarity. She already knew the dead woman had attacked my work, so there was motive—if you lived in the crazy world of the Devil.

It was time I accepted that I was a fellow inhabitant of his underworld.

The only way to catch him was to be as pitiless as he was.

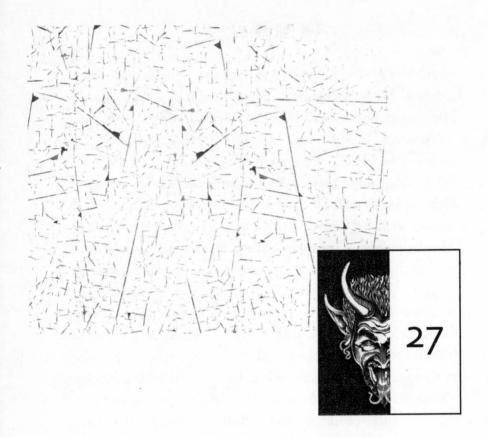

27

The White Devil was sitting in front of the bank of screens in his penthouse overlooking the Thames. Only one of the screens was in operation. It showed a dimly lit enclosed space with no furniture apart from an old armchair that was losing its stuffing. On it was a figure bound around the calves and chest, the head covered by a sack with a hole cut in it to aid the passage of air. There was no way the Devil wanted this captive to expire yet. That would be a tragedy of Jacobean proportions.

He smiled. The stench in the room would be almost unbearable by now, the urine and sweat joining with the reek of the rotting building. Originally, he hadn't intended going anywhere near the place again. The captive would eventually die of thirst.

Not a pleasant death, but there were worse ones. Matt Wells was a wanted man now, so he'd be prepared to take risks. That called for original thinking and flexibility. The Devil was a past master at those.

He thought back to the events of the morning. It had been a classic example of how good planning was rewarded by an unexpected bonus. He had always planned to carry out this murder on his own. It would be broad daylight and going with his partner was too risky. Besides, he wanted to deal with the woman on his own. He'd been in the audience when Dr. Lizzie Everhead had taken Matt Stone's novels to pieces in what was a very public humiliation. To be fair to Matt, he took it in good part, making jokes at his own expense and appearing to forgive the good doctor for what was an overscholarly attack on fiction for the mass market. Then again, as the novelist once said himself, if crime fiction wanted to be taken seriously, its writers had to expect to be judged by the same standards applied to literary fiction. Dream on, my friend, the Devil thought. The only people taking you seriously from now on will be members of the Metropolitan Police, the media and the judiciary.

Getting into the building had been easy. He'd been inside numerous times over the past three months, wearing overalls and cap, and using a fake but convincing maintenance man's pass. He'd spotted the absence of cameras beyond the entrance hall, and he'd also worked out the doctor's timetable. He knew exactly when she was on her own in her office. But how was he to know that Matt was going to turn up with his muscular friend a few minutes before him? It had been a close call—he'd seen them leave—but it had led to Matt being put solidly in the frame for the murder. That really was funny. Originally he hadn't intended using the modus operandi from the Zog novel, but since the writer had been messing him around, he wanted to pay him back. An anonymous phone call to the Yard later on would make sure the bitch Oaten had yet more to hold against Matt.

Moving over to the penthouse's tall windows, he looked out at the boats on the Thames. The worm of doubt he had felt about the murder at the Hereward and the men on Corky's tail was growing. His accomplice was continuing to keep ahead of the Orion, his well-developed sense of self-preservation functioning well. But for how long?

The White Devil shook his head and told himself to ignore Corky. It wasn't as if he knew where to find the Devil. No, he'd already brought his plans forward and the end was in sight. Soon, he'd be far away where he could never be found. With his partner.

In the meantime, he had work to do.

People to pick up.

Skin to pierce.

And blood to spill.

"I'm in, Matt!" Rog shouted.

Peter Satterthwaite and I dashed over to the desk and watched as he navigated his way skillfully around the lottery site. In a few seconds he'd accessed the list of big winners and typed in the date of the Devil's win. A couple more clicks and we had it.

Leslie Dunn—Flat 12, Vestine Building, Bermondsey Wall East, London SE16 OPY.

"You did it!" I shouted, grabbing Rog's shoulders.

"Just a second," he said, hammering away at the keyboard. "I'm deleting my identity so there's no way they can trace me. Done."

He turned round and smiled. "So, let's go and nail the bastard." He got up and went to the door. "Andy! Get in here. We need you."

I sat them all down to think things through. "Look, if the Devil really is in this flat in Bermondsey, we need to be pretty careful about going in mob-handed. He's cunning enough to have taken precautions."

"You and Andy can't go anywhere," Bonehead pointed out. "Your faces will be all over the evening paper."

He was right, but he could also provide a solution. "Aren't you into fancy dress?" I asked.

Andy guffawed. "Yeah, I remember when you turned up at the end-of-season dinner wearing a grass skirt."

Pete gave him an aloof stare. "I'll have you know that was a genuine South Seas fashion item." He laughed and turned to me. "As it happens, I have got a wardrobe full of outlandish gear. You'd look great as a Morris dancer, Matt, though maybe you'd attract a bit too much attention. As for you, Andy, I've got this great pair of leather trousers with the arse cut away."

The American looked appalled. "You must be joking, man."

I raised a hand. "All right, sober up. Yeah, we can disguise ourselves. The question is, how many of us go?"

"All of us," the three of them said in unison.

I shook my head. "It's too risky. What if he's got the place booby-trapped? I wouldn't put it past him."

"Why don't we get Dave to check it out?" Rog asked. "He's a demolition expert, after all."

I thought about it. "No, Dave needs to get back to Lucy and his family."

"So," Bonehead said, "who goes?"

"Since when were you part of this elite squad?" Andy asked.

The multimillionaire smiled at him. "Since you guys invited yourselves here, Slash."

"Fair enough," I said. "We need all the help we can get. But we also need someone here to check out any leads we come up with. That means someone who can handle a computer." I looked at Rog. "And that means you, mate." His disappointment was obvious. "Don't worry, you'll get your chance."

"I suppose I'd better stay here, as well," Bonehead said. "In case there's more financial stuff to chase up. You never know, I might find the identity he's using now."

I nodded, happy he'd worked that out before I had to tell him. "Looks like it's you and me again, Andy," I said. "Boney, show us your disguises."

He led us upstairs. "You do realize that the police might have found out about this place you're going to and put surveillance on it?"

I nodded. "It has occurred to me. But they've been busy with the killings. Maybe they haven't been into the lottery archive yet."

Half an hour later we left the house, this time driving our host's brand-new pale blue BMW 6 Series coupé in case the Jeep had been picked up on CCTV at Waterloo. I was wearing a shoulder-length blond wig and a blue boiler suit, while Andy had a hard hat, a fake Zapata mustache and an anorak. I suppose we might have been taken as genuine workmen. By a blind man.

I parked a couple of hundred yards away from the Vestine Building. We walked along the cobbled streets to what turned out to be a converted warehouse. There was a waist-high wall around it, the enclosed parking area filled with luxury cars. There wasn't any sign of coppers on surveillance, but that didn't mean they hadn't hidden themselves. I took a deep breath and tried to slow my breathing.

"Right," Andy said in a low voice, putting down his toolbox. "What's the plan?"

"We haven't got much choice. We'll have to go in the main entrance." We pulled on gloves, then I led him through the pedestrian gate. There was a panel covered in numbers by the heavy door. "We aren't going to press number 12," I said, as he raised his hand. "This usually works in my books." I pressed several other numbers. When a voice came through the panel, I said "Electricity."

There was a buzz and the door opened.

A woman holding a howling child poked her head out from a door as we headed for the stairs. "Problem on the second floor," I said, flashing my bank card—fortunately it had a photo on it. She nodded without interest and disappeared. We raced up the stairs, following the signs to Flats 10 to 13. We approached number 12 cautiously.

I listened outside the door for a while. I could hear nothing inside. "Right, Andy. You're on." He'd often boasted about his underage criminal activities in the suburbs of Newark, including burglary. Now was his chance to show he hadn't lost his skills. "Is there an alarm?"

"In a place like this? Gotta be. Don't worry, I can handle it." He took out a set of short steel rods, some flat and some with bent ends that he'd fashioned in Bonehead's basement before we left. In under ten seconds he had the door open. I watched as he ran to the beeping alarm box, pulled off the cover and fiddled with a screwdriver. The beeping stopped. I waited for the full-scale apocalypse to be triggered, but nothing happened.

"Christ, you really do know what you're doing," I said, closing the door behind me.

Andy raised his hands to his lips. We were in a long hallway.

I found the light switch. There were three doors on either side, all of them closed.

"Here," Andy whispered, pressing a hammer into my hand. He was holding a long screwdriver. "You go left, I'll go right. We'll open them together, on three."

I went to the first door and looked round at him. He mouthed "One, two, three." I turned the handle and shoved the door open. The room was completely dark. With my heart thumping, I located the light switch. The place was empty, not even a shade on the lamp. The blinds on the windows were drawn. I looked round to Andy and saw that he'd had the same experience.

It didn't look like anyone lived here. Tension slackening, we went to the next doors. Same procedure, same result. I had a bathroom with cobwebs in the corners, he had a kitchen—again, the blinds in both were firmly closed. We came to the last doors. One, two, three. This time I found myself in a wide-open space, with the light of the late-afternoon sun coming in through spaces between the blinds. Again, the room was emptier than a ransacked tomb.

"Jesus!" I heard Andy shout from the other side. I went over quickly. The room was the mirror-image of the one I'd opened. I guessed they were sitting and dining rooms as there was a glass partition between them. I opened it.

Andy was squatting on the floor next to a row of shriveled objects lying on a tarpaulin. There was a rank smell in the air, like game that had hung for far too long.

I put my hand over my mouth and nose. I counted five cats, four dogs and two rats, in varying stages of decomposition. As I went closer, I saw that all had been split open from the breast-bone to the anus, the desiccated entrails spread around on the tarp. I immediately thought of Happy. It looked like this was where the Devil had practiced. But why had he kept the corpses? I shivered. Because he was a sick bastard, that was why. Then I looked toward the far corner and saw things that were even worse.

"Oh-oh," Andy said, following the direction of my gaze.

On a larger tarpaulin lay several gray masses of flesh. This time, they hadn't been cut open. Instead, they'd been flayed, their skins nailed to the wall behind. There were a couple of large dogs and a cat. But that wasn't all. In the farthest corner was a large heap of skinless flesh. I made out human arms and legs. Hanging above them were two objects like deflated sex dolls. They were flayed skins.

"Holy shit!" Andy said, his hand to his mouth.

I couldn't speak. But who were these two victims? They were nameless, unidentifiable without detailed forensic investigation. I felt rage course through me. How could someone have such disregard for his fellow human beings? How could he turn them into anonymous pieces of flesh?

We retreated and checked the rest of the place but found nothing that might lead us to the owner. It was clear from the dust on the floor that he hadn't been here for some time. We'd left footprints all over, but I didn't care. I was already in deep enough trouble, both with the Devil and with the police.

"Let's get out of here," I said.

"Good thought." Andy attempted a smile. "There's a chance that, when I disabled the alarm, a light started flashing in the local police station."

"Why didn't you tell me before?"

"We were having such a good time." He turned away. "Come on."

We left at speed, encountering no one in the corridor or on the staircase. We were about to open the main door when I saw a panel of mailboxes.

"Can you get into that?"

"With or without damage?"

"It hardly matters now. As quick as you can."

He forced open the box marked 12 with his screwdriver. I stuck my hand in and came out with a single envelope. I stuffed it into my pocket. "Come on." It was only as we went out of the door that I saw the CCTV camera on the inside above it.

Too late. Too bad.

When we got back to the BMW, I took the envelope out. It was an electricity bill. "Mr. Lawrence Montgomery," I read.

"Who's he?" Andy asked.

I felt a shiver run up my spine. "He might just be the Devil himself."

We drove off into the evening's deepening shades.

The three men in the aged Orion were all looking to the front, the passengers' eyes fixed on the figure weaving in and out of the traffic ahead.

"Pity we haven't got a bike like that," the driver said.

"I didn't hear you volunteering to buy one, Geronimo," said Wolfe, his tone sharp. There was a dull ring from his pocket. He took out his mobile phone. "Yes?" He listened for a while. "Don't worry," he said finally. "We haven't done anything to the piece of shit." He cut the connection and looked round at Rommel. "Yet."

"Our friend the detective?" the man in the backseat asked.

"Yup. Wetting himself that we're going to chop the guy on the bike up like we did with Smail."

"We are, aren't we?" Geronimo asked.

Wolfe gave a hollow laugh. "Assuming he did for Jimmy Tanner, as I'm sure he did, you bet we are."

The motorbike was about fifty yards ahead of them, moving toward London Bridge. The traffic lights changed and vehicles began to slow. So did the man on the bike. But when he'd come to a complete stop, he suddenly accelerated, narrowly missing a taxi that was turning right.

"Fuck!" Geronimo smacked his palms on the steering wheel.

Wolfe got out quickly and looked ahead. He saw the motorbike disappear over the bridge.

"Now what?" asked Rommel.

"I call our contact," Wolfe said calmly, taking out his mobile. "It's me," he said. "We've lost our target." He listened for a few seconds. "All right, but I'm expecting reliable information. Remember, you owe us."

The traffic was moving again.

"Where to?" asked Geronimo.

"Find a parking space in Holborn. We'll be centrally positioned there. Don't worry, the copper will put a trace on him. After all, Jimmy Tanner saved his uncle's life in the Falklands."

"So we just sit and wait?" asked Rommel.

"What else do we do between ops?" The team leader moved his hand to the 9 mm Glock in his shoulder holster. "And when the time comes, we nail the fuckers before the Met get near them."

The other two men nodded, their expressions set hard.

Karen Oaten looked down over Victoria Street from New Scotland Yard. The last of the commuters were on their way home, some already well lubricated as their erratic movements showed. Why wasn't she normal? she wondered. Why couldn't she go down to the pub like everyone else? Because there was a pair of heartless killers on the loose, she told herself. Whether they were called Matt Wells and Andrew Jackson was another matter.

"Guv?"

"Yes, Taff?" She sat down at her desk and massaged her aching neck.

"There have been several calls reporting sightings of Wells and Jackson. We're checking them out." He shrugged. "Nothing definite yet."

That was the problem with public appeals, the chief inspector thought. Some people wanted to be helpful, but gave unhelpful information; other people wanted to shop those they didn't like; and then there were the crazies who only wanted attention.

"What about the National Lottery?"

"The warrant should be through any time now." The Welshman shook his head. "Tossers. You'd think they would understand this is a multiple-murder case."

"They're bureaucrats, Taff," Oaten said, staring at the heap of files on her desk. "Like us."

"Oh, yes," Turner said, a smile spreading across his lips. "And this call came in for you when you were with the A.C. I had it transcribed." He handed her a piece of paper.

"'At 1705 hours, muffled male voice,'" she read. "'For Detective Chief Inspector Karen Oaten. It may interest you to read pages 171 to 175 of the novel *Tirana Blues* by Matt Stone.'"

Turner was holding an open book out to her, his smile even wider.

She read through the description of an Albanian's murder,

taking in the similarities with that of Lizzie Everhead. The details hadn't been released to the public, so the message was obviously either from the killer or someone close to him.

"Pretty conclusive, isn't it?" the inspector said.

"You think so, Taff?" She was getting irritated by her subordinate's dogged determination to nail the novelist. "If Matt Wells is the killer, why's he taking the trouble to frame himself? Think about that."

"He's a psychopath," Turner said, his smile disappearing. "He's playing games."

"It was a mistake, making that public appeal. All it's done is make him even more determined to keep his head down. The idiot's trying to find the Devil himself."

"All he has to do is look in the mirror."

"What else have we got?" Oaten said wearily.

"No fingerprints at the scene except Jackson's on what looks like an ancient dildo, no significant physical evidence found by SOCOs. And everyone who appeared on the CCTV has been accounted for. Apart from Wells and Jackson." The inspector suddenly became less assertive. "And one other man, dressed in workman's clothing and wearing a hard hat."

Oaten looked up. "So there was someone else at the scene. That could be the killer. I'm telling you, Taff, there's more to this than Matt Wells and his mate."

"Maybe it was another of Wells's mates."

"Christ, you don't give up, do you?"

"I've been doing some checking," the Welshman said, looking at his notes. "When Wells gave you those names to be put under protection, he missed out several of his closest friends. I got their names from his ex-wife and cross-checked them with the rugby league club they're members of. There are two others we can't trace—David Cummings and Roger van Zandt. Neither of them is as tall as Wells and Jackson. And they haven't been seen at home for more than twenty-four hours." He glared at Oaten. "Why are you so dead-set against the writer as our main man, guv?"

It was the same question the A.C. had asked her. She'd only been able to cite the height of the figures on the CCTV at Dr. Keane's building and Borough Market. But, as her superior had pointed out, such images were often misleading because of the skewed perspective they gave. And there were the other potential suspects. She couldn't embarrass herself by giving him the main reason, but Taff should have been able to understand it.

"I've met him," she said. "My gut feeling is that he isn't capable of these killings."

Turner shrugged. "I've got to disagree with you there. I've met him, too, and my gut's telling me that he is. He's written about murder often enough. He's also got a reputation as one of the most gruesome crime writers."

"Writing about it is hardly the same thing as doing it for real," the chief inspector said. "How many writers have we done for murder over the years?"

"None that I can remember," the Welshman said reluctantly.

She nodded at him, and then looked away. She wasn't comfortable thinking about Matt Wells. He'd had more of an effect on her than any man for years.

There was a knock on the door. Paul Pavlou stuck his head round. "Excuse me, guv. The warrant for the lottery's here."

Karen Oaten stood up. "Right. Let's find out where the mysterious Leslie Dunn has got to."

Turner followed her out, shaking his head. Leslie Dunn was

a false trail, he was sure of that. They would be led round in circles, while Matt Wells went on killing people.

For the first time in nine years, he'd begun to doubt his boss's judgment.

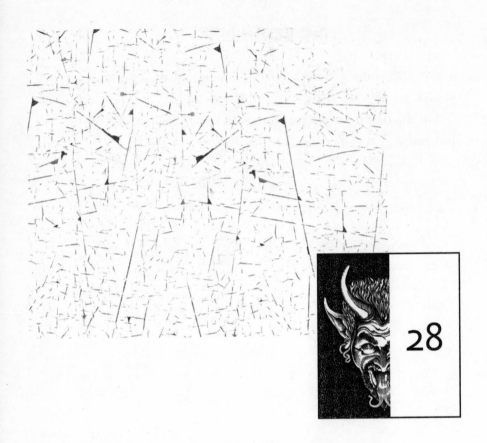

28

I drove back to the house in Blackheath. There was no point in calling ahead about the name we'd found as we were so close. As soon as we got there, Peter Satterthwaite rang his computer expert while Rog checked for Lawrence Montgomery in the online directories and search engines. Andy went off to the kitchen to make more food—even what he'd seen in the flat hadn't put him off eating. I called my mother. Again, there was no answer. Now I was getting seriously worried about her. I told the others.

"Why don't you let the police know?" Rog said. "It can't do any harm."

That made sense. I left the house and went out onto the Heath to avoid being located at Bonehead's, then rang Karen Oaten's mobile.

"Matt!" she said eagerly when she heard my voice. "I'm very glad you called. Where can I meet you?"

"I'm not coming in."

"You have to. It's the only way you can clear your name."

"What do you care about that? You're the one who made me public enemy number one."

She sighed. "I had no option. You're on the university's CCTV recording. Answer this question. Did you have anything to do with Lizzie Everhead's murder?"

"No, of course I fucking didn't!" I shouted, unable to control my outrage. "I told you, I'm trying to protect the people I care about."

There was a pause. "You can't tell me you cared about Dr. Everhead. Why did you go to see her? I presume you don't deny that's why you were in the building."

"No, I don't. I went to ask her about the Devil's use of the quotations from the play. And to warn her about him." I decided to play hardball. "Obviously that never occurred to you. Where was her police protection?"

There was a longer pause. "All right, Matt, I hear you. But I still need you to surrender yourself."

"Forget it."

"In that case, why are we talking?"

"Because my mother's not answering her mobile phone again. Can you find out from the airlines apart from British Airways if she left the country from Heathrow on Friday?"

"You mean you've already checked with BA? They don't give out that kind of information to the general public."

"Just take my word for it. If she's not on any flight list, then I think the Devil's got her."

I heard her breath whistle between her teeth. "All right, we'll look into it. At least give me a number to call you."

"Good try, Karen. I'll call you. Bye." I hung up. Jesus. Did the bastard really have my mother? The full horror of that idea struck me as I walked back across the open grassland in the darkness, the wind whipping about me like a mad dog. When would there be an end to the anguish the Devil was visiting on me?

When I got back, Pete yelled at me to join them in the study.

"Progress," he said, a wide grin on his face. "I just heard from my man. Lawrence Montgomery is the name of the holder of the accounts I tracked down before. Don't ask me how he did it, but he managed to verify that."

I nodded, not particularly impressed. "Where does that get us?"

"It gets us precisely here," Rog said, swinging round in his chair. He held up a printed page. "Properties listed in Lawrence Montgomery's name. All of them in London and the Southeast."

"Wow." That *was* interesting. I ran my eye down the page. "Bloody hell, how many are there?"

"Twenty-three apart from the one you've already been to," Rog replied. "Everything from a semi in Golders Green, to a penthouse near Tower Bridge, to a cottage near Hythe. Some of them are registered as owner-occupied, some as rented out."

"How the hell are we going to be able to check all those places?" I said with a groan.

"You could give the list to the cops," Bonehead suggested.

"What if the Devil's got my mother at one of the houses?" I said, slamming my hand on the desk. "What if he or one of his sidekicks kills her the second the law shows up?"

"The same thing could happen if we show up," Rog pointed out.

"That's why we have to be careful. Ultracareful."

Andy appeared in the doorway. "Chow time. I've made chili."

We went through. I didn't think I'd be able to get anything down, but Andy was a good cook and I suddenly discovered I had an appetite. When everyone had finished, Andy having scraped the bowl and licked the wooden spoon, I sent Dave a text message. He replied saying that all was okay. At least Lucy was secure.

"What are we going to do, then?" Andy asked, putting down the spoon at last.

"It's time we took the game to this tosser."

"Easier said than done," I said, suddenly remembering the notes that the Devil had sent me about Lizzie Everhead's death. He'd be expecting another chapter, but I wasn't going to play according to his rules anymore. I went through to the study and logged on to my e-mail server. As I'd expected, there was a new message from him, with yet another identity, this time WD999. No doubt he thought using the emergency number was very funny.

Matt, Matt, I read. You've been a bad boy. Who gave you permission to break into Flat 12 in the Vestine Building? That was really dumb. I hope you liked my collection of humans and fauna. Tonight I'm going to make you pay for your nosiness. People you love are going to die in agony, Matt, and all because you thought you could take me on. Do you remember what John Webster wrote? "As in this world there are degrees of evils, So in this world there are degrees of devils." I'm the worst kind, as you're about to find out.

"Shit," Bonehead said, reading over my shoulder. "What's the bastard up to?"

"I don't know," I said, "but I've got to work that out fast. I'll have to risk using someone's mobile from here." He gave me his, a small silver device. I rang my ex-wife's number. To my relief, she picked up immediately.

"It's me," I said.

"Matt!" she said, as if the word was a deadly insult. Obviously the Devil hadn't got to Caroline. "Where's Lucy, you…you criminal?"

"She's safe. Are the police still watching you?"

"Yes. What do you mean, she's safe? Don't you understand? I can't trust you. Your face is all over the news bulletins, you're a wanted man. I have to see Lucy, I have to—"

"You'll see her soon," I said gently, then rang off. I wished I could have done more to comfort her, but I knew she wouldn't listen. I'd been the enemy for years and now she had official confirmation of that.

The guys looked at me awkwardly.

"All right, say something!" I shouted.

Before they could, my new mobile rang. Very few people had that number.

"Hello."

"Oh, Matt, it's Sara." She was breathless. "You've got to help me, there's a man…he's been following me…oh, God, I'm frightened…I think it might be—"

"Where are you?"

"Um…near the office, at the meat market, oh shit, he's right behind—"

"Sara?" I tried to make out what was going on. I heard her shout and then scream. Not long after that, the line went dead.

"Jesus," I said, staring at the others. "He's got Sara." I told them what I'd heard.

"I can drive up there," Bonehead suggested.

"What the point?" I replied. "They'll be long gone. This is

what the Devil meant about making me pay. Christ, Sara..." I buried my head in my hands.

"What about telling the police now?" Rog said.

"How will they find Sara without putting her life in danger?" I said, looking up. "We've got the list of the Devil's properties. It's down to us." All three of them nodded. "We'll divide up the areas and each check out some properties. I'll get Dave to come up, as well. That makes five of us. Four or five places each. All we're doing at this stage is seeing if anyone's there. If there are lights on, check for movement. Ring the bell and ask for directions. See who answers. Keep in touch by mobile. Andy, you and I will have to use our disguises again."

"Oh, great," the American said. "I really like having a slug on my upper lip."

I called Dave from Peter's landline.

"Sorry, Psycho," I said. "I need you up here after all. How's Luce?"

"Bit down in the dumps. You'd better talk to her. Ginny's made sure she hasn't seen your ugly mug on the news."

I waited as he called her.

"Is that you, Daddy?" she said, her voice making me tremble.

"Hello, darling." I tried to make my voice sound normal. "Are you having a good time?"

"Ye-es," she said doubtfully. "Why aren't we at school?"

"Extra holidays. Isn't that good?"

"Ye-es. When am I going to see you and Mummy?"

"Very soon, sweet pie. In the meantime, have fun with the kids. Are they being good to you?"

She went into a lengthy description of the games they'd been playing. I finally managed to get her off the line. At least she was happy in her own little world. The idea of her finding out that I was a wanted man was repellent. I asked Dave if he was anywhere near Hythe. He said he wasn't far off, so I gave him the address of the cottage to check out. After that, he'd be given his next destinations by Bonehead, who was going to act as co-ordinator.

"Right, let's plot the properties on a map and work out who goes where," I said, turning to find the other three already doing that. It didn't take long. There were five places in the area of Camden. Andy took those because he could do them by Tube and bus. Rog took five to the north and west of that. Pete was going to do four south of the river. That left five to the north and south of the City for me, and three more for Dave to the southeast of the center.

"Listen, guys," I said, when we all had maps and annotated copies of the list. "What you're doing is way beyond the call of friendship. If you want to—"

"Forget it, man," Andy said. "We're all in this because we want to help you out."

The others nodded firmly.

"All right, all right," I said, raising my arms in surrender. "Pete, you're in charge of stores."

"Lucky I have such a well-stocked toolbox, eh?" he said, grinning lewdly as he handed screwdrivers, torches and chisels to everyone.

We headed for the door. I was going to take the BMW and drop Andy and Rog on their way north. Pete was going south in the Jeep. The three of us waved him away.

Then we drove into the pounding heart of the city, each of us sunk in his thoughts. Mine were full of a burning desire for vengeance on the Devil, who looked to have taken my mother and my lover.

I remembered another line from Webster's play—"To fashion my revenge more seriously."

That was what I had to if I was going to save Sara.

Karen Oaten was standing next to the array of human and animal corpses in Flat 12 of the Vestine Building in Bermondsey.

"It's them," John Turner said, coming into the room. "Wells and Jackson. They're wearing disguises, but the CCTV shots are clear enough. I'm sure of it."

His superior nodded. "The question is, what were they doing here?"

"Maybe they had some other dead body to get rid of."

Oaten frowned. "And how did they do that, Taff? They didn't carry it out, did they?"

"No," he admitted. "But they took a letter from the post box."

"Has it occurred to you that they're doing exactly the same as we are?" she said, giving him a piercing look. "Trying to find the Devil."

Turner looked perplexed. "How did they know to come here?"

"Christ knows. Maybe they've got a friend who's a computer expert."

The Welshman turned pages in his notebook. "Bloody hell, you're right. This Roger van Zandt guy, one of the pair we can't locate. He runs his own computing consultancy."

"There you are, then. They're several steps ahead of us." She pressed buttons on her phone. "Paul, any news on Matt Wells's mother?" She listened. "Nothing yet? All right, get them to keep checking."

Turner moved closer. "What's that going to tell us?"

"Whether the Devil's got his next victim." She walked out of the stinking room where the murderer had honed his skills. Dr. Redrose had confirmed that the human remains were months, even years old.

"And what if it was Wells all along, taking the piss out of us?"

"Then I'll buy you a very large drink, Taff." She turned back to him. "And you'll buy me one if I'm right."

He shrugged and followed her out. The fact was, they were playing catch-up and they knew it. Until the Devil—whether he was Wells or not—struck again, the Met's finest were nowhere. Civilian staff were trying to find out who owned the flat, but he had the feeling they wouldn't get on the killer's trail that way.

Christ, he wished his boss hadn't mentioned drink. He could have done with numerous pints of Brains, his favorite Welsh beer.

I got out of the BMW in Evelyn Street in Deptford, having dropped the others off at the station. The first property on my list was in Benbow Lane, a few minutes' walk away. As I turned into the street, I realized it was classic criminal territory—a derelict factory on one side and a row of extremely suspicious-looking lockup garages on the other. Almost all had reinforced doors and heavy padlocks. Number 35 was even better protected than most, with a steel roll-down door over the original wooden one. Not even Andy at his most creative could have found his way through that. I stepped back and saw that there was a small window in the roof. No light shone through it.

I was about to mark the place off with a cross on my list when I saw a ladder lying on the ground a few doors down. A length of guttering was next to it, obviously in the process of being re-attached. Both were chained to the garage door. I took the chisel from my pocket, found a loose cobblestone and started hammering. Fortunately the padlock wasn't a strong one and it soon gave way. I put the ladder against the wall and scrambled up it, then inched my way up the slate-covered incline.

There was a layer of heavy-duty wire over the window, but I could see inside by shining my torch down. I almost dropped it. Jesus. There was an old chair in the middle of an open space. The leather straps on the arms and legs made it obvious that someone had been held captive there. The chair also had dark stains on it. I had the feeling that something very bad had happened here.

But there wasn't anything I could do about it now. As far as I could see, there was no one living or dead in the lockup. I would send the police to it later, but in the meantime I had to move on.

The next property on my list was a flat in what I reckoned was an exclusive block near Tower Bridge.

What would I find in Number 6, The Royal Brewery?

The White Devil was driving a nondescript blue van through the sparse traffic on North End Way. Hampstead Heath was in the darkness to his right. He turned to his accomplice, whom he'd met half an hour after Corky gave the men in the Orion the slip.

"Not long now. Tonight we'll get them all."

"Then what?" answered the bearded figure in the padded black anorak.

"You know that," he said, smiling broadly. "The Caribbean, and then the world is ours."

"How can I trust you?"

The Devil laughed. "After all we've been through? Come on,

Corky. We've known each other since we were in primary school."

"That's what I'm worried about. You never did tell me if you had anything to do with what happened to Richard Brady."

"What, the bully? He was found dead in a wood outside Watford, wasn't he?"

The other man gave a sharp laugh. "Yes, and I remember how pleased you were with yourself after the summer holidays. Come on, you can tell me. Did you do him?"

The driver looked over his shoulder. "She's moving around a lot. Make sure her gag's okay. And the ropes round her wrists."

His accomplice sighed as he climbed between the seats, then inched past the motorbike he'd loaded earlier. He'd had a gutful of being ordered around. Still, the payoff would make that all worthwhile—as long as he never turned his back on the man who used to be Leslie Dunn.

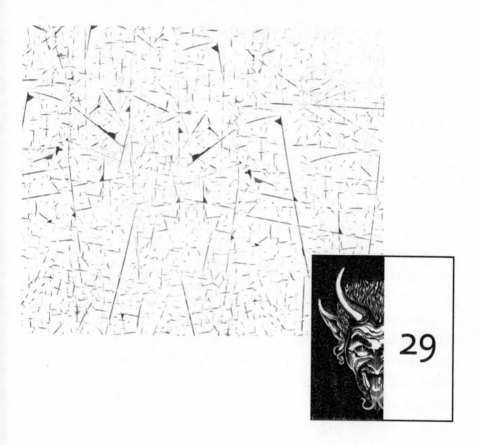

29

I was driving through Bermondsey in the BMW when my mobile rang.

"Matt? It's Dave. I've been to that cottage outside Hythe. There were no lights on. I had a snoop around. No sign of life."

"Okay. Call Bonehead. He'll tell you where to go next."

"Yes, I know, lad. I just want to tell you that I'm behind you one hundred percent. We'll get this lunatic. See you soon." He cut the connection.

I was glad I had him on my side. Dave Cummings wasn't known as "Psycho" just because he liked taking out opposition players for the Bison. He'd told us some seriously nasty stories about his time in Northern Ireland with the Paras, and later with the SAS. To be fair to him, he wasn't proud of what he and his brothers-in-arms had done. But if there was one of us capable of taking on the Devil, it was Dave.

I looked out at the lights in the buildings as I went through the southern Docklands. The place was full of people even at ten in the evening. Pissed-up commuters, young people out for a night on the town even though it was the middle of the week. There were so many of them. The city was packed to the rafters with millions of human beings. How were we going to find the Devil among them? Christ, what had happened to Sara? And to my mother?

I parked near Tower Bridge, paying no attention to its fairy-tale appearance. In the backstreets beyond, I passed through a chic area full of trendy wine bars and cafés. They were busy, the inhabitants of the recently developed former warehouse district out in force. It didn't take me long to find the Royal Brewery. It was a free-standing Victorian block next to the river, its brick facade lit up by well-positioned spotlights. There were lights on in a couple of the flats, but not in the penthouse. I was about to go in the gate when my phone rang again.

"It's Rog, Matt." He sounded anxious. "Where are you?"

I told him.

"Well, if there's nothing going on there you'd better get up here sharpish."

I felt a twinge of alarm. "What is it?"

"I'm in East Finchley, opposite the house in Howard Avenue that the bastard owns. There's something funny going on. A van just pulled up and a couple of guys got out. They checked to make sure no one was watching and then carried something inside." He paused. "Matt, it was tied up in a blanket. I reckon it was a body."

The twinge was replaced by an adrenaline rush. "Shit." I turned and ran away from the former brewery toward Jamaica Road. "Did you...did you see any movement?"

"Yeah. There were some wriggles. The person was probably conscious."

I started to run back toward the BMW, the phone to my ear. "What's going on now?"

"Nothing that I can see. The curtains are all drawn and they're obviously pretty thick. I can only see a dull glow at the edges of the upstairs windows."

"Jesus." Thoughts were flashing through my mind. Was it Sara? Fran? Should I contact the police? I decided that would be too risky. If it was the Devil, maybe I'd be able to reason with him. "Stay there. I'll park on the main road. Put your phone on vibrate mode. I'll contact you when I'm in walking distance."

"Right. I'm behind a hedge. Do you think we should get Andy and the others up?"

"Let's see how it looks when I get there." I was loath to pull the guys off the other properties until I was sure we had the Devil in our sights.

"Okay." He rang off.

The drive through Islington and up Holloway Road seemed to take an eternity. I was trying to work out what to do, how to approach the Devil, but I couldn't come up with any coherent plan. If he had one of my loved ones in his possession, I didn't have many options. Could I persuade him to take me instead?

At last I got to East End Road in East Finchley. My mother lived about half a mile away. Was it possible she'd never left home? Had the bastard got to her that early? And what about Sara? Her mobile was still switched off.

I forced myself to walk at medium pace into the back streets, the worn heels of my shoes not making much noise. The area was solidly middle-class—overpriced cars on the roadsides, Victorian artisans' houses that had experienced an astronomical increase in value over the past decade, normal families trying to spend some time together after the rigors of the working day. Curtains were drawn, blinds were down and everyone was studiously ignoring what their neighbors were getting up to. I was as liberal as the next man, but not where abduction and murder were concerned. How did the Devil and his sidekick manage to move around without attracting attention?

I slowed my pace as I approached number 14, looking at it from the other side of the road. The first-floor lights were still on, a blue van parked outside.

"Matt!" The loud whisper made me jump. I'd forgotten to warn Rog of my approach. "Come in the gate."

I went up the path that led to number 13 and saw his back. He was hiding in a hedge that wasn't too dense.

"There doesn't seem to be anyone in this place," he said, inclining his head toward the house behind us.

"Anything new?" I asked, pushing through the foliage beside him.

He shook his head. "I got shots of the bastards," he said, holding up his mobile phone. I remembered the ribbing we'd given him when he'd shown off the model that was equipped with a camera. Now I was glad he'd bought it, but I couldn't make out any faces. The long bundle they carried inside definitely could have been a person.

"What are we going to do?" Rog asked.

I'd come to a decision about that after I'd got out of the BMW. "We check the place out. There's no use just hanging around here. If they really have got a prisoner, God knows what they might be doing to her."

"Or him."

I shrugged. I hadn't considered that the captive might be a male, but it was perfectly possible. I had plenty of male crime-writer friends, as well as other former teammates from the Bison. Where would the Devil stop?

"Right, you go to the front," I said. "I'll check the back. If you spot any obvious way in that we can use our tools on, ring me. My mobile's on vibrate, too. I'll let you know if I find anywhere interesting."

"We're going in?" Rog said with a slack grin.

"Hold your horses, you headbanger. Only if we reckon we can surprise them."

He nodded, and then retreated from the hedge. Looking around and seeing that the coast was clear, we moved quickly across the road. I opened and closed the gate of number 14 as quietly as I could and left Rog at the front. As I skirted the side of the house, its flower beds tidy and the hedges trimmed, I felt my heart begin to pound. Was this innocuous-looking place really the Devil's lair? What horrors were we about to uncover?

The back garden was equally well tended. Had Rog only seen a house-proud owner and his mate bringing in a new carpet? No, that wasn't likely. The property was owned by Lawrence Montgomery, a multimillionaire who'd taken every step to cover his tracks. Something suspicious was going on.

The curtains hadn't been closed at the back. There was a thick, high hedge between the garden and that of the house behind. The kitchen door was well secured with a lock that looked new. But the window of the dining room was original and there was a gap between it and the frame. I reckoned I could get it open with the chisel Boney had given me. I rang Rog. He appeared a few seconds later.

I pointed at the window. He nodded and watched as I inserted the shank. It took a bit of work, but I finally managed to get the latch to move. I pulled the window outward and stuck my head in. I couldn't hear any noise inside the house. Rog shone the narrow beam of his torch on the ledge as I climbed over it, then I did the same for him.

We went through the dining room on tiptoes. Fortunately the floors were carpeted so we didn't make a sound. I glanced into the sitting room, and then shone my torch round. It was a typical suburban front room—widescreen TV, leather sofa, armchairs. But there was a total absence of photographs, artwork, CDs, videos—anything to personalize it. I had the feeling this was what the secret services would refer to as a safe house—where the Devil could bolt in times of need.

I took a deep breath. The men were presumably upstairs. Was I about to make a fatal error? I couldn't see any other way ahead. The Devil had shown what little regard he had for human life. If a prisoner had been brought here, that person's time was surely running out. I nodded as encouragingly as I could to Rog and set off up the staircase. There were a few creaks, but nothing too loud. When we got to the first floor, I pointed him to the back. There were three rooms there, all with their doors open. He checked each one and shook his head. That left the two front rooms. The doors to both of them were closed.

Rog came forward and took up a position outside the one to the left. He put his screwdriver between his teeth—that would have made Dave laugh—and held his torch and chisel in his hands. I had my chisel in my right hand and screwdriver in my left. I mouthed "One...two...three."

We put our shoulders to the doors and burst in. I saw no sign of the men, but something a lot worse. Rog was at my shoulder a few seconds later.

"Clear," he murmured, his breath catching in his throat. "Jesus Christ."

We stepped forward like automata, engrossed by what was in front of us. On the double bed lay a naked female figure. There were ropes attached to her wrists and ankles, binding them to the wooden bedframe. She had a gag round her mouth and she was unconscious, her eyes half open. But that wasn't the worst of it. Her hair was soaked and she was lying in a pool of blood that was dripping off the bedcover onto the carpet.

Suddenly there was the roar of an engine from outside. I ran to the window and wrenched the curtains apart. The blue van was already at the end of the road. Jesus Christ, the Devil and his accomplice had been lurking in or around the house when we broke in. I'd been that close to him, but he'd manage to evade me.

"Shit!" I yelled, turning back to the bed.

It was only when I stepped close and bent over the face of the captive that I recognized her.

Andrew Jackson turned onto Plender Road in Camden Town. He'd checked two of the properties on his list and seen no sign of anything suspicious. He was feeling like a complete dickhead with the fake 'tache on his upper lip and the baseball cap pulled low over the wig, but that wasn't his worst problem. He'd stopped for a pint in between each of the previous places and his bladder was now in urgent need of emptying. He pulled out his best friend and was letting rip between two parked cars when he saw a blue van pull up on the other side of the road—

right outside number 36, the property he was meant to be watching.

A man of medium height got out of the driver's seat. He was wearing a boiler suit and a workman's cap. Another man of similar stature opened the passenger door. He was dressed in similar clothes, but had a baseball cap low over his face like Andy did. He appeared to have a beard.

The American zipped up and crouched down. The street was quiet, but he didn't want his considerable bulk to stick out. He watched as the men went to the back of the van, looked round to satisfy themselves that they were alone, and pulled out a long object wrapped in blankets. Andy immediately felt a surge of concern. Was that one of Matt's family or friends? Shit, he should call him. No, there wasn't time. He could take that pair of halfweights easily.

The lead man put a key in the door and opened it while still holding the package. Andy clenched his fists and ran forward.

"Hey, you guys! What are you doing?" He reached the men and pushed the rear one away, grabbing hold of the object. "Stand still!"

Suddenly he found himself with all the weight in his arms. Before he could do anything to protect himself, he felt a blow on the back of his head.

Andy Jackson had started his journey into the depths of night.

"Mother?" I said, leaning over her. "Can you hear me?" I took her wrist and felt a faint pulse. "She's alive. Fran? Mother?"

She let out a faint groan.

"Matt?" Rog said from the other side of the room. "Look at these." He pointed to two plastic buckets. "They're empty, but there are drops of blood in them."

"Have you got a knife?" I said, trying frantically to undo the knots on Fran's bonds.

He came over with a penknife and started hacking at the ropes. In a couple of minutes we were able to lift her off the blood-drenched bed and onto the carpet. We turned her over into the recovery position. Her breathing became more regular, her lips parting.

"Get blankets," I said. I started looking over my mother's body for wounds.

"Here," Rog said when he came back from the other front room, his arms full.

"I don't get it," I said as we spread the covers over her. "She hasn't been cut, just tied up. Where did all the blood come from?"

"That's what I'm saying." Rog inclined his head to the buckets. "It wasn't hers."

I rocked back on my heels. "What did the bastards do? Pour someone else's blood over her?"

"We need to get her to a hospital," Rog said.

He was right. But how were we going to do that and avoid the police, let alone the Devil and his accomplice?

"The bastards must have been waiting for us."

I nodded. "But why? Did they know they were being watched?"

Rog raised his shoulders. "I'm pretty sure they didn't see me."

"The Devil's working to a plan," I said. "He and his sidekick could easily have surprised us, but they preferred to escape." I looked at Fran. "All right, I'm going to call the police." I rang Karen Oaten's mobile. It no longer mattered if she was able to trace me. I wasn't planning on sticking around for long.

"Matt!" she said, sounding surprised. "I've got news for you.

There's no record of your mother having got on any flight from Heathrow."

"I know," I said, holding Fran's hand. I told Karen what we'd found.

"Where are you? She needs an ambulance."

"Yes, but I don't need you taking me in." I looked at my mother desperately. I didn't want to leave her, but I had no choice. She seemed to be stable and there were other lives at risk, in particular Sara's. I wasn't going to tell Oaten what had happened to her. The Devil was playing a game that was between him and me, and I couldn't risk bringing the cops any closer. "I'll give you the address when we…when I'm clear."

"You're only making things worse for yourself, Matt."

"Bye, Karen."

"Wait!" she shouted. "There's something else I have to tell you."

The tone of her voice, a mixture of anger and regret, made my stomach flip. "What is it?" I demanded.

"Your ex-wife. She's…she's disappeared."

"What?"

"Unfortunately our people lost her between her office and Blackfriars Station. She hasn't shown up at home."

"Have you called her mobile?"

"It's switched off. I'm sorry, Matt."

"Bloody hell, Karen. Now do you see why I can't trust you?" I cut the connection.

"What is it?" Rog said, as I checked my mother for the last time. She seemed to be reasonably stable. I hoped she wasn't aware of what had been done to her.

"Caroline's gone."

"Fuck. Do you think—"

"It's the Devil? I'm sure of it." I led him downstairs.

"We can't just leave her on her own," Rog protested.

"I'll let the police know the location when we're away from here," I said, not feeling at all proud of myself. "You continue checking the places on your list, okay? I'll be in touch."

We climbed out of the window we'd come in.

"Matt? Don't you think we should stay together?"

"In a perfect world, yes," I said, squeezing his arm. "But this isn't one of those. This is the Devil's world and we can only catch him by risking everything."

He nodded and gave me a determined smile. "Got you, Matt."

We split up at the gate, Rog turning right. I headed back to the main road. The nearest property on my list was in Moorgate. It was only as I passed under a streetlight that I saw the blood on my hands. I spat on to them and wiped them with my handkerchief. If it wasn't my mother's, then whose was it?

That thought made me quiver with apprehension. It was likely that the Devil had both Sara and Caroline. Was either of them still alive?

I called Oaten from a public phone and gave her the address, then got into the BMW.

If I didn't find my tormentor soon, there wasn't going to be anybody left for me to protect. Then a thought struck me. The Devil could easily have killed my mother, even though he'd made an unplanned exit from the house in East Finchley. Christ, he could probably have done for Roger and me.

Why hadn't he?

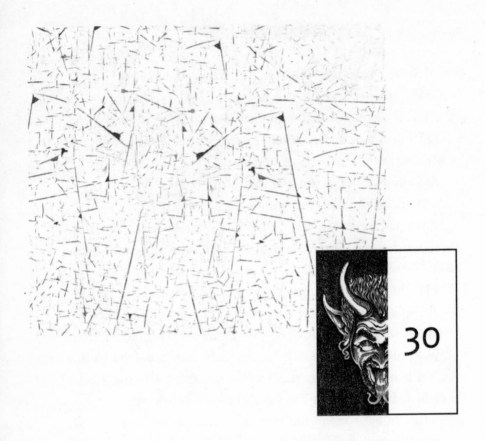

30

Karen Oaten watched the paramedics lift Matt Wells's mother onto a stretcher and take her out of the bedroom. Their preliminary examination had found only suppurating grazes on her wrists and ankles, suggesting that she'd been tied up for several days. She was suffering from extreme dehydration and a saline drip had been inserted in her arm.

"What's the story, Taff?" she asked.

The Welshman was standing over the SOCO team leader, who looked up from the buckets and twitched his nose. "I don't think it's human blood," the technician said. "You'll have to wait for the analysis, but my guess is that it came from a pig."

"Jesus," the inspector said, shaking his head. "I haven't got the faintest idea what happened here, guv."

"We're getting several sets of prints," the SOCO added.

"Wells was here, wasn't he?" Turner said to Oaten, his voice low.

She nodded. "He admitted as much."

"And then he disappeared, leaving his own mother behind?" The Welshman's tone was scathing.

The chief inspector shrugged. "He ascertained that she was okay, and then told me where to find her. What's your point, Taff?"

"He's playing you like a big juicy trout," her subordinate said, glaring at her. "There's nobody else involved, just him and his mates. Some of them are tall and some of them are short, but all of them are missing. You can't just let him mess us about like this."

Oaten returned his gaze coolly. "Have you got a better idea? None of this adds up, but it will do soon. I'm telling you, Matt Wells is one of the good ones."

Turner's expression was grim. "You'd better hope so. The word back at the Yard is that you've run out of lives with the A.C."

"Is that right, Taff?" she said, stepping closer to him. "In that case, you've got a decision to make. Are you going to stay as my number two or do you want out?"

The inspector's eyes dropped after a few seconds. "No, I'm tied to you whatever happens. It's too late to do anything about that."

Oaten laughed dryly. "Thanks for the rousing support."

"What now?" he asked, opening his notebook. "The constable outside Sara Robbins's place has reported that she's not shown up there this evening. And she's not answering her phones."

The chief inspector's forehead was furrowed. "So Matt's girlfriend may have been taken, as well. I'm not looking forward to telling him that."

"He already knows," Turner said acidly, "since he was the one who took her. Simmons has tracked down the owner of the flat with the flayed bodies and disemboweled animals in it. It's a guy by the name of Lawrence Montgomery."

Karen Oaten ran her fingers slowly down her cheek. "So it looks like Leslie Dunn became Lawrence Montgomery. He's a wealthy man. Get Morry to find out if he owns any other properties. No, on second thought, get Paul to do it."

The Welshman looked at his watch. "The council offices are all closed, guv."

"Well, tell him to squeeze their nuts. The stuff's all in databases. It won't need many people to work overtime."

Turner took out his phone and moved to the landing.

The chief inspector watched him go and then turned back to the crimson bed. All her experience was telling her there was more blood about to be spilled, and that this time it would be the human kind.

If Matt Wells had set her up, she'd personally spill his.

I had just checked out an upper-floor flat off Old Street—no lights or sign of movement—when my mobile rang, making me jump.

"How's it going, Matt?"

"Bonehead. The bastard had a go at my mother. I sent the cops round. She should be okay."

"Jesus. What do you mean she should be okay?"

I explained, feeling like a piece of shit for having left her behind.

"Oh, right," he said, obviously unconvinced that I'd made the right decision. "Have you heard from our American friend?"

"No. Haven't you?"

"He isn't answering his phone."

I felt a cold finger move down my spine. Bloody hell, what was going on? Was the Devil picking up everyone I knew? I should have expected it. He'd warned me often enough.

"Where was he the last time you heard from him?"

"Half an hour ago. He was about to go to the place in Camden Town. Plender Road. You see it on your map?"

I found the cross I'd made. "Yes." I got into the coupé. "All right, I'm on my way. What about the others?"

"Dave's between Bexley and Eltham, nothing to report. Rog has just finished in Cricklewood. He's going to Kilburn next."

"What about you?" I asked, as I accelerated up the City Road.

"I haven't seen anything worth talking about. I'm about to check the place in Norwood."

"Okay. Listen, Boney, keep in touch with the guys as often as you can. The lunatic seems to be picking us off one by one."

Peter Satterthwaite gave a dry laugh. "Not me, my friend. He doesn't know anything about me, remember?"

"Unless he trailed one of us back to your place." That shut him up. "Don't worry," I said, relenting. "It isn't that likely." I cut the connection, wondering how right I was. The Devil seemed to know everything about all of us. I was hoping Pete was the joker in my pack.

I parked off Camden High Street and walked down the darker back streets. It was after ten and there wasn't anyone around. Plender Road was narrow, and filled on both sides with parked cars. Number 26 was a terraced, three-story building. There were no lights on inside.

Andy Jackson still wasn't answering his phone. I felt my heart begin to pound. I had to try to get inside. What if he was tied up like my mother? Or worse. Making sure the coast was clear, I approached the front door on the balls of my feet. As I was going up the two steps, I noticed that there was a piece of paper protruding from the letter box. I went closer and shone my torch on it. My stomach flipped as I made out my name in red letters. I pulled on my leather gloves and removed it swiftly and silently. At least it looked like the lettering was in ink rather than blood. I unfolded the sheet and read:

Is it you, Matt? Are you hot on my trail? I really hope so. But you're too late here. Oh, you'll be wondering about your American hunk. I thought I'd dealt with him the other day, but he just keeps coming back for more. I don't think he'll be coming back this time. Don't bother breaking the door down. He's not inside. Can you save the others, or will you be the only man left standing? What does it feel like to be responsible for so many people's lives? Is it a heavy weight? No, I don't think it's troubling you so much. You're like me, aren't you, Matt? In the final analysis, all you care about is yourself and your own pathetic concerns—your writing, your inventing stories, your lying. Come on, let the anger out! You can track me down if you really want to. But have you got what it takes? Can you walk the walk? Remember what John Webster said. "Noble friend, Our danger shall be like in this design." We're two of a kind, Matt. You'll see that when we meet.
When, not if.
WD

The bastard. What had he done to Andy? I called Pete and let him know. He'd call Rog and Dave, and tell them to be especially careful.

I walked down the street. The Devil was playing with me. He knew that we had found out about the properties he owned. The question was, which one was he in? Or was he on the move? I felt that things were racing to a climax. Unless he had bought other properties under a false name, he would have guessed that the police would soon be on his trail whether we told them or not. So what was his plan? And where were Sara and Caroline?

I called Dave, breathing hard.

"Are you sure Lucy's safe?" I asked as soon as he answered. "Is there any way the Devil could have tracked you down to wherever it is you've been staying?"

"I don't see how," he replied. "But, if you like, I can tell Ginny to get the kids into the car and hit the road."

I thought about it. "Where are they, Dave? In an isolated place?"

"Yeah. Friend of mine who's on holiday. He's got a farm up on the Downs above the Elham Valley."

I didn't know it. "Where's that?"

"About ten miles beyond Canterbury."

I took the decision. "All right, tell her to get on the motorway and head toward London. Tell her not to go home, but to keep driving round the M25 till she hears different, okay?"

"All right, lad. Is everyone else okay?"

"No." I told him about Andy and the contents of the Devil's note.

"Christ, what a devious fuckwit. Wait till I get my hands on him."

"Hold your horses, Psycho. There's a lot of people at risk.

Hang on a minute, what's Ginny driving? I thought you were driving the four-by-four."

"Nah, I left it there. My mate's got this brilliant Chevrolet pickup, an Avalanche, that he lets me drive. I've been going to work in it."

Something bothered me about that, but I couldn't put my finger on it. Whatever the case, Lucy and Dave's family would be safer on the move.

"All right, keep in touch with Boney," I said.

"Aye, lad. Mind how you go."

As I walked back to the main road, I wished I had Dave with me. He'd been in the SAS. He could kill a man with his bare hands, as he'd frequently told us. Even the Devil would be scared of him. Then I remembered that my adversary had already dealt with two hundred and thirty pounds of American beef. Christ, Andy. Where was he?

I looked at my list. The next property was on Leadenhall Street in the City. I headed there.

The White Devil looked in the mirror. The two bound bodies in the back of the van were motionless and silent now. The big man had been groaning, but he'd stopped when Corky belted him about the head again. The other shrouded form had been motionless for more than two hours. The injection wouldn't wear off for at least another one. By that time the Devil would be close to his goal—and Matt Wells would be facing the ultimate test.

His accomplice squeezed between the seats. Corky's breath was rank, a mixture of roll-ups and dirty teeth. The Devil could remember the stink, not quite as strong, from when they were kids. But now Nicholas Cork's face was covered in a salt-and-pepper beard. He'd traced him a year back, then found a down-and-out with the same build and smashed his head in before leaving the body on the rocks in Cornwall with ID suggesting he was Corky. That would have kept the cops guessing—or rather, fumbling around without a clue.

They both leaned forward as the van coasted to a stop. The Devil owned a shop in Brondesbury Road with a flat above it. He rented the place to a Pakistani family via an agency. There were lights on upstairs and he knew that would attract Wells's friend. They could have taken him in East Finchley, but it had been more fun to get Matt himself up there. Seeing his mother like that would have put the shits up him, as would their daring escape.

The Devil looked down at the portable screen beneath the glove compartment. Someone was using a mobile phone across the road from his property.

"Got him," Corky said. "He's behind that tree on the opposite side of the road."

The Devil drove past and then took the first right turn. He circled round until they were approaching the main road from the rear. The hunched form of Matt Wells's friend was just ahead of them. He slowed and then stopped, checking they were alone.

"Oy, mate?" Corky shouted. "Any idea how to get to Belsize Road?"

The man watching the shop turned and walked toward the van. He was a lot shorter than the American, though he was solid enough—like all the rugby-playing fools.

He leaned in the open window. "You need to turn—"

The sentence was never finished. Corky slammed his head into the roof, and then, when it dropped, the Devil brought his short steel bar down on the top of the cranium. Roger van Zandt slumped unconscious as Corky held on to him. In a few seconds, the Devil had gone round, grabbed their victim and dragged him to the back of the van. Under a minute later, he was driving toward the city center, while Corky tied up captive number three next to the motorbike.

"Turn off his phone," the Devil ordered. He was tempted to call Matt Wells on it, but he didn't want to risk that. There was always the possibility that he'd invested in a scanner and was monitoring his friends' mobiles. Besides, they were about to move to the next stage. It had been easy nailing the first three, as he'd known where to find them. For the rest, they'd be using a different strategy. Matt Wells was smarter than he'd thought. By getting himself a new phone, he'd put himself temporarily out of the Devil's reach. But not for long. He wouldn't be able to resist the bait that was being prepared for him.

He'd be seeking revenge. That made the Devil smile. What would mankind be without the lust for vengeance? Nothing better than the animals. No animal was driven by the desire for revenge, whatever Herman Melville thought about the great white whale. Revenge was what distinguished man from lower beasts. Revenge was mankind's most salient feature.

The Devil laughed as he turned on to the Marylebone Road.

He was pleased to see that Corky jerked backward apprehensively.

I'd been watching the building in Leadenhall Street for ten minutes. It was a small foreign bank a hundred yards away from the Lloyd's of London Building. There were lights on all the way up to the fourth and top floor, but I found it unlikely that the Devil was there. There were cleaners moving around on all the floors, and a few eager-to-please employees were still at their desks. It was pretty clear that he'd rented the place out.

My phone vibrated in my pocket.

"Matt, thank God I got you."

"What is it, Boney?" I asked, concerned by his fraught tone.

"It's Rog. Now *he's* not answering his phone."

"Shit." I lashed out at the base of the streetlamp with my foot and felt a sharp pain. "The mad bastard." The net was closing around us. I tried to think clearly. How many accomplices did the Devil have? Had he set people on all of us, or did he have some kind of top-of-the-range tracking equipment? He was certainly wealthy enough.

"Matt?"

"Yeah, hang on, I'm thinking." Peter Satterthwaite should have been outside my tormentor's loop since he was a late arrival at our party. As for Dave, he had a new phone. Maybe the three of us were still undetected. But what about Ginny? Christ, that was the thought that had eluded me earlier. What if the bastard had put a bug on Dave's four by four? "Boney, how many properties have we still to check? Leadenhall Street's a no go."

There was a brief silence. "That leaves seven. There's one on Dave's list, one on mine and one on yours. The last I heard from Rog, he was outside a shop in Brondesbury Road. He didn't think it was interesting, but he was going to hang on a bit to be sure. He had two more. And there were two more on Andy's list."

"Seven? Bloody hell. Okay, I'll do my last one, that converted brewery near Tower Bridge. You do yours, and then get over there to pick me up."

"What about Dave?"

"I'll get him to drive there, too. Assuming those three are all clear, we'll check out the ones Andy and Rog didn't manage."

I broke the connection and called Dave.

"Matt, thank Christ. There's something funny going on with Ginny. No one's answering their phones—not her or either of my kids."

My stomach twisted like an oyster suddenly drenched in lemon juice. Lucy. She didn't have a mobile. Had the bastard caught up with them?

"Wellsy?" Dave said desperately. "We've got to tell the police. The children…"

"Tell them what?" I countered. "You said they were in an out-of-the-way place. Did you always get a phone signal there?"

"No," he admitted with a rush of breath. "No, you're right. But she should be on her way by now. There's no answer on the landline and she should be back in the network."

"Let's give it a bit more time," I said, struggling to beat back the onrush of panic. I told him where to meet me when he'd done his last place.

After I rang off, I drove to the Royal Brewery in Bermondsey. On my earlier abandoned visit, it had looked a much more impressive property than any of the others apart from the bank. Did that mean it was more likely to have been used as a base by the Devil?

I tried not to envisage the horrors that might be waiting for me there.

Karen Oaten stood outside a semidetached house in Neasden. A team of uniformed officers was searching the place, overseen by John Turner. The elderly residents were less than impressed. It wasn't long before her subordinate reported to her.

"This is a waste of time, guv," he said, shaking his head. "They don't have any idea what we're on about and there's no sign of any criminal activity. They rent the place through an estate agent and they've never met the owner."

"The place is on that list Pavlou got from the council's database," she said lamely. "We have to check all the places that Lawrence Montgomery owns."

"How many have you got on that list now?"

The chief inspector ran an eye down the addresses. "Eight, including the one where we found Matt Wells's mother."

The Welshman stared at his superior. "You realize that Matt Wells could be Lawrence Montgomery, don't you?"

"No," Oaten said firmly. "Lawrence Montgomery is the guy who used to be Leslie Dunn." She fixed him in her gaze. "The guy who won the lottery and who had motives for the first four murders, including the bank manager in Hackney."

Turner shrugged. "Wells could have killed him and taken over his identity, not to mention his money."

The chief inspector groaned. "Have you been reading far-fetched crime novels?"

"Like the ones written by Matt Stone, aka Wells?"

Oaten stepped toward the car. "Get D.C.I. Hardy's lot on to these two addresses," she said, pointing at the top ones on her list. "We'll go to Brondesbury Road."

As she drove away with Taff speaking on the phone, she squeezed the steering wheel hard. Where was the data from south of the river? She was sure that there must be some properties down there. Did all the useless sods from the council offices in South London turn their phones off at night?

And where was Matt Wells? Had she allowed her emotions to get the better of her? Maybe Taff Turner was right. But could it really be that she'd been taken in so completely?

The idea made her tremble with rage.

★ ★ ★

"Nothing yet," Wolfe said, putting his phone back in his pocket. He stretched his legs in the Orion's front passenger seat.

"Are you sure your contact in the Met is on the level?" Geronimo asked from behind the wheel with a scowl. "We've been sitting here for hours."

"He's all we've got. Never mind the guy on the motorbike now—he's gone to ground. But they're checking a list of properties he and his nasty friend might be at. There's no point in us going charging around London until we know which one the bastards are at."

The man in the back took off his woolen cap and scratched his crew-cut head. "But when the cops find out where he is, they'll be heading there, too."

Wolfe laughed emptily. "You think they'll get there before us, Rommel? We don't need long to find out what the scumbags know about Jimmy. And to take appropriate revenge."

The others shook their heads.

The three men settled back, their eyes half closed. They'd been on so many operations that their bodies responded automatically. When they could grab rest, they did so. When they had to go into action, be it a helicopter raid on an enemy listening post or the assassination of an IRA killer, they set off with only enough adrenaline in their veins to ensure success. This would be no different.

They were trained and experienced in death, and their list of victims was already long.

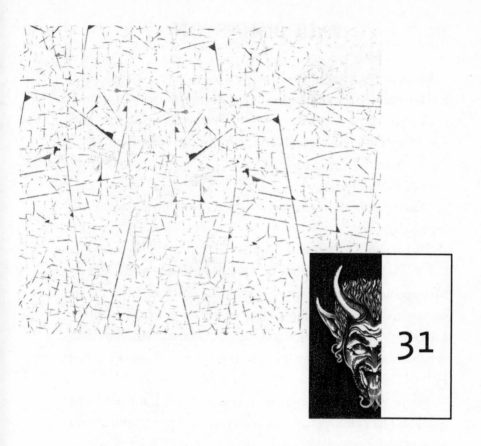

31

I came round the corner and looked up at the floodlit facade of the Royal Brewery. It really was a luxury block. I could tell that the flats were large from the patterns of light. Some had people at home, some not. It wasn't far to the main road to the south, but the noise of traffic was muffled by the large buildings behind, more of which were being converted into seriously desirable— and expensive—properties.

Alarms were dotted around the walls. I was pretty sure there would also be more sophisticated equipment to keep me out— cameras, motion sensors, who knew? There was a selection of high-performance cars in the enclosed parking area. I wondered if any of them belonged to the Devil.

I approached the main door. It was steel and looked like it had been made from the side of a battleship. There was a camera in the top-left corner. I was going to have to act a part. I psyched myself up for a few seconds and then hit the bell to number 3. After a long silence, a male voice that was distorted electronically came through.

"Lawrence?" I shouted in what I hoped sounded like a drunk's voice.

"Who is this?" the man demanded.

I waved my arms around. "I want Lawrence...Lawrence Montgomery. He invited me round to celebrate." After I said the words, I wondered how close to the truth that was.

"Oh, all right," the voice said wearily. "But tell Mr. Montgomery that the next time his friends ring my bell, I won't let them in."

There was a buzz, the door opened and I moved inside quickly. The entrance hall was opulently decorated, with abstract bronze sculptures in recesses in the walls and a thick gray carpet. The lift had glass doors and was unusually large. There was a sign telling visitors on which floor the various flats were to be found. I went in the lift to the third floor, the one below number 6, and then climbed the stairs as quietly as I could. Poking my head round the corner cautiously, I saw that there was only one door. Lawrence Montgomery's penthouse must be huge.

The door was a near replica of the one on the street, fashioned of metal that could have been used for armor plating. There was a camera fixed in the corner high above, well out of my reach. Whatever happened, my presence in the block and on the top floor was recorded for posterity. Too bad.

Then, as I approached the door, I noticed something that stopped me in my tracks. There was a space of about two centimeters between it and the frame. The bastard had left it open. Was it a trap? Or had something happened to make him get out in a hurry? I stood where I was, running through my options. The best thing to do would be to wait for Dave and Pete. If I were a normal, law-abiding citizen, I would have called the police, but I was long past that. What if the Devil had left one or more of his victims inside, as he'd done with my mother? What if they were in pain, struggling to breathe through tight gags, bleeding their lives away? No, I had to go in.

I took the screwdriver from my pocket and held it out like a weapon, steeled myself and nudged the door open gently with my shoulder. There was no light in the broad hallway inside, but a glow spread into it from the far end. The doors on both sides were open. That reduced the tension that had gripped me. I still approached each one carefully, shining the torch to check that it was empty. Apart from plenty of highly expensive furniture and fittings, all the rooms were unoccupied. That left the illuminated area at the end of the hall. I padded toward it, my heart pounding. It was inconceivable that the Devil would have let me into his lair without some surprises. Those had to be ahead of me.

As I stuck my head round the door, I froze. There was a noise, a weird, regular creaking that I couldn't place. I forced myself onward. The first thing that struck me was the enormity of the space. The room must have been fifty meters long, taking the whole of the north side of the building. The blinds were up and there was a view across the Thames to the renovated buildings on the north bank. Then I saw that the farthest blind on the left was down. In front of it was the source of the noise. Before I could stop myself, I threw up on the parquet floor.

The body was hanging from a varnished ceiling beam, secured

by a rope. It was naked, hands tied behind its back and, although it faced me, I couldn't determine the gender. That was because the head was covered in a black hood, and because the chest and abdomen had been cut open. I blinked, trying to block out the awful vision, but it was impossible. The intestines dangling to the floor, the great explosion of blood all around indicating that the victim had been alive when the mutilation had been carried out, the angle of the lifeless feet pointing downward—all of the images would remain with me for the rest of my life. But who was it?

I went toward the corpse, trying to get a grip on the thoughts that were flashing through my brain. Was it Sara? Caroline? One of my friends? At least it couldn't be Lucy, and it wasn't tall enough to be Andy. But could it be Rog? As far as I could tell, the upper body had good muscle tone. As I got closer, the stench from the ruptured internal organs washed over me. But the full horror didn't hit me until I was standing next to the loosened coils of the entrails. I was going to have to cut the victim down and take off the hood to identify him or her. At close range, amid the blood, I could see that well-formed breasts had been hacked apart. The victim was a woman. My stomach heaved again, but this time only a single, bitter mouthful was ejected.

I looked around for a chair and pulled one over from the dining table at the other end of the room. Positioning it to the rear of the body, I put my arms round it, feeling the movement of the innards in my gloved hands and swallowing back bile. The rope had been looped over a large steel hook in the beam, so by lifting I was able to slide it off. I took the full weight of the dead woman and lowered her slowly to the floor, stepping off the chair as her lower half splashed into the surrounding pool of blood. My shoes were drenched in it, my hands and arms soaked, but I didn't care. I had to find out who she was. Sara? Caroline? Oh, Christ…

I squatted down and fumbled with the hood. It had been tied tightly around the neck. Finally I got it off and was confronted with black hair. She couldn't be Sara, who had brown. But Caroline? The matted strands seemed too long. I had to turn the body round. I managed to do that, wishing I'd been able to block my ears to the squelching sound as the flesh and organs moved in the blood. I leaned forward, my heart almost bursting from my chest, and then kicked backward involuntarily, falling into the pool of gore. Jesus, how much worse could this get?

The woman had been beaten about the face. Her eyes and ears had been removed, and her nose crushed. I couldn't recognize the damaged features. To round off his work, the Devil had left a plastic bag protruding from the split lips. The bastard. Now I knew why he'd left the door open. I scrabbled to open it, my gloves slick with blood. There was a folded piece of A4 paper inside. I opened it and read.

Is that you, Matt? I do hope so. If not, maybe you'll be passed this message soon enough. Did you really think you'd find me? We'll meet where I want, when I decide. In the meantime, this is my gift to you. Did you think it was Sara? Caroline? You see, I can read your mind like a cheap paperback—like one of yours, in fact. We're two of a kind. We could have been brothers separated in childhood. Did you think of that? Birth brothers adopted by different parents, one growing up to a life of true crime and the other becoming a leech, a parasite pandering to people's baser instincts. Ha! I made it as hard as I could for you to identify the poor slut. Do you want to know who she is? Here's a clue. You spoke to her in person not long ago. Still stumped? She's, I mean, she was the receptionist at your publishers.

I let out a sob as I remembered the enthusiastic girl who'd told me she liked my books. Mandy was her name. I had a flash of her attractive face, and then it was replaced by the horror in front of me. The heartless monster. Was no one safe from him? I forced myself to continue reading.

Amanda Plimpton, she was called. The police obviously didn't think she was a likely target, so she didn't get protection. Did you include her in your list to the bitch Karen Oaten? No, I didn't think so. Oh, by the way, Matt, did you notice the box on the beam, a meter from the hook?

I looked up and saw a black metal object the size and shape of a shoebox. There was a wire leading from it to the hook.

No, you didn't, did you? It's packed with Semtex. The detonator's attached to a timer, which was activated when you took the body off the hook. It's set for seven minutes. How long have you got left to get out?
    Run, Matt, run!

I scrambled backward and got to my feet. I had no idea how much time had passed since I'd taken the poor woman down, but it must have been several minutes. As I headed for the door, I caught a glimpse of a couple of dioramas covered with tanks and soldiers, then a bank of screens on the rear wall. This must have been where my tormentor had been watching me from. Was he really going to blow up all his precious gear? I wasn't going to wait and see.

I ran down the stairs rather than risk being trapped in the lift if the explosion was as big as I suspected it would be. When I reached the front door, I opened it and pressed all the buttons to the other flats.

"Get out!" I yelled. "Get out now! There's going to be an—"

There was a muffled crump from the top floor. I ran back across the parking area, then out into the street. I could see fire in the penthouse. Then there were more explosions, more smoke and flame. The Devil had obviously rigged a whole series of charges. People appeared at the door, screaming and ushering children out. I retreated and ducked down behind a van. The smoke was roiling up into the night, caught in the floodlights. All the windows in the block had shattered. I hoped that no one had been hurt—no one apart from the innocent young woman that the bastard had butchered. Now I had yet another reason to hunt him down and exact vengeance.

I was sitting on the pavement, trying to stomach the fact that I really was turning into the Devil's twin, when I heard a vehicle draw up. It was a large American pickup truck. I staggered over to it.

"Dave," I gasped. "You made it."

He eyed me up. "Christ, is that blood?" Then he looked up at the blaze. "Not much of a job," he said. "I could have done a lot better."

Maybe he would soon get the chance to show how lethal he really was.

D.C.I. Oaten was sitting in the Volvo outside the terraced house in Plender Road, Camden Town. They had just finished searching it and found nothing of significance. It was rented to a man who was an airline pilot. Although he was absent, there were several uniforms in a wardrobe.

"Where to now?" John Turner asked.

"Pavlou's finally managed to get people to wake up south of the river. A place called the Royal Brewery near Tower Bridge is the nearest. Hardy's people are on the last property we've got in the north. Some dump off Old Street. It doesn't sound hopeful. Let's get down to Bermondsey." She drove off.

A few minutes later her mobile rang.

"Get that, will you, Taff?"

The inspector reached across, picked the phone gingerly from between her legs and answered it. He listened, his expression growing somber.

"Jesus Christ, Morry, didn't anyone notice earlier? Yeah, all right, get over there and take their statements. Find out if there's anywhere else she could be."

"What is it?" Oaten asked, with more anxiety in her voice than she wanted.

"Amanda Plimpton, known as Mandy. Twenty-two-year-old receptionist at Matt Wells's publishers, Sixth Sense. Her flatmate's just reported her missing. Fortunately a smart desk sergeant in Hammersmith got on to Morry."

"Shit," the chief inspector said. "We didn't have her protected, did we?"

The Welshman shook his head. "Matt Wells didn't give us her name, guv." He shook his head. "Christ, what more do you need to convince you? The guy's got this all thought out."

Oaten glanced at him, this time less fiercely than earlier. Before she could answer, her phone rang again.

"Yeah, Paul, what is it?" Turner said, and then listened.

"What? Fucking hell. All right, we'll be there soon." He cut the connection and turned to his superior. "Guess what."

"Just tell me, Taff," she said resignedly.

"This Royal Brewery we're headed to. Apparently the penthouse owned by Lawrence Montgomery blew up fifteen minutes ago. The neighbors got out when they were warned via their entry phones."

"Warned? Who the hell by?" The chief inspector glanced at him, and then ran a red light on Moorgate. "What's going on?"

"Our friend Wells is covering his tracks," Turner said. "What's the betting we find a charred female corpse inside?"

"You can stick those odds," Oaten said. Her stomach was aching and her throat was dry. If she didn't catch up soon with the White Devil, the New Ripper, Lawrence Montgomery, Leslie Dunn, Matt Wells, whatever his name was, her career would be his next victim.

There was no way she was going to allow that.

"Boney, where are you?" I shouted into my phone. I started the BMW as Dave flung the Chevrolet round the corner ahead of me. We were leaving what remained of the Royal Brewery behind as fast as we could. Before we parted, Dave had told me that his wife and kids still weren't answering their phones.

"Coming up Tower Bridge Road. I'll be with you in—"

"Change of plan, my friend. The Devil's just blown up his own penthouse."

"Jesus. Where are you guys?"

"Getting as far away as we can. The place will be swarming with firemen and cops. Did you find anything at that last property?"

"No. Bunch of students playing loud music."

"Rental, obviously."

"Yeah. So, do we head for the places Rog and Andy didn't get to?"

"They still not answering their phones?"

Bonehead sighed. "Afraid not."

It looked like the Devil or one of his accomplices had caught up with Lucy, and Dave's family. He had everything to bargain with, we had nothing—that was, if he was serious about us meeting. The killer was obviously in the process of destroying all traces. The easiest thing for him to do now would be to dispose of his victims and activate his escape plan. I had no doubt that he had one of those worked out to the last detail.

"You there, Matt?"

"Sorry, Pete." I looked out of the window. Dave and I were driving in convoy past the eastern end of Southwark Park. "All right, go back to your place. We'll meet you there."

I called Dave.

"The Devil wants me," I said, trying to reassure him. "Ginny and the kids will be okay."

"What about Lucy?" His voice was low and menacing, as it used to be during games when we were getting a pummeling. "What about you? Do you think I'm just going to let you walk into the fucker's arms?"

I was touched by his concern, but I'd already put Rog and Andy in mortal danger, as well as his family. I wasn't going to let Dave make any needless sacrifices.

We got back to the gated street in Blackheath and were admitted by the sour-faced guard. Pete arrived a few minutes later. As soon as he let us into the house, I headed for the study and booted up a computer. All I had to go on was the Devil's last e-mail address. There was no guarantee he would be checking his messages—he was obviously very busy with his other activities—but it was the only chance I had.

I hammered out a message.

I just came from your penthouse. You want to meet me, so name the time and place. I'll do whatever you want as long as you let my daughter and the others go. Anything. Please, answer.

I sent it, hoping the tone was suitably craven, and left the e-mail program online. Then I sat down with my two remaining friends. We talked about what we would do if the Devil got back to me, we tried to plan and we kitted ourselves out as best we could with what Peter had in the house.

Then we waited, unable to eat or rest.

Answer, I kept saying to myself. Answer, you crazy freak. I swore to myself that if the Devil had done anything to Lucy, to Sara, to Rog and Andy, to Ginny and the kids, to Caroline, I would have no mercy on him.

After half an hour there had been no reply. We decided to drive up to north London in the Jeep and check the properties that Andy and Rog hadn't got to. Fortunately Boney had a state-of-the-art laptop with an Internet connection via his mobile phone.

As we headed toward the Blackwall Tunnel, I had the distinct feeling that we were going in the wrong direction.

I sincerely hoped I was mistaken.

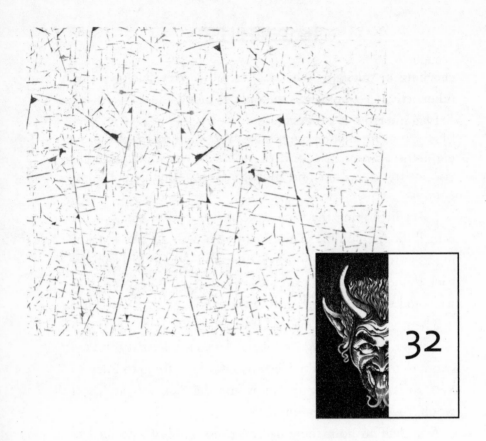

32

The White Devil stopped the van outside Free Forests Timber Supplies in Bethnal Green and waited while Corky unchained and opened the gate. He had set the company up under his mother's name and it wasn't likely that Matt Wells or the police would be on his track here—at least not yet. His accomplice unlocked the left-hand shed and the Devil drove in. Now they were completely out of everyone's view. There was a converted Victorian school about fifty yards away, but the occupants of the flats were all young professionals. They were too busy getting pissed or stoned, shagging each other or catching up on their shut-eye to pay attention to the wood yard.

Between them they carried the three bodies through to the

main shed and laid them out on the tables that had been prepared. There were leather straps to tie the comatose victims down. Another six spaces were awaiting the arrival of Dave Cummings's family plus Matt Wells's daughter, and then Matt and Dave themselves. The last one, behind a partition, the Devil had set up himself. Corky didn't know about it. He didn't know about the explosive charges that had been set all over the building, either.

He checked for messages on his laptop. Matt's desperate plea for an answer was gratifying. It meant that he knew he was at the Devil's mercy. It was always good to put the opposition on the back foot. No doubt that applied in rugby league, as well. Soon Matt would have his answer, but in the meantime there was something else to be done.

The Devil selected one of several mobiles in his briefcase and found the number he wanted in the memory.

"Six six six," he said when his partner replied.

"The number of the beast," came the smooth reply. "All's gone according to plan."

"Where are you?"

"Should be with you in ten minutes."

He cut the connection. That accounted for the Cummings family and little Lucy. They had all succumbed to the knock-out gas and wouldn't come round for at least an hour. By which time Matt and Dave would be on site for a tearful reunion.

"What's so funny?" Corky demanded, a roll-up in the corner of his mouth. "This is bloody sick, if you ask me."

"I'm not asking you," the Devil replied, his tone sharp. It was just as well that his school friend hadn't seen what he'd done to the succulent receptionist in the penthouse. It was a pity he'd had to destroy the flat—he'd had some good times there and he'd have liked to take his dioramas. But if Matt hadn't found the place, the police eventually would have. Watching the writer's horrified reaction to the sight of the strung-up girl on the video link had been a lot of fun, and it got even better when the writer had forced himself to put his arms round the body. "Ah, Matt," he said to himself. "I'm going to miss you."

It wasn't long before he heard the sound of the van outside. Corky opened the doors again. The Devil waved to his partner behind the wheel of the white vehicle and received a tight smile in return. The three of them transferred the comatose bodies to the tables. Matt's little girl really was a looker. On the other hand, his friend Dave's wife looked like she'd been several rounds with Mike Tyson.

"What happened to her?" he asked.

His partner shrugged. "The gas didn't knock her out completely. She was stumbling around trying to protect the kids, so I had to lay her out."

"Nice work," the Devil said admiringly. "You didn't have any trouble getting them into the van?"

"Do I look like an eight-stone weakling?"

He laughed, and then looked at Corky. "All right, it's time for the end game. You both know what you're doing?"

After they'd nodded, he turned to the laptop and tapped out his final message to Matt Wells.

I whistle and you'll come to me, my lad...

And then the Devil felt an icy finger run up his spine. What if the men who had been on Corky's tail, the men he was sure had cut up Terry Smail, had found a way to locate the wood store? Could his plans really be in jeopardy at the very last moment?

No, he told himself. He could take on anyone. He was the King of the Underworld, Beelzebub, the Lord of the Flies.

Let them come, whoever they were. They would burn in the fires of hell with all the rest.

We were near Euston when I heard the chime from Bonehead's laptop. The Devil had answered. Boney pulled off to the side as I read out the message, my breathing shallow.

Matt—how nice to hear from you. I hope you enjoyed the gift I left you in my penthouse. And the fireworks. I'm so glad you got out in time. You want to see your loved ones, do you? Lucy, Sara and...well, I don't suppose Caroline is a loved one anymore. Don't worry, I can oblige. Your mates Roger van Zandt and Andrew Jackson are with me, too. As is Dave Cummings's family, all three of them.

I heard Dave curse under his breath from the backseat. Then he started checking the gear he had with him in a large holdall. I went on reading aloud.

So, why don't we meet up? Just you and your friend Dave. No police, if you want any of your people to stay alive. Understood? Here's where to come. Free Forests Timber Supplies, Mace Place, Bethnal Green.

Hurry on down!!

"He doesn't know about Boney," Dave said.

"I knew I was in the clear." Peter Satterthwaite laughed humorlessly. "That means I can creep up on the fucker and brain him." He drove forward at speed and managed to complete a U-turn in front of a lorry.

"Watch it," I said. "The last thing we need is to attract the cops' attention."

"Wrong," Dave said. "The last thing we need is to waste any time. He's got our kids, remember?" There was a metallic sound that made me look round.

"Jesus, what's that?"

"It's a 9 mm Glock automatic pistol with a fourteen-shot magazine," he said, putting it into the pocket of his leather jacket.

"Where did you get it?" I said, touching the useless Luger in my pocket.

"Never you mind. There are some dodgy people in the demolition business. It's a good idea to have your own protection."

I was staring at him. "Dave, you can't use that. The bastard's got our families. And he's obviously not on his own. It's too risky."

Dave held my gaze. "You remember what I did in the army?"

I nodded.

"So leave the violence to me, okay?" He handed Bonehead a baseball cap. "Put this on. You're going to pretend to be me."

"Oh, great," the driver said, accelerating down the City Road.

I turned to the front. "You don't have to get involved, Boney," I said. "Just take us to the place and wait outside."

"What, and miss all the fun?" Pete said, his voice shrill. "Just because I'm gay, you think I can't put myself about?"

Dave leaned forward. "You putting yourself about is exactly what worries me. Now, listen, here's what we do."

He spoke, we heard what he had to say and we agreed. Then we sorted out the equipment. By that time we were heading down Bethnal Green Road. Another few minutes and we'd be at the Devil's lair.

Did I have it in me to save Lucy and Sara, let alone all the others? To my surprise, I found that my breathing was regular, my heart wasn't racing and my hands were still.

I was calm and I wanted payback.

It seemed that I was even more like the Devil than I'd thought.

★ ★ ★

Karen Oaten was standing outside the Royal Brewery. Ahead of her, fire engines were pumping water onto the blaze on the top floor. All the other flats had been evacuated, none of the occupants suffering worse than shock and minor injuries. John Turner was beside her, his phone jammed between his ear and his shoulder as he scribbled notes.

"Okay," he shouted above the noise, "get going with the list, Morry. Give some of the properties to Hardy's lot. And make sure the bomb squad go in first every time. Out." He put the phone in his pocket.

"I wonder how many places he's wired to blow," the chief inspector said, her eyes on the clouds of smoke that were ascending from the burning building.

"We haven't found any more explosives yet," the inspector said. "That makes thirteen that have been checked. There are another seven."

"And more to come, I suspect." Oaten glanced at her subordinate. "Of course, the Devil's smart enough to have bought properties under other names. In fact, I'm wondering if the reason he kept so many in the name of Lawrence Montgomery was to tie Matt Wells and us up."

"What do you mean?" the Welshman asked, his eyes narrowing.

"Think about it, Taff. The Devil sends us running all over the city while he's happily installed in some secret location with the people he's been abducting—Matt Wells's girlfriend, his ex-wife, God knows who else. Maybe he's even got the little girl."

Turner was chewing his lip. "And if the Devil turns out to be Matt Wells?"

"Come on, Taff, you don't really believe that." Oaten could

see that he still wasn't convinced. "Didn't you just take a statement from one of the residents identifying Wells as entering the building not long before it blew?"

The inspector raised his shoulders. "So? Maybe he had the explosives on a timer."

"Why?"

"To destroy the evidence, of course. We aren't going to find much up there when the fire's eventually out, are we?"

Karen Oaten sighed. "Didn't we just also hear from the same resident that the owner of the penthouse is a man of medium height with short fair hair. Meaning he is *not* Matt Wells."

"So?" Turner said stubbornly. "That guy might be an accomplice of Wells."

"All right, forget it," she said, giving up. It made no difference to the investigation at this stage. Until they could locate Wells or the Devil, they were up sewage river with no form of propulsion. "Come on, where's the next property on your list?"

"Deptford," he said. "A lock-up garage."

Oaten looked at him. "Really? That sounds interesting. Have you told the bomb squad?"

"They're on their way. As you can imagine, we're stretching them tonight."

"It's part of his plan, Taff," she said, heading for the car. "I'm telling you."

"Yes," he said, catching her up. "But who is he if he isn't Wells?"

The chief inspector drove away, flames dancing in the rearview mirror.

It was like a vision of hell in some medieval painting.

The Jeep slowed after we turned off the Roman Road.

"First right," Dave said, his eyes on the map. "Okay, stop here."

There was a Victorian school that looked to have been turned into flats. I saw a sign for Free Forests pointing round the back of the block.

"There it is," I said. "How long do you want, Dave?"

He grinned at me. "Ten minutes, Matt. You both clear about what we're doing?"

Pete and I nodded.

"Christ, look at him," Bonehead said. "No wonder they call him Psycho. He's actually enjoying this."

"I can't believe I'm riding in a puce vehicle." Dave's grin faded. "My kids are in there. No one messes with my kids."

"Right," I said. "The same goes for Lucy."

"Okay, check the time. It's 12:14 in three, two, one, zero."

We synchronized watches.

"Just like in those war movies I used to hate when I was a young lad," Boney said. "I always preferred musicals."

Dave gave him a despairing look, then squeezed my arm and moved away round the corner.

"You sure you're up for this, Pete?" I asked, checking the gear I'd filled my pockets with.

He did the same. "Of course. This is what friends are for, isn't it?"

I hadn't even regarded him as a close friend until the last couple of days. I still felt guilty about the prejudice he'd suffered from the Bison.

Those ten minutes were the longest I had ever lived. My mind was filled with images of the ones I loved. How would Lucy be coping with this horror? She was only eight years old, for Christ's sake. Dave's son, Tom, wasn't much more. And what about Sara? She was tougher than most women I knew— she'd fought off a security guard once when she was doing an undercover story about banking fraud—but the Devil had a way of finding people's weak spots. As for Caroline, I couldn't bear to think what she'd have to say to me if we got out of this. *If* we got out of it. Bloody hell, what were we thinking of? Did we seriously imagine we could take on a genuine psychopath and his accomplices, however many they were? I felt for my phone.

"Steady," Bonehead said, sticking out his hand. "Remember what the scumbag said. No police."

"How did you know I was going to call them?"

"It's logical, isn't it?" he said with a faint smile. "Any normal person would. But we aren't normal, are we?"

"You certainly aren't."

He nudged me hard in the ribs. "Don't push your luck, Mr. Writer."

I returned his smile, then thought about the way he'd addressed me. I didn't remember him having referred to me by my profession often. Someone else had, though. The Devil...

"Right, this is it," Peter Satterthwaite said, his eyes on his Rolex. "Five, four, three, two, one...go!"

He started the engine and drove slowly round the edge of the former school. There was a low wooden building about fifty yards ahead. It was surrounded by a wire fence, but the gate was open. I made out three adjoining sheds, the central one larger than the others. Stacks of cut timber were dotted about the yard. It looked like a genuine business.

"I'll park outside," Boney said.

"Remember what Dave told you. Turn round so that we can make a quick getaway if we have to."

He did that. The Jeep made enough noise to alert the people inside, but I was pretty sure they were keeping a lookout anyway.

"Stay here till I call you," I said, opening my door. "And remember to pull that cap down low."

Bonehead reached across and touched my hand. "You can rely on me, Matt," he said, giving me a vacant smile.

I walked away from the vehicle. He must have been nervous, but he wasn't showing it. Peter Satterthwaite had hidden depths. But now I had to concentrate on my own job. I could only hope that he and Dave would be able to carry out theirs. I felt tension in my shoulders, but nowhere else. I was as ready as I'd ever be.

Slowing my pace as I approached the left-hand door, I glanced around. There was no sign of anyone. Then I heard the clang of a bolt being drawn and the door slowly swung outward.

"Matt Wells," came the Devil's voice. It sounded reedier that it had on the phone. I narrowed my eyes and tried to see in the bright light that was flooding out. I made out a single figure. Could it be that he was on his own, after all? A surge of optimism ran through me.

I went inside, and then heard a noise at the door behind me. The optimism vanished. A figure of medium height wearing gray overalls and a black balaclava was standing there, a wicked-looking, snub-nosed machine pistol pointing at me. I turned to face the Devil.

"As you see, Matt, I am not alone." He was wearing ov ralls, too, but his were white. I might have known. The face under an orange safety helmet was clean-shaven. The features were un-exceptional, the brown eyes cold and the lips thin. I could see what looked like dyed blond hair above his ears. Then I saw his teeth. Jesus, the canines were pointed like a vampire's. He, too, was carrying a machine pistol. "But you suspected that, didn't you?" He glanced beyond me. "Get the other one in here." He looked back at me. "I take it that's Dave Cummings in the Jeep."

I shrugged.

"Nice wheels," he continued. "Where did you get them?"

"I borrowed them from a friend." I was relieved to hear that my voice held firm. I turned my head toward the open space at my right. My heart skipped several beats. There was an array of wooden worktables. Secured to them were motionless figures under white sheets. Christ, had he killed them already? I rapidly counted six.

Three were small, clearly children. Lucy...

"Don't worry," the Devil said. "They're not dead." He smiled slackly. "Yet."

I resisted the urge to run at him.

"What have you done to them?" I demanded. "Is Lucy there? Sara? Caroline?"

"All in good time, Matt," he said. His voice was almost accentless, but I picked up a hint of Cockney. He was back in his old haunts now. "What have you got in your pockets, by the way?" He raised the gun to my upper chest. "Empty them."

"All right," I said, dropping to the floor screwdrivers, a torch, the Luger and various other bits of junk Dave had given me. I was hoping he wasn't going to subject me to a body search—I had one of Peter's kitchen knives in my belt under my jacket. I needed to distract him, and quickly. "Ah, I get it. You want the story of your life so far to end where it began, don't you? That's why we're back in Bethnal Green, Lawrence. Or should I say Leslie?"

There was the sound of footsteps.

The Devil was looking beyond me again. "Welcome to the party, Dave," he said, his expression growing suspicious. "Take his hat off."

The figure in the balaclava flipped the baseball cap off Bonehead's shaved skull.

The Devil's eyes knifed into mine. "Where's Dave Cummings,

Matt?" he demanded. He moved quickly to the first worktable and yanked the sheet from the figure on it. It was Ginny. Her face was a real mess. "I can kill his wife in a matter of seconds." He slung the machine pistol over his shoulder and took a double-edged knife from his pocket. "Where is he?"

I heard the shrill note of panic in my tormentor's voice. Dave's tactics were paying off.

"He...he wouldn't come," I said, playing my part as best I could. "He was too scared."

The Devil laughed. It was a humorless, chilling sound. "Dave Cummings was a paratrooper, Matt. Did you think I didn't know that?"

"Did you also know he left the regiment after the first Gulf War?"

"Yes, I did," he countered.

"And do you know why?"

The Devil's eyes were suddenly less certain. "Tell me," he ordered.

"He was serving in Iraq," I said, relating the story I'd agreed upon with Dave. "He refused a direct order to go into action, so he was kicked out. They didn't mention anything about cowardice because he had a good record up to then."

For a few moments I thought the Devil wasn't going to buy it. That wouldn't have surprised me. If he'd done his research, he'd have discovered that Dave had been mentioned in dispatches twice when he was in the Paras, though his SAS service was classified. The reality was that he'd been helicoptered into Iraq before Desert Storm and had single-handedly knocked out an Iraqi guardpost.

"All right," the Devil said. "I suspected there might be uninvited guests. Who have you brought to replace him? Kojak?"

"Up yours, shithead!" Bonehead yelled. Immediately the guy in the overalls smashed the butt of the machine pistol into his belly and dropped him to the floor.

"This is Peter Satterthwaite," I said. "Another friend."

"I hope *he* wasn't in the Paras." The Devil laughed. "It doesn't much look like he was."

I looked at the sheet-covered figures. "Can I see Lucy?"

"Just wait, Matt," the Devil said, raising the hand that wasn't holding the knife.

"First you'd better see who you're up against." He turned his head. "You can come out now, Number Two." He gave a dry laugh. "Here's my Dr. Watson."

I watched as another figure in gray overalls appeared on the far side of the tables. This one was also wearing a balaclava and carrying a machine pistol. My heart began to beat faster as the figure came nearer. There was something familiar about the gait, something very familiar....

"All right," the Devil said, a wide smile spreading across his thin lips. "Show him who you are."

The figure nodded and then raised a hand. It seemed to me that whoever it was deliberately moved slowly. Finally the top of the balaclava was grasped and pulled upward.

I felt my breath freeze in my throat.

The person in the overalls was Dave Cummings.

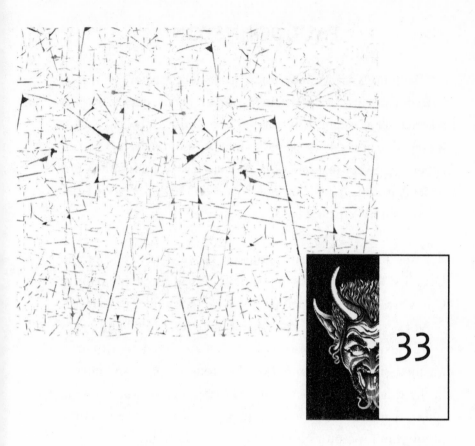

33

D.S. Paul Pavlou went to the corner of the ops room and called a number on his mobile. "I've got something," he said in a low voice.

"Shoot," Wolfe said.

"Wood supply depot in Bethnal Green. It's under the name of our man's mother."

"Give me the address." Pavlou did so, hearing the team leader repeat it, and then the sound of an engine being gunned. "Are your lot on the way?"

"Not yet. I haven't reported the location."

"Hold off for a bit. We won't need long."

Pavlou swallowed nervously. "There better not be another dismembered corpse."

"We'll do what we have to do. Your debt is paid."

Pavlou put his phone back in his pocket. He felt queasy, but also relieved. The weight of his uncle's obligation to the old soldier Jimmy Tanner had been passed to him by his mother, his Cypriot father being kept unaware of it. At last a few seconds of heroism under Argentinian fire in the South Atlantic had been canceled out.

But at what cost in blood?

I was so shocked that I couldn't move. Dave, one of the Devil's sidekicks? It was impossible. What about his family? Ginny was lying unconscious. Who else was under the sheets?

Not everyone was as stricken as I was. I turned when I heard a loud expulsion of breath. Pete had managed to extract a medium-size kitchen knife from his trouser pocket and bury it in the thigh of the other figure wearing a balaclava. Showing agility that I wouldn't have credited, he wrested the machine pistol from his captor's grip and drove the butt into the covered face. But before he could pull the balaclava off his victim, a volley of shots made both of us dive to the ground. I watched as the Devil ran behind a screen, Dave firing after him.

"What's going on?" I shouted, my ears ringing.

"I improvised," Dave said. "I came across one of his accomplices and relieved her of her gear."

"Her?" I said as a burst of fire was returned by the Devil. Forgetting the question, I ran to the tables and pulled the sheets off the smaller figures. Dave joined me. In a few seconds we'd freed Lucy and his kids, and pulled them under the worktops. They all had their eyes closed, but I could feel a pulse in Lucy's neck. Thank God, she was breathing normally.

Bonehead joined us, bullets kicking up dust behind him as he ran. "Jesus," he gasped. "For more than a moment, I thought you were with him, Psycho."

"What about the one who hit you?" I asked.

"Dead," Peter replied. "Your Devil got him instead of me."

That reminded me. I turned to Dave. "You said 'her.' You mean the other person was a woman?"

"Genius," Dave grunted. "We've got to turn the tables into barricades now. You guys do it. I'll cover you."

There followed a blur of activity as Boney and I struggled to turn the heavy wooden objects over, while Dave blasted away at the Devil. Finally, we managed to get them all down. Ginny was mumbling, apparently coming round. Caroline, Rog and the three kids were still out, but apparently unharmed. Andy was swearing loudly, a fresh wound in his forearm pumping out blood. We undid the leather straps and got them under cover. But where was Sara? Had the monster killed her already?

Dave and I were crouching behind the worktops. Pete stood up and loosed off some bursts from the machine pistol, a wild look on his face. I signaled to them both to stop firing.

"Lawrence!" I shouted. "Leslie! Give it up. The police will be on their way."

"They'll never take me," the Devil called back. "And neither will you."

"For Christ's sake, it's finished. Throw out your gun."

There was a pause. "Don't you want to know why I chose you, Matt?"

"Keep him talking," Dave said, preparing to move to the right. "By the way, I disabled the detonators on three caches of high explosive that the bastard planted inside the warehouse. Okay...now!"

"Yes," I shouted to my tormentor as Dave ran out in a crouch.

There was no firing from the Devil. "There's plenty I want to know. Why me will do for a start."

I heard a bitter laugh.

"Why not you?" the Devil said. "There's no shortage of bloodsucking crime novelists I could have used. It just happened that I'd met you. Twice."

"What?" I said in amazement.

"Oh, you wouldn't remember. Your career was on the up then. You didn't register the faces of the people who queued to have their copies of your books signed. Then again, the second time I met you, things weren't looking quite so good. It was when Lizzie Everhead tore into you."

"You were there, at King's?"

"Yes. I knew you wouldn't remember. You signed my copy of *Red Sun Over Durres*. Not that you bothered to make your signature legible."

I saw Dave scuttle unnoticed behind a partition wall.

"You mean you got me into all this shit because you met me twice?"

"Well, I felt sorry for you, Matt." He sounded distracted. "Your books aren't as bad as Dr. Everhead, rhymes with 'dead,' made out. I killed her for you. I hope you appreciate that."

I clenched my fists to restrain myself. The vicious, scheming bastard. "Why my family? What were you going to do with them?"

"That was to depend on you, Matt. You did well to get as close to me as you have. I'd let you sacrifice yourself for them if I thought you had the guts."

"What about my mother?" I shouted. "Why did you spare her?"

"When I saw your friend Roger outside the house, I decided

to leave her alive. She was in a drug-induced stupor, with a knife to her throat, the times you called her. Killing her might have made you lose your grip and hand over the chase to the police. I hope you liked the pig's blood. Good touch, wasn't it? I slaughtered and drained the animal myself."

I kept my head behind the tabletop. What the hell was Dave doing? "But you did your best to frame me for the Drys murder and Lizzie Everhead's, as well as my publisher's employees."

"I wanted to keep you on your toes." There was a long burst of gunfire from the vicinity of the Devil. "There you are," he said. "I was wondering where you'd got to."

I looked at Bonehead. His expression was grim. "Dave?" I yelled.

There was a pause.

"Dave's got his hands full," said the Devil, his voice stronger. "Or rather, his legs—full of bullets. Now, here's what we're going to do. My partner and I are going to bring your friend Dave out. He's still alive—just. Before we do that, I need you to throw the Uzi—the machine pistol—as far as you can to the front."

Boney and I exchanged desperate looks.

"We have to defend the others," I said to him.

"What, and leave Dave to take his chances? No way."

I watched as Pete took a matte black automatic from his boot. It looked to be the identical twin of Dave's. What the hell was going on?

"He gave it to me earlier," Bonehead explained. "Showed me how to use it, too. He reckoned I might find myself in a better position than you."

"Looks like he was wrong," I said. "The only way to save the others now is to cooperate with the lunatic. Toss that thing out."

He did so, along with the machine pistol.

"All right!" I shouted. "Don't hurt Dave any more."

"Stand up so I can see you," the Devil ordered.

Boney and I glanced at each other, and then obeyed.

After a pause, the Devil appeared. There was a twisted smile on his lips and he was pointing his machine pistol at us steadily. Dave, moaning, his trousers heavily bloodstained, was being dragged along the floor by his accomplice. As they came closer, I realized who the person wearing only a white T-shirt, knickers and socks was.

"No," I gasped.

"Hello, Matt," Sara said brightly, dropping Dave and aiming the Uzi she had picked up at me.

"You never suspected?" the Devil asked sardonically.

Suddenly, everything fell into place—Sara's forcing herself on me at the party where we first met, the hard edge she had that I'd put down to her job, her strange moods recently. What a blind idiot I'd been.

"No, you didn't, did you?" she said. "How's that for authorial imagination?"

The Devil laughed. "Here's another surprise for you, Matt. Sara's my little sister. By twelve minutes."

I didn't want to believe him, but the expression on her face confirmed it.

"It took me a long time to find her, but finally I tracked down the family who adopted her. They'd moved near to Inverness. I prevailed on them to tell me her whereabouts."

My stomach constricted as I remembered the unsolved double-murder of a retired couple in the Highlands of Scotland a few years ago. Jesus, was there no end to what the Devil had done? As for Sara, she'd obviously picked up some moves, too. She must have managed to sneak out of her flat without the police guard noticing.

"So you set up the relationship with me," I said to her, shaking my head.

"It wasn't difficult," she said contemptuously. "I suppose you thought a common-as-muck journalist should have been grateful that an award-winning crime writer took an interest in her. I've been playing with you for months, Matt. Right up to tonight. Who do you think took care of Ginny and the children, in particular your precious Lucy? I located them by the tracker we put on the four-by-four and sprayed them with knock-out gas before they got far from the house in Kent." She laughed harshly. "And you fell hook, line and very heavy sinker for my supposed abduction on the phone, you egotistical fool."

I stared at the Devil. "How long have you been planning this?"

"A long, long time," he replied. "I started writing my death list after my mother died. I knew from the start that wasn't going to satisfy me." He smiled. "Deep down, I'm a generous soul. I wanted to write a death list for somebody else, as well."

"You're insane," Pete said.

"Clinically?" the Devil said. "I doubt it." He frowned and glanced at Sara. "So, what are we to do with them?"

She gave him a look that was full of lust. I realized that the Webster quotation left in the old schoolteacher's body had more than one meaning—she had been in an incestuous relationship with her brother. Was Sara with the Devil in that way, too?

"You haven't told him the best bit yet, darling," she said. "His father?"

"Oh, yes, his father. Or rather, his adoptive father—Paul Wells." He gave me a sick, malicious grin. "I was the one who ran him down on the street in Muswell Hill."

I felt what remained of my world crumble. Before I could control myself, I was climbing over the tabletop. I heard sirens in the distance, then realized that Bonehead was coming with me.

There followed a cataclysm of noise—gunfire, shouts, screams, some of the latter coming from me. I saw that Andy had crawled round the table and grabbed the Devil's ankles. Sara turned and ran, her head down. I hit the Devil with a crushing tackle in his midriff before he could bring the machine pistol to bear on Andy.

The three of us lay in a heap. It was then that I became aware of footsteps drawing close.

"Well...done...Matt," my tormentor said, gulping for breath. He attempted a smile, and then scrabbled at the front of his overalls.

"The explosives have been deactivated," I said, taking in the remote control pad on his chest and the blood that was flowing freely from several bullet wounds.

"Drop your weapons! All of you!"

I looked round and saw three men approaching fast. They were dressed in black, balaclavas over their faces and automatic pistols in two-handed grips pointing at us. "Who the—"

The man in the lead shook a finger at me to shut me up. "You," he said, directing his aim at the White Devil. "You. Jimmy Tanner. Tell me what happened to him."

The Devil gave a choked laugh. "So you finally got here. Who are you? Brothers-in-arms of the old piss-head?"

The man in black stepped forward and grabbed the Devil by the throat. "Where's Jimmy Tanner?" He looked at the weapons on the ground. "He taught you how to use those, didn't he?"

The White Devil nodded slowly. "And I put what I learned to good use."

"You're the fucker who's been slaughtering people, aren't you?" said one of the other men.

"Shut it, Rommel," said the first man. He bent low over the Devil. "Where's Jimmy? Did you kill him?"

"Among many others." He squealed as his assailant took his nose between thumb and forefinger and twisted it hard to one side. Then he moved his head slowly toward me. "Remember what Webster said, Matt?" he asked. "'If the Devil Did ever take good shape, behold his picture.' This will make a great ending for your book."

The other men in black stepped close, grabbing the Devil by his armpits. That made him yelp.

"Execution time," the first man said.

I averted my eyes as a fusillade of shots rang out. Then I saw the men turn away. But before they made off, the one called Rommel leaned over Dave.

"What the fuck are you doing here, Patton?" he asked, and then headed quickly away with the other two.

I took in my tormentor's head. It was a broken mass of crimson and grey, his white overalls splashed liberally.

"Jesus," Andy said, his hand clamped over his wounded arm.

"Christ," completed Pete. "Who were those guys?"

"Armed police!" came a yell from the door. "Move away from the weapons!"

We did as we were told.

I cast one last look at the monster who'd ensnared me. The White Devil's soul had left his body.

I hoped it had gone straight back to hell.

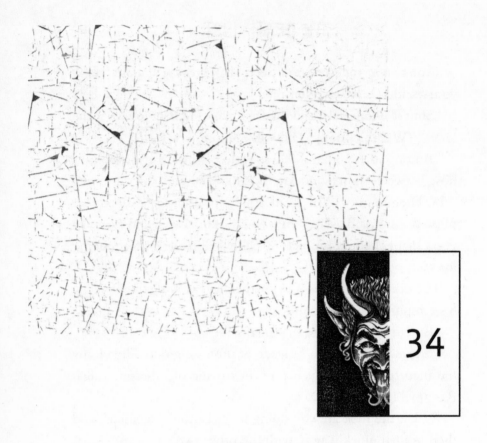

34

Karen Oaten stood watching as Matt Wells's family and friends were loaded into ambulances. As soon as she and Turner heard the report of gunfire in Bethnal Green, they'd driven over at high speed. The fact that Leslie Dunn had grown up in the area was too much of a coincidence to pass up. But, by the time they got there, Pavlou having confirmed that the property was in the name of Leslie Dunn's mother, the action was over.

She'd talked to Matt briefly before he was allowed to accompany his daughter and ex-wife to hospital. There would be plenty of time to question him in detail over the following days. She found the fact that his girlfriend, Sara Robbins, had been the Devil's partner and sister almost as astonishing as he did. The problem was, she had disappeared. A general alert had been issued, but if she'd learned her trade from her brother, there wouldn't be much chance of catching her. As for the men who'd killed the Devil, there was no trace of them whatsoever.

"I guess you were right, guv," the inspector said with a rueful smile. "Sorry I doubted you."

"I'll let you off, Taff," she said, returning the smile, "if you buy me several very large drinks. To be honest, I don't think even Matt Wells could have dreamed up a plot like this in one of his books."

He nodded. "Wonder if he'll be using it in his next one."

"More crap odds," Oaten said, moving to the car. "Come on, the commissioner's waiting to shake our hands." She sniffed. "Not that we did much to solve this bloody case."

"Who cares?" the Welshman said. "It goes down in the book as one of ours, and the press will plaster your picture all over the front pages."

"Wonderful," she said, pushing a loose strand of hair back. "Who do you think the assassins were? Hit men put on to the killer by some gangland scum he'd offended?"

"As likely as not," Turner said with a shrug.

Karen Oaten headed outside to face the cameras, her hand on her hair again. Now that the White Devil had gone, maybe she'd finally get the chance to tart herself up. But what was the point? Who would fancy a hard-faced detective with blood on her hands?

Then again, she'd noticed Matt Wells giving her a look that made her entertain some hopes.

Peter Satterthwaite and I went to visit the guys in hospital. They'd managed to talk the doctors into putting them into a room together. It probably hadn't been too difficult. That way the myriad reporters could be kept at bay.

"How much have you been offered by the vultures, then?" I asked, after I'd established that the three of them were on the mend.

"Twenty-five thousand and counting," Andy said, grinning.

"Ditto," Rog said. His head was covered in a bandage.

"Thirty-five," Dave said. "I was the military mastermind, after all. Problem is, Ginny wants half of it. Says she's traumatized, but I know she's harder than that. Shit, I'm the one with shell shock."

There was a flare-up of laughter and abuse, then they all looked at me seriously.

"What about you, man?" Andy asked. "Lucy's okay, isn't she?"

I nodded. "Fortunately she slept through almost everything and there have been no serious ill effects of the gas my lunatic ex-girlfriend sprayed them all with."

"How about Caroline?" Rog asked.

I looked at the floor. "Fighting fit. If she could have got out of bed, she'd have beaten the hell out of me." I shrugged. "I can't blame her."

"Aw, come on, Matt," Dave said. His legs were enclosed in a kind of tent. He'd been lucky. The bullets had missed his arteries by millimeters. "It wasn't your fault the lunatic dragged you into his filthy scheme."

"No, but I still put Lucy and her in danger. I should never have taken his money and written up his notes. But writers are whores and I couldn't resist a good story." I shook my head. "I couldn't resist taking him on. I must have been mad."

There was an uneasy silence.

"I also put my best friends in danger," I said, looking at each of them.

"Never mind," Dave said. "The good guys rescued us in the end."

I took in the wide grin that had spread across his face. "What do you mean, Psycho?"

"They were SAS," he said in a low voice.

"I get it. One of them knew you," I said. "The guy called Rommel. Why was your code name Patton?"

"Because he's a crazy bastard who never stops an attack," Andy said with a wide smile.

"What the hell were they doing there?" Roger asked.

Dave shook his head. "Don't tell anyone who they were if you want to stay alive. Just be thankful they came when they did."

There was another silence. Eventually it was broken by Bonehead.

"I hope they come again soon," he said in his campest voice.

The resulting uproar brought in several nurses.

I spent two days being questioned by Karen Oaten and her lugubrious Welsh sidekick. It wasn't a serious grilling. The chief inspector seemed to be inclined to believe me from the start, and even the man she called Taff was reasonably sympathetic, although he wouldn't hear a word about rugby league being superior to the union code. We parted on pretty good terms. There were some details left and I was sure it wouldn't be long before I saw them again. Actually, I wouldn't have minded seeing Karen again on her own. It seemed I wasn't cured of my weakness for strong women.

When I finally went back to my flat, I used the equipment Rog had obtained to debug the place. The Devil had been very thorough. There were seven separate pinhole cameras and as many microphones, all wired to my electricity supply and linked to a common transmitter hidden in the loft. He'd presumably managed to install them when I was with Lucy in the mornings and afternoons.

My daughter and Dave's kids were soon back at school. They were dying to tell their friends what they'd been through. The head teacher had to ban the press from school property. I spent the nights with Luce at my mother's. The journalists hadn't been told about Fran's involvement in the case. She was three days in hospital before she was discharged. Her wrists and ankles were painful, but she had come through the ordeal with her customary strength of will. I decided against telling her that the Devil had killed her husband, my adoptive father. What good would it have done? She was embarrassed by the fact that the lunatic had been able to catch her so easily. He'd arrived outside the house as she was preparing to leave for Heathrow, saying that he was a minicab driver booked by me. Before she knew it, she'd been sprayed with gas and tied up in a deserted building—I never found out where, but I reckon it was the lockup garage in Deptford that I'd checked out.

I spent a lot of time trying to avoid my ex-editor Jeanie Young-Burke. She'd come back from Paris as soon as the Devil died, desperate to sign me up to write a true crime book about the case. She was upset about Reggie Hampton's murder, and the receptionist's, but the deal took precedence. I wasn't sure if I wanted to do the book, although the amount of money on offer was so huge that I wasn't able to resist for long. Besides, the desire for revenge in me that the Devil had played with needed to be written out. Even my tormentor's execution in cold blood hadn't made me feel any better disposed toward him. I wasn't proud of that.

My former agent Christian Fels called, offering to represent me in the negotiations. I decided that, since he'd lost his lover and been terrorized by the Devil, he was entitled to a cut, so I signed up with him again. As for the ten thousand pounds

I'd been given by the bastard, I wrapped it up and had it cou-
riered to a charity that helped adopted children with psychological problems.

Relations with Caroline went from bad to worse. One of the
Devil's final acts had been to send a digital image to her office
e-mail address. It showed me burying the neighbors' dog near
Farnborough. I managed to convince her not to show it to
Shami and Jack, but explaining why I'd done it was a tough one.
I was protecting Lucy, but she couldn't see it that way.

Things got more or less back to normal two weeks later.
Dave and the others were out of hospital, Lucy was highly
enamored of the neighbors' new Husky puppy and summer
seemed to be on its way. I even managed to set up a date with
Karen Oaten at a new Mexican restaurant in Covent Garden.
She said yes with unexpected alacrity.

Then, that morning, I got an e-mail from the person I'd been
trying to forget. As with the Devil's messages, it was impossible
to trace the account holder. The first part of the sender's address
was "sarakills."

Matt, Matt. You came through it. Or rather, you think you did.
I saw that interview with you in my ex-paper. You said that the
desire for revenge was immature, that people in a civilized
society should be able to control it. My beloved brother
wouldn't have agreed. Neither do I. Although he trained me
in the basics, it seems I have an excess of natural aptitude. It
was difficult at first, but I soon got used to killing. Now I have
access to the funds that he stashed. I've moved them, in case
you're wondering. I owe him. I'll live in luxury. I'll never have
to work again. But I still have an account to settle with you. I'll
be making my own death list. Look over your shoulder every
day for the rest of your life.

John Webster put it well. "I must first have vengeance." And I will, Matt.

Stay well—until we meet again.

Deep down, I'd expected the lover who betrayed me to get in touch. Now I knew for sure that, sooner or later, the horror would begin again.